NUBIAN PASSION

NUBIAN PASSION

A collection of six sensual romance short
stories

By
Gwendolyn R. Morris

iUniverse, Inc.
New York Lincoln Shanghai

Nubian Passion
A collection of six sensual romance short stories

iUniverse, Inc.

For information address:
iUniverse, Inc.
2021 Pine Lake Road, Suite 100
Lincoln, NE 68512
www.iuniverse.com

ISBN: 0-595-31397-3

Printed in the United States of America

DEDICATION:

To all women of Nubian ancestry,

celebrate your splendor

Contents

THE NILE

The land was Egypt, ancient empire of the Nile River, the continent of Africa. It was during the reign of Pharaoh AmenhotepIII and his Nubian wife, Queen Tiye, around the year 1358 B.C., that their son Prince Sekhaten and the woman Lady Nuith lived out their drama. Prince Sekhaten was one of their middle sons in age, Djutmose being the eldest and Tutankhamen being the youngest.

Prince Sekhaten was a handsome young man with golden-colored skin and light brown eyes. His hair was long, the color of midnight, and was braided into a single plait on the side of his head, the sign of royalty. However, because he was only third in line for the throne, he was not required, at that time, to shave any of the hair from his head (as were his elder brothers). That day the braid was adorned with delicate gold chains and tiny jewels, and he wore several gold and jeweled necklaces. He was attired in a long white tunic tied at the waist by a red and gold sash, and wore jeweled leather sandals.

It was a day of excitement around the palace, Queen Tiye's father, who was a nobleman of Nubia, would arrive soon. Things were in an uproar in preparation for the royal guests. Prince Sekhaten entered his mother's living quarters in an effort to calm her down. He found her scurrying around giving instructions to her lady servants as they rushed in and out of her rooms to carry out her desires. "Mother, please sit down and have a rest. You will either be exhausted or dead by the time they arrive if you do not ease your stressful state of mind," Sekhaten implored.

"Yes, my dear son, I know, I know. Thank you for your concern. I think I will sit down and take a few breaths," Queen Tiye said as she took a seat on her mosaic and gold chaise. Sekhaten walked over and sat down on the chaise with her, then took hold of her hand. Queen Tiye did not want to say she had a favorite son, but should she need to choose, she would have to choose Sekhaten. He was always the most caring and loving of her sons and he never failed to put her or the other family members' well-being before his own. Sekhaten had seen his Grandfather only three times in his life, the last time was 5 years ago. Sekhaten understood, though, that a nobleman could not so easily leave his kingdom during precarious times, and these were indeed such times. There was a great rivalry between Egypt and Nubia, the fact that Egypt's current Queen was of Nubian origin helped quell the atmosphere for now. But, it would be unwise for anyone to depend upon that situation.

In a few moments, a young girl about 11 years old ran into the Queen's quarters. She ran so fast that she almost slipped and fell on the shiny, marble floor. "Now, now child, be careful or you will injure yourself," Queen Tiye said in a serious tone.

"I am sorry, My Queen, but the nobleman from Nubia is here," the child replied breathlessly. Queen Tiye and Sekhaten both jumped-up from the chaise, dashed out of her rooms, and began to hurry down an elaborately decorated hallway.

"Thank you, little one," Sekhaten called back to the girl as he followed his Mother. The little girl smiled, pleased that she had delivered her message and the Queen and Prince were appreciative of her efforts.

Queen Tiye and Sekhaten entered the Great Hall and found her husband, Pharaoh Amenhotep, was already there and seated on the throne. She rushed to take her place next to him. Sekhaten walked to his assigned seat amongst his brothers and sisters. Then, there was the sound of drums and reed instruments. The Nubian nobleman entered the Great Hall preceded by male and female servants carrying gifts of animal furs, jewels, and gold. As the nobleman approached, Pharaoh Amenhotep and Queen Tiye stood and walked down the two steps to the main floor. When they were close enough, Queen Tiye threw her arms around her Father and hugged him as tightly as she could. He returned the hug and included a kiss.

"My daughter, it is so good to see you again. It has been too, too long," her Father said.

"Yes, my Father, it has been too long. Come, let us all go to my quarters and get re-acquainted," Queen Tiye requested. The whole family, including all the siblings, retired from the Great Hall to the Queen's suite of rooms.

The conversation was jovial and affectionate between the re-united family members. Queen Tiye's father told stories of her childhood, Queen Tiye and the Pharaoh told stories of their own, most particularly of their sons and daughters.

"Dearest Tiye, I have brought you a very special gift. One that shall remind you of me and our beloved Nubia everyday," her Father said as he beckoned a servant to retrieve the gift.

"What is it, Father? Tell me," Queen Tiye asked excitedly.

Her Father chuckled and said, "You will see in a moment. Be patient, the way I always taught you."

In a short while, the servant returned with a lovely young woman. "Ah, here she is," the nobleman said proudly.

"Is this lovely girl my gift, Father?" the Queen asked.

"Yes, my dear. A beautiful Nubian woman to be your personal lady," he explained.

The new addition to the family re-union caught Sekhaten's attention. She was truly the most beautiful woman he had ever seen. She had smooth dark bronze skin, the same as his Mother, and large dark brown eyes. Her black hair was styled into many long braids adorned with tiny bits of gold. She wore a long white tunic underneath a top layer of sheer white material that fell into pleats around her body and was tied with a gold and jeweled roped sash. He had yet to have seen an Egyptian woman who compared to her. He wished she was of royal blood, such as himself, for then the path that he knew he was about to take would be easy. But, she was the 'lady-in-waiting' to the Queen, a required virgin; a very difficult situation for him to maneuver.

"What is your name, my dear?" Queen Tiye asked the lovely woman.

"Nuith, My Queen," she answered softly.

Sekhaten thought Nuith's voice as sweet as the first chirps of the birds in the morning. How he loved the sound of her sweet, sweet voice.

"What a pleasant name. I welcome you to the palace," Queen Tiye said happily.

"Thank you, My Queen. I am happy to be here to serve you," Nuith replied.

Sekhaten was pleased that his Mother was so kind to Nuith, but then, his Mother was usually kind to everyone. That was one of the reasons he admired and loved her so much. A quality he hoped was a part of his own personality.

"You need not concern yourself with any work tonight, Nuith. You've had a long and difficult journey. Rest yourself and I will see you in the morning," Queen Tiye said affectionately.

"Thank you, My Queen. I shall rest and be anxious to serve you tomorrow," Nuith answered with a smile and a bow.

Sekhaten quickly stood-up from his seat and addressed his Mother, "Where will Nuith be living during her stay with us?" he asked boldly.

"I think she should live in the third set of rooms down the hall to the left. What do you think my husband?" Queen Tiye inquired.

"That is an excellent choice. Far enough away for you to have privacy, but close enough to be summoned quickly," Pharaoh Amenhotep reasoned.

"Fine, there it shall be then," the Queen said.

Sekhaten quickly added, "May I show her the way, Mother?"

Queen Tiye, as well as the others, was rather shocked at Sekhaten's request, a Prince asking to show a servant to her living quarters. But, Queen Tiye, remembering Sekhaten's kind nature, did not want to deny him. "All right, my son. You may show her, but please return swiftly, you will not have many opportunities to visit with your Grandfather."

"Yes, I will return quickly," Sekhaten promised.

Then, he turned to Nuith and she fully noticed him for the first time. How handsome he was, she thought, and how kind he must be, this Prince, who offered to walk her to her rooms. They looked into each other's eyes and for a moment or two forgot anyone else was there. Their gaze was broken only by the voice of the Pharaoh who requested that Sekhaten hurry a little. Consequently, their attraction to each other was noticed by everyone, but not everyone found innocence in it. In particular, the high priest Heptshoten, who had recently joined the gathering, was clearly bothered.

Sekhaten and Nuith walked down the hallway in silence at first, of course, she could not be the one to initiate the conversation. But, momentarily, Sekhaten began to speak; he could not miss this opportunity. "I, too, would like to welcome you to the palace, Nuith. I hope you will be happy here with us," he said softly.

"Everyone has been so kind to me. I could not be anything else but happy here, My Prince," she replied gratefully.

"Please, Nuith, call me Sekhaten when we are alone. I truly dislike the formalities of being a prince," he explained.

Nuith was very surprised that he would ask such a thing of her. She knew it was against the religious laws of his land to disrespect the son of 'Egypt's Living God', Pharaoh, by addressing the Prince without his title. "But, My Prince, will I not be punished should someone hear me or find out?" she questioned.

"I will protect you. I will never let anyone harm you," Sekhaten said warmly, then smiled. She returned his smile and felt a chill of excitement come over her body. Still, she knew that she must not entertain hopes or desires of love with him. She was a servant and he was the son of the Pharaoh of Egypt, a few heartbeats away from being Pharaoh himself.

"Well, here we are already. Sleep well, sweet Nuith. I will see you in the morning," Sekhaten said cheerfully.

"Goodnight, My Prin…um, Sekhaten. I will wait with anticipation to see you again tomorrow," Nuith answered softly, stunned by her own boldness. Sekhaten held back the layers of sheer material that covered the entrance to Nuith's suite, allowing her to pass through and into her rooms. He watched her for a second and then let loose of the material, once again concealing the rooms and Nuith from his view. Yes, he thought, tomorrow would be a day of anticipation for both of them. Indeed…it would most certainly be an excellent day.

The next morning, Nuith awakened early and immediately prepared herself for her day's work. She had just finished dressing and had sat down on her chaise, when she heard the voice of a child calling out to her. "Lady Nuith, My Lady," the child said sweetly. Nuith quickly ran to the entrance of her suite and pulled back the sheer curtains. There she saw a lovely little brown-skinned girl about 7 or 8 years old. The girl wore a short dark blue tunic tied with a wide red-colored rope belt. Her hair was dark brown and in two large thick braids bound together behind her back by a red-colored cord.

"Yes, my child, what is it?" Nuith asked puzzled by the encounter.

"Queen Tiye requests that you attend her now, My Lady," the child explained.

"Oh, all right, I am ready," Nuith said excitedly, "Let us go."

They both rushed down the hall, and then calmly entered the Queen's chambers. Queen Tiye stood at the doorway to her balcony, where she caught the morning breeze each day. She turned around as she heard the footsteps of Nuith and the girl, Karin, behind her. "Ah, good morning, my lovely Nuith," the Queen said joyously.

"Good morning, My Queen. I hope you slept well," Nuith remarked, once again with a bow.

"Yes, my dear, I did. You are certainly a pleasant girl. I am quite pleased with you," the Queen complimented. Nuith smiled.

And, so the morning passed, Queen Tiye continued to visit with her Father as well as to help the Pharaoh with affairs of State. For the most part, Nuith did a lot of standing and sitting around, careful to pay attention to any of the Queen's needs. When it was time for the mid-day meal, Nuith was allowed to have hers alone. That was arranged by the Queen, so that Nuith might rest a bit and not have to serve the Queen at least a little while during the day. Nuith chose to eat in a garden just behind the Great Hall. She took a seat on an alabaster bench and began her meal of fruit, bread, and cheese. Shortly after she had begun, she saw a figure emerge from around one of the many fountains in the garden. Oh, no, she thought, it is Sekhaten. What on earth shall I say to him? If he does not speak to me first, I cannot say anything to him. And, if he passes and says nothing to me, I will be quite upset. Oh…why did I come out here? Sekhaten came closer and closer and was soon upon her.

"Good afternoon, sweet Nuith. Are you well today?" he said with a smile as he sat down beside her.

"Good afternoon, Sekhaten. Yes, I am well and am pleased to see you," she answered, now relaxed by his gentle and caring manner.

"I am pleased to see you as well. I have been looking for you," he said.

"Have you? Why?" Nuith inquired respectfully.

"I cannot really explain. It felt good when I was with you yesterday. It seems I liked being around you and being able to look so closely upon such remarkable beauty," Sekhaten admitted.

Nuith was thrilled by his comments. "Sekhaten," she said in a shy whisper, "I liked being around you, too. And, I dare say for the same reasons as those of your very own."

They smiled at each other and their eyes re-entered the dream world that they had experienced the prior day, when each saw nothing but the other and preferred things that way. As Sekhaten reached for her hand, they heard the voice of Karin calling Nuith back to her duties. "I must go now, Sekhaten. It was lovely being with you. I hope we shall meet again soon," Nuith said as she reluctantly stood and began to walk away.

"Nuith," Sekhaten called softy, "I will miss you until that time."

Nuith turned around and gave Sekhaten a quick smile of approval then scurried back to the Queen's side. The rest of the day Nuith was on a cloud. Sekhaten was in her heart and would be forever. She accepted the fact that there was no future with him, except to be a servant in his palace, and, to watch him marry someone else. But, she would still feel deeply for him and give him aid whenever possible, and that she would do until she no longer existed in this world.

Once the Queen had gone to bed, Nuith walked back to the garden and sat on the same bench she and Sekhaten had been on that afternoon. She smiled as she remembered his words, 'I will miss you until that time', and then prayed that the gods would allow them to be alone together just one more time. She watched the night sky as the multitude of stars twinkled and the large white

full moon shone brightly. There was a warm sensuous breeze and her hunger
for Sekhaten grew. Suddenly, out of the shadows, she heard a voice.

"Nuith, it is wonderful to see you. I could not sleep for thought of you and
now you are here," Sekhaten said happily as he walked towards her.

Nuith looked-up in surprise, but also in fear, she knew she was treading on
dangerous ground. Were they caught, his penalty would be light, but despite
his declarations of protection, her penalty would be death…Just this last time,
she thought, then she could let go. "Sekhaten," she said nervously, "I, also,
could not sleep for thought of you."

Sekhaten's heart filled with hope. "You truly care for me. then?" he asked
affectionately as he again sat down beside her.

"Yes," she answered, "Very much…very much indeed."

He took her hand, held it between both of his, and caressed it lovingly, "I
have cared for you from the moment I saw you," he whispered. "More than for
any other woman I have known." Then, he let go of her hand, pulled her
towards him, and embraced her tightly. Nuith slowly put her arms around his
neck and returned his tight embrace. She knew this would be the last time they
could engage in such affection, so she hugged him as if she was saying good-
bye, and essentially, she was saying good-bye. Sekhaten gently kissed Nuith's
neck…then her forehead…then her nose…then her lips, and filled her mouth
with his tongue. He moved his tongue swiftly and erratically around the inside
of her mouth and deeply down her throat. He moved one hand up from her
torso and cradled the back of her head, pushing her head towards him as his
tongue continued to thrust down her throat. It was building a passion in his
groin that he knew could not continue unless there was to be a release.

Nuith had never felt such emotions; she had never 'known' a man and had
never been in love. Suddenly, she was very conscious of her breasts, she was
feeling stimulation there, particularly in her nipples, that was unfamiliar to
her. And, each time Sekhaten caressed her breasts with his hands, or rubbed
her nipples with his fingers, despite she being fully clothed, her body became
inflamed and she could not hold back her moans. As well, there was an equally
unfamiliar feeling between her legs, one that provided even more pleasure. She
continuously felt his warm and rapid breaths on her face, and heard the
sounds of his muffled moans, and they aroused her more and more each second. After several minutes, Sekhaten withdrew his tongue from Nuith's mouth
and sweetly kissed her lips, ending their long and passionate kiss. He could
stand no more without completion of the lovemaking and that was impossible,
at least for now. Nuith had to remain a virgin as long as she was the Queen's

personal servant, but also, Sekhaten knew enough not to expect any honorable woman to quickly engage in sexual intercourse without marriage, even for the son of Pharaoh.

Nuith wished she could make love to the fullest with Sekhaten, she wanted him enough to do so right then and there. But, she knew it was improper and that he would most surely think ill of her after all was done. She had planned to end their intimacy that night, but, she knew she could no longer live with that decision. And, as of that night, her commitment to virginity no longer mattered to her. If need be, she would find a reason to leave her position, her desire to have him 'enter' her was so great. They ended their brief time together with a short kiss and a long, ferocious embrace. Sekhaten massaged her back as she, having her arms around his neck, played with the back of his soft black hair. Neither was ready to part from the other, but the hour was late and soon the palace guards would make a patrol through the area. They must not be seen there together at night. They parted, anxious for morning when they would see each other again. But, after their departure, someone else emerged from the shadows; someone who had been there almost from the beginning of the meeting, Heptshoten, the high priest.

It had been several weeks since Nuith had come to live at the palace. She had settled nicely into a routine with Queen Tiye with whom she got along splendidly. She continued her secret meetings with Sekhaten and they now had fallen deeply in love with each other. These were difficult times for Nuith and Sekhaten, though. They were seldom able to meet alone, perhaps only one or two days a week and only for a short amount of time. They chose various meeting places, but all within the palace walls. Their public appearances together could consist only of formal polite conversation despite the fact that, inside, each burned with passion for the other. And, though it might be all right if they were observed alone for a moment or two, any prolonged such behavior would be strongly reprimanded.

But, this was one night they were able to meet; they had chosen the hanging garden at the far end of the palace. Sekhaten had arrived first and was sitting on a marble bench when he saw Nuith walking towards him in the moonlight. He stood, smiled lovingly as she approached, and outstretched his hand to her. She smiled and took hold of his hand, at which point he gently pulled her close to him, and then hugged her as if he had not seen her in a million years. She hugged him equally as hard, her heart began to beat wildly at his touch upon her body.

"Umm...My Love...I have missed the feel of your body," Sekhaten whispered, his hands moving up and down her back.

"Yes, I have been longing to be in your arms for what seems like forever," Nuith replied softly. Sekhaten began to kiss Nuith on the neck, and then ran his tongue down the front of her chest until he reached the edge of the low-cut outfit she was wearing. His hands left her back and proceeded to pull the top of her outfit down until her soft warm breasts were fully exposed. He passionately began to massage them with both hands, as she leaned slightly backwards and held tightly onto his waist. When the massaging caused her moans to become continuous and her nipples to become enlarged and hard, he engulfed one of her nipples with his mouth. He sucked and licked it maniacally and eventually sucked each nipple in turn with much fury and exhilaration. He ultimately was stimulated to a point at which he had to abruptly stop. His penis was hard and throbbing and he would soon need to relieve himself without her. They had not yet had intercourse; the danger of being found out seemed far too great a chance to take right now. So, they stopped their activity, both frustrated with the lack of completion.

"What will we do, Sekhaten? We cannot continue like this," Nuith asked sadly as she covered herself again.

"I do not know yet, my Love. But, you are right, we cannot continue in this manner. It is all too painful this way. I do not know what kind of future we can have together, but, I promise you, I will find an honorable life for us. Somehow, someway, I will arrange it. I will never consent to have another," Sekhaten assured her with eternal love in his heart.

Three weeks later, Sekhaten was summoned to the Pharaoh's chambers. It was very early morning and Sekhaten wondered what could be of such urgency that he need be summoned immediately. Was Egypt perhaps at war? he thought. When he reached the Pharaoh's chambers, the soldiers guarding its entrance bowed and then pulled back the heavy curtains that covered the entrance. As Sekhaten walked into the suite, he saw his Mother and Father seated side-by-side at a large decorative table. "Come sit down, my son," his Father said with a smile as he beckoned him to the table. Sekhaten did as the Pharaoh asked. The presence of smiles on the faces of both his parents, as well as the absence of his brothers, signaled that the subject was not war. Once Sekhaten was seated, his Father began, "My son, I have this very morning received wonderful news. The Sultan of Arabia has accepted our terms of negotiation and agreed to a marriage between you and his daughter," he explained happily.

Sekhaten was stunned. That was the first mention of any kind of marriage plans made to him, regarding anyone. He looked at his Mother, she was smiling at first, but, having realized his reaction, was rapidly reversing her expression. "Why?" he replied respectfully. "I have never indicated a desire to marry any time soon, Father…and I tell you now, I do not wish to do so."

"I know we should have come to you when we first received the inquiry from Arabia, but, we got caught-up in negotiations and almost turned them down," Queen Tiye answered.

"I wish you had," Sekhaten said in disgust. "What about my brothers? Cannot one of them marry her?"

The Pharaoh laughed slightly. "Be realistic, son. Djutmose is too sickly, Akhenaten is strange in his thinking and actions, not suitable for marriage at this time. Smenkhare and Tutankhamen are just babes. Besides, you were specifically mentioned as their choice."

Queen Tiye tried to reconcile the news. "You are of the age when it is time for you to marry. And, this marriage in particular is your duty as a Prince. There had been talk of an invasion from Arabia, this alliance might save the lives of many of our people. Should we reject it at this time, the consequences could be disastrous," she stated in a most serious tone.

Sekhaten released a be-labored sigh of defeat. There was nothing he could say that would change anything. His mind now went to Nuith, his one and only acceptable love. How could he tell her this? Had he not just several weeks before promised her he would find a way for them to be together? He would have to tell her immediately, before she heard it around the palace or from his Mother.

Queen Tiye and the Pharaoh disliked seeing Sekhaten so obviously unhappy. "I am sorry, my son. But, those of us of royal heritage must live our lives in accordance with what is good for the people and the State, not for ourselves," the Pharaoh explained.

"I understand, Father. It is all right…May I leave now?" he responded solemnly.

"Yes, Sekhaten, you may leave. We will talk with you again," the Pharaoh said sympathetically.

"Fine," Sekhaten replied as he rose from his chair and quickly left the chambers. Sekhaten hurried down the hallway to Nuith's suite. Since it was still very early, and thank the gods, Nuith was not with the Queen, he assumed she was still in her chambers.

When he reached the entrance of her suite, he pushed through the curtains without prior announcement. He found her sitting on a chaise leisurely eating her morning meal. She was startled by his sudden appearance. "Sekhaten, what are you doing here? It is too dangerous," Nuith said fearfully.

"I know, but, I had to talk with you before you heard from someone else what was to happen," Sekhaten explained. Nuith became even more fearful at hearing Sekhaten's words.

He sat down beside her and took hold of both her hands. "My Love, I have just come from the chambers of my Father. He and my Mother summoned me early this morning. I was informed that they had arranged a marriage for me to one of the daughters of the Sultan of Arabia, without my knowledge," he explained in distress.

Nuith's heart seemed to stop for a moment, but then, she stoically maintained her composure. Though she was in great pain, his words were ones that she had expected to hear someday. As much as she wanted to believe they could have a life together, deep inside, she always knew it was impossible. She only wished she had been able to have more time with him before he married. "I see," she said calmly.

Sekhaten was puzzled by her reaction. "Are you well, Nuith? Do you understand what I have just told you?" he inquired softly as he massaged her hands.

"Yes, I am well and I understood your words, My Prince. They were as they should have been," she replied.

Her formal words and tone took Sekhaten by surprise. He was so used to hearing affection in her voice and thinking of themselves as one. This formality and separateness would require much painful adjustment on his part. When Nuith pulled her hands away from him, it was almost more than he could stand. Did she not realize that his heart was in misery as well? "Nuith," he whispered sorrowfully, "Please, do not end it like this…we mean more to each other than this," he pleaded.

Nuith rose from her seat and looked-down at him. "I think it would be better for both of us if you left me now, My Prince. Of course…it is your decision to make, but, I think the pain would be lessened for both of us would you do so," she answered honestly.

Sekhaten stood and tried to embrace her for the final time, but she quickly moved away from him. He reluctantly followed her lead and slowly walked back to the entrance of her suite. He turned to take one last intimate look at the woman with whom he would always be in love, but, would never be allowed to hold in his arms again. "Good-bye, my true wife," he said softly, then turned and left her chamber.

Once he was gone, Nuith sat back down on the chaise and began to cry. Good-bye, My Heart, she thought, I wish you happiness.

As the weeks passed, the time grew closer and closer to the wedding. The atmosphere around the palace became more and more frantic with each passing day. Besides the extravagant wedding, there was a national celebration in a few weeks in honor of the gods. Ironically, Queen Tiye had Nuith helping with the wedding preparations. But, Nuith's love for Sekhaten made her work even harder to ensure a perfect wedding for him. Afterall, in her eyes, he still deserved the best of everything. However, as the weeks passed, neither Nuith nor Sekhaten could turn-off what each so strongly felt for the other. The love and sexual stimulation that they felt became excruciatingly unbearable for both of them. And, though she tried to avoid his presence as often as possible, Sekhaten finally cornered Nuith alone one night in the palace and re-iterated his undying love for her.

He pushed her up against a limestone wall that was hidden in shadows and was decorated with a colorful scene of a royal procession. He whispered to her in a tone of desperation as he pressed his body against hers, "My Love, my life. I cannot continue without the touch of your lips on mine and the feel of your body against me...I need you...Please, do not let us part." One of his hands began to caress her large soft breasts while the other hand did the same to her buttocks. He quickly lowered his head and began to lick her on the neck, breathing heavily and rapidly.

After hearing his words and feeling his touch, Nuith could hardly restrain herself, but she tried. "I suffer enough. Why do you torture me with your tongue and your touch?" she lamented. Sekhaten ignored her words and continued his physical expression of love to her body. Nuith became uncontrollably wet between her legs as her passions reached a height they had not attained in the past.

Sekhaten pleaded with her once more, "Come back to me. Please, come back to me...We must not part. Promise me, you will remain with me always."

Nuith soon knew she had lost the battle and ultimately repeated the words that Sekhaten hungered to hear. "We shall never part," she replied softly, "Never."

They then engaged in a marvelously fanatical kiss, with tongues and hands sliding everywhere. Sekhaten earnestly made a commitment of his own. "I will make it right for us. You will not be merely my sexual convenience or merely my lover. I do not know what I will do, but I will do something…something of which you will approve. We shall be happy and together. On that, I give you my word," he promised.

Regardless of the danger involved, they decided that night upon a plan that would provide for a private place far from palace eyes and ears, where they could finally consummate their love. The plan began when, with the permission of Queen Tiye, Nuith was allowed one full day and night away from her duties as a time to rest before the arrival of the national celebration to the gods. The celebration would require Nuith's aid in many of the preparations. And…as a rest from her duties with the wedding preparations, an event which would closely follow the yearly national celebration. Since Sekhaten had requested it for her, Queen Tiye, again, found it difficult to deny. With that arrangement in play, all that was necessary was for Sekhaten and Nuith to meet each other, just before dawn of said day, and travel to the royal summer house up the Nile in Gebelein. There would be no one living there nor should there be anyone around, it was a secluded area, built particularly for privacy. As far as Sekhaten's whereabouts were concerned, no one would wonder about him being gone all day. Being third in line for the throne, he had no pressing duties to perform and he was, occasionally, gone from the palace all day anyway. The day that was chosen was only two days away now, yet, both felt the amount of time to be an eternity.

The high priest, Heptshoten, was well aware of the relationship between Prince Sekhaten and the Lady Nuith. He had purposely viewed their encounters many times. And, despite the fact that she should have been put to death by now, he had done nothing. He loved the Prince and hoped the affair would quickly burn itself out. But, instead, the relationship had intensified. Even the impending marriage had not ended the affair. Though Sekhaten had thought himself alone with Nuith when he cornered her that night, in reality, he was not alone. In Heptshoten's mind, the affair was now a double threat to Egypt. Should the Sultan of Arabia somehow discover that the husband-to-be of his precious daughter was sexually and romantically involved with a servant, it would be an unspeakable insult. It would most surely lead to war. Additionally, the gods would be merciful for a time, but soon they would be angered by the denigration of 'Egypt's Living God', Pharaoh, and the royal family by Sekhaten's minglings with a servant. The gods would punish Egypt for allowing Heptshoten to be high priest, a high priest who would permit such sacrilege. Then, the gods would take vengeance upon the unworthy priest himself. Heptshoten was determined not to let any of these happenings occur.

The morning was cool and it was still dark as Sekhaten and Nuith rode their horses south, following the Nile River up to Gebelein. As the sun began to rise, the air warmed, and the shadowed shapes of sandstone houses and palm trees came into focus. By the time the sun had fully arisen, they were far from any familiar houses or people and almost at the outskirts of Gebelein. They did not ride into the city, but rather around its borders, directly to the summer quarters situated on the banks of the Nile.

Nuith saw the enormous alabaster building come into view. It sat on a bed of soft white sand, had multiple tall colorfully decorated columns supporting the large flat roof, and was surrounded by fragrant flowers and lush green palm trees. The sheer white curtains at the windows fluttered in the warm river breeze. Truly, it was a house of the gods, Nuith thought, for who but the gods could live in such a dwelling. They stopped at the front entrance and Sekhaten helped Nuith down from her horse. He tied the horses to a long stake that was already driven into the ground and left some water from the river for them to drink. Then, Sekhaten put his arm around Nuith's waist and guided her into the house.

The large entrance room of the house was equally 'god-like' to Nuith, with many colorful wall paintings and beautifully carved furniture. Sekhaten led her down a wide hallway and into a large suite of rooms that had a view of the Nile. "These are my quarters when we stay for the summer…Come," Sekhaten said softly. They walked through a pair of white curtains and out onto the terrace attached to the room.

"What beauty," Nuith said breathlessly as she beheld the magnificence of the Nile. Its gently rolling blue waters against the background of graceful palm trees, a white sandy shore, and hundreds of multi-colored flowers. A flock of birds glided through the clear blue sky, several peacocks strutted near the water's edge, and one small boat with a slightly fluttering white sail, floated down river.

Sekhaten, his arm around Nuith's waist, pulled her closer to him and kissed her cheek. She turned her head, looked-up at him, and smiled. He leaned down and passionately kissed her lips for a few moments. But, he needed to ask her a question before they went any farther. "Are you sure you want to do this, Nuith? The possible consequences for you are far greater than anything I would experience. The priests might overlook us merely meeting, but the breaking of your vow of virginity would be fatal. I love you and I want you more than anything in life. But, should you now not want to continue, I would understand and could not blame you. I will love you no matter what you decide," Sekhaten explained with great concern.

Nuith thought for a moment. She had decided long ago to take the chance she was about to take and she saw no reason to change her mind now. "Sekhaten," she whispered affectionately, "I have wanted you ever since we first spent time together by ourselves and nothing has changed that for me. I am fully aware of what might happen to me. But, I love you and I will not leave this life without having had you in me."

With the speaking of those words, Sekhaten smiled and kissed her hand, then they lovingly walked back into Sekhaten's suite and over to the bed. Nuith pulled her white tunic up and over her head, exposing her shapely, naked, dark-bronze body. She had very large breasts. Her nipples were round and long, almost an inch in length, beckoning his mouth to engulf them. The look of them always excited Sekhaten. He could hardly wait to wrap his lips around them again. She had a tiny waist and a wide pubic area covered with thick curly black hair between two firm shapely thighs. The sight of which was over-whelmingly arousing to Sekhaten, as this was his first viewing of her naked lower body. He quickly removed his own tunic, pulling it up and over his head. His long straight black hair fell gracefully and loosely passed his shoulders and again down his back once the tunic was fully taken off. The removal of his tunic revealed his muscular golden-colored body and large, partly hard, penis surrounded by silky soft slightly curled black hair. He grabbed her buttocks with both hands and pulled her to him, smashing their bodies together, her hard nipples burned into his bare chest as they pressed against his skin. He feverishly fondled her buttocks, squeezing and pulling at them, in a manner similar to someone kneading bread. His head quickly moved downward; where he took one of her enormous nipples into his mouth.

He sucked it hard and rapidly, as if he thought he could actually pump milk from it. First one nipple, and then the other, until each was engorged to almost another inch in size. Nuith held the back of his head with both hands, and in turn, pushed as much of each nipple into his mouth as she could. She wanted his mouth filled with it. And, each time Nuith saw one of her nipples fully dis-appear into his mouth, she was thrilled at the sight of it. They ultimately lost their balance and both fell sideways onto the bed. Now in a more comfortable and sturdy position, Sekhaten increased the force of his sucking on her nipples. But, in a few moments, he stopped, put his arms around her, and held onto her as he shifted their position, placing their heads towards the top of the bed. His breathing became heavier as he resumed his tongue caress of her nipples.

Because her legs were more spread apart, he moved one of his hands from her buttock area to her thoroughly wet genital area, where he massaged and pulled at her slippery clitoris. It caused both of them to cry-out in pleasure. Nuith reached down with one hand and took hold of his now hard penis, slippery with its own wetness. She repeatedly rubbed the head of it with her thumb in a lovingly circular motion that caused a gush of wetness to stream down her hand and long loud moans from Sekhaten. Then, with her hand, she guided the head of his penis to her clitoris and began to massage her clitoris with the head of his penis, sliding the head back and forth, up and down, their wetness mixing. Sekhaten suddenly slid her nipple out of his mouth and quickly moved his body downward, breaking her hold on his penis. In an instant, he was licking and chewing her clitoris and running his tongue across her vagina opening, provoking screams of ecstasy from Nuith. She thought her breasts would burst, they were so swollen with passion. Her nipples were fully hard and pointed, like the tops of pyramids.

Within a few minutes, Nuith whispered to Sekhaten, "I want you in my mouth too." Sekhaten lifted his head and moved his body back towards Nuith, then he turned around, his back to the head-end of the bed. On his hands and knees, he straddled Nuith's head, allowing his penis to hang directly above her mouth. She opened her mouth and he slowly lowered his groin, filling her mouth with the head of his large hard penis. She used one hand to fondle his muscular buttocks and one hand to hold the shaft of his caramel-colored penis, while she licked and sucked its large and slippery head. His soft hairy sacks rested comfortably on her forehead. Sekhaten closed his eyes and began to moan loudly, but after awhile, leaned down and continued to engulf Nuith's clitoris with his mouth, his head buried in her pubic hair, as he held one thigh in each hand.

When Sekhaten could hold his ejaculation no longer, he pulled himself up, withdrawing his penis from Nuith's mouth, turned around, and laid on top of her, face to face. He gently 'entered' her wet warm vagina, and then began to pump her furiously, thrusting his penis deep inside her again and again, attempting to touch her very soul. But, in Nuith's mind, he had already done just that...many weeks ago. Within several minutes, Sekhaten's liquid began to pour into Nuith, so much so, that it began to flow back out of her vagina. Their passionate love-filled screams of ecstasy floated loudly across the calm and glorious waters of the marvelously bountiful Nile.

Once they had ended all the lovemaking they were physically able to withstand, they laid in bed for a very long time. They held each other tightly.

Sekhaten's penis softened, but remained resting in Nuith, neither of them was ready for him to take it out. But, the hour was growing late and they would have to make it back to the palace before daybreak, they must be leaving soon. It was dark, but still warm, when they arrived at the back of the palace. Sekhaten and Nuith quickly kissed goodnight, then Nuith hurriedly passed through the garden entrance, through the garden, passed the Great Hall, and finally through the large wooden door, which led to the hallway of the living quarters. No one was in view, so she quietly dashed down the hallway and through the sheer white curtains of her suite.

The moment she entered, she knew her fate was sealed. For there stood the high-priest, Heptshoten, along with three of the royal guards awaiting her return. "So, there is no end to your insolence!" he shouted angrily. "Was it not enough that you met with the Prince right here, under my very nose?! Did you need to go away with him as well?!" He abruptly paused, calmed himself, then came very close to her ear and gently whispered, "You understand...I cannot save you now."

Nuith stood silently, she was frightened and guilty. She had no defense for what she had done. There was nothing for her to say. She knew that whatever she said would not matter anyway. At Heptshoten's beckoning, a guard took hold of each of her arms and they all left her chamber, her presence never to be seen there again.

Sekhaten casually returned the horses to the stable, handing their reins to the stable keeper. He strolled back to his room with the memories of his love-making with Nuith on his mind. Upon opening the white curtains to his suite, he found his Mother sitting at the large table in the middle of the room. "Mother, what are you doing here at this late hour?" he asked with astonishment.

"Where have you been, my son?" Queen Tiye inquired, though she already knew the answer.

"Why? What do you mean?" he answered attempting to avoid the truth.

"I am sure you know exactly what I mean, Sekhaten. What on earth possessed you to leave the palace alone with her? Have you lost your mind?" Queen Tiye said in an annoyed tone.

"I love her, Mother. I needed to be with her and I did not know what else to do," he tried to explain.

"You did not know what else to do?" Queen Tiye repeated as she quickly became enraged, "You did not know what else to do! You are a Prince! The son of Pharaoh! You should have had more sense and more control! You have killed her! That is what you have done!…You have killed her!" Queen Tiye exclaimed angrily. She was quite fond of Nuith and felt horrible over the entire situation.

"What will happen?" Sekhaten asked softly, now as frightened as was Nuith.

"That which will happen has already happened. She has been arrested and taken to the prison beneath the palace," Queen Tiye told him with sorrow, her rage now somewhat subsided. "Your father will hear her case tomorrow and she will most surely be condemned to death."

Sekhaten crouched down on one knee so that his head was almost even with that of his Mother's, who was still seated at the table. He held both of her hands in his and looked straight into her eyes. "Mother, please help me save her. I know there is something you can do. Father will listen to you if you ask him to spare her. Will you not give me aid in this matter?" he pleaded softly and in anguish.

Queen Tiye replied with tears in her eyes, "There is nothing I can do to help her, Sekhaten. The law is what it is, I cannot change it…not even for you."

Sekhaten rose to his feet, slowly walked to the terrace entrance, and pulled opened the curtain door. He looked out into the night sky and soon raised both of his hands, covering his face with his palms. In a few moments, Queen Tiye heard her favorite son, Prince Sekhaten, crying and it broke her heart. She could not endure the sound of it, so she stood and downheartedly left his suite, leaving him alone with his pain.

Queen Tiye was correct in her predictions. Nuith was found guilty of blasphemy and sentenced to death. Her execution was to be in 3 days. Sekhaten arranged for a secret meeting with his two older brothers, Djutmose and Akhenaten, to request their help in the escape of Nuith. They agreed to help him and they all devised a plan that was to be carried-out the day before the execution.

It was a quiet night around the palace as Sekhaten gathered together all of the jewels he had been given over the years as gifts and wrapped them in a piece of cloth. He then placed the bulging cloth within a sack containing some of his clothes. He could not merely set Nuith free, he must go with her, into exile from Egypt. He would not survive his life without her. In a short time, his brothers, Djutmose and Akhenaten, arrived at his rooms; it was time to leave. They all walked cautiously and quietly down the main hallway to a flight of stairs that led beneath the palace main floor. They descended the stairs and continued on through one of the torch-lighted narrow hallways that led to the prison area and down another flight of stairs, finally reaching the prison cells.

Sekhaten hid behind a corner wall as his two brothers approached the guard. Because of her arrest, Sekhaten was forbidden to see Nuith again, and should he accompany his brothers, his presence there would have caused suspicion in the guard. As the Princes approached, the guard, shocked at their arrival, jumped to his feet. "Good evening, My Lords," he said nervously with a bow.

"We want to talk with the prisoner," Akhenaten demanded sternly. Nuith was the only prisoner there at the time as these cells were only for criminals who had once lived in the palace.

"Oh, most certainly, most certainly," the guard replied as he stepped aside, allowing them full view of the cell.

"Open the door, man!" Djutmose exclaimed with a scowled look, pretending to be angry.

The guard untied the knot that held tight the door, his hands shaking at the thought of possibly having displeased the Princes. Then, he flung the reed door open so that the Princes might enter. Nuith looked-up from the straw mat upon which she sat. Her eyes widened as she realized who her visitors were. "Is Sekhaten all right?" she asked in a worried and weakened voice.

"Come, Nuith," Akhenaten whispered as he helped her up from the ground. "He awaits you outside this cell." Then, Djutmose pretended to feel ill; it was well known that Djutmose was sickly, so his pretense was quite plausible. "Guard! Go to the house of the physician and bring him here immediately, my brother is ill!" Akhenaten shouted. "And take the guard at the stables with you! NOW GO!"

The guard was puzzled over the reason for the additional guard; but, he must perform as the Prince ordered and hurried to do so. When the guard disappeared, they all quickly left the cell. Halfway down the hallway, Sekhaten stepped from behind the corner wall. Nuith saw him and ran to his arms, where they hungrily embraced and kissed each other. Then, at Akhenaten's prompting, Nuith and Sekhaten released their clinch and all hurried on their way. They ascended the first staircase, but then detoured to follow an underground tunnel that led directly to the stables. As they neared the entrance to the outside, a figure came into view that stood between the group and the doorway. Upon a closer distance, the figure was seen to be Queen Tiye. The group nervously stopped once it neared the Queen and stood silently, fearful of what her actions might be towards their criminal act. Queen Tiye looked at Nuith with a slight smile and then at her sons. Seeing the large bundle in Sekhaten's arms confirmed her suspicion that he would be leaving along with Nuith. She handed Sekhaten a large sack. He gently took it from her, making sure to touch her hand. "Here are some gold and jewels to take with you, Sekhaten…Be happy in the life you have chosen, my son," she said mournfully as a tear streamed down her face.

Sekhaten smiled at her and nodded in recognition of her sincere wish for his happiness, despite her fervent disapproval of his actions. "The princess, Mother? Will there be trouble?" Sekhaten asked with concern for Egypt's and his family's well being.

Queen Tiye frowned mildly. "We will pay the Sultan enough gold to satisfy any need he might develop for retribution. And, as you know, we have plenty of gold to spare. Do not worry yourself about us or Egypt…we will survive," Queen Tiye replied as she took a last pain-filled look into his eyes. Suddenly, she threw her arms around him and embraced him tightly. "I will miss you terribly, my sweet loving son," she whispered in despair, her tears now flowing profusely.

Sekhaten returned her tight embrace and whispered, "I love you, Mother. You shall be in my heart each moment of everyday, forever…Please, always remember me favorably regardless of what others will say." He leaned down and kissed the top of her forehead and then continued, "Try to believe, that at least in the Afterlife, we shall be together once more."

Overwhelmed with grief, Queen Tiye quickly turned loose of him and distraughtly returned to her quarters without looking back at him. Sekhaten turned to his brothers, grabbed each with an arm, and pulled his brothers to his chest, hugging them. "Thank you my kind and gentle brothers. I love you deeply and always will…I leave with Egypt in excellent hands." He kissed each on the side of the head. Then, he and Nuith were gone, never to be seen on Egyptian soil again.

The high priest, Heptshoten, decided not to send soldiers to capture and return the couple. He felt the gods would be satisfied enough with Sekhaten's departure. Deep in his heart, Heptshoten actually wished the couple well. But, as high priest, it was his duty to set the proper example for the people of Egypt. So, shortly after Sekhaten and Nuith escaped, Heptshoten decreed that Prince Sekhaten was disgraced and ordered his name removed from all records, past, present, and future, for all time.

And so, in whatever land you now reside, in whatever life you now have established. Multiply and live long Lady Nuith and handsome Prince Sekhaten…

Third Son of Pharaoh Amenhotep III and his Nubian Wife, Queen Tiye.

PEACE…out.

THE BEAUTY AND THE IRISHMEN

The land was the continent of Africa in the year 1656. The sun was warm, but there was a cool breeze as Master Whelan sat on the front porch of his 'part African-part Irish' styled house. He was an older man with a gray beard and long gray hair that he wore in a ponytail. However, he was handsome, with a muscular, well-built body that could have been taken for that of a man in his thirties were that all of him one saw. Alas, though, he was a man well into his fifties. It was his last morning at that home, for he was returning to Ireland that very afternoon.

Everything was packed and ready to go, including his beautiful African servant woman, Mjouli, whom one day he happened to call Beauty and had done so ever since. Beauty seemed a more fitting name for her, he had thought. Mjouli understood that Master Whelan was giving her a compliment, and since he was always very kind to her, did not object to his special name. Her family was of Ethiopian ancestry, thus she was tall and slender, but extremely curvaceous with hour-glass figure. Her skin was soft and smooth and the color of rich cedar wood. Her hair was a mixture of medium and dark brown in color; and was very long with parts of it almost to her waist. Its texture was somewhere between naturally curly and straight. She had big dark brown eyes that sparkled all the time, and full lips that she often stained with berry juice that gave them a reddish color.

Master Whelan loved having Mjouli around to look at everyday. He never gave her very much work to do; he let the other servants do it. Mostly, he talked with her. He had lost his wife to malaria 2 years ago, and though Mjouli was young enough to be his daughter, he found her very mature and a very pleasant conversationalist. He had never tried to seduce her, though he wanted to do so. But, because Mjouli was a servant and not a slave, he knew there would be unpleasant consequences to pay from her family members, as well as the other members of her African community, should he 'take her' against her will. It was also for this reason he was required to ask the permission of both Mjouli and her parents before she could accompany him back to Ireland. He had informed them all that it would only be for a period of 2–3 years, after which time he would return. His only child, Kevin, had reached the point at which he was now running the Ireland-based portion of the family enterprise. Master Whelan felt he should travel home to confer with Kevin and to see if he needed any guidance. He also had some new ideas he wanted to try and thought it would take a few years to get them up and running.

As Mjouli stood on the deck of the huge ship, she waved good-bye to her family with tears streaming down her lovely soft brown face. Master Whelan had begun the purchasing of an extravagant European wardrobe for Mjouli that he planned to continue in Europe. So, he advised Mjouli that she need not bring any of her native clothing. Thus, she was no longer dressed in her African attire, but instead, now wore the clothing of aristocratic mid-17th century Europe. Her hair was pinned-up and confined under a satin champagne-colored bonnet. She had on a floor length silk and satin champagne-colored dress, a thin satin champagne-colored cape, and the most uncomfortable footwear she had ever experienced.

"Are you all right, my dear?" Master Whelan asked as he walked over and put his arm around Mjouli's shoulders.

"Yes, sir, I will be fine," she answered as she wiped her tears away. She wanted very much to travel to Ireland with Master Whelan. She desired the adventure of going new places and meeting new people. But, she also feared that for some reason she might not see her homeland again and that thought sent a cold wind through her heart. The dock and all of its inhabitants soon disappeared from sight.

Master Whelan, in keeping with his regard for Mjouli, had purchased a cabin for her right next to his own. He took Mjouli by the hand and led her to the room, where he gave her the key and kissed her on the forehead. "I will see you shortly. I will have our dinner brought to your room and we can eat together here," he said lovingly. Mjouli did not like any of that behavior. Master Whelan had never kissed her before and she did not like the tone of his voice. He had changed already since leaving Africa. She must be vigilant in maintaining her dignity. She knew it was close to dinnertime, so she freshened-up and sat on the bed nervously awaiting dinner and Master Whelan.

Momentarily, there was a knock at the door and Mjouli reluctantly opened it. "Master Whelan, sir, good evening," she said softly.

"Good evening, my girl. Our food is right here behind me," he answered cheerfully.

One of the sailors followed Master Whelan into the cabin, carrying an assortment of African fruits and vegetables as well as bread, pork, beef, and wine. He had great difficulty keeping his mind on his duties as he stared almost continuously at Mjouli, overwhelmed by her beauty. Eventually, he left and Master Whelan and Mjouli quietly ate their meal. Mjouli had only a little wine, despite Master Whelan's prompting. She had never had it before, and though it tasted good, she did not like the way it made her feel.

After Master Whelan finished all of the wine, he walked to the bed and asked Mjouli to join him so that they might talk. She was not as innocent of the world as he imagined, Mjouli thought. Why could they not talk at the same table upon which they had just eaten their meal? She suspected he had something else on his mind and was not about to join him. "Master Whelan, it is not proper for me to do that, it was not even proper for me to eat in my room alone with you. My family would be most ashamed of me."

"Come now, girl. I am not going to hurt you. We are not going to tell your family what we did in private," he replied in an annoyed tone, he knew full well that his intentions were to 'persuade' her to bed him.

Mjouli was becoming frightened, she had trusted Master Whelan in the past, but perhaps she had been wrong about him. "Please Master Whelan, you have always been a good man, always kind and gentle to me. Why are you treating me like this?" she asked.

He saw the distress in her face and the fear in her eyes and these observations weakened his sexual desires towards her. He truly did care for her in an honorable way. "Now, now. I told you, Beauty, I was not going to hurt you," he said as he got up from the bed and walked back to the door. "I just wanted to talk, the way we always did. But, perhaps you're tired or upset by the separation from your family, so I will leave you now," he said impatiently as he walked out of the cabin and closed the door behind him. He did not attempt to seduce her for the remainder of the trip. He even let her eat her meals alone in peace, only approaching her on deck, except for saying goodnight. Mjouli's faith in the goodness of Master Whelan was unquestionably restored.

The trip was long and the sea was often rough, but eventually the ship docked in London. Master Whelan had business to attend to in the city, but then they were on their way to Ireland by private coach and ferry. Mjouli only saw a little of London for they only stayed 2 days. She did not like it, though. It was crowded, dirty, cold, and had a foul smell about it. It was not like her fragrant, warm, open-spaced home in Africa. She was thankful when they finally were on their way to Ireland.

The arrival at the Whelan Estate was an exciting one; most of the servants were lined-up at the front entrance to welcome Master Whelan home. When he stepped out of the coach, there was applause and cheers as the servants greeted the Master. He smiled and thanked them and then turned to help Mjouli out of the coach. As she stepped from the coach, the servants were all stunned into silence. Though they had all, on occasion, seen Africans, they had not before seen one so close or one so beautiful and elegant. Denny O'Meara, who was to be Master Whelan's "gentleman's gentleman" was particularly smitten by Mjouli and was sparked into a desire for her that consumed him thoroughly. Denny was following in the footsteps of his father who had also been a "gentleman's gentleman" and had trained Denny in the profession. Denny himself was a strapping young man in his late twenties. He was tall with a muscular build and wavy red hair that hung slightly passed his shoulders and complimented his blue-green eyes. He was a known 'ladies man' and always looked quite dashing in his required 'formal' work attire. However, that day, his heart had been stolen completely and forever by a sensuous, beautiful, African woman named, Mjouli.

When Master Whelan and Mjouli entered the manor, a servant girl rushed to take their outer clothing. She promptly hung the garments in a closet located on the side wall of the foyer. The foyer itself was decorated with a white background and floral-designed wall covering. The furniture in the foyer was covered by light green upholstery with its visible wooden portions gilded with gold leaf, which gave the appearance of solid gold furniture. "Thank you, Molly. Please show the lady to the blue room," Master Whelan said cheerily.

"Yes, Master Whelan and welcome home sir," she said softly.

"Thank you, Molly," he said. Then, turning to Mjouli, "I will see you at dinner, Beauty. One of the servants will come for you at sundown, my dear," Master Whelan said affectionately.

"Yes, sir," Mjouli answered. She was in awe of her surroundings; she had never seen a mansion, much less one so beautiful.

"Please follow me, My Lady," Molly requested then started up the elegant winding staircase.

Mjouli followed the servant until they arrived at a closed door. Molly opened the door and beckoned Mjouli to enter. Upon entering, Mjouli's eyes widened as she saw that the size of the room was enormous, almost as large as her parents' entire dwelling. An entire wall was composed of latticed windows that allowed one to observe a magnificent view of the gardens. The decor was magical with more gilded furniture. All of the chair and drapery material was powder blue with gold-colored embroidery. The bed covering and multiple shams were also powder blue and gold. The bed itself was gilded and ornately carved. It had a huge headboard and four bedposts, all of which were connected at the top by long golden rods from which hung sheer powder blue curtains. The curtains could be drawn together for some minimal privacy. The floor was made of two-foot wide, powder blue mosaic tiles that shone as brightly as glass, almost giving the appearance of a mirrored lake. Master Whelan must care for me very much, she thought. She wished she could love him the way he seemed to want her to love him. But, she only saw him as a second father and could never of her own free will be his lover. She hoped that he already understood her feelings.

"Is everything all right, My Lady?" Molly asked politely.

"Yes, everything is wonderful. Thank you," Mjouli replied kindly.

"I will return shortly with some hot water for your basin, so you may wash before dinner," Molly added with a smile.

"Oh, thank you very much, that would be lovely," Mjouli answered gently.

Mjouli found dinner to be most enjoyable. The huge dining hall table was only set for two with Master Whelan at the head of the table and Mjouli sitting directly next to him on the right. Master Whelan had learned that Kevin was in France conducting business, but would be returning within a month. The meal consisted of Irish stew (Master Whelan's favorite meal), biscuits, pastries, and wine. Mjouli chose to have water with her meal. The servants all wondered amongst themselves about who this lady was and what her relationship was to the Master. Was she his lover?

But, Denny was concerned more than anyone else. If she was the lover of the Master there was no hope that he could have her. If she was merely a companion, then she, too, was a servant, though on a higher level such as himself and possibly attainable. He lingered around the kitchen peeking through the door to the dining hall now and then to catch a glimpse of the Lady. At that point, she had not been introduced to any of the servants and none of them even knew her name. As the hour became late, Denny was forced to remove himself from the kitchen, so that he could start preparing the Master's bed and sleepwear for the night. It would not do should the Master arrive at his room and Denny not be there to assist him.

That night, Mjouli laid in her large soft bed confused, yet excited about her new world. She no longer understood her relationship to Master Whelan. She had not been given any chores and he was treating her in the same fashion that he would a woman of his own stature. She would have to follow his lead, but beware of any improprieties in accordance with her own African customs and morals.

The next morning as Denny was leaving the Master's bedroom, he saw Mjouli enter the hallway from her bedroom. When she started towards the staircase, Denny called to her. "Good morning, Madam," he said nervously. When she turned to answer him, he thought he had never seen such loveliness. And, when she smiled at him, he thought his heart would melt from the heat of his simmering passion.

"Good morning," she said in a pleasant, but formal, tone.

"My name is Denny O'Meara. I am Master Whelan's manservant," he explained.

"I am called Mjouli. It is a pleasure to meet you. I..." At that moment a voice rang-out from the bottom of the staircase.

"My Dear. My Beauty. Good day to you," yelled Master Whelan as he ascended the staircase. Mjouli smiled. She and Denny both watched until the Master arrived at the top landing. "So, have you introduced yourself to my companion, Denny?" the Master inquired.

"Yes, sir, I have," Denny replied respectfully. He was pleased to hear the Master refer to her as his companion and not as his lady. Now, he would have a chance to court her.

"Excellent, excellent. My dear, go take a look around the manor and the grounds. I will send Denny to find you when the morning meal is ready," Master Whelan suggested enthusiastically.

"I would enjoy that very much, sir. I shall do exactly what you have suggested," Mjouli answered happily.

"Capital, capital," Master Whelan added as he continued on to his room. Since he had been out for an early ride on his horse, he needed to wash and to change clothes. So, of course, Denny returned to the room with him. Making her way downstairs, Mjouli thought what an attractive and seemingly agreeable young man Denny was and she hoped she would get to know him better.

Master Whelan continued the relationship with Mjouli that he had cultivated in Africa. They had long enjoyable conversations and walked the grounds of the estate together daily. He did not assign her any duties and the truth be known, he had never intended to do so. However, his full intentions towards her were unclear even to himself. He knew he desired her sexually and he knew he felt love for her. But, he also knew that her feelings towards him were quite different from his own towards her. Yet, he hoped against hope that still he might win her.

After several weeks, Master Whelan decided to give a small party for the servants as his 'return home' gift. He had food prepared and brought in from the village so that his servants would not have to cater their own party. The party was held in the large storage house where there would be plenty of room to dance. The night of the party, Master Whelan and Mjouli arrived at the function together. When they entered the party, the music stopped and there was applause as the servants expressed their gratitude to the Master. He had provided Mjouli with a light pink, satin and lace gown, low-cut in front and off-the-shoulder, with large puffed-sleeves (which was the style of the period). Her long, mostly curly, brown hair hung loosely as it had in Africa. She wore two small diamond and ruby earrings and an elaborate diamond necklace with small rubies sprinkled within it, all gifts to her from a loving Master Whelan. She was truly an enchanting sight, and no one in the room could refrain from watching her, especially Denny.

Once Master Whelan and Mjouli were seated, the music resumed playing and the people resumed dancing. There was a series of about 5 fast, catchy tunes to which the people danced an Irish jig and an assortment of other dances. Mjouli found the dances to be very different from what she had known in Africa, but much fun to watch. Then, the musicians played a slow song, and as couples began to dance, Denny quickly walked over to Mjouli. "Excuse me, Madam, would you care to dance with me?" he asked politely.

Mjouli looked at Master Whelan, and though he did not like it, he indicated that the dance would be proper behavior. "I do not know how to do your dances," Mjouli explained.

Denny smiled at her with an outstretched hand and affectionately replied, "That is all right. I will teach you."

Mjouli took hold of his hand and rose from her seat. All eyes were on them as they walked to the dance area. Denny guided Mjouli's arm around his neck, placed one of his arms around her waist, and held her other hand with their arms bent-up at the elbow. Then, he began to take slow steps forward, which forced her to take slow steps backwards. Soon she was in-step with the movement and they were able to glide across the floor as well as any other couple there. Mjouli had never been this close to a man's body before, she could feel the large muscles across his broad shoulders as her hand held on to the back of his neck. And, each time her breasts happened to brush against his chest, she felt a tingle over her whole body. Denny was in his own heaven with Mjouli in his arms. The feel of her torso as it moved beneath his arm around her waist was ecstasy to him. And, each time her breasts happened to press against his chest, he, too, felt a tingle. But, his was limited almost exclusively to below his belt. All too soon for Denny, the song ended and he escorted Mjouli back to her seat. Once she was seated, he eloquently said, "Thank you, Madam, for a most enjoyable dance. I hope you will give me the pleasure of another shortly."

"Of course I will, sir," she replied with a smile.

Master Whelan was feeling a tinge of jealousy, he could see there was an attraction between them. And, though he doubted that he could ever have her, he would not let his servant have her either.

Suddenly, there was a lot of commotion at the entrance to the building. The servants at the party seemed to be excited over someone who was entering the party. In an instant, Master Whelan saw who it was and elatedly jumped-up from his chair. "Kevin! Kevin! My son!" Master Whelan exclaimed as the crowd parted and allowed Kevin to pass through to where his father was standing. Mjouli watched as a lone figure emerged from the crowd. She thought her heart would stop at the sight of him. There walking towards her and Master Whelan was indeed the most handsome man she had ever seen. He was highly sensual with his long, straight, black hair, piercing blue eyes, and clean-shaven somewhat tanned complexion. He had a smile as warm and bright as the sunniest day in Africa. His tall, muscular build was absolutely flattered by his attire, which consisted of a three-quarter length, A-line, burgundy coat with gold braid trim around its borders, a gold and burgundy embroidered vest, a white shirt with a ruffled front, black trousers (resembling those of the musketeers), and black knee-high boots. She watched as he hugged and kissed his father and as Master Whelan hugged and kissed him as well.

"My son. I am so pleased to see you. Are you well?" Master Whelan said breathlessly.

"Yes, Father, I am well. How are you? How are things in Africa?" Kevin replied lovingly.

"All is fine, all is fine…Oh, let me introduce you to the companion I have brought back with me from Africa. My boy, this is Beauty."

"Beauty? Is that her true name?" Kevin asked in a tone of disbelief.

"Well, no, it is not. I have called her that for so long, I have forgotten her true name. What is it, my dear?" the Master inquired.

"My name is Mjouli, sir," she said with a shy smile.

"Oh, yes, quite right, I remember now. Yes Kevin, this is Mjouli. Mjouli, this is my son Kevin," Master Whelan said proudly.

Kevin bowed at the waist, took her hand and kissed it, then, softly said, "I am pleased to make the acquaintance of such a lovely and elegant lady. The name Beauty does indeed suit you perfectly."

Mjouli smiled and again felt a reaction she had never experienced. The touch of his lips on her hand made the area between her legs feel warm and more moist than usual. Her nipples tingled as well, even without direct contact from him. Her mother had explained to her what happened when a man and woman made love. She thought that what she felt now must be the beginnings, because it felt so very pleasurable.

Kevin was also experiencing the pleasure. As with Denny, now his heart was also hers; he knew right away there could never be another woman for him. He must have her no matter what it took. He would first determine her relationship with his father, as there may exist a 'situation' that would have to be 'handled'. But, as great as Kevin's love was for his father, no matter what the relationship might be between his father and Mjouli, he was resolved to have her. He took a seat next to Mjouli and they talked and laughed with each other the entire party. They became as close that night as they would ever be, so strong was their attachment. Master Whelan saw that there was a true affection between Mjouli and his son. And, as painful as it was, he felt that since he probably could not have her, his son having her would be the next best thing. He would indeed give his blessing to their union should Kevin come of mind to ask for it.

Denny, too, saw something happening between Mjouli and Kevin. He would not stand for it. And, though he had engaged only in minimal formal conversations with Mjouli during all of her time there, Denny was sure Mjouli loved him. He was sure that she was being forced by these men of wealth to submit to them. But, he would find a way to save her and take her away from this rich man's manor forever.

Kevin and Mjouli spent long periods of time together strolling through the beautiful emerald gardens and sumptuous massive woodlands of the estate. They spoke of anything and everything and found many similarities in their personalities and philosophy of life. So many similarities, that at times, they could have been one person, one entity, attempting to make a way through life following the least complicated, yet most beneficial path. On one of their strolls, Kevin proceeded to inquire of Mjouli her plans and desires for the future. "May I ask whether my father ever informed you of the length of time he planned to keep you here in Ireland, Mjouli?"

Mjouli answered quickly, "Yes, he did. He expressed to my parents and to me that I would be here 2 or 3 years."

"Apparently, that amount of time was agreeable with you at that moment. But, how do you feel now? Are you lonely? Do you wish to return home shortly?" Kevin questioned cautiously.

Mjouli thought for a moment and also wondered why Kevin was asking her about returning home. Was he attempting to rid himself of her? Did he wish she would leave soon? She answered him softly, but truthfully, "No, I am not lonely and I like it here very much. I would not care to leave anytime soon."

Kevin was elated. "Excellent, excellent! Then, that shall be our plan. You and I shall travel to Africa in 2 or 3 years, together. You can show me all of the wonders of your homeland…the ones besides yourself, that is."

Mjouli looked at him, smiled, and shyly lowered her head. Kevin returned her smile, then, reached over and held her hand. In a moment or two, each gently holding the hand of the other, they slowly continued their stroll through the ever-enchanting, fairytale-like grounds of the estate. Kevin's heart sang. He was surer than ever that Mjouli would one day love him. She was certainly agreeable to holding his hand and that was an encouraging sign. Mjouli's heart was beating so fast, she could hardly breathe. And, the touch of his hand was again causing that pleasurable feeling between her thighs and producing that now familiar wetness there as well.

One cool sunny day as they strolled adoringly in the most magnificent of the gardens, Kevin found he could no longer contain the feelings he had for Mjouli. He knew that it was improperly too soon for any romantic declarations, but, it could not be helped. He kissed her hand and they became lost in each other's eyes as he attempted to express himself. "My dearest Mjouli," he said softly, yet passionately, "I must convey to you that our times together have felt as though I entered heaven's gate, into a land of milk and honey, where all is warm, sweet, and filled with magic. And, I must now say, in all truth and sincerity, how ardently I love and desire you."

Mjouli's heart began to pound for she felt the same emotions towards him. "Sweet, precious Kevin," Mjouli whispered with great affection, "I, too, love and desire you. From the moment I first saw you, my soul did belong to you for all time. Our frequent encounters have only served to enhance and strengthen my feelings for you, so much so, that I do not feel life without you would be worth living. You are my life."

Kevin grabbed Mjouli around the waist with both hands and quickly pulled her against his body, embracing her tightly. Mjouli slid her arms around his neck and hugged him with all the strength she could harness.

"Oh, My Love," Kevin said breathless with zeal and a racing heart, "I was hoping with every part of my being that you had such feelings for me. I am filled with happiness and delight. I treasure even a single strand of your hair as though it were my entire fortune. My world is now complete for the sun that lights it and keeps it alive loves me."

They continued their unyielding and loving embrace, his hands massaging her back. But, they did not kiss. The European protocol and etiquette of the time did not allow for it until after marriage nor did Mjouli's African traditions. So, they derived what pleasure they could as they pressed their bodies tightly together during this ephemeral, but sensuous, embrace.

Denny continued to observe the couple with an irrational intensity. He could barely keep-up with his duties because of his attempts to follow Mjouli, either alone or with Kevin, around the estate. He often stayed awake nights enjoying fantasies about making love with her, which produced climax after climax for him. He craved to taste her nipples in his mouth and to feel his fingers between her thighs. Each time he saw her, he was forced to restrain himself from grabbing her, pulling down the top of her dress, fondling her large breasts, and thrusting one of her nipples into his mouth. He had a small collection of her things in his room hidden in a box under the bed, making for easy access while lying down. They consisted of items she had used such as napkins, and inexpensive things that belonged to her such as a ribbon or a small hair comb. He tried to add to it everyday. Every night, he ran his fingers around each item, his only way of caressing her for now. That 'fingering' of her items always ended in an ejaculation for him and the subsequent euphoria increased with each session. Despite the fact that Mjouli paid him practically no attention, he was convinced that she was truly in love with him and not with Kevin. He still believed that she was somehow being controlled, remaining there against her true will, and needed him to save her from these powerful evil men of wealth.

Several days after Kevin and Mjouli had declared their love for each other, which was unknown to Denny at this time, Denny traveled to England on a short vacation in search of some kind of emotional relief. He found his way to a seedy area of London where he began to drink heavily at one of the low-life pubs. He was solidly 'high' when he walked out into the chilly night and promptly engaged the services of a streetwalking prostitute. She took him to an area behind a deserted building. "Is this all right, Dearie?" she asked in a high pitched voice.

"Sure, sure. Let us get on with it," Denny replied gruffly. Denny leaned his back against a wall of the building. The prostitute unfastened Denny's pants and pulled them down to his knees, exposing his large, but not yet hard, penis. She got down on her knees and took hold of his penis with her hand. Then, she placed the head of his penis in her mouth and began to suck and lick upon furiously. Denny closed his eyes and began to moan in pleasure. Within a few moments, he began to call-out Mjouli's name over and over again, which provided more and more passion to the fantasy in his mind. As his penis grew hard and his ecstasy was about to reach an extraordinary level, the prostitute made the mistake of stopping her activity and asking a question.

"What the hell does this 'mjulie' you keep shoutin' mean?" she asked with annoyance, "It's gettin' on me nerves."

Denny became enraged! How dare this whore intrude upon his fantasy! He opened his eyes and looked down at the prostitute's pale, fat, and painted face. He frowned. She disgusted him. He leaned over, reached down, and wrapped his hands around her throat. He squeezed her neck tightly. She tried to cry-out, but could not. She began to struggle and flail about erratically. The more she struggled, the tighter Denny squeezed. Until, finally, the struggling stopped and the prostitute's body went limp. She was dead and Denny was glad of it. He smiled. The area was still totally deserted, so Denny remained for a few moments and masturbated his already hard penis to the completion of his orgasm. He stood over the prostitute as he ejaculated, allowing his 'fluid' to spray across her head, covering almost her entire face with the creamy substance. After he finished, he pulled-up his pants to their proper location and disappeared from the area.

When he returned to his room, he laid in bed and thought about what he had done. He had never killed anyone in his whole life. He was surprised at how good it made him feel. 'It' was only a slut afterall, not worth anything to anyone. 'It' would not be missed. The act did seem to enhance his sexual stimulation and ejaculation, especially in combination with his thoughts of Mjouli. He would try the act again in the near future. Within a few days later, he was already back in Ireland and only a few miles from the Whelan Estate. He had not yet committed another murder of a prostitute, but, he knew that in due time, it would happen. At the moment, though, he deeply missed his Mjouli and needed to be with her again.

Within a month after Denny's return, Kevin did ask Mjouli for her hand in marriage and she accepted his proposal. Master Whelan gave his permission and within another month there was to be an extravagant garden wedding with multitudes of guests, wine, and food. Upon hearing of the wedding, Denny became abnormally on edge. He was unable to concentrate on any of his work and had now received several reprimands from Master Whelan. He became obsessed with the thought that he must speak with Mjouli, so he could tell her that she did not have to marry the Master's son. He wanted her to know that she could leave with him and he would take care of her. He felt sure she was being forced into the marriage. He was desperate to catch her alone, but it seemed she was always with one or the other of the Masters, truly a prisoner, he thought.

Then, one cloudy afternoon, Denny saw Mjouli walking alone in the garden close to the storage house. He rushed out of the mansion and over to the garden in which she slowly strolled. "Mjouli, Mjouli!" he called, somewhat out of breath from running.

She turned and looked at him with a slight smile as he rushed to her side. "What is it, Denny? What is wrong?" she inquired, no longer smiling after seeing the disturbed expression on his face.

"I had to let you know. You do not have to marry the Master's son. Come away with me, I will take care of you. I love you and I know you love me!" Denny exclaimed almost incoherently.

Mjouli was stunned; she did not know Denny felt that way about her. She had never encouraged him and she certainly did not love him. And now, his tone of voice and unusual behavior were making her feel alarmed. "Denny, you are mistaken. I love Kevin. I am sorry that you care so much for me, but your feelings are not returned," she explained kindheartedly.

"You do not mean that, I know you do not," Denny replied as he abruptly took Mjouli by the arm and aggressively attempted to pull her against him.

Mjouli struggled to break loose, "Stop it, Denny! What are you doing!" she cried-out fearfully.

"I love you! I love y...." But, before he could finish, he was grabbed by the neck, breaking his hold on Mjouli, and landing him on the ground.

"Get your things and get off my land!" Kevin shouted angrily, as he waited to see if Denny would continue to fight. He did not. He stood-up and lovingly looked at Mjouli.

"You do not have to marry him," Denny repeated softly.

Kevin gave Denny a forceful push. "Get out of here before I have you put in prison!" Kevin shouted in a controlled rage.

Denny angrily walked to his room, gathered his things, and left the estate within a half hour. Kevin closely oversaw his departure and made sure Denny did no lingering. But, Denny knew it was not over yet. He was not finished.

The day of the wedding was a joyous one, except to Master Whelan. In his mind, it was a bittersweet day. As pleased as he was to see Kevin married, for it was time that Kevin produced heirs to the estate, he truly wished that Kevin's choice of wife had not been the one woman in the world that he wanted for himself. The weather was perfect for a garden wedding and both Mjouli and Kevin looked magnificent. She wore a low-cut, white satin and lace, partially balloon-skirted gown. And, sheer silk white veils that covered the top of her head and hung gracefully down her back into a 20-foot long train. Her face was left uncovered and was adorned by a pearl and sapphire tiara with matching pearl and sapphire earrings and a matching six-strand pearl and sapphire necklace. Her hair was styled into one large braid down her back, held together at the bottom by a pearl and sapphire clasp.

Kevin wore an extraordinary outfit that consisted of a knee-length, A-line, white, satin jacket with gold embroidery down the front panels and a pair of white satin musketeer pants. It was completed with a pair of white knee-high boots, a white satin vest embroidered with gold thread, and a silk shirt with a ruffled front-button panel. His long black hair was parted down the middle and hung sensuously down his back. No additional adornment was needed to accentuate or otherwise enhance his phenomenal handsomeness.

Master Whelan walked Mjouli down the aisle in the place of her father. He gave her hand to Kevin who took it lovingly, then Master Whelan gave Kevin a pat on the shoulder as he walked to Kevin's right side and stood in the role of 'best man'. As Kevin and Mjouli said their vows, Master Whelan became overwhelmed with feelings of sadness and emptiness that he knew could only be relieved by having Mjouli for himself. He watched as Kevin and Mjouli kissed each other for their very first time, sealing their bond of marriage. He vehemently wished he could take Kevin's place at the altar and especially tonight…in the marriage bed.

Kevin and Mjouli celebrated with the guests for several hours. Then, they said their good-byes to their friends and left the celebration to be alone. The wedding reception was held in the huge main ballroom. As Master Whelan observed Kevin and Mjouli leave the ballroom together, his feelings of envy towards Kevin increased. He knew that they were on their way to a night full of glorious promises of love and passionate acts of sex…However, Master Whelan remained strong and weathered the storm of his heightened sexual imaginings and feelings of love towards Mjouli. And…no one who interacted with him that night was able to tell that his heart was broken.

Since Kevin and Mjouli had only been at the estate a short while, they decided not to leave for a wedding trip. The estate was so beautiful and there were so many secluded areas in which to be alone, they were sure that no other place could possibly be more lovely. Kevin led Mjouli to their new rooms on the other side of the manor, away from Master Whelan's room and most other activity in the mansion. The guests continued to celebrate into the early hours of the morning, but the rooms of Kevin and Mjouli were far enough away that they were not disturbed by the noise. He opened the bedroom door and held her hand whilst they entered the room. Mjouli viewed the room's appearance as a scene from heaven. Once again the wooden portions of the furniture were all the color of gold, but all the material used in the room was white silk and satin. The room was fragrant with the scents of the hundreds of colorful flowers that filled it. The soft yellow glow of the many candles added to the warmth and romance of the scene.

Kevin closed the bedroom door as Mjouli walked towards the bed. She saw a beautiful white silk nightgown laid across the bed for her. Kevin walked over to her and put his arms around her waist. He kissed her lips, but in a second, slid his tongue into her mouth. Her mother had never mentioned anything about this, but she liked it very much. His hands began to move up and down her torso. She put her arms around his neck and ran her fingers through his long, thick, black hair as his tongue swirled in her mouth. As their passions grew, the result of his tongue continuously thrusting down her throat and their bodies tightly meshing together, their breathing became heavier. Kevin withdrew his tongue from her mouth and glided it down her neck and onto her partly exposed breasts protruding over her low-cut gown. Once the tops of her breasts were thoroughly wet from his licks, he ran his tongue back up her neck, then around the inside of her ear and whispered, "Let us get in bed."

Mjouli smiled. "Yes, let us do so," she said softly then turned her back to him. "Will you unfasten my gown for me?"

"Always and forever, My Love," Kevin replied adoringly.

When he finished unfastening her gown, Kevin walked to the other side of the room to allow her to remove her wedding gown, veil, jewelry, and to put on her bed clothing. It also allowed him the opportunity to change his clothing as well. Mjouli nervously crawled into bed and Kevin followed shortly. He pulled her close to him and gently stroked her face with his fingers as he whispered, "I love you, Mjouli…more than life itself. I shall never leave you…even death will not part us. Our spirits are one and shall remain so…throughout eternity."

Mjouli realized that she was no longer nervous. She wanted to feel him inside her and she could wait no longer. She lifted her head and kissed Kevin's lips, but this time, she slid her tongue into *his* mouth, an act which unleashed a torrent of passion in Kevin. He quickly pulled-off Mjouli's nightgown and dropped it on the floor beside the bed. He held the back of her head with one hand as he kissed her lips and their tongues entwined. He massaged her large breasts with the other hand. Soon, once again, his tongue left her mouth and traveled down her neck to her breasts. He licked every inch of each breast several times, making sure that his tongue missed no part of them, until each entire breast shimmered from wetness. Then, both hands caressed her breasts as his lips and tongue alternately surrounded her bronze-colored nipples. He vigorously sucked and licked them for over half an hour. At some point during that time, one of his hands left her breasts and moved down to her pubic hair, then slipped between her thighs, where he slid his fingers up and down her large wet clitoris and in and out of her soft warm vagina. His fingers and hand dripped with her wetness. The more Mjouli moaned, the more intense and frantic Kevin's movements became, and it was not long before Kevin's heavy breathing turned into moans of his own. Mjouli assumed that her body could not stand much more pleasure. Certainly, she had reached the epitome of such feelings now.

But, then she felt a pleasure she was sure would burst her heart. She looked to see the cause of it and found Kevin was sliding his tongue between her widely spread legs and each time he thrusted into her vagina with his tongue, her already hard nipples would throb wildly. She felt his fingers pull at her skin to widen her vaginal opening, so that more of his tongue could 'enter' her. Once his entire tongue filled her, its soft thrusting movements inside her vagina caused her indescribable additional pleasure. Her wetness streamed unbelievably heavy, and it covered his lips and chin. She held his head with her hands, massaging it and playing with his hair. His intense breathing, his moans, and the wet sounds of his tongue as it squished between her legs delighted her, and she wished it could all go on forever.

In a short time, he moved his body up, pulled-off his own nightwear, and laid on top of her, wrapping his arms around her shoulders and torso. She grabbed hold of his muscular naked buttocks and held onto them tightly. Soon afterwards, she felt his large, hard penis 'enter' her dripping tight vagina. His rapid forceful thrusts and the feel of his pubic hair rubbing against her engorged clitoris provided further sources of extreme pleasure for her. After multiple orgasms for Mjouli and as much arousal as Kevin could withstand without ejaculation, the climax was reached for both of them. They then rested for awhile, snuggled together in a tight embrace, but there were two more such sessions that night before they both drifted off into a satisfied sleep.

A few weeks later, on a night that was dark and cold and with rain just starting to fall, Denny sneaked to the back door of an old apothecary shop on the outskirts of Dublin. He had chosen that shop because it was far from the Whelan Estate, and being in a city, he would be less likely remembered by anyone. The elderly shop owner heard his knock, slowly opened the door, and allowed Denny inside through the back room of the shop. There was a previous agreement, which had been arranged by a third party, for an illegal purchase of poison herbs. Denny handed the old man a number of silver and gold coins, at which point the old man walked to a cabinet and opened a draw. He took a small cloth sack tied with a short piece of rope from the draw and gave it to Denny. Denny kept his head down and in the shadows as he accepted the sack. Neither man spoke a word and Denny immediately slipped out of the back door from whence he had come. Denny mounted his horse and rode furiously down the road, the rain beating against his face and the wind howling in his ears, enroute to the main road, which would take him east to the Whelan Estate.

Kevin and Mjouli had been married for 3 weeks when Denny returned to the manor. He presented himself at the kitchen entrance where Clancy, the butler, greeted him. None of the servants knew why Denny had left, thus they were not leery of his return, indeed, they were happy to see him. "Denny! Where did you go, man?" Clancy asked.

"I had to leave. Family problems you know," Denny said casually.

"Have a seat. Let us talk," Clancy continued affably.

"No, I cannot stay. I just wanted to get something from my room that I accidentally left behind, if you do not mind," Denny explained. He knew he had to hurry before he was seen by the Masters or Mjouli.

"Go right ahead, my man. Do come say good-bye," Clancy requested.

Denny nodded that he would, as he rushed out of the kitchen and up the back staircase. He reached the landing of the second floor and waited while he listened for any sounds. He heard none and then proceeded down the hallway to the area he knew now belonged to Master Kevin and Mjouli. He wished he could have saved her from the wedding night and these following nights, but he was sure she would understand and forgive him. He remembered that Master Kevin had chosen the white room for their sleeping residence, so he headed straight to it. He listened at the door for a second for possible noises inside, but he knew that at this time in the afternoon, it was not likely that Master Kevin and Mjouli were still in there, even as newlyweds. Not proper you know.

He opened the door and quickly entered, closing the door quietly behind him. A look around the room afforded him the object he was after, a decanter of wine on the small table beside the bed. He knew Master Kevin always drank a glass or two of wine shortly before bed and that Mjouli never drank wine. He removed the cloth sack from his pocket and emptied it into the decanter of wine, then shook the bottle vigorously to dissolve the poison herbs. He returned the decanter to its place and sneaked downstairs using the same path by which he had come upstairs. Clancy was not in the kitchen when Denny returned and he did not seek him out to say good-bye. He left the estate and traveled into town to await the news of Master Kevin's death.

Kevin and Mjouli entered their bedroom after a full afternoon and evening of shopping, dining out, and the theater, all located in the city not far from the estate. "I am so tired," Mjouli said wearily.

"I, as well. The bed looks so alluring. I cannot wait to get into it," Kevin agreed equally as wearily. They both prepared for bed, but nowadays, Mjouli was usually the first to get under the covers. The main reason was that Mjouli had begun to wear only slips under her dress, eliminating her cumbersome pantaloon undergarments. That was basically for Kevin's convenience. They never walked to or rode to anyplace where Kevin did not at some time during the venture want to lick between her thighs or 'enter' her. He would always find the opportunity to secretly do one or the other or both, and she always gladly accommodated him.

Even during their coach rides, with the coachman driving atop, Kevin might kneel on the coach floor, push back the bottom of her dress and bury his face between her thighs, engulfing and sucking her clitoris with extremely great zeal. He always simultaneously inserted a finger or two or three into her vagina using them to feel inside, as her juicy clitoris became harder and harder, setting her entire body afire. However…after such coach episodes, it was always necessary for them to make a 'mad dash' to their private suite either at the theater or at one of the exclusive eating establishments or back at the estate in order that Kevin might relieve his erection. Once in awhile, Kevin would misjudge the timing of his ejaculation and would have to 'enter' her as they traveled along the road in their highly decorative, elegantly gilded, aristocratic coach.

Though Mjouli was already snug beneath the sheets, Kevin was true to habit; he sat on the side of the bed and poured himself a glass of wine. He took a few sips, it tasted a bit strange, he thought. He took a few more sips and decided not to finish it. He told Mjouli he thought it must have gone bad somehow and he would be sure to have the contents of the decanter thrown away tomorrow and replaced with a different bottle. He joined Mjouli under the covers where they embraced each other, then, each quickly fell asleep wrapped tightly in the other's arms.

The next morning, Mjouli awakened and was surprised to see Kevin still in bed, much less still asleep. He was always up and about long before her in the morning. He must really be tired from yesterday, she thought. She leaned over to kiss his cheek and found his breathing to be labored and shallow. He was also soaked with perspiration. She shook him in an attempt to wake him, but he would not awaken. She jumped out of bed and ran down the hallway screaming for help. First, came some of the servants and then came Master Whelan. "Father! Father! Kevin is ill. I think he may be dying!" Mjouli screamed, tears flowing down her face.

"Clancy! Go fetch the physician, now!" Master Whelan yelled, as he ran to Kevin's side. Mjouli followed close behind and stood by the bed as Master Whelan examined him. "Kevin, my son, can you hear me, boy?" Master Whelan pleaded. Kevin made no movement and his breathing was still labored. "What happened, Mjouli, do you know?" Master Whelan asked in distress.

"No, Father, I do not." She thought for a moment and then added, "He did mention last night that the wine tasted badly and that he was going to have it thrown away this morning."

Master Whelan picked-up the wine decanter and sniffed inside, it did have an unusual, foul odor. He put a drop on his finger and stuck the tip of his tongue into it. He recognized the taste; it was an herb that he knew to be poison. "The wine has been poisoned," Master Whelan lamented.

"Poisoned! Who would do such a thing? And, how did someone get in here?" Mjouli inquired in disbelief.

"I do not know, but I will find out," Master Whelan promised angrily.

At that moment, the physician rushed into the room. Master Whelan apprised him of the circumstances and the physician advised that he knew just what to do. He asked Master Whelan and Mjouli to leave the room and informed them that they could see Kevin when he was finished. Mjouli and Master Whelan waited in the hallway in front of the door to the bedroom.

Master Whelan had a chair brought for Mjouli, but he was too worried to sit still. He paced back and forth for what seemed like hours, until finally the physician entered the hallway, his face with no discernable expression.

"He is going to live, but it was extremely close," the physician said exhaustedly and with an earned sense of comfort.

"Thank God," Master Whelan whispered with relief as he took Mjouli's hand. Mjouli thanked God as well, while tears of joy poured down her cheeks.

"May we see him now?" Mjouli asked softly.

"Yes, he is asleep, but you may see him. He will need to remain in bed a few days, but after that, he may get up if he wants to do so. Do not let him go outside for about four or five days. He will be quite weak and that may be too much for him. I will be back tomorrow to examine him again," the physician explained.

"Thank you, friend," Master Whelan replied with much gratitude. The Master and Mjouli walked quietly into the bedroom and stood by the bed. Kevin was indeed asleep, but his breathing was now normal and he was no longer perspiring. Master Whelan bent down and kissed his son on the forehead. Then, he quietly left, leaving Mjouli to be alone with her husband.

Denny sat at a table in his dingy room. It had been two days and he still had not heard anything about Master Kevin. He also had not heard that Master Whelan was searching for him. Clancy had informed the Master of Denny's recent visit, and knowing the truth of Denny's dismissal, the Master supposed him to be the culprit. Denny could not wait a day longer, he thought, and decided to sneak onto the estate and investigate the matter.

Kevin was healing quickly, though he was still very weak. He convinced his family to allow him to sit in the library and read. Kevin was always very active and had great difficulty staying in bed. Master Whelan and Mjouli thought perhaps it would be more beneficial to his recovery to adhere to his wishes. And, there he sat, when the door to the library opened and he saw a familiar, but unwelcome figure. "Denny! What the hell are you doing here?!" Kevin said in an almost inaudibly weak voice of exclamation.

"You not dead, yet, Master Kevin? I prompted your demise long ago and thought you would be eliminated by now," Denny said angrily.

Master Whelan had informed Kevin of what had happened and of his suspicions, so Kevin was well aware of Denny's possible attempt to murder him. A possible attempt that Denny himself had just confirmed. Denny began to walk towards Kevin's chair. Kevin was too weak to cry-out for help and too weak to fight Denny when he picked-up a pillow and placed it over Kevin's face, cutting off his ability to breathe. Kevin struggled, but he had so little strength that he was not able to free his face from the pillow.

"Denny!" a voice cut through the air. He turned and saw Mjouli standing in the doorway with a cross-bow that she had taken from the wall decorations, pointed straight at him.

"It is almost done, My Love. Soon, he will be dead and we can be together. I still love you and I know you still love me," Denny said adoringly. "I'm sorry about the wedding night and all these days after it. You forgive me for being so late, do you not?"

Mjouli shouted in despair, "Denny, I do not love you and I never did!"

In a state of confusion, Denny loosened the pillow slightly as he looked at her and thought for a few seconds, which allowed Kevin the chance to breathe a little air. "I do not believe you. For some ill reason, you want to save his life, but you cannot," Denny said as he turned back around and added more pressure to the pillow.

"Denny! Let him go, NOW!" Mjouli screamed frantically. She really did not wish to cause Denny harm. She knew he must be unwell in his thinking.

Denny made no movement to free Kevin, so Mjouli let the arrow fly. She shrieked in anguish as it was released, a shriek that almost sounded like crying for she was regretful at having to perform the act. Denny screech in agony as the arrow sliced into his back and halfway out of his chest before it rested in his body. He turned and looked into her eyes with puzzlement, then whispered in a tone of incredulousness, "I loved you." A moment later, he fell to the floor, gasping for air. Tears filled Mjouli's eyes as she saw blood begin to drip from Denny's mouth and nose. Despite the fact that he had twice tried to murder the one person she loved most in the world, she felt sorrow at his suffering.

In the next instant, she hurried over to Kevin, who by that time had left his chair and was laboriously walking towards her. They passionately embraced, and then both turned to take a last look at Denny. He laid dead on the floor in a pool of blood, pale and still, the murderous pillow now innocuously laying there beside him. Deeply tormented over their few moments of terror and over the horrendous sight of Denny's body, they quickly turned back around and slowly walked out of the room, Kevin leaning on Mjouli, as much needed help came running towards them.

But, lo, a foul plague was afoot
A plague that wouldst spread both near and far
A plague that wouldst no longer allow the union
Of those such as Kevin and Mjouli
And did this plague haveth a name?
Indeed it did…t'was called
THE ATLANTIC SLAVE TRADE

PORT ROYAL

In the early part of 1692, Port Royal, Jamaica was a longstanding, bustling pirate city well established in the 'new world'. But, it was a city that was about to experience a disaster of monumental proportions; a disaster which was entirely unexpected and from which it would nearly not recover. Our story, though, began 15 years earlier, in England, at the estate of the Duke of Havenshire. The current inhabitants of the estate were the Duke and Duchess Oliver and their son.

It was a night like many others at the estate. The Duke and his family had just finished an excellent meal and had retired to the sitting room for the daily out-loud reading of the Bible by the Duke. He settled comfortably into his favorite chair as did the Duchess in hers. She wrapped her arms tightly around their 10 year-old son, Ian, who sat firmly on his mother's lap. The Duke had read only a few passages when he heard tremendous amounts of noise coming from the foyer of the mansion. He rose from his chair to investigate, signaling to his wife to remain in her seat. But, before he could reach the door, several men, clad in heavy armor and filthy with sweat and blood, burst into the room. Within seconds, the group of men parted and a singular figure walked through to the front.

The outraged Duke confronted the man, a man whom he knew well. "Count Archibald! What is the meaning of this!? How dare you invade my home!" he shouted angrily.

The equally angry Count replied with venom, "Good evening, My Lord. Pleasant night is it not?"

"Do not be ridiculous…you spawn of Hell!" the Duke replied with even more anger.

"Ridiculous, am I? Spawn of Hell, am I?" the Count repeated, now becoming enraged at the Duke's obvious arrogance.

"I order you to leave my home immediately!" the Duke bellowed with indignation.

"I am finished taking orders from you! And this will be your home for only a few moments more, My Lord," the Count answered sternly. By that time, the Duchess had arisen from her seat and was standing with her arms tightly surrounding Ian. The boy had a reciprocally tight hold around his mother's waist and tears flowed gently down his face.

The Duke was absolutely puzzled by the Count's actions; he had always thought their relationship to be an amiable one. "What has brought you to this madness, John? What in God's name have I ever done to you to provoke this insanity?" the Duke queried more calmly in the effort to avoid escalation of the incident. The tactic worked for the moment and the Count did reply in a more calm tone as well.

"We and our families have served you faithfully and well for most of our lives, is that not true?"

"Yes, of course it is, and I have provided well for all of you," the Duke replied sincerely.

"No, My Lord, you have not. We receive next to nothing in return and now we want a much bigger share. I have found a sponsor who will present my case to the king, in the hope that I may be elevated to the new Duke of Havenshire. All my sponsor asked of me was to eliminate you. However, he stressed that I must leave no witnesses alive," the Count informed. Fear overtook both the Duke and the Duchess upon hearing the Count's words. They were particularly distressed over the fate of their son. But, their hearts were lifted slightly after the Count's next words.

"I cannot spare the life of you or your wife, but, I will spare the life of your son. I have made arrangements with the captain of a pirate ship docked only a few miles away. He has agreed to pay handsomely for the boy. Ian will be taken to the captain this very night."

"My God, man. You *have* gone mad," the Duke uttered in disbelief. At that moment, the Count beckoned one of his men to take Ian outside. As the Duke tried to prevent it, the Count slapped him forcefully and he fell to the floor. The Duchess began to scream and violently resisted the man's attempts to pull Ian from her. But, the man's strength prevailed and over the cries of the Duchess, he carried Ian outside to the estate grounds with Ian kicking and screaming the entire way.

Once outside, the man put Ian down, but maintained a tight hold around his shoulders. In a few minutes, Ian heard his mother emit a blood-curdling scream. His tears began to flow uncontrollably as he cried-out to her, "Mother! Mother! Are you all right, Mothe!?" His cries were answered when he saw the Count and the group of men exit the mansion without his parents and walk towards him. As the Count stood in front of Ian, he spoke to the child coldly. "You are an orphan now, boy. And, unfortunately, you are by birth the new Duke of Havenshire. Too bad you will not be around to rule over your domain. You shall grow to manhood in a pirate world. Not in the aristocratic world that I am sure you feel you deserve."

The Count's words about the demise of his parents angered Ian and he stopped crying. He mustered all of his 'aristocratically taught' nerve and angrily replied to the Count. "It is true, sir, I may grow to manhood as a pirate. But, I will always know my heritage. I am Ian Oliver, the Duke of Havenshire. And, one day I will return and find you. Then, I shall promptly slice-off your head!"

The Count frowned with disgust, "Just as arrogant as your father, you little bastard." Ian spit at him and that was enough for the Count. "Get him out of here before I do the brat some real harm. Take him to the ship. The captain awaits him."

Ian was taken to the ship, the money was paid, and the ship immediately took sail. Captain Red, so named equally because of his flaming red hair and because of all the blood he had spilled, took an instant liking to Ian. He had never had a son and saw Ian as his first opportunity. The captain handed Ian over to the cook, Sully, for safekeeping. Sully was an aged man with a full head of gray hair. He, also, took an instant liking to Ian. In fact, within a few days, Ian and Sully had grown quite fond of each other and had become fast friends.

Fifteen years had passed and Ian had grown into a strikingly handsome man. Both Sully and Captain Red had gone to meet their maker. And Ian had become the most excellent swordsman on the ship. It was that fact, plus the fact that he was known to be a fair man with everyone, that resulted in him being voted the new captain. He had been captain for almost two years now, and the treasures that the ship had accrued increased magnificently. But, Ian had recently heard of a rich city in the West Indies that was supposedly controlled by and overrun with pirates. It was a city known by the name of Port Royal and was the current destination of the ship.

It was the year 1692 when Ian's ship first sailed into Port Royal. The greatness of the city could be seen even from the ship. Many of the buildings were colorful and architecturally elegant. There were crowds of people everywhere and, more importantly, plenty of well-dressed women of every color. Ian and most of the crew disembarked and began to explore the city as a group. One-by-one, though, the men went their separate ways as something or another caught their eyes. Ian ended-up with only his first mate at his side when they entered a rather expensive-looking drinking and eating establishment. They found an empty table and immediately sat down. A rather pretty copper-colored woman quickly came to their table and they ordered a hearty meal of meat and two mugs of rum.

The rum came first and as they sat sipping their drinks, Ian noticed a very elegantly dressed man sitting at a corner table. The man had brownish-red hair that was extremely straight and which hung several inches passed his shoulders. His skin was pale for such a tropical climate and he had very light blue eyes. Ian could not tell if the man was a pirate. But, if he was, his attire proclaimed him to be a very successful one. Then, Ian noticed the woman who was sitting next to the man, she was as elegantly dressed as was the man. In Ian's eyes, though, she did not need such embellishment. Her beauty was incomparable to anything on this man's earth. Her skin was of a darker tone than the waitress, more of a dark bronze color. Her eyes were large and were only slightly darker than her skin tone. Her hair was as black as a raven and hung a quarter-way down her back in tight bushy curls. Her nose was the most perfect he had ever seen. Her lips were full and seemed filled with passion. He could not turn his gaze away from her. And, then, as if by his very will, she noticed him as well.

Her name was Fola. She was an African captive, kidnapped from her home in Africa by the very man with whom she sat, a pirate captain, Sean Macgregor. Fola did indeed notice Ian staring at her, but, she did not mind. He was surely the most handsome man on the island. His hair was parted in the middle, tied in a ponytail that hung to the middle of his back, and was the color of the golden sun. His facial features were remarkable, most certainly the face of a god. She could tell that his body was perfect even though he sat behind a table. As she stared into his large green eyes, she became lost in them, as did he in hers. That first flicker of passion between them had been inescapably ignited. Ian smiled at her and she returned his smile. But, their exchange was abruptly interrupted by Sean's voice as he informed Fola that they were leaving. Fortunately, Sean had not become aware of Fola's flirtation...fortunately for both Fola *and* Ian.

The next day Fola strolled through the crowded open-air market of the city. It was one of those frequently occurring warm and sunny days on the island. She had not eaten breakfast and it was already mid-day, so she stopped at a table full with fruit and picked-up two bananas. As she reached over to pay the vendor, she saw the face of the handsome stranger smiling at her from the other side of the table. She again returned his smile and with her sign of encouragement, he walked around the table until he was at her side. "Good day to you, Madame," he said softly.

"Good day to you as well, sir," she replied nervously.

Ian continued confidently, "Let me introduce myself. My name is Ian Oliver. I am the captain of the ship named the 'Devil's Heart', which is presently docked at port. It is a pirate ship, of course."

Fola was disappointed with his profession. She was hoping that he was a more gentle man. Since her abduction, the only men she had been around were pirates, and they were always coarse and often cruel. Though, she had to admit that Sean did not quite fit that mold, he was more often than not a gentleman. But, Ian's handsomeness was overwhelming her, so she suppressed her objections to his lifestyle. "I am pleased to meet you, sir. I am Fola Obewetu of Africa," she replied sweetly.

Ian was intrigued by her answer. "You are African?…Why is it you have come to this place?"

Fola replied truthfully and with sadness in her voice, "I was taken from my home in Africa by the pirate, Sean Macgregor, the man who was seated at the table with me. I was taken only a year ago."

Ian was totally amazed. "You are a slave?"

"Not so much a slave as a captive. While it is true that I am not free to leave, I am treated more like a companion than anything else. I never do any work. But, unfortunately, Sean desires me to be his lover, thus he forces me to remain with him. So far, I have been able to elude intimate relations with him," Fola explained.

Ian was disturbed over her general predicament. But, he was more than pleased to hear that she had not yet been 'seduced' by her captor. "I am distressed by your circumstance. Is there no way I may assist you?"

"I am grateful for your offer, sir. But, there is nothing you can do. Sean will never release me," she replied in anguish.

Ian thought., one day, My Love, I indeed *shall* release you.

Fola knew it was growing late and that she needed to make her exit. "I must be leaving now. Do have a pleasant day, sir," she said as she started to make her way passed him. But, as she passed, he grabbed her wrist and began to caress it. She stopped and watched as he then softly kissed the top of her hand. After which, Ian whispered to her sensuously, "Please…meet me here again tomorrow," he requested.

Fola was impressed with his gentle and caring manner. Perhaps, he was not like the other pirates she had known. Perhaps, he was a man of agreeable disposition afterall. "Yes," she answered, "I will try to meet you, but, not here. Sean has eyes almost everywhere and it would be too dangerous for us both. I know of a place near the beginning of the highlands. It is easily identifiable by the waterfall which spurts forth from the mountain."

"That sounds excellent. I shall meet you there tomorrow at this same time of day," Ian agreed.

Fola explained to Ian how to reach the waterfall, then quickly returned to Sean's mansion on the outskirts of town.

Ian arrived at the waterfall first. He had started for it exceptionally early, not only because he was unfamiliar with the terrain, but also because of his burning desire to see Fola alone. It was indeed a beautiful location. The waterfall was small but wonderful at which to look. It poured into an equally wonderful looking pond surrounded with exotic plants and flowers. The soothing sound of the running water added to the peacefulness of the environment. It was certainly a scene ripe for romance. Ian soon sat down on a large rock and anxiously awaited Fola's arrival.

In a little while, Ian heard rustling noises amongst the shrubs, which surrounded the clearing around the pond. He stood and immediately saw Fola step into the clearing. His heart began to pound quickly as he once again beheld her beauty and the closer she came to him, the more it pounded. Fola smiled brightly at the sight of him. As she walked towards him, she became more and more sexually excited, and her nipples began to prickle incessantly. Once she reached him, he again took her hand and kissed it. They looked at each other for a moment, then, their heads slowly moved towards each other until their lips softly pressed together. In short measure, their mouths opened and their tongues whipped into a whirlwind of hot and heavy passion. They embraced tightly as they indulged in their kiss, but in a few moments, Ian abruptly interrupted the kiss. He lifted Fola and carried her over to a grassy area of the landscape. He gently laid her down, then, joined her there. He leaned over her as she laid supine on the grass and lovingly whispered, "I adore you…My mind, soul, and body need you. My love belongs to you…and so it shall be forever." Fola reached upward and wrapped her arms across his shoulders hugging him lightly. Ian fervently resumed the abruptly interrupted kiss.

Such went the afternoon, filled with fiery kisses, the fondling of each other's body, and endearing words of undying love.

That evening Fola sat at the long dinner table opposite Sean as usual, but she was unusually quiet. Her thoughts were on Ian and the time she had spent with him that day. Sean was becoming increasingly annoyed at her. He had attempted to engage in conversation with her several times, but Fola's replies had been short and lacking in enthusiasm or emotion. He thought it all very strange and wondered what disturbance was in the making.

The following day, Fola and Ian met at the same place and at the same time. It was an extremely hot day, so they decided to take a swim in the pond. Fola knew she would need to swim naked. She would have to leave early that day and she could not chance encountering Sean with her clothing not yet dry. He was extremely jealous and would be suspect of any explanation she might give for her uncharacteristic appearance. But, she had always swum that way in Africa, so it did not bother her. Though, this would be the first time that a male was present. Ian decided he would do the same. He certainly did not have to do so, but the very idea of the situation aroused him. He allowed Fola to undress first, which she did amongst the trees. When she was ready, Ian turned his head and allowed her to enter the pond unseen by his eyes. Then, he also undressed and emerged from the trees naked. He had expected that Fola would also turn her head and allow him to enter the pond unseen. But, instead, she looked straight at him. He did not notice her watching him until he was halfway to the pond. However, he enjoyed having her eyes upon him.

Fola watched as Ian's naked, muscular, tan body came towards her across the grass. He was a sight of indescribable beauty. He had removed the tie from the back of his head and his long blond hair blew alluringly the gentle wind. And, just as she had thought, his body was indeed perfect in every way. She longed to feel the long thick penis that she was now able to observe, inside of her. Ian entered the pond and waded directly to her; they immediately embraced. Ian's penis began to harden as he felt Fola's breasts press against his chest. His arms slowly moved downward until her round soft buttocks filled both of his hands. He pulled her groin tightly against himself and Fola moaned as she felt Ian's penis press upon her abdomen.

Ian slid his tongue into her mouth and began to forcefully plunge it down her throat for several minutes. Then, he ran his tongue down the front of her chest until his head was between her bronze-colored breasts. The water covered some of each nipple, but he was able to view her large fudge nipples adequately, each of which was the size of a small cherry tomato. He took one into his mouth and began to swirl his tongue around it relentlessly. Fola's moans became louder and soon were joined by Ian's. He began to chew her other nipple as she began to feel his fingers massaging her between her thighs. The bliss she started to experience was so intense, she was not sure she would be able to withstand the sensation for very long. She stooped a bit and parted her thighs farther so that his fingers would be able to reach every inch that he desired. After a few minutes, she felt his large hard penis 'enter' her, its size filled her vagina to the very limit. The size of it caused her to utter a short cry of pain, which provoked concern in Ian. "Are you well, My Love?" he whispered gently.

"Yes, I am fine," Fola replied with affection.

Then, with his face buried in her hair, his hands tightly holding onto her buttocks, and her arms tightly wrapped around his neck, he began to thrust his penis back and forth into her at an unearthly pace and level of power. It caused their bodies to bounce uncontrollably in the water, causing a circle of waves and foam to develop around them. Their dual cries of pleasure echoed through the cave located just behind the waterfall, which sent their sounds of love deep inside the huge majestic floral-covered mountain.

Because of her unexpected sexual experience with Ian, Fola lost track of time and returned to the mansion late. Sean sat in the foyer waiting for her. As she entered the house, he rushed to the door, grabbed her by the arm, and pulled her into the sitting room. "Where have you been until this late hour, Fola!?" he asked angrily.

"I was at the market and then I went for a walk across the island. I forgot the time and also walked farther than I had intended. I am sorry if I caused you concern, Sean," she replied calmly.

Sean did not quite believe her. It was unusual behavior on her part, as was her lack of conversation the previous night. "You have not forgotten that I own you and that your freedom to roam is dependent upon my permission?" he reminded her coldly.

Fola replied in an equally cold voice, "No, Sean…I have not forgotten."

"Very good. Now, go change for dinner. Though, it is nearly time to retire for the night," he answered sarcastically.

The next day Ian and Fola again met at the waterfall. They embraced and kissed passionately. Then, Fola informed Ian about her encounter with Sean. Ian suggested that they enter the cave behind the waterfall and have their visit there to help avoid detection. But, it was already too late for that; Sean had ordered one of his men to follow Fola whenever she left the house. The man saw her meet Ian and enter the cave with him. The man remained amongst the trees and took a seat on the ground to await their exit.

Ian and Fola noticed a large patch of moss-like growth near the entrance to the cave and chose that spot upon which to sit and kick-off her shoes and his boots. Then, Ian questioned her about Sean. "Do you think he believed you? Or do you think he is suspicious of you?"

Fola thought for a moment and then responded, "I really do not know. He seemed to accept my explanation. But, his reminder of my status did not feel right to me."

Ian knew that the situation must change…and soon. "I shall have to find a way to remove you from his hold," Ian answered.

"As I told you when first we met, Sean will never let me go," she answered back in despair.

"I shall ask him for your hand in marriage and offer my entire fortune in payment for you. The payment should be enough to sway him. Afterall, he *is* a pirate and the acquisition of fortune *is* for what we live," Ian explained confidently.

But, Fola was still absorbing the word 'marriage'. "You want to marry me, Ian?" she asked in disbelief.

He put his arm around her shoulders and pulled her close to him. He looked into her eyes and softly answered, "Yes, my sweet, sweet Love. Will you have me as your husband?"

Fola smiled, quickly leaned her head upward, gently kissed his lips, and whispered, "I love you, Ian."

Ian grinned at her with affection and jokingly replied, "So…does that mean yes?"

They both laughed and Fola answered, "Of course. How could you ever have doubted it?"

They lavished in a feverishly zealous kiss with Fola's tongue thrusting as much and as forcefully down Ian's throat as his tongue down her throat. Fola began to pull at Ian's pants and they stopped their kiss as he assisted her in pulling-off all of his lower clothing, which left him naked from the waist down. He did not know what she was planning, but, he would allow her to do her will. She hurriedly rose to her knees and maneuvered her body until she was kneeling between his legs. She thought his penis undeniably beautiful with its long, thick shaft surrounded at its base by light brown and blond hairs. She gently embraced it with her hand and began to softly lick across and around its enormous head.

Within a few seconds, Ian began to moan lightly, but the longer and harder she continued with the licking, the louder and more frequent his cries became. She soon began to simultaneously massage his large hair-covered sacks, which increased Ian's cries three-fold. She started to taste the saltiness of his wetness in her mouth as his clear fluid began to flow excessively. In a few minutes more, she inserted the entire enormous head of his penis into her mouth. Her mouth was just barely able to open wide enough to accommodate it. She began to suck at it ravenously as she was now extremely aroused herself and was producing deep sighs of her own. She continued to fondle his sacks at the same time, and in a short while, Ian grabbed her shoulders with both hands and closed his eyes. He yelled three tremendous cries and could no longer restrain his ejaculation. His 'climatic fluid' shot into her mouth like a bullet from a gun. Some of it slid straight down her throat, the rest of it filled her mouth. Fola tried to quickly swallow as much as she could, but, his flow was so heavy that it seeped out of her mouth. When the flow finally stopped and Ian's penis began to return to its normal large size, Fola removed it from her mouth and wiped her lips and chin with the bottom of her dress. Ian opened his eyes and reached-out his arms to her. Still on her knees, she reached over and hugged him around the neck. He wrapped his arms around her waist and pulled her down until she sat between his bare legs. Her torso was pressed against his body and his naked penis was still exposed to her view.

They remained in that position for at least an hour, embracing each other tightly, kissing each other frequently, and making plans for the future. Fola intermittently fondled Ian's penis, which caused it to slightly harden now and then, providing sexual pleasure to the both of them. But, after an hour or so of kissing and fondling, Ian reached that arousal point at which his penis could not return to normal without some kind of sexual completion. So, all of a sudden, he hurriedly pulled the bottom of Fola's dress up to her waist and quickly pulled-off her pantaloon type undergarment entirely. He rolled over on top of her and positioned himself between her legs. As that was his first time at actually viewing between her thighs, he played with her clitoris with both hands for several minutes holding-off his ejaculation with much difficulty. He was pleasured as he watched the liquid that began to flow from her vagina opening and as he watched Fola experience several orgasms from his touch. Within several more minutes, he inserted his warm penis into her and they lovingly moved up and down, synchronized in their passion, immersed in their pleasure once again.

She returned to the manor early as she did not want a repeat of the prior night. Sean was in the library; she greeted him. She was thankful that he had no complaints about her time of arrival. After a short conversation with him, she continued up to her suite to prepare for dinner. But, the man who had followed her was now at the backdoor of the mansion asking to speak with Sean.

Fola awakened early in the morning, she was nervous and fearful. Ian had promised to come to the mansion around midmorning to speak with Sean about her release. She hoped it would be a civilized meeting, but, she had her doubts. She washed and dressed, then sat by the window to await Ian's arrival. The household was not big on breakfasts, so if either she or Sean did not show-up for it, there was no problem. True to his word, around mid-morning Ian rode-up to the manor. She watched him enter the mansion and she began to pace back and forth as she awaited the outcome of the meeting. She rushed out of her suite and reached the head of the stairs just in time to see Ian exiting the front door. Sean was in a tyrate as he shouted at Ian to never come to his home again. As soon as Ian left, Sean began to ascend the stairs, but, upon seeing Fola at the top of them, began to ascend them three steps at a time. Fola ran back to her suite and closed the door, though she knew the door would not deter Sean. And, in a few seconds, he came bursting through it, his face distorted and red with rage. "You have been meeting with this man behind my back? You lied to me about your whereabouts? How dare you deceive and dishonor me in such a manner!" Sean shouted.

Fola tried to reason with him, "If I had come to you and asked to be allowed to see him, would you have allowed it?"

"No!" Sean screamed at her, "And, I shall make sure that you never see him again!"

"Please do not separate us, Sean! I love him! I will always love him!" Fola begged desperately.

Sean became even more infuriated at her words. He picked-up a rather large chair and threw it across the room, crying-out with a loud grunt as he did so. It hit the wall with such force that two of its legs instantly broke off. When he turned to her again, his face was blood red, he again screamed at her with spit flying from his mouth, *"You shall not see him again!"* He then stormed out of the suite, slamming the door behind him. Though fearful of what Sean still might do, she was thankful that he had exhibited his violence towards the chair rather than towards her. But, she was disconcerted over Ian's departure. What would he do now and how would he contact her?

Ian returned to his ship instead of his rooms. He needed to think and thought it better to be in a safer environment at the moment. As he sat in his cabin, he came to the realization that he would have to obtain possession of Fola in the same manner as did Sean. He would have to kidnap her from Sean, then, sail instantly out of port. Should Sean choose to follow, there were cannons enough on the 'Devil's Heart' to make light work of Sean's inadequately equipped ship. Ian immediately began to make his plans. But, Sean was making plans as well and his would be carried-out that very night.

It was midnight and 'Old Jack' sat in the shrubs drinking down another bottle of rum. He was an elderly man with long dirty gray hair. In his youth, he had been a pirate, but those days were long passed. He was merely a drunken alcoholic who begged around the city for money to drink. He had just finished his bottle when he felt several sharp pains in his back. He had been stabbed multiple times and shortly afterwards, he was dead. Two men carried his body to the edge of the city where it could be quickly reached. Then, the two men entered the dwelling that housed the rooms Ian had rented. Unfortunately, Ian had remained on the ship the entire night, so the men were easily able to break into his rooms and hide the bloody murder weapon there. Afterwards, pursuant to orders, they immediately rushed to the office of the island Constable to report that they had just seen the captain of the ship named the 'Devil's Heart' argue with 'Old Jack' and savagely stab 'Old Jack' to death.

Ian sat-up abruptly on the side of the bunk in his cabin. There was a lot of commotion seemingly coming from the deck of the ship. He rushed out of his cabin and up the steep wooden steps that led to the deck. Upon his arrival 'top side', he observed several of his men blocking entrance aboard ship to a group of unfamiliar men from shore. He hurried towards the group to investigate the matter. When he was almost at their sides, he called to the strangers. "What goes on here? I am the captain of this ship. State your business, gentleman," Ian said in a formal tone of voice.

The large bearded man who seemed to have been doing all of the talking spoke. "I am Constable Sedgwick and if you are the captain of the 'Devil's Heart', I am here to arrest you for the murder of 'Old Jack' whom you stabbed to death this very night."

Ian could not believe his ears, "What the hell are you talking about? Who the hell is 'Old Jack'?" Ian questioned in bafflement.

The bearded man continued, "It is an even more foul situation when one does not even know the name of the person one has murdered. It is…."

Ian interrupted, "I have not murdered anyone! Who charges me with this crime!?"

Sean's cohorts stepped forward at the Constable's beckoning, "These two men saw you do it and reported it to me," the Constable explained.

"Then, they are lying! I tell you that I have murdered no one!" Ian exclaimed.

"The court will decide your innocence, sir," the Constable said authoritatively as he signaled to his men to grab Ian. The small group of Ian's men who were involved in the incident attempted to defend their captain, but Ian waved them away. "Do not endanger yourselves men. I shall prove in court that I have murdered no one on this island."

"But, sir," the first mate answered in frustration.

"It is all right, Talbot. You are in charge while I am away. Take good care of the ship and beware of strangers," Ian said reassuringly.

"Aye, sir," Talbot replied with even more frustration.

The Constable, his group of men, and Ian all left the ship and traveled immediately to the small prison in the center of town. Ian was quickly thrown into a dark and dirty cell.

Very early in the morning Sean received word of Ian's arrest. He could not wait to advise Fola of the situation. He hurried to her room despite the fact that he knew she had not yet awakened. He stood outside of the door to her suite and banged upon it until he heard her voice.

"Yes...what is it?" she called-out hoarsely.

"I am coming inside," Sean replied as he opened the door and entered the room.

Fola sat-up in bed and covered the top of her body with her sheet. She was puzzled by Sean's early and unwanted intrusion into her quarters. "Why are you here, Sean?" Fola asked nervously.

"I have a bit of news for you. Your 'lover' has just been arrested for murder. What a good judge of character you are, my dear," Sean said smugly.

Fola could not believe what Sean was saying. Surely, he was only trying to upset her in revenge, she thought. "I dare not believe you, Sean. Arrested for murder? Who was supposed to be his victim?" she asked with much skepticism.

"None other than Old Jack," Sean replied sarcastically sympathetic.

Fola laughed out-loud as she shifted her body to sit on the side of the bed. "Old Jack? How ridiculous," Fola answered in total disbelief.

"Ridiculous or not, it is the truth," Sean verified.

Fola quickly realized that Sean was not lying and continued her reply angrily, "This is your doing, is it not, Sean?"

Sean was proud of his accomplishment, but did not want to admit his treachery. He knew that Fola would be lost to him forever should she know the truth of his actions. So, in a forced tone of indignation, he avoided the truth, "Do not try to displace the low character of your 'lover' on me! You have dishonored me sufficiently already! Do not overstep your importance to me!" he exclaimed. Fola jumped-up from the bed and began to dress herself despite Sean's presence in the room. "For what reason do you dress at this hour, Fola?" Sean inquired curiously.

"I must see Ian as soon as possible. I must see how I may help him," she said fearfully.

"You cannot help him and you will not see him. At least…not until later today, at his trial," Sean explained joyfully.

"His trial is today? How could that be? How could it be so soon?" Fola cried out in despair.

"Who knows? Perhaps the judge is going on holiday and wants to clear his business," Sean suggested. But, he knew that the swiftness of the trial was also of his own making, he wanted to rid himself of Ian as rapidly as possible.

The courtroom was packed with people by the time Fola and Sean arrived. Since most citizens of Port Royal were pirates or associated with pirates, there were not that many trials in the city. So, when there was one, everyone knew about it and everyone wanted to see it. But, Sean's reputation for violence was so well known, he was immediately allowed to enter the courtroom. Though, at the expense of several persons who were abruptly kicked-out of the room. Sean was offered seats in the front for Fola and himself, but he declined them. He preferred that they stand amongst the crowd in the back of the room, so that Ian and Fola could not easily make eye contact, if at all.

Fola's heart began to beat rapidly as she watched the Constable and one of his men bring Ian into the courtroom from a side door. They all walked to the middle of the room and stood by chairs that faced the judge's seat. Within a few seconds, the judge also entered. He sat down and the others quickly followed his lead. It was obvious from the beginning of the trial that there was no element of fairness in the proceedings. Ian was not being allowed to speak in his own defense and there was no other person there to defend him. When the two 'witnesses' appeared and Fola recognized them to be Sean's men, she could not endure the farce any longer. As Fola attempted to cry-out in Ian's defense, Sean quickly grabbed her around the waist, covered her mouth with his hand,

and dragged her out of the courtroom door. Fola struggled to free herself, but was unable to do so. He released her once they were outside in the hallway. When she tried to re-enter the room, Sean blocked her way to the door. "Let me through, Sean! Please…let me be with him!" Fola begged tearfully.

Sean looked into her love-filled eyes and became angry and hurt at the same time. He again grabbed her around the waist, but that time, pulled her to him and embraced her tightly. "Why do you not love me?" he asked, his voice filled with pain. "My God…the things I have done to try to make you love me…Have I not been good to you? Have I not given you everything you have desired? Have I not respected your honor and not 'taken' you, because *you* did not yet desire it? Why do you not love me?" Sean lamented fretfully as he tightened his already backbreaking hold. He hoped she would return his embrace, and, she did, but not out of love for him. It was more out of pity or a mere act of comforting. The words he had spoken were true. He had given her many expensive, elegant, clothes and jewelry, the spoils of his pirate activities. She was the envy of every woman on the island. And, he had not forced her to 'give herself' to him. Though, the sexual aspect was one that she did not expect to last much longer. Yes, it was true that he had always been rather kind and gentle. But, the fact that he was the one who had kidnapped her from her family in Africa would not allow her to fall in love with him, no matter what he did. His lust for her had separated her from all she had known and loved; and she could never forget or forgive him for that cruelty. He had promised to take her home for a visit someday. But, in reality, she doubted he would ever bother to return to her homeland.

Fola soon felt Sean loosen his embrace. He then began to maneuver his head so that they were face-to-face. In an instant, he pressed his lips firmly against hers and attempted to slide his tongue into her mouth. Fola forcefully pulled herself away from him and broke his hold upon her body. She quickly backed away as she looked at him with distain and began to shake her head 'no'. He looked at her with the pain and desperation of an unrequited lover. Then, he outreached his hand to her in a last attempt to possess her. She again shook her head 'no', then quickly bolted out of the court building onto the crowded street.

She rushed back to Sean's manor, ran straight to her room, and hurriedly locked her door. She did not know whether Sean was close behind her, but he would not have easy access to her suite. Since it was dusk now, she lit the candle lamp on the table next to her bed. She heard no signs of Sean, so, she laid down on the bed and began to cry profusely. Her thoughts were swimming with confusion. She was worried about Ian and did not know how to help him or even help her own situation. Perhaps, she should gather some things together and escape while she could. Though, where she would hide she did not know. She may have to lose herself in the forest of the highlands on the other side of the island. Sean's sudden sexual advance towards her now made her fearful of his next actions. Yet, somehow, she could not bring herself to really believe that he might force her to submit to him. Still, before she could ponder the subject in depth, she fell asleep.

It was early morning when Fola opened her eyes abruptly. She thought she was awakened by a loud sound and sat-up on the bed. There standing in the doorway of her suite was the shadow of a man. He had busted through the lock on her door and left the door hanging by one hinge. The man stepped into the light of the lamp and she saw that it was Sean. He started to walk towards her and she could tell by the swagger in his walk that he had been drinking heavily.

"What is it you want, Sean?" she asked alarmed by his demeanor.

Sean continued to walk towards her as he answered in slurred words. "I thought you might be interested in what happened with your...friend," he teased.

Fola's heart began to beat erratically at the prospect of his potentially devastating information. "What has happened?" she asked irritably.

"Ah...I see that, now, I have your undivided attention," Sean slurred.

"Why do you pain me so? Tell me what has happened!" Fola implored impatiently.

Sean continued towards her until he was able to sit on the bed next to her. He reeked of liquor and Fola could hardly breathe from the stench of it. "He was found guilty of murdering poor 'Old Jack' and sentenced to hang this very day," Sean explained joyfully.

"*Oh my god! I must go to him, now!*" she screamed. She attempted to jump off the bed, but Sean pushed her flat down on the bed with both hands.

"You are not going to him! I will not allow it!" he yelled back at her irately.

"*You must let me go, Sean! Please!*" Fola begged as tears ran down her face.

"No! I will not let you continue to dishonor me!" he bellowed angrily.

Fola became filled with anger herself. "*I hate you!! I hate you!! I will always hate you!*" she exclaimed as she once again struggled to free herself from his grip. She reached-up with one hand and dug her nails into the side of his cheek, then slid her fingers down to his chin. It caused several long, deep gashes down his face that immediately began to bleed. Sean grimaced with pain.

"So, you hate me, do you!? Until now, you have had no reason to hate me! *But, so help me that will end!*" Sean shouted as the pain of his injury shot through his entire head. Despite his words, he was still in love with her. And, had he been in his right mind, things would not have progressed to such a violent point.

Sean quickly moved his position from that of sitting on the bed to that of lying on top of Fola. Her valiant attempts to prevent him were thwarted by his superior strength and size. He again tried several times to kiss her, but she continuously moved her head out of his way. Frustrated with that dilemma, Sean began to pull down the top of Fola's low-cut gown. Fola's entire body was pinned down by Sean's weight and she could not stop his actions. He continued to pull down her gown until both of her large breasts were fully exposed. He immediately began to suck one of her nipples with great vehemence and much moaning. He alternated between nipples for multiple seconds and his penis grew harder each second that he continued.

In a minute or two, Fola began to feel Sean moving his body downward and pulling-up the bottom of her gown at the same time. She decided to stop struggling. She thought perhaps if she let him do his desire, he would leave and she could make good her escape. He continued to move himself downward until her legs were spread and his head was opposite her pubic area. He almost simultaneously completed lifting her skirt and pulling her pantaloons off of her body. As he viewed between her open thighs, he passionately uttered the word, "Lovely." He buried his mouth between her vaginal lips and began to forcefully lick her clitoris.

Fola soon realized that she could no longer stand his touch upon her body; she could not go through with the submission. She carefully reached over and took a firm hold upon the candle lamp on the table next to the bed, which was remarkably still burning. She instantly swung it around and smashed it over Sean's head. He immediately lost consciousness, his head now motionless between her thighs. She quickly slid her body away from him, jumped off of the bed, and hurriedly re-dressed. Fear gripped her heart when she heard Sean begin to make noises as if he were waking. But, within a few seconds, he was quiet and did not move again. She rushed out of the suite, down the stairs, and through the front entrance of the large manor. Fola had not noticed as she rushed out of her suite that several sparks from the smashed lamp had begun to catch fire to the large thatched rug next to her bed.

She ran towards the main part of the city, the sun was rising and she had to get to Ian at the prison. Suddenly, she noticed that crowds of people were noisily running and pointing in the opposite direction of her path. What is happening, she thought. She stopped and turned in the hope of seeing the cause of the commotion. What she saw was an alarming sight. There was a huge fire burning furiously, located in the direction from which she had just come. She ran back in that direction for a few minutes, but stopped dead in her tracks when she realized that it was Sean's manor that was burning. For a few seconds, she worriedly wondered if he had awakened and made it out alive. Then, she wondered why she should care. She was sure that it was the broken lamp that had started the fire. But…it was a fitting ending for a house of hell, she thought.

She resumed her desperate journey to the prison. Upon her arrival at the prison, she found there to be only one guard and he was deep in sleep. All of the other guards had gone to help with the fire. Fola quietly picked-up a pitcher and knocked the guard over the head. He fell off of his stool and onto the floor, his keys jingled as he fell. She reached under his jacket and removed the keys from his possession, then quickly ran down the hallway to the cell area. Once there, she called-out, "Ian, it is Fola, where are you?"

He immediately answered her, "I am here, Fola, at the end of the aisle." She rushed to the end of the row of cells and found him standing with both hands gripping the metal bars of the cell door. His face filled with joy at the sight of her. "My dearest, beautiful, Love. What are you doing here in such an unspeakable place?" he asked softly.

Fola showed him the keys and responded lovingly, "I have come to take you out of this horror."

She hurriedly unlocked the cell door. Ian was in shock at her actions and as he exited the cell, questioned her. "How have you accomplished this, Fola?"

As they rushed back down the hallway, she replied, "Sean's manor is on fire. Everyone has gone to help put it out…so, we must hurry and reach the highlands before the guards return."

They raced up the mountainous hillside, but constantly checked to see if they were being followed. Upon reaching the very top of the highlands, they turned and found they had succeeded in their escape, there was no one behind them. But, in the same instant, they viewed the most astonishingly ghastly sight that either of them had ever seen. It was a tidal wave, at least 30 feet high, still out at sea, but bearing down fast upon the island. The ground began to shake slightly, but, before they knew it, the shakes turned into major tremors. Ian took Fola's hand as they watched multiple buildings in Port Royal crumble into piles of rock. Large crevices opened up in the ground, swallowing whole buildings and hoards of people at the same time. The screams and cries of the frightened and the injured could be heard even from the highlands. And, people could be seen scrambling to ascend the very mountain that Ian and Fola had themselves just climbed. Some pirates, being the thieves that they usually were, could be seen stopping to rob persons who were already dead, even as the pirates themselves tried to make their way to higher ground. Of course, many of those greedy men ended-up being killed by the quake as the result of their delay in departure.

Ian and Fola watched terror-stricken as the tidal wave finally came crashing onto the shore. Two-thirds of Port Royal was engulfed by the wave before it smashed against the rocky walls of the highland mountains and lost much of its force. Its foaming waves settled down into a continuation of the ocean as most of Port Royal was now underwater. The couple remained in the highlands for about a week. But, within only a few days, they ran into several other people who had also escaped to the highlands and were able to tell the anguished stories of their experiences.

Ian decided that he and Fola would leave Port Royal on the first ship to England. He would return and attempt to re-claim his estate. Now that he was in love, he wanted a different life. Luckily, his room on the island had been spared, unlike Sean's mansion and his ship 'Devil's Heart'. Ian's fortune of jewelry and gold was still in its hidden place in his room. It was only a few days after their return to Ian's room that they learned a ship was leaving for England. Ian purchased their passage and within two days they were sailing on the Atlantic. Ian's first action upon boarding the ship was to have the ship's captain marry him to Fola. And, it was on the voyage to England that Ian first told Fola about his boyhood and how he came to be a pirate. Among other things, he wanted her to be prepared for the happenings that would unfold upon their arrival.

The winds and the currents were excellent and it took them only a month to reach England. Ian immediately began to inquire about Count Archibald, the murderer of his father and mother. He was pleased to hear that the Count had been defeated and executed for his crimes over 10 years ago. The ranking aristocrat in charge now, the Duke of Collingswood, had been friends with Ian's father to the best of Ian's remembrance. So, he confidently went to speak with the Duke. The Duke of Collingswood was elated at Ian's return and exclaimed, "My dear boy, I am overwhelmed and overjoyed! You are indeed the very image of your father. Count Archibald informed us of his dastardly actions towards you shortly before his death. I have prayed frequently that you might somehow find your way home. My prayers have now been answered."

Ian thought, truly my father had a kind and loyal friend in the Duke. And, Ian was determined to faithfully continue the friendship, not only because the Duke was such an agreeable man, but also in honor of his father.

The Duke of Collingswood did all that was necessary to restore Ian to his rightful place in society and to secure the return of Ian's estate. In a short time, all was once again put right. And, with his mighty pirate fortune in hand, Ian was able to make his estate a showcase of beauty. The estate became the envy of all who lay eyes upon it. The Duke and Duchess of Havenshire were the hosts of many an elegant ball at their estate and everybody who was anybody was always anxious to be invited. A year after their arrival in England, a son was born to Ian and Fola. Thus, the circle was now complete. The magnificent and noble Havenshire Estate was again inhabited by its rightful royal family:

Duke and Duchess Oliver and their son.

GRAY-EYES

Part One

It was a night like many others of the season. The weather was warm but rainy, with a wind that occasionally howled and slammed raindrops noisily against windows. Sheriff Mirinda Durham sat on an old mahogany chair behind a large, somewhat worn, mahogany desk in the front office of the newly renovated jailhouse. Mirinda was mostly of African ancestry; her parents had both been runaway slaves who met in the West. She was a tall, shapely, chocolate-brown woman, 24 years old, with hair that hung down to her waist in a thick bushy braid. She had an incredibly beautiful face displaying large dark brown eyes and luscious full lips. She wore a black, high-collar man's shirt and a pair of dark brown leather pants. She also wore a dark brown leather vest, upon which was pinned her sheriff's badge, and, wore a pair of newly purchased brown leather cowboy boots. Her gun belt and gun were strapped to her waist, her supply of bullets readily attached to the side of the belt. She was elected sheriff simply because she was the fastest gun in the town of Sanctuary Meadow. It was so named because it was an all African-American and Native-American town where both groups intermingled and lived in peace with each other.

The town was quite prosperous and had seen the birth of multiple businesses. The standard of living was high, driven by both business and spirituality. And, there was a high-class social environment that was based on African and Native cultures. The year was 1875, Sanctuary Meadow was located in a sparsely populated mid-western state. It was the end of Spring and the warmer weather was making some townspeople restless for action, a malady which was presenting itself in the more active saloon activity and the spur of the moment fights. There were no prisoners in the jail right now and the night had been very quiet, but Mirinda feared it was the 'quiet before the storm'.

Momentarily, a young boy came bursting through the heavy jailhouse door. "Sheriff! Sheriff! There's a dead body in the blacksmith's barn!" the boy shouted. The boy was Thomas, jr., the son of the bank teller, Thomas G. Keys. He was a good-looking boy, about 12 years old. He had almond colored skin and slightly curly black hair. He obviously had some kind of racial mix in his genes, as did Mirinda, but in both cases, it was too far back for anyone to have knowledge of the particulars. Mirinda jumped-up from her chair and quickly followed the boy to the barn. She usually liked to be right with her predictions, but this time, she wished her 'quiet before the storm' theory had been incorrect.

When they arrived at the barn, there was already a small crowd gathered. The blacksmith, Isaiah Adams, rushed to Mirinda's side and grabbed hold of her arm as he pulled her into the stables. He was a large, dark-brown man, tall, with bulging biceps and a bald shiny head. He was somewhat dressed-up, at least he had on an almost new pair of pants and a clean white shirt. He had just returned back to his barn from the saloon when he found the body. He spoke nervously yet softly as he led her towards a horse stall at the far end of the barn. "You have to see this, it's horrible. It must've been a wild animal. Nothing else would have torn at the body with such savagery."

Mirinda noticed that the closer she came to the last stall, the more blood she saw splattered around on the hay. Then, at last, she was upon the death scene stall. She looked inside and did, indeed, see a horrific sight. It was pretty, 21 year old, Sadie Jefferson, stretched-out on her back in the middle of the horse stall, partly covered with hay, her gray and white calico dress, and neatly braided hair covered in blood. Mirinda could tell right away that it was not done by an animal. The wounds and the torn clothing were too neat. Sadie was stabbed, not ripped by savage teeth. "This was not done by a wild animal, Isaiah, this was a human act of savagery," Mirinda stated. Though the condition of the body was a blood-curdling sight, Mirinda was not overly repulsed by it. She had grown-up on a farm and had seen hundreds of slaughtered animals. True, this was a human being, but there was not a whole lot of difference in the actual appearance, for in many ways, slaughtered meat looks like slaughtered meat, human or not.

"Holy mackerel, Mirinda," Isaiah whispered in disbelief, "Some person actually did this?"

"I'm afraid so, my friend. Did anyone go get undertaker Douglass?" Mirinda inquired.

"Yeah, Chauncey went to get him," Isaiah answered.

Mirinda bent down and reached for an item in Sadie's hand. "What's this doing in her hand?" she said out loud, but to herself.

Isaiah replied, not realizing that she was not actually speaking to him. "An eagle feather? I don't know. Do you think maybe a Native did it?"

"Could be, but an eagle feather represents honor and respect to them. It would not make sense for a Native to leave it with someone he killed under less than honorable circumstances," Mirinda reasoned.

"Maybe she just grabbed it off of him during a struggle," Isaiah suggested.

"That could be an explanation," Mirinda said as she placed the feather in a small empty burlap sack that she found on the hay in a corner of the stall. She then searched around the stall and the rest of the barn for a murder weapon or some other clues, but found nothing. Isaiah watched her every move, fascinated with her detective work. "I can't believe that any of our residents would be capable of such an act. Has there been anyone new in town lately, Isaiah?" Mirinda asked.

"There were three strangers the other day, but so far as I know, they've left already. There's one more who came today, the man's still here, too, I saw him at the saloon tonight. And what do you think, he's a Native. Or, I should say, he looks to be a half-breed. Half Native and half white," Isaiah informed.

"I'll go talk with him right now. See who he is, where he comes from, and why he came to Sanctuary Meadow," Mirinda said as she walked out of the barn with the sack.

"I'll come with you," Isaiah volunteered anxiously.

The small crowd was still assembled at the entrance to the barn when Mirinda and Isaiah came out of the front door. The rain had stopped, but the wind was still quite brisk, which put a bit of a chill in the night air. Mirinda thought it was best that she let the crowd know something, though she knew next to nothing herself. She stood-up on a small wooden box and addressed the crowd. "Folks, Sadie Jefferson has been murdered. Right now, I am in the process of investigating the murder. If any of you, or anyone you know, can give me information about the murder, please notify my office. If anyone saw something out of the ordinary within the last few days, let me know that, too. Other than that, I ask that you all go home and keep your doors and windows locked and try to stay in groups of two or more as much as possible."

A soft murmur rose from the shocked crowd as the people slowly dispersed. Mirinda proceeded to the saloon with Isaiah close behind her. She saw the undertaker hurrying towards the barn, so she knew the body would be taken care of shortly. The music from the saloon drowned out the quiet of the night as Mirinda came closer and closer to the building. She pushed through the gold-painted, wooden, swinging doors and entered the noisy establishment. The main room was full of smoke and crowded with well-dressed men and fancy saloon ladies. There did not seem to be much gambling going on tonight, but the drinking and the fondling of the ladies appeared to be making up for it. Mirinda did not understand how women could let men paw over them like that, just for money. She did not see the stranger she was looking for at any of the tables, she recognized everyone. She walked farther into the room to see the entire bar. Isaiah pointed the stranger out to her. "There he is Mirinda, there in the corner, at the end of the bar."

Mirinda took a few steps forward, then the stranger came into view. Mirinda felt an instant sexual attraction to him. He was a tall, well-built man, his large muscles evident even fully clothed. His skin was the color of a golden wheat field, his hair was thick and hung halfway down his back, it was light brown in color, but had streaks of dark and even light blond in various places. His Native blood provided him with a smooth, hairless face, but his white blood provided him with unusually colored gray eyes. He wore a white, open-collared shirt, and a thigh length buckskin jacket with fringe down the back of both sleeves and across the top of both side pockets. His attire included a pair of dark brown pants that were tucked into a pair of knee-high buckskin boots trimmed with fringe around the top. He had a red and white beaded choker around his neck, from which hung a collection of several feathers about 3–4 inches in length, attached to the bottom center of the choker. His gun belt was partially in view at his waist, but there was no mistaking the bulge of his gun beneath his jacket.

Mirinda walked over to him, Isaiah at her side, as the patrons watched, wondering what could be the problem. The stranger realized her approach and immediately turned all his attention to what he thought would be some sort of racial confrontation. His half-breed status caused him trouble wherever he traveled. Someone always disliked one side of his heritage or the other. He had never fully been accepted anywhere or by anyone since the accidental deaths of his parents over 3 years ago.

"Good evening, sir. I'm Sheriff Durham, may I ask you a few questions?" Mirinda inquired in a pleasant tone.

"What's this about? Have I done something wrong?" the stranger replied cautiously.

"Not from what I know, but a few questions should clear things up," Mirinda explained. As they looked at each other, the sexual attraction felt by Mirinda became a mutual sexual attraction, and each knew that the other felt the stimulation.

"All right then, sure, why not," the stranger said, succumbing to what he knew was a futile effort to avoid the law.

"First of all, what's your name?" Mirinda asked.

"GrayEyes Le Clair," he answered proudly.

"Le Clair. What kind of name is that?" Mirinda queried curious about its origin.

"It's French. I'm from Canada. My father was French and my mother was Native," GrayEyes replied defensively.

"I see. Why have you come to Sanctuary Meadow?" she continued to pry.

Not seeing the usual adverse reaction to the breakdown of his ethnic background from Mirinda, GrayEyes felt an ease and a comfort that he had not experienced in many years. His initial instinct to stay there awhile was a good one. "I had no plans to come here. I never knew the town existed. I just happened upon it today. I liked what I saw and decided to linger, that's all," GrayEyes explained cordially.

Mirinda nodded. "O.K., well, enjoy your time with us and be careful, there's been a strange murder in town and everyone should be on guard," she warned with true concern for his safety. Then, she turned around and casually walked out of the saloon, Isaiah still at her side. GrayEyes felt the warmth in her voice and his attraction to her grew at the sound of it. He watched her walk away and enjoyed seeing the movement of her buttocks underneath her leather pants as she moved across the floor. He smiled slightly as he viewed the invigorating sight.

Isaiah was confused about the shortness of her talk with GrayEyes. "Is that all you're going to say to him, Mirinda?" Isaiah questioned in frustration.

"What else can I ask him? You said he was in the saloon with you tonight and I did not see blood on him anywhere. His clothes were not messed or torn and his hair was neat and clean. The knife he had in his boot looked clean, there was no blood around the knife area and he surely had no reason to murder her. He did not even know her. In fact, he doesn't know anyone here, why would he murder any of us?" Mirinda answered calmly.

"Well, I didn't see him every minute of the time. Maybe he left and came back," Isaiah pounded.

"Maybe, Isaiah, but I have no proof of anything like that happening. Perhaps someone will let me know if they remember seeing him leave and come back to the saloon. But, even if he did, it was not against the law and does not prove that he committed a murder. His only crime is that he is a stranger and the murder happened to occur the day he arrived. But, don't you think that would be a very stupid way to commit a murder and hope to get away with it?" Mirinda asked him.

"Yes, it would be...unless he's a madman," Isaiah replied.

Mirinda shook her head and gave Isaiah a cynical look, amazed at his persistence in the idea that GrayEyes was the murderer. Perhaps, like herself, he did not want to believe that someone with whom they were friends was the actual murderer. "I'll see you in the morning, Isaiah," she said as she walked back to the jailhouse.

The deputy, Carl Little Deer, was already there taking over the shift. They discussed the murder briefly, and then Mirinda went home to get some sleep. She opened the door to her small house and quickly lit the lamp by the door. She looked around the room and determined that no one was there, then entered the house, immediately closing the door behind her. After eating a light meal, she washed herself and crawled into her soft, comfortable bed. As she laid there, she began to have thoughts of GrayEyes. She thought about the look of his perfectly shaped lips as he answered her questions. And, the gentleness in his unusual gray eyes as he looked at her. She wondered what his muscular body looked like without its covering of clothing, and how it would feel to run her fingers all over his naked body. Her thoughts of him made her clitoris begin to throb.

The next morning Mirinda arose early. She had Sadie *and* GrayEyes on her mind all night, so was not able to sleep very well. She finished her morning grooming routine and then hurried back to the jailhouse. As she entered, she saw Carl Little Deer asleep in the chair behind the desk, his legs crossed as his feet rested on top of the desk. Mirinda smiled and then closed the door behind her, making sure to create lots of noise. Carl's whole body jumped, his hand automatically reached for his gun. "Carl! Carl! It's all right, it's just Mirinda!" she called, laughing.

"Oh, don't do that, Mirinda," Carl said breathlessly, "You liked to kill me, or I kill you."

Mirinda chuckled, "Your reflexes are still good. I'm glad to see that, I was beginning to wonder if you were getting too slow," she continued to tease.

"Yeah, right. Sure you were," Carl replied with a bright smile as he started towards the door. "Oh, there was a fight last night, so James McCurry is in a cell getting sober," Carl added.

"All right, thanks, Carl," Mirinda answered.

Mirinda walked to the back of the jail to check on James McCurry and see if he was in need of anything. Once she reached the back, she could see from a distance that Mr. McCurry was still in his drunken sleep, so, she decided to make her check around the town. As she strolled through the streets there were many expressions of 'good morning' and a few questions about Sadie's murder. By the completion of her rounds, she had answered all the questions that she could about the murder, but regretfully, had received no new information with which to work. Immediately upon re-entering the jailhouse, Mirinda heard James McCurry shouting at her. "Sheriff. I'm hungry. Get me some food!"

"Hold your horses, Mr. McCurry. I already told Mrs. Jackson to bring breakfast for you," Mirinda informed him.

"All right then, missy," Mr. McCurry replied. James McCurry was an older man with salt and pepper, tightly curled hair. He often initiated drunken brawls, usually with men half his age, in his attempts to prove that he was still a man with whom to be reckoned. He always ended-up in jail, though, and never remembered why he was there. Mirinda released him shortly after his breakfast.

The day continued without disturbance as Mirinda caught-up on her paperwork and took two observation strolls around the town. Then, about an hour after dark, there was another burst through the jailhouse door. "Sheriff! There's another body! Behind the mercantile store! Savage job, just like the first one!" a man shouted. This time it was Thunder Hawk, the trapper. Mirinda could not believe her ears. Another body just like the other one? What was happening? she thought. She accompanied Thunder Hawk to the murder scene.

Someone had brought a few kerosene lamps to the area, so the scene was lighted for sufficient observation. And, just as Thunder Hawk had said, this body was also stabbed multiple times. It was another woman, 22-year-old Sallie Red Clay, covered with blood, lying on her side in the dirt. Once again, a small crowd had assembled, but this crowd was considerably more frightened than the first crowd had been. Their incessant talking and distorted facial expressions revealed their confusion and fear. Mirinda again looked around for a weapon and possible evidence, but, none could be found. In a few moments, undertaker Douglass arrived on the scene.

"Wow! Unbelievable!" the undertaker exclaimed in shock. "What vile animal of a human could butcher people like this?" he added with distain.

Mirinda wondered the same thing. Truly, there must be someone in town who was 'mad', but, how could she stop the madness. As undertaker Douglass and his helper picked-up Sallie's body, Mirinda saw that beneath the body was a familiar item, another eagle feather splattered with blood. She picked it up to take back to her office and deposit in the burlap sack with the other one.

"When you gonna find the murderer!" a hostile woman shouted from the crowd.

"As soon as I can, as soon as I can," Mirinda replied sternly.

"You'd better hurry before the whole town winds-up dead!" another voice shouted angrily.

Mirinda ignored the comment and began to walk back down the dark alley to the front of the store that was situated on the main street of the town. As she approached the street, she noticed a lone man standing at the entrance of the alley. Upon closer inspection, she saw that it was GrayEyes. Her heart began to beat quickly at the sight of him. She looked at him and smiled as she passed through some moonlight and continued on to her office. He stepped into the moonlight, smiled back at her and tipped his hat.

He felt sad for her, he could see she was in pain over the murders and he wished that he could help her. He was surprised that he had such strong feelings towards her, especially so soon. The last time he had cared for a woman, she rejected him because of his mixed race. He swore he would never allow that to occur again. But now, here he was, his heart seeming to jump into his throat and choke him each time that he saw her. And, then, finding his body wet with perspiration each time she had left his view.

Mirinda returned to the jailhouse and placed the blood stained eagle feather in the burlap bag with the other one. Then, she sat down in the chair behind her desk. What could be the connection between Sadie's murder and Sallie's murder? Both of them had a first name that began with 'S', could that have something to do with it? she thought. Should I warn every woman in town whose first name begins with 'S' to be careful and not be alone? I don't know that to be the connection, so, I'd better not spread such information, she finally decided. The rest of her shift was quiet. Apparently, there was none of the usual Spring wildness. The two murders had frightened everyone and no one was in a social mood. Who would need any additional excitement, she thought.

In a few hours, Carl returned to provide her with some much-needed relief. "What the hell is happening, Mirinda? Two murders in two days. Two beautiful, decent, young women. Such a great loss to the town," Carl said as he walked towards the desk.

Mirinda rose from the chair allowing Carl to set things up for his shift. "Yes, Carl, you're right. It's truly a loss to us all. They were both kind ladies. Do you have any thoughts on the possible connection between the two?" Mirinda inquired.

"Well, no. They were both beautiful, both young, both kind, both had obviously affectionate steady man-friends. But, who would murder someone because of those characteristics?" Carl replied.

"There must be something. I don't believe they were selected at random. I must figure it out before someone else is murdered," Mirinda lamented as she waved goodnight to Carl and left the jailhouse on her way back home.

She walked down the long dirt main street, taking a thorough look around while she walked. Her eyes searched for any unusual persons or activities that might lend a clue to the murders. However, all was quiet, a circumstance that was comforting, yet disappointing at the same time. As she approached her house, she saw the figure of a man walking towards her in the dim light of the moon. Her heart began to beat quickly and she immediately stopped walking and placed her hand on the butt of her gun. "Who's there?" she called nervously, aware of the high possibility that this was the murderer she had been seeking.

"GrayEyes Le Clair," a voice answered amiably.

As he came closer, the moonlight shone more directly on the man and Mirinda saw the face of GrayEyes smiling at her. She felt somewhat relieved, but, she did not know much about him and he still could be the murderer. "Is there some way I may help you, Mr. Le Clair?" Mirinda asked curiously.

"Well, I came because I thought there might be some way that I could help you," GrayEyes replied with compassion.

"Help me? With what and how?" she questioned puzzled by his offer.

"With the murders. I belonged to the mounted police for a few years before I left Canada. We never had anything quite like this, but I do have some experience with investigating murders. I would like to help you if I may," GrayEyes explained caringly.

Mirinda was not sure she could trust GrayEyes. He could be telling her one big lie. But, her instincts told her that he was probably being truthful. She wanted to believe him and could certainly use his help if he was telling the truth. She decided to take a chance and see what he could contribute. But, she hoped she was thinking with her head and not with her heart. "All right, Mr. Le Clair," she said as she walked passed him and started up the steps and into the house, "Come inside with me and we will talk." GrayEyes followed her through the front door and waited at the entrance while she lit a kerosene lamp that was on a table by the door. "Have a seat here at the kitchen table," she said as she placed the lamp in the middle of it. Then, she continued around the room and lit three more lamps, providing more than enough light, before she joined him in a seat at the table. "Now, what is that you were saying? You used to be a member of the mounted police?" she inquired with alertness.

"Yes, that's right, about two years ago now," GrayEyes answered candidly.

"Why did you leave, Mr. Le Clair?" she asked in great anticipation of the answer.

"First of all, please stop calling me Mr. Le Clair. GrayEyes is the name by which I am always called," he requested in earnest.

Mirinda smiled, "Of course. Please call me Mirinda as well," she replied warmly.

He nodded and returned her smile, then continued with his answer, "I left because it became too difficult to function as a law officer. Because of my mixed racial heritage, I was only allowed to arrest Natives. I had no authority over any white people unless the person in question would submit to my authority, but, none of the whites would accept that situation. I was often able to help behind the scenes with the gathering and evaluation of evidence. But, even if I was the one to solve the case, if the suspect was white, I could not be in on the arrest. And, only the arresting officers got credit for the case, so my brains helped earn the white Mounties medals and bonuses, while I didn't even receive a 'thank you' from anyone. So, I left and here I am."

"Horrible. Sounds like Canada is not much different from the United States on racial issues. Of course, you know I could never be sheriff anywhere else but in a town of Color, don't you? What you see here is certainly not the normal situation," Mirinda explained.

"Oh...Yeah...I know. I've been in this country for over a year now. I've seen and experienced the racial hatred here. I'm well aware that Sanctuary Meadow is not the typical town," GrayEyes expounded in frustration.

Mirinda was pretty satisfied with his explanation, but she needed to remember that the fact he might have once been a Mountie did not mean he was not also a murderer. She decided she would try working with him, but not necessarily tell him everything she might come across during her investigation. "O.K., GrayEyes, we'll see if we can work together on the case. Have you come-up with any ideas about the murderer on your own yet?" Mirinda asked.

"Not yet, but give me as much information about the women as possible, perhaps there will be a clue amongst the details of their lives that will lead to a link between them," GrayEyes reasoned, in sync with Mirinda's own thoughts. Mirinda proceeded to tell him all she knew about the two women. Afterwards, GrayEyes saw no obvious connection between the two ladies that might have contributed to their deaths. Though, he stated that he would be sure to recount the information again later. He was determined to find a viable link between the women, one that would lead him down the right path to capturing the insane murderer.

But then, in the next instant, his thoughts turned to an entirely opposite subject, his attraction to Mirinda. She looked more beautiful than ever in the flickering light of the kerosene lamps. He wished she would undo the large braid in which her hair was confined and let her hair hang loose about her shoulders and down her back. Though, he supposed he would have to wait until another time. She was very much in a formal frame of mind and it was not likely she would relax around him in that manner just yet. However, he would wait. He would wait forever if needed. He knew already that he was never going to let her be without him.

Mirinda also began to have romantic thoughts. She had not noticed earlier that GrayEyes had removed his hat. His long, streaked with blond, light-brown hair was parted in the middle and hung straight and neat, passed his shoulders, halfway down both sides of his chest, and down his back. His gray eyes became an even more strange color as the yellow light of the kerosene lamps reflected in them. His lips were more full than the average white man and also more full than the average Native. Perhaps, he had some African blood about which he did not know. At any rate, his lips were full and luscious and she had the strong desire to kiss them. She wondered if he felt the same desire towards her. She hoped so.

They looked at each other for a few moments, each sexually excited by the other, each longing to touch the other, each a little sad at the uncertainty of the other's feelings. GrayEyes had no need to know her better before beginning a romantic relationship with her. But, Mirinda did need to know GrayEyes better before she could fully give herself to him. GrayEyes assumed and understood that fact, so he did not act upon his feelings that night. "Well," he said as he stood-up and started towards the door, "I'll be leaving now. We both have a lot of thinking and figuring-out to do."

Mirinda followed him, disappointed that he was leaving so soon, wishing their relationship had already advanced to where he would passionately kiss her goodnight. "Yes," she said softly. "We have much to figure-out concerning many things."

GrayEyes opened the door, stepped-out onto the dark porch, and put his hat back on his head. He turned around to take a last look at Mirinda. Once again, the sight of his handsome face in the lamplight made her want his lips on hers and his tongue in her mouth. And, her current level of stimulation was far more intense than when she was alone and would merely think of him. Tonight was indeed a pre-cursor to the orgasms she knew she would easily have with him, if and when they made love.

He smiled at her warmly and tipped the brim of his hat to her as a temporary goodbye. "Goodnight," Mirinda answered sweetly with a smile. GrayEyes turned and quickly left. His penis was slightly hard and stinging, and the old familiar perspiration was beginning to cover his forehead and body. Mirinda watched him with pleasure, until he finally disappeared into the dark dangerous shadows of Sanctuary Meadow.

Part Two

Mirinda awakened earlier than usual and her thoughts immediately went to those of GrayEyes. Actually, she had barely slept at all; she kept imagining sexual activities with GrayEyes and had masturbated herself out of a decent night's sleep. But, she was not tired. She could hardly wait to see GrayEyes again. She reminded herself that he still could be lying to her, so she decided she would send a telegram to the mounted police in Canada. Once she received their answer, she would know with more surety if he could be trusted. In the meantime, she would conduct her business with him as planned and work on the premise that he was being truthful with her about his past and present situations.

GrayEyes also had a sleeping problem. He, too, stayed awake almost all night. After he had left Mirinda's house, his already semi-hard penis became harder and harder at the thought of her beauty and body. Despite the men's shirts that she wore, he easily saw that she was endowed with large breasts, a particular liking of his. And, her tight leather pants allowed her other considerable attributes to be readily seen and admired. As he laid in bed, his fantasies that night had been more exciting than any he had ever experienced. He fantasized about her naked body pressed against his naked body and her large bare breasts digging into his chest. He fantasized about his hands between her thighs, how soft, sweet, and warm it must be there, he thought. The more he imagined, the more wet and engorged his penis became, until finally, it relieved itself, and he cried-out in a welcomed pleasure.

Mirinda arrived at the jailhouse at her usual time and found Carl eating breakfast and reading the early edition of the town newspaper. "Good morning, deputy," she said with a smile as she entered the office. She left the front door open, it was a lovely day and the office could use the airing-out. She had stopped on the way to the jailhouse and sent the telegram to Canada. She hoped for a swift answer.

"Good morning, Mirinda," Carl said with a mouth half-full of hash-brown potatoes. "The paper is all articles about the murders. Some people are really calling for your head. Some think a man ought to be in charge. They say a woman can't handle something like this. Some think that I should take over things."

"Is that right," Mirinda answered with disgust and a frown on her face. "Any business here last night, Carl?" She wanted to get off the subject of her ineptness. She was already shaky about her ability to solve the murders, she did not need further discouragement.

"No, nothing happened after discovering that body. The town is being quiet, the women are afraid to be out at night and without the women, the men don't come out very much," Carl explained as he finished his breakfast and cleaned off the desk.

At that moment, GrayEyes walked into the jailhouse office. Mirinda, who had been fumbling in the drawer of an old chest that was used to file papers, turned around as Carl addressed GrayEyes. "What can I do for you, stranger?" Carl asked cordially.

"This is GrayEyes Le Clair," Mirinda interrupted, "He will be helping me to investigate the murders. He used to be a Mountie in Canada and he offered his services, which I accepted."

Carl did not like that at all. He felt slighted. Why did she not ask him to help her if she needed it? Afterall, he was next in line for her job should she leave. Was he not smart enough or good enough to help? He controlled his temper and kept his composure. He knew he would gain nothing by not doing so.

"Good to meet you, Mr. Le Clair, my name is Carl Little Deer," he said pleasantly.

"Good to meet you also, brother, and please, call me GrayEyes," he said with equal pleasantry.

"So, you belonged to the mounted police? I didn't think they allowed Natives or half-breeds to become Mounties, no offense intended," Carl said somewhat suspicious of the stranger.

"They seldom do. My father was white and was a Mountie, so I guess they did not want to totally dishonor him by not letting me join. But, they made sure that I was not a bonafide Mountie," GrayEyes replied openly.

"Ah, I see. Well, my shift is over, I'm going home to get some MORE sleep," Carl said in jest. He was still a bit suspicious of GrayEyes, but, he liked him well enough. He was annoyed with Mirinda, though. "See you good people later."

"See you, Carl," Mirinda said softly.

"Goodbye," GrayEyes responded as he turned his attention to the magnificent Mirinda and she to him.

Now alone, each became extremely nervous. Each had masturbated over the other the night before, thus the sexual atmosphere between them was tense and heavy with passion. Mirinda spoke first. "Have any ideas last night that might help us with the murders, GrayEyes?" she asked as she excitedly looked at him across the room.

"I thought we should return to the areas where the bodies were found and take a look around the scenes. I know you did it once, but it was dark and things were emotional at the time. I think it would be wise to re-visit the places," GrayEyes stated in a most 'Mountie-like' professional tone.

"Sounds good, I agree with your conclusions. Let's go now," she answered walking towards the door. Being a true gentleman, GrayEyes waited and let her exit the office first, but once they were outside, she turned back around and shut the jailhouse door, then locked it with her key. They traveled down the wooden sidewalk of the main street side-by-side. Many citizens greeted Mirinda and most of them only looked at GrayEyes. But, everyone was wondering why they were walking around together. Who was he?

"I thought about you last night," GrayEyes said in a surprise move as they walked along the street.

"Did you? What was it you thought?" Mirinda asked softly and somewhat hopeful of the answer.

"I thought about what a gracious and lovely woman you are and about how much I would like to know you better," he said with great sincerity.

"How kind of you to think such of me and how honest of you to tell me. Actually, I thought about you last night also," she replied.

GrayEyes turned his head and looked at her with a smile, then asked, "And what were your thoughts about me?"

She looked-up at him and gingerly returned his smile, then answered, "I thought you to be the most handsome man I had ever laid eyes upon, and I wondered if I could trust you," she said truthfully.

"Oh…and what did you decide about my trustworthiness?" GrayEyes questioned slightly disappointed with her answer.

"I thought that you deserved a decent chance. And, that I would not judge you to be anything other than honorable unless I receive a reason to do so," she replied in earnest.

"That's all I can really ask of you right now. Of course, you do not know me or even if I have been telling you the truth. I would expect nothing less from you at this point. But…the situation will change in time, and I can wait for you to come to me," he proclaimed confidently, unhindered by possible rejection or embarrassment.

Mirinda, though taken by surprise at his rapid and open attachment to her, was also more than pleased. Her attachment to him was also in full force and had occurred as rapidly as his did. She never dreamed that he cared for her so much already. She wanted to come to him right now, that very moment. But, she must control her emotions. She must wait for an answer to her telegram first, then, she would decide what step to take next. She truly cared for him in the dearest way. And, his romantic declarations concerning her sparked a most urgent desire to make love with him. Yet, could he still be a liar and a murderer?

They arrived at the first site, the blacksmith's barn. The blacksmith, Isaiah, stood outside hard at work in front of a huge metal oven which contained a large pile of white-hot coals. He was banging away on a horseshoe when he noticed Mirinda and GrayEyes approaching him. He immediately stopped working and greeted them. "Goodmornin' Sheriff, and GrayEyes, wasn't it?" Isaiah spoke puzzled by the presence of GrayEyes. The suspicious Isaiah attempted to give some kind of questioning eye signal to Mirinda, but she ignored his display and began her conversation.

"May we take a look around your barn, Isaiah? It's possible I might have missed something that night and perhaps in the light of day GrayEyes and I might find something new," she explained to him.

"Sure, sure, go right ahead, stay as long as you like. I want that crazy man caught," he said sternly.

"Crazy man or woman," GrayEyes added.

"Woman? Do you think a woman could have done it?" Isaiah asked with surprise.

"Why not? Any adult could stab someone multiple times. After the first stab, the victim is usually so much in shock and disoriented that the other stabs are relatively easy to do. There's not much struggle any more," GrayEyes informed him.

"How do you know so much about stabbings?" Isaiah asked cautiously.

Mirinda responded in defense of GrayEyes, "He used to be one of those mounted police in Canada. He's had experience with such matters and has unselfishly agreed to help us with our problem."

Isaiah nodded in understanding and replied, "All right, good." Then, he simply returned to his work.

Mirinda and GrayEyes slowly made their way back through the barn to the stall where Sadie had been found. The blood stained straw that had been there the night of the murder was gone and there did not appear to be anything new to be found. Then, GrayEyes stooped down and picked-up something which was partially hidden beneath some hay. "Have you found something?" Mirinda asked when she saw GrayEyes stoop down.

"Yes," he said, "A pink ribbon stained with blood."

"A pink ribbon? Do you think it has some importance? Perhaps it was just lost by someone before the murder and so ended-up getting blood on it merely because it was there," Mirinda reasoned.

"That's certainly possible, but, perhaps its presence here has more bearing on the murder than we might imagine," GrayEyes answered.

"Well, all right, we can take it back to the office and save it the way I did with the feathers," Mirinda informed him.

"Feathers? What feathers?" GrayEyes asked her with surprise in his voice.

"I found a small eagle feather with each of the bodies. I wondered if that was a sign that a Native had done it, or someone's attempt to throw me off the trail. But, I have them in the chest at the office if you'd like to see them," Mirinda told him.

"Yes, I would like to see them, but first, let's go over to the other murder site and see what's around there," GrayEyes suggested humbly. He did not want to make her think he was trying to take charge of things.

"O.K., let's go. Give me the ribbon for safe keeping, though. I'll put it in this small sack attached to my gun belt until we return to the office," she requested. GrayEyes handed her a wrinkled, pink ribbon covered with maroon-colored speckles and splotches. She tucked it away in the sack and they headed out of the barn over to the mercantile store. "Thanks Isaiah," Mirinda called-out as they passed by his oven.

"You find anything else?" he yelled greatly curious about the answer.

"Maybe. Maybe," She shouted back to him.

They arrived at the back of the mercantile store where the second body was found. Again, any previously visible signs of blood were no longer in view, but once again, in the light of day, there was a blood-stained pink ribbon partly hidden amongst some grass. GrayEyes and Mirinda were both surprised and both puzzled by its presence.

In mild frustration, GrayEyes explained, "Two pink ribbons and two eagles feathers. Very strange. Either they both mean something, only one means something, or neither one means anything and are only decoys."

"That makes things nice and easy doesn't it?" Mirinda teased with a grin, "We may as well head back to the office, now. It's getting late and you can take a look at the feathers, if you still want. Also, Carl will be coming back on duty soon." GrayEyes handed her the ribbon and she put it in the sack with the other one, then, they returned to the office.

GrayEyes examined the feathers, but saw nothing of significance about them. He was pretty sure, though, that a Native did not leave them. Like Mirinda, he, too, felt that the eagle feather was too revered an object to be used in such a manner by a Native. But, on the other hand, who knows what a 'mad-person' who happened to be a Native might do. He returned the feathers to the sack and Mirinda gave him the ribbons to put in the sack with them. He did so; and then put the sack back in the chest.

"So, what's your opinion about the feathers?" Mirinda asked anxiously.

"The same as yours, probably not left by a Native, but who knows what an insane person might do. We can not rule-out Natives," he answered plainly.

At that moment, Carl walked in ready for his shift. "You folks still here? I thought you would have moved by now. This is how I left you many hours ago," he said with a chuckle.

GrayEyes and Mirinda laughed. "I guess it would seem that way," Mirinda replied, "We're leaving now, though." She turned to GrayEyes and said, "I'm not the best cook in town, but, I'm not half-bad. Would you like to come to my house for dinner tonight?"

GrayEyes smiled admiringly at her and answered, "Yes, I'd like that very much."

"Come along, then…you can wash-up and have a drink while I prepare the food," she said with affection.

As he watched them leave, Carl again became upset. It was obvious that there was more than the murders between Mirinda and GrayEyes. And, though he never really thought he had a chance to have her, as long as there was no one else in her life, the hope was still alive. But, now, with GrayEyes being so tall and handsome and an ex-Mountie, too; he knew he could not compete with him. Disappointment after disappointment today. Carl hoped tomorrow would bring forth sweeter fruit for him to swallow.

Mirinda set a basin of hot water for GrayEyes on a small table at the far end of the living room/dining room of the house. GrayEyes turned his back to the kitchen area where Mirinda was and removed his buckskin jacket and white shirt, exposing his broad, muscular, golden-colored back with its smooth, clear, subtle skin. His long light-brown hair hung mid-way down his back, and laid flatly against it. Mirinda took frequent glances as he gently rubbed his face, chest, and arms with a soapy cloth. She wished she could walk over and do it for him, though she would love to wash more than just those areas. She felt herself feeling more and more sexually aroused, so she turned around, cutting him out of her view. She did not want him to 'take' her yet. And, if she continued to watch him, she would not be able to control herself. He soon finished, put his shirt back on, carried the basin out the back door, and threw the water into the woods behind the house. He came back in and sat down at the table.

Mirinda came to the table carrying two glasses and a bottle. "I hope you drink wine," she said as she placed all the items on the table.

"I'm part French, remember? I grew-up drinking wine," he answered with a smile.

She filled a wine glass for him and one for herself. "Dinner is ready, I'll be back in a moment with the food," she said happily.

"Take your time. I'm not going anywhere for quite awhile," he replied sensuously. He was overjoyed at the chance to be with her like this, he would make the most of it. But…he knew eventually, somewhere down the line, every night would be like this, and every night would include lovemaking as well. Mirinda came back to the table with two bowls of beef stew that she had warmed-up from yesterday's meal and placed them on the table, one in front of GrayEyes and one in front of her own seat, then sat down. GrayEyes took a big spoonful and put it in his mouth. He must have been hungry because he swallowed it very quickly, almost seeming not to chew. "This is very good. Best I've ever had," GrayEyes said as he continued to eat. Mirinda wondered if he meant it or if he was just being nice.

GrayEyes seemed to sense what she was thinking so he reinforced his compliment, "Really, it's quite delicious and I've tasted a lot of different stews," he said giving her a re-assuring glance.

"Thank you. I'm glad you like it," she replied shyly.

Then, GrayEyes began to question Mirinda in a non-chalant manner, but, which was far from non-chalant in his own mind. "So, Mirinda, how much longer do you plan to remain sheriff?" GrayEyes questioned.

"I don't know. I haven't thought about it. I've only been sheriff for about 10 months," she answered.

"Are you interested in getting married and having children in the near future?" he continued to pry.

"Well, yes, I guess so. But, no one has asked me to marry him yet," she expressed.

"Someone will, just wait a little," he said confidently.

"Are you sure about that?" she asked hoping he was talking about himself.

"Yes, I'm absolutely sure about it. Absolutely sure," he said gently.

She lowered her head and smiled. She felt hopeful that he was speaking of himself.

"I've decided that I'm going to stay in Sanctuary Meadow. It's a nice town and the people don't seem to care about my mixed race. Also, and more importantly, I don't want to leave you," he said softly, looking at her with great desire.

Her mind began to spin in circles. There were so many contradictory thoughts in her head. Yet, she could not bear to discourage him or seem not to return his feelings. She wanted him more than anything in the world and hoped she would not be forced to let him go, or even worse, arrest him. "I'm glad you've decided to stay. I would have been very unhappy to see you leave. I think I would have missed you constantly for a very long time," she replied. They had both already stopped eating in the middle of their meal, GrayEyes reached across the table and took hold of Mirinda's hand. He held it tightly as he expressed even more of his feelings to her.

"Mirinda," he said softly, "I know it's only been a short time since we met, but I care for you so deeply that all I can say is I must be in love with you. There have been other times when I thought I was in love, but none of those times ever felt anything like this. I want us to be together, now, and always, and I will do whatever you need me to do in order to have your love."

Mirinda could not hold back anymore, the touch of his hand sent shivers through her body and the words he was saying were perfect in every way. He had said everything beautiful that she wanted to hear from him. She could not believe that he was anything other than what he claimed to be and she knew when she did receive the telegram, it would all be confirmed.

"I believe I'm in love with you, too," she whispered, "Like you, I don't know how it happened so quickly, but it did. I've thought of you each night and day since we first met. I've laid in bed at night and longed for you to be next to me, I've…"

GrayEyes could not restrain himself, he swiftly rose from his seat and rushed to Mirinda's side. He pulled her up from her chair and wrapped his arms around her waist, embracing her tightly. She threw her arms around his neck and hugged him as hard as she could. "My wonderful, beautiful, Love," GrayEyes whispered in a passionate sigh as he began to position his head to kiss her lips. When he was aligned appropriately, he gently pressed his lips against hers; she instantly opened her mouth and he immediately thrusted his tongue into it. Her nipples quickly hardened and her undergarment became soaking wet between her thighs as he continued to thrust deep down in her throat with his soft, warm, sensuous tongue. They both knew they would only go so far that night. So, after a few minutes of what could be called 'heavy petting' and after both felt GrayEyes getting somewhat 'hard', they stopped and said their goodnights. They still, afterall, had two murders to work on in the morning.

It was another sleepless night for the both of them. Each was so sexually aroused that neither could sleep for want of the other. So, when Mirinda heard an early knock at her door, she was already wide-awake and quickly answered it. The man at the door was Percy Jenkins, the helper at the telegraph office. The answer to her telegram had arrived. She took the message and thanked Percy for bringing it to her right away. She was afraid to read it. After last night, she did not know if she could break from GrayEyes no matter who he was or even what he had done. But, she knew she must find out the truth, so with her heart beating wildly, she began to read:

ھ

Sheriff Durham,

Received your query regarding GrayEyes Le Clair.

He was given an honorable discharge from the Royal Canadian Mounted Police two years ago.

Good family, good man, honest, trustworthy.

Ernest B. Wellington, Major
Royal Canadian Mounted Police

Mirinda's heart filled with relief. GrayEyes was telling her the truth and there was no reason whatsoever to suppose he was involved in the murders. She felt free to plunge fully into her relationship with him now. She hurried to get dressed and get down to the jailhouse. He would be meeting her there shortly and she could not wait to see him. When she arrived at the office, she told Carl that he could leave early. Carl jumped at the chance and left immediately. She wanted to be alone when GrayEyes came. She had sat down at the desk and started searching in one of the drawers for the new box of bullets she had bought, when she heard the front door to the office open. She looked-up with excitement because she knew it must be GrayEyes. But, she found out she was wrong. It was Mr. Keys, the bank teller.

"Good morning, Mr. Keys, what may I do for you?" she asked with a smile.

"Good morning yourself," he replied angrily.

"What's wrong? Have I done something to you?" she asked astonished at his behavior.

"Why are you so lovey-dovey with that stranger, that GrayEyes? Stay away from him! He's no good! He's going to hurt you in the end!" he exclaimed in annoyance.

"How do you know? Have you found some information about him that I may not know?" There was only silence. "If not, I can pick my own friends, Mr. Keys," Mirinda answered, puzzled and a bit concerned.

"I know, that's all," Mr. Keys began to explain a little more calmly, "He's trouble, he…." At that moment, GrayEyes walked through the front door. Upon seeing him, Mr. Keys immediately stopped talking, quickly brushed passed GrayEyes, and exited the front door.

"Whoa, what's his problem?" GrayEyes asked as he strolled over to where Mirinda was sitting.

"I don't know. For some reason he doesn't seem to like you. He wanted me to stay away from you," Mirinda told him.

"Umm, that's odd. He doesn't even know me or anything about me, so far as I can figure…Well, anyway, good morning, my Love," GrayEyes whispered as he leaned down to kiss her lips.

She lifted her head to meet him and their tongues gently entwined into a soft, wet swirl of excitement. When they finished their morning 'hello', GrayEyes made a suggestion. "What would you think about us splitting-up today? I could hang-out at the saloon and see what information I might hear during the course of the day. People get mighty loose lips once they start drinking. A day at the saloon could turn-out to be of great benefit," he said.

"All right, there's a lot of truth in what you've said. I'll circulate around town and talk in depth with folks. Perhaps something unintentional will slip during a conversation," Mirinda informed.

"Good. I'll meet you back at your house at the end of your shift and we'll discuss our findings," GrayEyes concluded.

"Fine, see you later," she said as he walked out of the door.

It was dark by the time Mirinda finished her sweep of town and her shift ended. She stepped onto the dark porch of her house and unlocked the door. As she stepped through the entrance, a figure rushed from the bushes and pushed her through the door, knocking her on the floor. The figure quickly entered the house and grabbed her around the neck with its arm, then pulled her back-up from the floor. The figure slammed the back of her body against the front of its body, and began choking her by squeezing her neck in the bend of its elbow. She tried to scream, but her air was cut-off and she could only emit muffled sounds. She heard a man's voice talking to her erratically, saying the same things over and over again, "I have to punish you. You have to be punished." Then, he would repeat a name, but she could not quite understand it.

Unknown to Mirinda, the man was fumbling in his pocket to find the knife that he had brought with him. She struggled furiously to get loose, which made it difficult for him to retrieve the knife. In the course of the struggle, two chairs were knocked over and a kerosene lamp fell and smashed into pieces on the floor. It was these sounds that caused GrayEyes to come tearing through the open front door. The man immediately freed Mirinda when he saw the form of GrayEyes entering the house. The house was dark, Mirinda never had time to light a lamp before she was attacked, so in the time it took for GrayEyes to adjust to the darkness of the house, the man had run out of the back door. It was obvious that the man had some familiarity with the house. However, because of the absence of lights, neither Mirinda nor GrayEyes could recognize or describe the man. GrayEyes rushed to the figure of Mirinda that he could now discern in the moonlight from the open front door. "Are you all right, Mirinda?" he asked worriedly as he put his arms around her and held her tightly.

"Yes, I'm okay," she replied softly as a few tears trickled down her face.

"Come sit down," he whispered, gently guiding her to a chair at the kitchen table. She sat down, extremely shaken by her brush with death. But, she was beginning to regain her composure.

"I'll light some lamps," GrayEyes continued.

Mirinda sat wiping her eyes and wondering why the murderer had come after her. Was she getting too close to his identity or was there some other reason?

"Look at this place," GrayEyes said, picking-up the knocked over chairs. "I'll remove this broken glass from the floor for you right now."

"It was a man," Mirinda said to him in monotone.

"Are you sure?" GrayEyes asked as he put the glass and the broken lamp into a burlap sack.

"He spoke to me. He kept saying that I needed to be punished and calling me by some name. Cara, Clara, something. I can't quite figure-out what it was," Mirinda said with a frown of disappointment.

"Knowing it's a man rules-out quite a number of people. Could you tell anything about his race by his voice?" GrayEyes asked.

"No, there was nothing distinctly racial about it, but I wasn't really paying attention either," she answered.

"Well, why don't you go lie down, maybe you'll fall asleep. We can talk more about it tomorrow. I'm going to spend the night right here by the fireplace, so don't be afraid," GrayEyes assured her confidently. "Would you throw me out a pillow and a blanket when you get to your room?"

"Of course I will," she said. She stood and picked-up one of the now lighted lamps, which she carried with her into the bedroom.

GrayEyes removed his jacket and hat and sat at the table waiting for Mirinda to bring him the pillow and blanket. When she returned to the bedroom door, he saw that she did not have the items with her, and, that she was totally naked. Her bushy, long, black hair hung loosely about her shoulders and down her back just as he had been desiring to see it. "I think I'd rather you spend the night a little closer to me than in another room," she said softly. Her brush with death had increased her urgency to make love with him. GrayEyes smiled at her seductively, stood-up from his chair, and slowly walked to Mirinda. He could see by the lamplight, that just as he had imagined, her breasts were large and sensuous. Her nipples, which were already swollen with passion, invited him to partake of them. His eyes followed down the rest of her shapely, chocolate body to her firm, muscular thighs and her thick, black pubic hair...his mouth watered at the sight of them. He wrapped his arms around her back and followed its curve with his hands, downward, to the soft, smooth skin of her waist. He held her firmly, while he engulfed one of her engorged nipples with his warm wet mouth. She placed both of her hands on his head and began to caress it, stroking his hair, and, holding his head close, while he suckled at her breast. His lips cuddled each nipple extensively, causing Mirinda to experience her first intense orgasms.

He maneuvered her against a wall in her bedroom and began to lick his way down her body. He ended up on his knees. He slid his tongue across her pubic hair several times causing the entire area to become damp. Then, sliding his tongue in and out between her thighs, he ran his tongue back and forth along her large warm clitoris. GrayEyes lifted one of her legs and placed it over his shoulder, which spread her thighs far apart and allowed him to submerge his face between them. She grabbed his head and held it tightly to her lower body as she became lost in the paradise that GrayEyes was providing. Her stimulation increased dramatically each time she caught a glimpse of his tongue as he maneuvered it between her thighs. And, the more engorged her clitoris became, the more sensitive it became to the feel of his tongue. Until, finally, she reached a point at which she thought she might faint. Deep gasps and pantings of delight and pleasure were continuously emitted from each of them as passion and fire burned throughout each body. GrayEyes reached upward, grabbed hold of each breast, and began to vigorously massage each nipple as he continued to lick her dripping enlarged clitoris into multiple orgasms for her.

After a considerable amount of time, they slowly made their way to the bed. Mirinda laid down, her knees bent up and back, her legs spread far apart. GrayEyes hungrily absorbed the sight between her legs while he quickly undressed and revealed the beautiful, tall, muscular body that Mirinda had salivated over only yesterday. His large golden-colored penis was hard and dripping with clear fluid. He laid on top of her and immediately inserted his penis into her open, drenched, and waiting vagina. He was already aroused into a sexual frenzy and knew he would need to ejaculate any minute now. But, still, he was determined to hold it as long as possible. He began to thrust himself deeper and deeper into her at a lightening speed and with a thundering force, their strong arms locked around each other in a lovers' embrace. Soon a dual climax was reached, which produced fires of rapture so hot, the blazing inferno reached even unto the celestial heavens.

Part Three

GrayEyes awakened and sat-up in bed, full of spice and ginger after having experienced his highly anticipated sexual encounter with Mirinda. He looked over at her and smiled as he viewed the sight of her beautiful, peaceful face at sleep. He decided to lean down and kiss her lips until she, too, awakened. But, just as his lips reached hers, she popped-up, forcing him to dodge out of her way. She was now sitting-up next to him on the bed, her eyes wide-open. "I know who it is," she said breathing hard and fast.

"Who is it you think you know?" he asked startled by her sudden movement.

"The person who murdered those women. I know who it is," she repeated nervously.

"Who?" GrayEyes asked stunned at her admission.

"The bank teller, Thomas Keys," she stated sternly and definitively.

"Why do you think he did it? What led you to him?" he questioned somewhat uncertain of her revelation.

"Remember when I told you that the man who attacked me kept calling me by a name and that his speech was so muddled that I couldn't quite understand the name?" Mirinda asked him.

"Yes, I remember," GrayEyes said.

"It just hit me as I woke-up, he was saying Jarra…Jarra Keys, the daughter of Thomas Keys," she informed him.

"What would cause him to commit such acts?" GrayEyes questioned still uncertain of her conclusions.

"I'm not sure why he would murder anyone, but I'll tell you about Jarra. She was beautiful, inside and out, but started keeping company with a young man by the name of Delano Barrett. We all grew-up together here in Sanctuary Meadow and were all about the same age. Delano was always a very aggressive, violent little boy, and, unfortunately, grew-up to be the same type of man. He was always in fights and seldom had a job. But, for some reason, Jarra was madly in love with him. Mr. Keys tried desperately to break them apart, especially when Delano took to beating Jarra on occasion, but Jarra would not hear of it nor would she press any charges against him. One day, when Jarra was home by herself, Delano came to visit. And, because she didn't have any food ready for him to eat, he beat her unmercifully, to death," Mirinda explained sadly.

"A disgusting pig wasn't he?" GrayEyes said solemnly.

"Yes, to say the least. Anyway, Delano was arrested for murder by the sheriff whose job I took over and after a swift trial was hanged. But, Mr. Keys has never been the same since it all happened. This month is the one-year anniversary of her death. And, now, I recognize that the voice last night was indeed Mr. Keys," Mirinda explained.

"It would seem that you could be right," GrayEyes said still somewhat skeptical about the case.

"And, one more thing, ever since Jarra was a little girl, she always wore some kind of pink ribbon in her hair every day. For what reason, I never knew," Mirinda added to further strengthen her analysis.

"All right. We'll go pick him up right now," GrayEyes said as he got out of bed and proceeded to get dressed. Mirinda quickly followed his lead. GrayEyes was still concerned about their ability to prosecute Mr. Keys. Mirinda's knowledge about the family and her personal familiarity with those involved were certainly heavy evidence. But, would that be enough to hold-up in court without a confession?

As soon as they finished dressing, they rushed out of the bedroom and towards the front door, each with a gun belt strapped around the hip and each hoping that neither would have to use a gun. Just before they reached the front door, GrayEyes grabbed Mirinda around the waist and pulled her body against him. Then, he gave her a short, but extremely passionate kiss, rolling his tongue around in her mouth with tumultuous vigor. He withdrew his tongue, kissed her lips, and smiled at her. She looked in his eyes lovingly. She already wanted him deep inside her again. But...within a few seconds, they were on their way to capture a 'madman'. They hoped to arrive before the 'madman' could avoid them and murder again.

When they approached the house of Mr. Keys all was quiet. It was still pretty early in the morning and the streets were rather deserted. Both Mirinda and GrayEyes were happy about that circumstance; it would be safer for everyone. They quietly walked-up the front steps of the large white house, onto the wide front porch. Mirinda knocked on the door, but no one answered. She looked at GrayEyes, who motioned to her to knock again. She did so, and a few moments later Mr. Keys opened the door. Upon seeing them, he immediately bolted for the back door. He knew what he had done and he knew why they were there. GrayEyes took off after him and was able to tackle him around the legs as they reached the kitchen. Mr. Keys struggled, but he was almost 20 years older than GrayEyes. The police training as a Mountie enabled GrayEyes to pin Mr. Keys to the ground, on his stomach, with his arms behind his back. Mirinda quickly handed GrayEyes a pair of handcuffs, which he promptly locked around the wrists of Mr. Keys.

Within seconds, Mrs. Keys and their 12 year-old son came running down-stairs into the living room. "What's happening? What are you doing to him?" Mrs. Keys cried-out, her face distorted and tears running down her cheeks. The boy grabbed hold of his mother and clung tightly to her waist. He began to cry loudly as he watched his father being pulled-up from the floor and dragged towards the front door. Mirinda wanted to comfort them, but she did not know quite what to say, yet. "I'll be back shortly and explain things to you, Mrs. Keys," Mirinda said, upset herself by the whole occurrence. She was glad GrayEyes was there to help. She was too emotionally involved with the family. Afterall, she had known them all of her life.

But, before they were able to leave, Mr. Keys began a 'rant and rave' directed at Mirinda. "I warned you, Jarra! I warned you! I told you to stay away from men. They're no good! I saw you kissing this GrayEyes two days ago. I warned you at the jailhouse to leave him alone! You wouldn't listen! You never listen! I warned you! I've punished you two times for not listening! Now you have to be punished again! I'll be back! I'll punish you again!" he rattled on in a delusion-ary tyrate.

Breaking her son's hold around her waist, Mrs. Keys cried-out as she ran over and hugged her husband around the neck, "Thomas, stop! She's not Jarra! She's not our daughter! Please, don't do this to yourself anymore!"

He quieted down, but continued to whisper to his wife, "I warned her, I warned her."

GrayEyes pulled Mr. Keys towards the door and Mrs. Keys let loose her hold on him. In a few moments, GrayEyes, Mr. Keys, and Mirinda were enroute to the jailhouse. The few people who were up and about watched the trio as they passed, all wondering what was happening. What in the world could the bank teller have done? Within a few days, the whole town knew what Mr. Keys had done. There was a brief hearing where it was determined that Mr. Keys was not of sound mind and required hospitalization rather than a hangman's noose. He was sent to a mental institution somewhere in the East. Mrs. Keys and her son moved East so they could be near him. And...the murders in the town did indeed stop.

GrayEyes remained in Sanctuary Meadow. He and Mirinda were married and he became her additional deputy. Once Mirinda and GrayEyes began to have children, she resigned her position as sheriff. The town elected GrayEyes as her replacement, much to the disappointment of Carl Little Deer. Carl stayed on as deputy anyway, though. The town returned to its usual prosperous and peaceful existence. There were still a few saloon brawls, especially at the end of Spring. But, that was normal for Sanctuary Meadow.

BUTTERFLY

The struggle between the BAND and BUTTERFLY had been engaged upon for many years. The BAND was a 'right wing' group, white supremist, and more concerned with individual benefits than the benefits to humanity. BUTTER-FLY was a human rights group fighting police, racial, and governmental oppression. There were members and sympathizers of each group who wore the uniform of the FORCE. But, most of the FORCE were typical military types who generally just followed orders without much, if any, thought to the human rights aspect of any situation.

Anti-human rights sentiments were running high in some areas even without BAND influence. The reason for this phenomenon was not very clear. Half of the world's population had been destroyed during the war, but apparently old fears and hatreds continued to be passed on from generation to generation. With the decrease in jobs, food, clothing, and housing, some factions seemed to need a scapegoat to justify their ills. There seemed to be an emerging 'all for me' mindset even amongst former humanists. Thus, instead of working together for the common good, some chose to hoard resources and murder competition for survival. Many buildings were destroyed or badly damaged. Large numbers of people were homeless and living on the streets. Violence erupted at any time, any place, by anyone. It was supposedly the 29th of April. But, no one was totally sure of the days, months, or even the years. The calculation was not exact, but an attempt was made to reconcile the time before the war with the time after the war. However…the sun was bright, the sky was blue, and it seemed that Spring was beginning to show its face. Buds were on the trees and a few multi-colored flowers were starting to bloom.

Kazi traveled his usual route to work, riding his motorcycle along the poorly paved suburban road enroute to his city job. Kazi was one of the elite of the FORCE; he was a WARRIOR, and a striking figure indeed. In ancient Earth terms, his appearance would have been one of Mediterranean decent. He was approximately 32 years old with short, almost black, wavy hair. Dark brown eyes, a clean-shaven, naturally tan complexion, 6'3" tall, and a muscular build. He wore tight, black, leather pants with heavy knee-high boots, a burgundy t-shirt, and a black leather jacket. The jacket had an emblem sewn on the shoulder of the sleeve that read, 'Warrior 888'. He had removed his helmet for a time so that he might enjoy the sun and the air. Kazi was the product of a rather isolated country family. Most people lived in the city or close to it because of the lack of transportation and lack of gasoline. But, Kazi's parents were self-contained farmers who could function without much dependence on the city. Kazi, being a member of the FORCE, was privy to ample gasoline, so it was not a problem to commute from the country. As his parents were now elderly, he thought it best to remain living with them. He was a loner, the last of the children. His younger brother and sister had died in the last flu outbreak 5 years ago.

Except for his work environment, Kazi had no real dealings on any social level with those varied individuals who composed the masses. Nor was he aware of any particular human rights infractions perpetrated upon them by the FORCE or the government. He just did his job in accordance with the law, and then rode back to the country. Law breakers must be controlled! As he traveled the road, he thought how nice it would be to go by the lake and just stretch-out all day…Peace. But, he knew it was impossible. He wondered what would happen today. Would he make it back alive tonight? Or would this be the day his luck ran out? Kazi could see the tops of the buildings appearing over the hill. He rode to the crest of the incline, stopped at the top of the hill, and put both feet on the ground straddling the motorcycle. There it was, the 'city', decaying and dirty at its entrance, but signs of new life and civilization at its core. He removed his gun and holster from the black side-pouch of his motorcycle and strapped them around his waist. He checked his gun; it was loaded and clean. He made sure his extra ammunition was readily available (anything could happen upon entering the city). He placed his helmet on his head. All was in order. The WARRIOR rode into battle.

The WARRIOR briefing room was nearly filled when Kazi arrived. Something had happened during the night. He took a seat in the back of the room. The WARRIOR chief walked to the podium and the room quieted down. There had been a bombing around 1:00 a.m. The building bombed was a known BAND hangout and three bodies were found, all identified as BAND members. The BAND was blaming BUTTERFLY and demanding action. Since

BUTTERFLY had always had the philosophy of nonviolence, it was thought that the best thing to do would be to infiltrate them to get evidence. The high-level BUTTERFLY members were to have individual surveillance. Kazi was assigned to a leader by the name of Taifa. The name seemed somewhat familiar, but he could not picture the individual. There was to be a BUTTERFLY rally in the park at 2:00 p.m. and Taifa was to be a key speaker. He would begin his surveillance then. Kazi went to his locker and proceeded to change out of his uniform into the street clothes he always kept in his locker. His attire consisted of a pair of jeans, a plain white shirt, and a brown tweed sports jacket. Even his plain manner of dress could not lessen the effect of his handsome face, though.

The day was awfully warm, but then maybe it was not April at all. The crowd was much larger than Kazi thought it might be, perhaps the bombing had something to do with it. It consisted of people from all races and creeds, all ages, and both genders. He worked his way up to about the third row from the stage. He wanted to be sure he could keep his eye on Taifa while she spoke and then keep sight of her after the speech. The crowd began to cheer as a tall red-haired man approached the podium. Once he reached the microphone, the noise of the crowd subsided, and he began to speak. His name was Yi' Sen; he spoke of injustices that had been occurring. Incidents that Kazi had never heard of and was having trouble believing. Kazi was fascinated, yet disturbed, over the climate being projected. He had been at BUTTERFLY gatherings before, but never listened to the speeches; he had always been in uniform and was too busy helping to control the crowd.

The crowd was angered and excited at the same time. Kazi heard the announcer introduce the next speaker, Taifa. Kazi's eyes searched the stage waiting to see the subject of his surveillance. The crowd roared. A woman stepped from behind the curtain on the side of the stage. Kazi had never seen anyone so lovely, his eyes followed her as she crossed the stage to the microphone. She had black hair that hung in many braids 3–4 inches passed her shoulders and a small bang in front. Her skin was the color of deep copper. She wore a powder pink, silky, mid-calf dress with short sleeves. She smiled at the crowd, her large brown eyes gleaming with love for them. Her lips were colored red and to Kazi were perfectly shaped, the most beautiful he had ever seen. In the ancient Earth era, she would have been deemed a woman of African ancestry, and a more enthralling woman he had never seen. Suddenly, Kazi was aware of the roaring crowd. Taifa had finished her speech. He had not heard a word she said. She stepped away from the microphone and a group of

5 men came-up on stage and began to sing an old inspirational titled, 'Monarch...Fly Butterfly'. People in the crowd began to sway and sing along to the music. Kazi began to feel a twinge of comradery, but then the song ended and so did the feeling. Kazi quickly looked for Taifa; she had come off the stage and was talking with a group of people near the rear of the stage.

Taifa was raised in what could be called an upper-class family. Her parents were both scientists and were paid very well because of the great need for scientists. She herself was a physician. The group surrounding her was praising her speech. She felt a glow knowing that her friends were inspired by her words. In a few minutes, she excused herself, it was beginning to get dark, plus she would have a long day tomorrow visiting patients who were unable to come to her clinic. Kazi watched her as she walked to her jeep, he was in awe of her. These hours of surveillance would be the highpoint of his life. Fortunately, his unmarked car was parked only two spaces away from her jeep. He waited for her to pull-out of her space. She pulled-out and made a left turn at the first intersection, Kazi followed close behind. The streets were beginning to be deserted now. Most people tried to stay inside after dark because of the many youth gangs that roamed the streets at night in search of excitement. Not to mention the violence that the BAND perpetrated upon what it deemed to be undesirable members of the populace.

It was dark by the time Taifa arrived at her apartment building. She parked, gathered together her purse and medical bag, and took a look around the neighborhood before opening the jeep door. Kazi parked about 40 feet behind her. He had been driving without his lights and hoped she had not noticed him. He waited for her to leave the car, but, he too, was observing the neighborhood for possible gang members. He knew, however, that the gang would not be fearful of a lone FORCE member, if he should have to attempt to rescue her. The area seemed clear to him and he was glad she had chosen to park in front of an old-fashioned street light, it gave him a clear view of her and her immediate surroundings. He watched her safely enter the building. After about two minutes, he saw a light go on in a second floor window. He saw Taifa come to the window and pull down the shade. He could see her shadow behind the shade and wished he was in there with her. He watched as she began to undress and wished even more that he was in there with her. But, then he turned his head away from the window. Among other things, he had respect for her and did not want to reduce all he felt to something cheap and lustful. He knew it was more. Contrary to his orders, though, he decided to alter his assignment from only surveillance to general undercover. He knew he needed to be close to her. He would go to the clinic tomorrow and make contact.

Taifa felt exhausted as she undressed. She knew she would not be able to fall asleep right away. Although exhausted, she was still wide-awake. She took a short shower, water was rationed and the meter would inform the authorities of excessive usage. The warm shower relaxed her; enough that she thought she might be able to fall asleep soon afterall. She laid her head on the pillow; it felt so good. She reached over and turned out the light. Her eyes closed and did not open again that night.

Kazi saw the light go out. He continued to watch the building. He could not be sure right away whether Taifa had gone to bed or was coming back out. After about 10 minutes, he assumed she had gone to bed. He decided to get out and take a look around the building, particularly to see if there was a back door. He walked slowly down the alleyway next to the building. He turned the corner into the backyard and found the back door. It was all boarded-up, which made it impossible for anyone to get through it without a crow bar. The other side of the building was attached to the next building by a common wall, thus there was no way of entering or leaving the building from that side. He was satisfied that she had not left the building from another exit. He walked back to his car, got in, and locked the door. He figured he would get a few hours of sleep; he was sure Taifa would not be going out again that night.

Taifa was awakened by the alarm at 6:00 a.m. She quickly washed, then dressed by putting on a pair of kaki pants, black boots, white blouse, and a light, black jacket. She kept her hair in braids and slipped on some gold hoop earrings. She grabbed her purse and medical bag and walked out to the jeep. Kazi, who was half asleep, was fully awakened by the closing of the door to Taifa's building. He slowly stuck his head up over the dashboard and caught sight of Taifa as she descended the front stairs. How it pleasured his heart to see her. She was just as beautiful today as she was yesterday, maybe even more so, he thought.

She arrived at the clinic with Kazi still behind her; it was 7:15 a.m. and the clinic opened at 8:30 a.m., but she was not staying anyway. Kazi watched her as she went into the clinic. He assumed she would be there all day, so he decided he would clean-up before going in the clinic to make the contact he so badly wanted. He radioed into headquarters for a relief officer and reported his activities of the prior day and night. In about 15 minutes another WARRIOR drove-up in an unmarked car. Kazi informed him of Taifa's whereabouts as well as her description. He then pulled-out and drove back to headquarters. He shaved, showered, and changed clothes with great expectations of the day's coming events.

Taifa gathered together supplies that she thought she might need for her medical rounds to the homebound. She gave her nurse some last instructions on things to do while she was out of the clinic, and then started through the front door. Just as she stepped out, she was surprised by a man standing at the entrance. He smiled slightly as she softly gasped.

Kazi said in a convincingly distressed tone, "I'm sorry, I didn't mean to startle you. I need to see a doctor."

"I'm the doctor. How may I help you?" she asked with concern.

"I've been having pains in my chest this morning and I thought I should get myself checked-out," Kazi replied distraughtly.

Taifa was inclined to send him to the hospital, so that she could start her rounds, but she thought perhaps she should check him now in view of his purported symptoms. "Come in and have a seat. I'll be right with you," she said as she turned around and re-entered the clinic.

Kazi's heart began to beat quickly as he took a seat. He felt a little warm. He hoped he would not lose too much of his 'cool', but he felt very nervous. He watched her as she removed her coat and took a stethoscope from her medical bag. She began walking towards him, but stopped at an examining table. "Mister…aah, I'm sorry, what is your name?" she asked.

Kazi had not thought about having to give a fake name. "Oh, it's…Redfern. Vincent Redfern," he replied.

"Mr. Redfern, would you please come and sit on the examining table?" she requested. Kazi walked over and sat on the edge of the examining table. "Please unbutton your shirt, Mr. Redfern," Taifa added softly.

Kazi did as she asked. She came close to him and gently placed the stethoscope head on his chest. Her hair kept brushing across his face and it was beginning to excite him. Her mouth was so close to his. He wanted to taste her.

"You're very nervous aren't you, Mr. Redfern? Your heart is beating very fast. However, there doesn't seem to be any other problem with it. I think you must have just had a little indigestion this morning," she said in a reassuring tone.

"Well, that makes me feel more at ease," Kazi replied with pretended relief.

"I'll give you a small bottle of antacid you can use next time," Taifa responded in a kindly manner.

Kazi wished he could put his arms around her and hold her close for awhile. But, right now, he needed to come-up with some reason to be at the clinic on a daily basis. "Doctor, I was wondering if you might be in need of a handyman or helper around here. I recently lost my job and I am desperately looking for work," he pleaded.

Taifa thought for a few seconds and then said, "Sure, we could use a man around here. There are only women here. I hope that won't bother you," she warned.

Kazi smiled, "No, not at all."

"O.K., come back tomorrow morning at 8 o'clock, Vincent," Taifa said with a smile.

"Thanks, Doc. You'll never regret this, I promise," Kazi said trying to continue the act.

"I'm sure I won't. I must leave now to examine some patients. See you tomorrow," Taifa said as she rushed out of the door. Kazi was not on duty again until the following day; so, he returned to headquarters where he put on his helmet, jumped on his motorcycle, and headed back home. All he could see in his mind was Taifa's face and fantasies of making love with her. He rode with a renewed zest for life as he traveled the long and badly paved road. The day was cool, but he was feeling hot.

It was 11:35 p.m., the top leaders of the BAND were gathered in a large, dingy room located in an old brick building at the edge of the city. The building served as their headquarters. They had purposely demolished the buildings in the immediate area so as to have a clear view from all sides, should anyone approach them. Thus, it stood much like a fortress in an open field. It was heavily armed and had guards posted at strategic windows. The head leader, Cray Brookline, addressed the group from a seat at the table around which they all sat. He was an older man with mixed gray hair and dark blue eyes. Peter, Cray's brother, sat at the far end of the rectangular table. He was sort of a 'leader in training', a position he was allowed to have basically only because he was Cray's brother. Peter was a recent joiner and technically should not have been in the meeting at all. He was about 33 years old with light brown hair, tall, well-built, and generally a very attractive man. The discussion centered on the bombings. Cray had received word that the FORCE was not going to take much action to flush out the bombers in BUTTERFLY, so the BAND would have to do it. "We must exact our own revenge," Cray said angrily, "The authorities won't help us take care of BUTTERFLY without solid evidence and they don't seem to want to try too hard to get it."

"Let's handle it then, the sooner the better," one of the others agreed enthusiastically. A plan was devised, all the top leaders were given their assignments, and the membership was divided into teams.

Kazi sat outside the clinic. He had seen the nurse go in, but not Taifa yet. It had been a restless night for him with his thoughts of Taifa, particularly of making love with her. Taifa's jeep pulled-up, she jumped-out and ran into the clinic. Kazi realized that once again his heartbeat had quickened as he watched her. He knew he would have to learn to keep his emotions intact if he planned to pull-off his deceptions. Suddenly, Kazi realized it was almost 8:00 a.m.; he rushed out of the car and dashed into the clinic. The nurse, who was an older woman, immediately looked-up from her desk.

'Good morning. May I help you?" she asked in a kind voice. Then, she added, "Weren't you here yesterday?"

Before Kazi could answer Taifa walked in from the examining room. He glanced over at her and felt his heart melt as he looked into her eyes. "Good morning, Vincent," she said with a smile.

Kazi smiled softly and replied, "Good morning, doctor."

"Carole, this is Vincent Redfern. I hired him yesterday to help us out around here," Taifa explained.

"Great. I'll show him around," Carole happily volunteered.

"Thanks, Carole. Vincent, you're in good hands now. She'll get you started," Taifa said reassuringly, then walked back to her office.

Kazi turned to Carole, she was already looking at him. "You're certainly a strikingly handsome man, Vincent," Carole said in a somewhat seductive manner.

"Thank you, Carole," Kazi replied feeling a bit embarrassed, yet uplifted by the compliment.

The days passed and Kazi became more and more accustomed to the clinic operations. He also felt more and more admiration for Taifa. She always worked extremely hard and was totally concerned with the well being of others. How could such a person ever have anything to do with a bombing? He knew she did not, and he stated such conclusions in his reports. He had been following her for some weeks now. Luckily, she remained in the clinic all day, almost every day. He never saw anything suspicious. In the evening, he followed her and she almost always went straight home, stayed in all night, and had no visitors. However, he knew that his benign reports would soon have surveillance of her halted due to lack of evidence. So, he would have to make a move to get closer to her right away.

Taifa quickly found that she liked having Vincent at the clinic. She found herself very attracted to him, feelings she kept trying to fight. But, each time she saw him, she lost the battle. This was a new experience for her, at least new for a very long time. Her previous relationships had not worked well, and, in recent times, her dedication to medicine had consumed her. She was fearful of becoming involved with anyone again. Her past break-ups had been painful ones and her heart had been broken each time. She had great difficulty trusting men now and no longer trusted her judgment in choosing a mate.

One evening when Carole had already left, Kazi and Taifa were doing the final cleaning-up for the day. Kazi decided he would take this opportunity to become more intimate. "Taifa, you've been working tremendously hard for many weeks, please let me take you to dinner tonight," Kazi said with affection. Taifa thought for a moment, should she pursue this more personal relationship with Vincent? So far, he had been a kind, helpful, most enjoyable person, and she did have romantic feelings towards him. Suddenly…a tinge of fear entered her thoughts. Then…she looked into his eyes and the fear diminished. "All right, Vincent, I would like that very much. Let me just lock my office and we'll be finished here," Taifa answered warmly.

In a few minutes, they were on their way. They decided to go to a little cafe just down the street from the clinic. They walked slowly down the street, both feeling rather nervous despite the fact that they had been working together for several weeks. "This is very nice of you, Vincent. Are you sure you can afford it? I know I don't pay you an awful lot," Taifa questioned.

"It's no problem. I have some money saved and anything I might spend on you would be worth it to me," Kazi said with sincerity.

What a sweet thing to say, Taifa thought. How easy it would be to fall for him. But, should she really take the chance of being hurt again? She would give the matter some thought when she got home. They reached the cafe where the host greeted them enthusiastically as they entered. The host showed them to a secluded, softly lighted booth; he must have thought they wanted romantic seating. They sat down and began to look at the menus that the host handed them. He left, but in a few minutes, returned and took their orders.

Kazi and Taifa looked at each other, neither knowing what to say because of their lack of recent dating experience. They each sensed what the other felt, which caused each to chuckle simultaneously. "So, where do you live, Vincent?" Taifa asked initiating the conversation.

"Right in the neighborhood, on Sunflower Avenue," Kazi replied naming a street close to the clinic and her apartment in case she happened to spot him near her building.

"Oh, not far at all. I live in the same general area, on Bird of Paradise Court," Taifa informed him.

Kazi did not want to betray the fact that he already knew where she lived. "Yes, I've heard of the street, pretty decent there," he said.

The waiter soon came with their meals. Fish, fried potatoes, and salad for Taifa. Spaghetti and meatballs for Kazi. Taifa was pleased to be in Vincent's company this way. She looked-up from her plate and watched him as he lifted a bit of food with his fork. He surely was a very handsome man. Pleasant as well. She watched as he parted his lips to consume the morsel of food, but then noticed he was watching her, too. His gaze was warm and kind; the skin around his eyes crinkled a bit as he smiled at her. She could feel the affection in his eyes. She smiled back at him, and then slowly lowered her eyes to resume eating. She felt more nervous in her stomach now, though. He continued to look at her for a moment, then he, too, resumed eating. As the meal progressed, neither one said very much. But, somehow each knew that the other cared, and as such, was all that was necessary.

Taifa offered Vincent a ride home since she did not know about his car. But, he told her that he had a car and would follow her to her apartment to make sure she got in safely. Taifa liked that very much. Once they entered her building and reached the door of her apartment, Taifa decided not to ask Vincent inside, but she was surprised at the intensity of her feelings for him. "Thank you for a lovely evening, Vincent. It was the nicest I've had in a long time," Taifa said in a grateful tone.

As they looked into each other's eyes again, the sparks between them began to catch fire. Kazi slowly began to move his head towards Taifa. She did not move away. He parted his lips as he pressed them against hers. Her heart began to pound. She parted her lips and at once Kazi's soft tongue slid into her mouth. Kazi wrapped his arms around Taifa's waist and brought her closer to him. Her breasts pressed against his chest and sent currents of electricity throughout his body. Taifa wrapped her arms around Kazi's neck as Kazi pressed her against her apartment door.

As he felt himself becoming more and more aroused, he uttered a low moan, and then drove his tongue deeper into Taifa's mouth. That stimulated Taifa to the point where she, too, could not restrain a moan. Kazi's breathing became increasingly heavy. At that point, Taifa thought it best that they stop their activity. She was not ready for things to go any farther yet. She gently pulled away and he immediately let her go. Kazi only wanted what she wanted. He took hold of her hand and said with an affectionate smile, "I'll see you tomorrow."

Taifa gazed into his eyes and beamed back at him, "Yes, you will…Thank you," she answered softly. Kazi knew that the 'thank you' was for his lack of lovemaking persistence. She opened her door, walked in, and turned on the light with the switch on the wall by the door. She turned back around and they gave each other a final smile. Kazi started back down the hallway and she closed her door. Yet, she began to wonder if she had done the right thing. Vincent seemed to care, but so had others in the beginning. She thought it would be best in the morning to act as though nothing much had happened between them that night.

The next day Taifa walked into the clinic and greeted Carole. Vincent was not in sight. She walked through the drapes that separated the examining room from the waiting room. There was Vincent sitting with his back to her at the supply table, hard at work. He turned his head to look at her immediately upon hearing her footsteps. His beautiful brown eyes and perfect smile went straight to her heart. He watched with bliss as she came closer to him. When she reached him, she placed her left hand on his left shoulder, bent down, and began to run her tongue slowly around the inside of his ear. She ran the fingers of her right hand through the hair on the back of his head. He groaned, reached his arm around her, and began to massage one of her buttocks. Then, Carole began to talk on the telephone, which reminded them that they were not alone. They agreed to continue their lovemaking at Taifa's place later, and then indulged themselves in a quick, but passionate kiss. They gave each other glances throughout the day. Sometimes their eyes met and sometimes one was watching the other without the observee's knowledge. The sexual tension built more and more as the day progressed and by the end of the day each was ready to open the sexual floodgates.

That night Kazi arrived at Taifa's apartment around 9:00 p.m. When he entered, he found the room was lighted with dim red and pink lights; they gave the room a warm, romantic glow. Taifa looked particularly fetching in a low cut, floor length, turquoise dress that buttoned down the front. Kazi put his arms around her and again pulled her close. He slowly moved his hands from her waist, up her torso, and around to her breasts, caressing them as he began to run his tongue all over her neck. In a few moments, Kazi took Taifa by the hand and led her to the couch. She laid down on the couch and he laid on top of her. He continued to lick and suck-on her neck while he began to unbutton her dress. Once her sizeable round breasts were exposed, he began to briskly pass his tongue in circular motions over her chocolate nipples. He watched as her nipples grew bigger with each stimulating lick. Taifa was having her third orgasm already as he continued to unbutton her dress until her pubic hair was revealed. Because he was lying between her legs, her thighs were apart and he was able to see her extremely moist, engorged clitoris ready for his mouth. As he began licking his way down her torso to reach the ultimate goal, there was a knock at the door.

"Tai, Tai," a man's voice called loudly as he continued to bang on the apartment door.

Taifa recognized the voice; it was Gordon. "All right, all right," Taifa answered. Kazi and Taifa both rushed to get themselves together. Kazi wondered who this man might be. He hoped it was not anything he would have to report. The assignment was making him very uneasy now. He knew he was serious about Taifa and he feared what she might do if she found-out who he really was before he could explain. Taifa opened the door and there stood a tall, handsome, brown-skinned man with a close haircut, beard, and mustache. "Hello," she said and hugged him.

Kazi did not like this much, he considered Taifa his lady. The man noticed Kazi right away, so he walked into the apartment and stood waiting to be introduced. "Vincent, this is my brother, Gordon," Taifa said with a smile. Kazi felt relieved. It was her brother not competition. "Gordon, this is Vincent Redfern, he works at the clinic," she added.

"Hey, man," Gordon said. But...times being what they were, Gordon was suspicious of the stranger. He would get him checked-out by BUTTERFLY as soon as possible.

"Hi," Kazi replied pleasantly.

"I need to see you in the other room Taifa," Gordon said anxiously.

Taifa nodded in the affirmative and said, "Excuse us for a moment will you please, Vincent?"

"Sure," Kazi answered curious about the urgent tone of the visit. He knew he should try to hear what was going on, but it was too risky. If he were caught, it would all be over...not only with his cover, but also with his Love, Taifa.

"Who's that guy?" Gordon asked once he and Taifa were alone.

"I told you, he works at the clinic," Taifa defended.

"Yes, Taifa, but what do you know about his background? Where does he come from? What type of work has he been doing?" Gordon questioned intently.

"I don't know any of that yet," she said a little embarrassed by her obvious lack of precaution.

"Taifa, you know the sensitivity of our organization and your position in it," Gordon reminded her. "You must be careful, baby." Taifa shook her head in agreement for she knew he was correct. "What's he doing here?" Gordon inquired most concerned about the stranger's presence.

"We're getting to know each other. That's what you want isn't it?" Taifa teased.

Gordon grinned cynically. "Stay alert, Taifa. Your life and the lives of others are all at stake here."

"Why are you here, Gord?" Taifa inquired as she attempted to limit another one of his incessant lectures.

"I needed to warn you. We've heard that the BAND is not going to wait for the FORCE to investigate the bombings. They are convinced that BUTTERFLY was responsible and there's some major plan of revenge at work as we speak. So watch your back more than usual," Gordon explained.

"Wow. All right, I will. Thanks for coming all this way to tell me," Taifa replied earnestly.

"Hey, I'm your brother, it's my job to do things like that," Gordon said with a smile. "I'm sorry if I sounded harsh in regard to your visitor, but you know now why I was so interested." He leaned over and kissed her on the cheek. "I've got to be going, see you soon." After which, they exited the room and walked down the hallway back to the living room. They found Kazi standing at the window looking out at the night. He turned back around as he heard them re-enter the room. "Good to meet you, Vincent. Perhaps we'll meet again soon," Gordon said as he walked to the front door, opened it, and walked into the hallway.

"Take care, man," Kazi replied just before Gordon closed the door.

Taifa felt a little uneasy after hearing Gordon's words. She really did not know much about Vincent; except that she felt him to be a good person and that she still cared for him a great deal. But, she thought, perhaps she would cut the evening short and cool things down a bit. She made her excuses to Vincent explaining that she no longer felt well and was also rather tired. He provided the necessary sympathies and left without further discussion. After he left, she drank a cold glass of orange juice and went to bed early. Kazi was very puzzled by Taifa's actions. He wondered what had gone on in the room between Taifa and her brother that caused her to send him away so abruptly. He would have to play it by ear and see what developed.

Gordon got back in his car where another member of BUTTERFLY was waiting for him. "Thomas, I want to wait here and follow the man that's at my sister's apartment right now. He's a stranger to her and to me. I don't like that, it will keep me worried," Gordon explained determined to get to the bottom of the 'Vincent' mystery.

"Sure, how long do you think he'll be?" Thomas asked cooperatively.

"There's no way of telling. It might be quite a long time…Whoa, wait a minute. Here he comes right now," Gordon replied with dedication. Kazi got in his car engrossed in thought about Taifa, so engrossed that he took no note of Gordon's car when it pulled-out behind his car and began to follow him. Kazi had decided to return to FORCE headquarters for awhile; he was behind on his reports and needed to turn a couple into the captain. He drove to the front of the headquarters building, and since he did not plan to stay long, grabbed one of the spaces that were usually meant for visitors. It was late, so he doubted that there would be a run on visitors. Gordon double-parked his car about 50 feet from the headquarters front door.

"So, what's this?" Gordon stated puzzled by Kazi's destination.

"Yeah, what's going on here?" Thomas answered softly.

"Follow him inside, Thomas. See what you can find out," Gordon requested quickly.

Thomas rushed out of the car and quickly ascended the staircase that led into the building. He walked through a set of double doors and into a fairly busy main lobby. Thomas spotted the stranger proceed passed the reception desk and on down a long hallway that led to the offices. Thomas was about to ask the reception officer about the stranger, when he heard a woman call-out, "Warrior Kazi." For some reason, Thomas looked to see who answered the call and to his disbelief saw the man he was following answer the woman. That was all Thomas needed. He ran back through the double doors, down the staircase, and straight to the car. He slid into the front seat, closed the car door behind him, and breathlessly reported his information to Gordon. "He's the law! He belongs to the WARRIORS! He must be a spy, doing undercover work to trap BUTTERFLY! A woman called-out to him using the name of WARRIOR Kazi!" Thomas exclaimed irate over his discovery.

Gordon was incensed and disappointed. Not only was the man a police officer, but was a member of the elite faction of the law, putting BUTTERFLY operations in considerable danger. Besides that predicament, Gordon had hoped that the guy would be an all right fellow for his sister's sake. It was obvious to him that Taifa was romantically interested in the man. But, such was not to be the state of affairs, so to speak. He patted Thomas on the shoulder as a sign of brotherly comradery. "Thanks, Thomas," he said gratefully, and then added sadly, "So there we have it."

The following day at the clinic was uneventful. Kazi did not notice any appreciable difference in Taifa's relationship with him. They still had plans to see each other that night, so he hoped she had worked through whatever it was that had bothered her the prior night. He left the clinic a little early so that he could buy some flowers to start the evening off with a romantic touch. However, Taifa was visited by Gordon that evening at her apartment just before Kazi arrived. Kazi cheerfully rang Taifa's doorbell holding a bouquet of two-dozen red roses. But, as soon as Taifa opened the door, he could tell something was wrong. She was not smiling and there was no kiss or hug. He stepped inside the apartment and she began to back away from him.

"What's wrong, Taifa? Did something happen?" Kazi asked troubled over her reaction.

"Why do you want to know? You want to investigate it, Kazi?" Taifa replied angrily. "How could you treat me like this?!"

"Let me explain, please, Taifa. It started out as a FORCE assignment, but from the second I saw you everything changed. I swear it. I love you and I'd never do anything to harm you," Kazi pleaded desperately.

"You're lying. You've been lying from the beginning and you're still doing it. Just get out of here," she requested in abhorrence and broken-hearted pain.

"Taifa, please, I…" Kazi started, but was instantly interrupted.

"*Get out!!*" Taifa shouted as she turned her back on him. Kazi discouragingly put the flowers on the table by the door and slowly walked out of the apartment.

Hearing him leave, Taifa turned back around and noticed the flowers that Kazi had left. She walked over to the table with tears in her eyes and picked-up the flowers. She held them tightly against her breasts. He said he loved me…he probably does, she thought. Her dilemma was that she knew she loved Vincent, but did she love Kazi? The two could not be that much different could they?…She needed to consider what she would do when he contacted her again…and she knew that he would.

The next day Kazi sat in his car near the clinic; he arrived early so that he could be sure to see Taifa. He had to resume his original surveillance. His heart was in turmoil, not only for himself, but also for the pain he had caused her. Momentarily, she drove up in the jeep and walked into the clinic. Kazi noticed that her usual bounce was missing and it saddened him. He decided when he followed her home that night, he would attempt to talk with her again. Within a few minutes, there was a transmission over the FORCE radio about some BUTTERFLY missing persons. He wondered what could be going on, some kind of BAND conspiracy?

It was closing time at the clinic. Kazi started preparing to follow Taifa home and try to speak with her again. He hoped she would not slam the door in his face. He saw Taifa scurry to her jeep. She started it and pulled-out of the space. He rushed to start his car. It would not turn over. He tried again. Still nothing. He looked-up and saw Taifa's jeep turn right at the first street. That was not her regular direction. Where could she be going? he thought. Frantically, he tried the car again, this time it started. He quickly pulled-out of his space and drove to the corner where he saw Taifa turn right. He made the same right turn and searched for Taifa's jeep. The street was deserted. There was no sign of her jeep or any other vehicles. He continued down the street looking in driveways and alleys hoping it was parked somewhere, but there was no sign of Taifa. He was worried; he decided he would go back to her apartment and wait for her to return. When he arrived at her building, he saw a light on in Taifa's apartment. Had Taifa beaten him here? There was nothing in the vicinity even resembling her jeep. He saw a shadow move across the window, and then suddenly, the light went out. In a few moments, a man came out of the front door. Had he been the one in Taifa's apartment? The man got into a car parked directly in front of the building and drove off down the street. The hour became late and still there was no inkling of Taifa. Where in this world could she have gone? If she did not show by morning, he would have to locate Gordon and see what information he could obtain from him.

Taifa tried to stretch, but she was unable to do so. The ropes around her ankles and wrists were tied together, forcing her to sit with her knees up. Her body ached as she sat on the floor of a dingy old room. Where was this? she thought, and who are these people? In a while, Cray and Peter entered the room and sat on chairs directly in front of her. Taifa looked up as Cray began to speak. "Taifa, you've been brought here to BAND headquarters because we want to find those persons responsible for the bombings. Tell me what you know and you'll be let go," Cray said gruffly.

"I don't know anything. It wasn't BUTTERFLY, we wouldn't do anything like that," Taifa remarked sincerely.

"You tell me the truth!!" Cray screamed in a sudden rage as he stood and was about to hit Taifa.

Peter jumped-up and grabbed Cray's arm. "We don't need to do that, Cray. I'm sure she'll cooperate," he said cautiously. Cray backed-off and walked to the other side of the room. "Forgive my older brother, Taifa, he tends to get carried away. He has sort of a horrific temper. Please, do tell us what you know about the bombings. Our only interest is to save lives," Peter said calmly. Despite his white supremist leanings, he still found himself quite attracted to the beautiful Taifa.

"I told you, I don't believe it was BUTTERFLY at all, it's simply not our way. We're humanists not murderers," Taifa replied proudly. She could see that the older man still wanted to beat an acceptable answer out of her, but it appeared that the younger man's presence was enough to delay that occurrence for now.

"Well, I'm afraid we're going to have to let you stay here and think for a while. Perhaps something or someone will come to mind a little later," Peter answered as he and a rancorous Cray left the room.

Kazi knocked on the door of the old warehouse. There still had been no sign of Taifa and he was forced to find the likely whereabouts of Gordon. According to his investigation, this warehouse was one of the main BUTTERFLY locations. A young man answered the door. "What is it, sir?" he asked politely.

"I would like to see Gordon, is he here?" Kazi replied sternly.

"I'm not sure. If he is, who are you?" the young man asked.

"Tell him one of his sister's friends would like to have a word with him," Kazi responded. The man left the door but returned instantly. He opened it wide and beckoned Kazi to come in and follow him. They went down a narrow hallway until it ended with an open door. Kazi stepped through the door and saw to his right a large desk with Gordon seated behind it. "Kazi, or was that Vincent?" Gordon said with a grimace.

"Yeah, well, I knew you were the one who told Taifa my real identity, but I'm here about something more important than that information," Kazi expressed honestly.

"Oh, really. And, what would that be, my man?" Gordon asked with suspicion.

"Do you know where Taifa is? She didn't come home last night," Kazi inquired anxiously.

Gordon could see that Kazi was sincerely upset about Taifa, so he did not play games with him. Although Kazi was a member of the FORCE, the man obviously had deep feelings for his sister. "Yes, I know where she is. According to our sources, the BAND kidnapped her last night on her way to one of our meetings. They're holding her in an old building at the edge of town that they use as their headquarters. We're preparing a rescue attack right now. As soon as it gets dark, we'll be converging on the place," Gordon admitted. "I'm taking a chance telling you all of this. I hope you can be trusted. I believe for the sake of my sister that you will not betray us to the authorities."

"Let me join you, Gordon," Kazi requested urgently.

"You? A member of the FORCE? You'd be committing an illegal act. Breaking the law," Gordon reminded him.

"That's not important now. We must get Taifa back before any harm comes to her," Kazi said with determination and deep emotion.

Gordon smiled. "All right, Kazi, you're in, meet me back here at 6:30 p.m. and we'll get the show on the road," Gordon said with gratitude.

Peter entered the small room that contained Taifa. His huge effort to refrain from seeing her was not working. He found he was drawn to her in a way he never thought possible or wanted to be possible, she being a woman of Color. What was happening to him? What about all the values he had learned that were the opposite of what he felt for her? What was he doing seeking her out? Taifa watched him as he entered the room. He stood at the door for a moment looking at her, then walked over and sat in one of the same chairs, directly in front of Taifa. "Have you thought of anything else yet?" he asked gently.

"No, I don't know anything," Taifa answered wearily.

He began to play with his fingers as he struggled to find something else to say. "I didn't come to talk with you about that anyway," Peter said nervously.

"Why did you come, then?" Taifa asked with great curiosity.

Peter stood-up, looked into her eyes, and gave her a brief smile. "I don't know," he said as he turned and walked out of the room. He returned to his quarters and laid down across the bed. He felt so stupid. He acted like a scared teen-ager when he tried to talk with her. He had wanted the encounter to be so different from what it actually turned-out to be. After a few moments, he supposed he must be a glutton for punishment, because he was determined to immediately go back and try again.

Taifa wondered if her brother or any of the members of BUTTERFLY had knowledge of what had happened to her and knew where she was at this time. She soon started to squirm from pain; the ropes were beginning to cut into her skin and she could see small specks of blood popping-up on her wrist. Her throat was dry and they had not given her any food yet. As she attempted to stretch, Peter came back through the door. She looked-up at him leery about what his real intentions might be, since they apparently warranted a second visit. Peter strolled back to the chair upon which he had previously been sitting. He sat down and looked Taifa in the eyes. "I regret that this was done to you. It was my brother's doing, he's in charge and the others follow him blindly. I'm new to the organization and am not totally in agreement with all of its actions or with all of its philosophy. I have no power here, except that from time to time I can influence my brother's actions, as you saw earlier. However, I'm not always able to calm him down as I did. He truly hates anyone who is not white and Christian," Peter thoroughly explained.

"Why did you join it in the first place if you're not actually committed to their cause?" Taifa inquired thankful for some show of kindness.

"Of course, you know the answer. I'm not sure why I joined. I grew-up in a white supremist household and have strong feelings against People of Color, yet, somehow, I have developed an attraction and an attachment to you," Peter told her blatantly.

"Really? In a strange way, that's nice to know. It's somewhat of a compliment, I guess…Yes, I truly feel a warmth within you of which your brother shows no indication. You seem to be a caring and kind man at heart. It's too bad you've chosen to join with the BAND. I think that without much 'awakening', you'd fit into BUTTERFLY quite nicely," Taifa remarked graciously.

They smiled at each other for a moment, and then Peter stood and started towards the door. "I'll see about getting you something to eat and drink," he said as he left the room, now satisfied with and optimistic about their time alone.

It was 6:15 p.m. when Kazi arrived at the warehouse. He was let in immediately and he went straight to Gordon's office. Gordon was there with several other top BUTTERFLY officials, everyone outfitted for battle. Gordon introduced Kazi to the others. Kazi's attire revealed to Gordon just how much Kazi cared for Taifa. It was the custom of the day to wear your family 'coat-of-arms' whenever you fought a battle in defense of family honor or a family member. This was not taken lightly by anyone and was always of a most serious nature. Tonight, Kazi was wearing his family crest across his armor, which announced to the world that he loved Taifa and that he considered her a part of his family. Only Kazi and Gordon wore their family crests that night.

The battle had begun an hour ago, and it now appeared that BUTTERFLY would be victorious. The BAND was caught completely off-guard and never regained its foothold. Cray and the other leaders all vowed not to be taken alive. Cray also decided not to let Taifa be taken alive. He sent Peter to take care of her. Peter entered Taifa's room. He knew when Cray sent him that he was not going to kill her. He walked straight over and began to untie her. "Come on, I've got to get you out of here," he said nervously.

"What's happening?" Taifa asked perplexed by his behavior.

"The butterfly has left its cocoon," Peter replied. Taifa did not understand what he meant, but she followed his instructions to her. They walked to the door and Peter checked the hall, it was clear. He took Taifa's hand and they quickly traveled down the hallway and around a corner, then straight out of a side door. Peter led her around the side of the building and then pointed-out an alcove where she could hide until she was able to rejoin her comrades. Taifa leaned-up and kissed Peter on the cheek. "Thank you," she said softly. "And, should you survive this battle, consider a new home within BUTTERFLY."

"You'd better hurry," Peter answered affectionately. He watched until she disappeared into the dark alcove. Suddenly, he felt a sharp pain in his back. He turned around and almost inaudibly said, "You?" then collapsed on the ground, a knife in his back.

Cray walked-up and stood over him. "So it shall be for all traitors, brother," he said coldly.

A few hours later, the battle ended. As the fates would have it, BUTTERFLY was indeed victorious. Instantly, Kazi began to look for Taifa, and then saw her coming from the side of the building. He started walking towards her, at which time she noticed him as well. He had been here fighting with BUTTERFLY to save her. He wore his family crest in her honor. His feelings for her must certainly be greater than his loyalty to the FORCE, she thought. And, surely the Vincent that she loved was only Kazi by another name. When they finally reached each other, no words were spoken. Kazi took Taifa in his arms and kissed her with all the passion of a lost love, found. As they walked back to the car, Kazi's arm around Taifa's shoulders, Gordon watched with a smile, pleased at the sight he was viewing.

Kazi sat on Taifa's bed drying his hair from the shower he had just taken. He wore only a white terrycloth towel that was tied around his waist and covered his groin. Momentarily, Taifa entered the bedroom from the bathroom having just finished her shower. She wore an extremely low-cut, extremely sheer, white nightgown. She walked over to Kazi and kneeled down on the floor between his bare legs. Then, she leaned over, placed a hand on each of his thighs and began to lick and suck his nipples. Kazi moved his hands up and down her body, and massaged every inch within his reach.

As Taifa started to travel down Kazi's body with her tongue, she untied the towel covering him. She opened it, exposing his large, tan penis surrounded by lots of soft, dark, curly hair. She began to lick the two large sacks that lay invitingly beneath the dark hair. They were soft and warm, and Kazi began to moan when she took one into her mouth and gently began to chew it. She chewed one and then the other, before moving up and proceeding to lick the now hard shaft of his penis. She reached the helmet shaped head, which overflowed with a clear warm liquid, the precursor of what was to come. As it dripped down the shaft, she caught it with her tongue. Then, she engulfed the entire head with her mouth, sucking it forcefully and massaging it wildly with her tongue. His clear warm fluid filled her mouth, covered her lips, and dribbled down her chin. Shortly afterwards, Kazi placed one hand on Taifa's shoulder and held the back of her head with the other hand, as he pushed his large, hard penis farther down her throat. He closed his eyes and let out several loud gaspy moans as his penis exploded…releasing him into a long desired rapture and releasing Taifa into the pleasure of a job well done.

That amatory episode was not enough to satisfy either one of them, though. Kazi pulled Taifa off of her knees and onto the bed, where he quickly removed her sheer, white nightgown and became thoroughly aroused by her totally naked chocolate-colored body. Her soft, round breasts were truly the most alluring he had ever seen and he was sexually provoked by the mere sight of them, even more than when he saw them for the first time. Her large dark brown nipples called to his mouth. He answered the call immediately. He took hold of her torso and wrapped his lips around one of her nipples. He ran his tongue back and forth across it numerous times and began to suck it with great vigor. After a few minutes, he engulfed the nipple entirely and filled his mouth with as much breast as he could without choking. He sucked and licked her breasts one after another for close to 20 minutes, then proceeded to concern himself with the lower half of her firm, shapely body. Taifa was highly charged herself by now and her moans of pleasure motivated more and more intense activity from Kazi.

The other night, Kazi had been interrupted at the very moment they had begun to make love. And, had been deprived the pleasure of her large, soft clitoris in his mouth. He had also been deprived of tasting her warm, clear wetness covering his tongue and trickling down his throat. The pleasure would not be denied this time, he thought, as he moved his body downward, placed his head firmly between her thighs, and began to glide his tongue up and down her delectable cocoa-colored clitoris. He licked her with such craze that Taifa could not restrain from crying-out loudly as she reached orgasm after orgasm. Kazi's penis quickly hardened to a wood-like firmness inspired both by her reactions and his independent sexual upsurge. He eventually laid on top of her and inserted his penis deep into her vagina as she wrapped her arms around his back. He grasped each of her shoulders with each hand and rested his head against the side of her head while he buried his face in her hair and the pillow. Kazi began to moan incessantly as he felt the pressure of Taifa's tight vaginal muscles surround his throbbing penis. And, when he began to thrust backwards and forwards inside of her, he almost immediately hit her 'G-spot' so to speak, intensifying Taifa's arousal into the production of indeterminate numbers of extraordinary orgasms.

When she awakened in the morning, after a night of continuous ravenous lovemaking, Taifa leaned over and gave Kazi a soft, loving kiss on the lips. He opened his eyes, looked at her, and smiled. His mind still swam in the ecstasy of their sexual eruption. His penis was beginning to harden at the sight of her and he wanted her again right away. But, before he could make his move, she rolled over in bed, and as was her norm, turned on the radio. The news was full of reports about the battle that had taken place between the BAND and BUTTERFLY last night. Kazi sat-up also as the news about the battle overshadowed his sexual desires for a few minutes.

Apparently, though badly damaged and having lost a considerable number of members in the battle, the BAND was still operational and had declared their new headquarters was located in another deserted building of which they had now taken possession. "I'd better get down to the station," Kazi said reluctantly as he rolled-out of bed and walked towards the bathroom. Taifa smiled from bliss as she watched his naked body move across the room. Each muscle of his body was highly pronounced, like that of a weight lifter, but he was tall and slender rather than thick and bulky. She knew it would be difficult to let him leave. But, life must go on and she must get used to not having him around all day the way it was at the clinic.

It had only been several months since the battle with BAND and since the re-uniting of Kazi and Taifa. But, already, Taifa was beginning to feel that the 'honeymoon' was ending. Between Kazi's work with the FORCE and his aggressive new commitment to BUTTERFLY, he seldom had time to spend in her company. Though, he did call her a few times each day. However, she, too, had long hours as a physician and was committed to BUTTERFLY, but she always made time for him. There was a major BUTTERFLY meeting that night consisting of all the top-level members. Kazi had worked his way up to top level quickly and she knew she would see him there. Hopefully, after the meeting they could get together and she could discuss their relationship with him.

The conference room was almost filled to capacity when Taifa entered. One of the men stood and gave Taifa his seat. She thanked him gracefully and sat down. A few moments later, Kazi entered the room. He spotted Taifa immediately and smiled at her lovingly. She, of course, saw him as he walked in and immediately smiled back at him. There were no more seats, so Kazi stood somewhat in the rear of the room, but in an area where he could still make eye contact with Taifa, if he so desired. The meeting began and after about half an hour, the president of BUTTERFLY began to make an introduction. The person was said by the president to be one of BUTTERFLY's best and most daring freedom fighters. A new member. Someone who had recently made some amazing infiltrations into the BAND organization and brought back huge amounts of highly confidential information at extreme risk to his own life each time. Everyone learned that the introduction was being made because the man was to be made one of the top-level officials that night. The president beckoned to the doorkeeper to bid the man enter.

As the man walked into the room, Taifa fell back against her chair in shock. It was Peter! The president continued with praises of Peter's accomplishments, Peter caught sight of Taifa sitting along the side of the huge cherry wood conference table. She was smiling at him warmly. He returned an excited and equally warm smile. Their exchange of pleasure was noticed by Kazi and the emotion known as jealousy, which he had never before experienced, made an immediate stop at his front door. When the meeting ended, each member made sure to stop and shake Peter's hand upon exit. Taifa decided to wait and make herself last. Once she reached Peter, they looked at each other for a second, and then embraced tightly.

"I'm so happy to see you," Peter whispered emotionally.

"And, I'm happy to see you, Peter," Taifa said softly. By the time they ended their embrace, Kazi was standing at their side. Taifa excitedly explained her actions to him, "Honey, this is the man I told you was with BAND and saved my life!"

"So, this is the valiant man," Kazi replied as he reached to shake Peter's hand. Peter grinned and firmly took a hold of Kazi's hand.

"Peter, this is my friend, WARRIOR Kazi," Taifa said cheerfully.

Kazi thought her choice of the word 'friend' was a bit misplaced. Surely, their relationship was more to her than just friendship. "Well, I have some legal work to do. It was an honor to meet you, Peter. I'm sure we'll meet again soon," Kazi remarked as began to make his exit.

"I hope so," Peter replied, but his mind was only on Taifa.

That night on his way to a WARRIOR meeting, Kazi stopped by Taifa's apartment. When he walked inside, he was disturbed to see Peter, seated at the dining table eating dinner. "Am I intruding upon something?" he whispered to Taifa as he passed-by her at the apartment door and entered the living room.

"Of course not, what are you thinking?" she answered surprised over his manner.

"I thought we'd have a chance to talk for a few minutes, Taifa. I thought that was something you wanted," Kazi replied annoyedly.

"Yes, it is something I want. But, you should have told me this afternoon that you were coming tonight," Taifa explained somewhat apologetically.

"I didn't think I needed an appointment," Kazi proclaimed even more bothered.

"You don't. You know that, but once in a while I have something to do besides wait here for you to drop-in for a few minutes," Taifa replied a little irritated now herself.

Kazi heard the irritability in her voice. That was the last thing he had intended to provoke. "You're right. I'm sorry. I'll come back tomorrow night. We'll get things straightened-out...Have a good night," Kazi said as he reluctantly started towards the door.

"All right, I'll see you tomorrow night," Taifa answered lovingly. Kazi quickly exited the door and left the building. He had decided he would immediately have to cement his relationship with Taifa before it became too late.

The night went quickly in Peter's company. Taifa liked him very much. But, soon it was time for him to leave. It had grown quite late and they both had very early meetings the next day. As they stood at the opened door to her apartment, they stared at each other for a few moments. Then, Peter slowly leaned down and gently kissed her lips for several seconds. Upon completion of the kiss, he sweetly whispered, "Goodnight, My Angel."

Taifa's heart was pounding as she affectionately responded, "Goodnight, My Hero."

After his departure, Taifa closed the door and leaned her back against it. She exhaled a long sigh and softly said, "Now what?"

The next night, Kazi showed-up at Taifa's door with a huge bouquet of wild flowers, a large basket of fruit, and an engagement ring. Taifa quickly accepted his proposal. She truly loved him with all her heart, despite her fleeting weakness because of Peter. As the sun arose announcing the new day, they were still engrossed in the consummation of their engagement. A consummation that had begun several hours ago. And, within a period of two months, Kazi and Taifa were blissfully married.

The battle for the planet continued as the BAND forces scrambled to re-organize. Peter's continued bravery and cunning against the BAND soon earned him the position 'President of BUTTERFLY'. Not long afterwards, he found another love amongst the BUTTERFLY women. Coincidently, she was of African ancestry as well. Both couples later produced several members of the next generation. A generation for whom they both hoped love and human rights would be the rule of the day.

VAMPIRE

(A Love Story)

Chapter One

It was a cool night and the half-moon shone brightly down from its cushion of black velvet, blanketing the densely wooded forest, casting eerie shadows across the moist, soft ground. The handsome young aristocrat strolled with the lovely Lucinda, one of the town prostitutes, through the silent misty forest. He had given her 10 shillings for her services and they were enroute to her small cottage located just beyond the massive group of trees. "How have you been, Lucinda? I have not seen you for some time," the young aristocrat spoke.

"I've been good, My Lord. Where were ya? You've not been in town for many weeks I've heard," Lucinda inquired with great interest.

"I was in France on shipping business," the young aristocrat answered.

"Ah, making more money to give to me. That's the way, all right, I say," Lucinda joked.

"Yes. Exactly. I have just arrived home today and you see I have flown to your arms to give you the money I earned," the young aristocrat replied with a chuckle. Lucinda began to joyfully laugh with him. Then, in an instant, the laughter stopped and only the passionate moans of distorted pleasure filled the air. Lucinda lay on the ground, her life's blood being drained from her body by a vicious male vampire. The young aristocrat also lay on the ground, a female vampire enjoying a meal of him. But, the female had seen the young man before and had no plans to drain him until dead. Instead, she wished to make him one of her kind, so that he could join her in her unholy existence.

The young aristocrat awakened into dark surroundings. When he attempted to move his arms, he found they were blocked on both sides. And, when he tried to reach up, he found he was blocked once again. However, he felt the top move when he pushed it, so he continued to push until the top was completely up and out of the way. He sat up and was stunned to find that he was inside the family mausoleum. He looked down and was even more stunned to find he was sitting in a shiny black coffin. Then, from behind him came a voice. "Good evening, My Lord," the strange voice said.

The young aristocrat turned around and saw a most unusual looking man with a rather odd expression upon his face, an expression appearing to be some combination of evil and glee. His skin was somewhat gray in color and his eyes were like none the young aristocrat had seen before, some shade of purple, he thought. His hair was very dark, almost black, and cut very short, not at all like the style of the time, that being the year of Our Lord, 1699. He was tall, but exceedingly thin and his all black clothing was ill-fitting and seemed to hang off his body.

"Who are you? What are you doing here?" the young aristocrat inquired, puzzled about his circumstance and still quite dazed.

"The Master has sent me. I am ordered to take you to him. Your transformation is not yet complete," the strange man replied in a polite manner.

"The Master? What Master, my father?" the young aristocrat demanded, frustrated and impatient.

"No, My Lord. The Almighty Master," the man answered with a gentle smile.

"Of whom do you speak? In God's name, who are you?" the young aristocrat commanded with even more anger as he proceeded to climb out of the coffin.

"In God's name?...I am called Jason, My Lord. Please...come with me," the man replied calmly, and then turned to exit the mausoleum. The young aristocrat suddenly felt an unnatural attachment to the stranger, one that he did not understand. It seemed to compel him to follow as the man had requested, so he did.

The year was now 2032 A.D., Friday, 8:05 p.m., Nia was waiting for a call from her friend Imani. They had planned to go to a new club that had opened. All ladies were to be admitted free that night, so she and Imani thought why not check it out. In a moment, the telephone rang. Nia picked it up and immediately Imani's lovely chestnut-colored, smiling face was projected across the screen connected to the phone. Imani always smiled. She had one of those effervescent, optimistic personalities. The kind that sometimes gets on your nerves. "Hey, Imani," Nia said smiling back at her friend.

"What's up, honey. What time do you want me to pick you up?" Imani queried.

"How about 9:30?" Nia replied.

"That's fine with me. See you shortly," Imani answered enthusiastically.

"O.K.," Nia said, then Imani's face disappeared as they both hung-up the phone.

Nia rushed to take a bath. As the water ran into the sleek violet-toned tub, she poured in her favorite bubble bath, raspberry orchids. She let the water run until the bubbles were close to the top of the tub, then turned the water off quickly. She lowered her chocolate-colored body into the warm sudsy water. It felt so good. She loved feeling clean and fragrant, and always looked forward to taking a bath. Perhaps, tonight would be different from so many other nights out, she thought. But, then, she hoped that would be the case on each of her ventures out. Nothing ever really turned out differently. The same creepy guys with the same stupid rap. She often wondered why her education as a psychiatrist never seemed to help her in relationships with men. She supposed that her constant analyzing was more of a detriment than benefit. Men usually found it to be threatening and/or insulting.

She reluctantly ended her bath, drying herself with a huge, fluffy, violet-colored towel that matched the color of her bathtub. She walked out of the bathroom into the bedroom. The plush rose-colored carpet felt soft and warm as it squished between her toes. She sat down on the corner of the bed and began to massage the complimentary raspberry orchids body lotion all over her long, shapely, brown body. The feel of the lotion stimulated her sexually as she spread the warm, fragrant lotion gently over her large breasts, muscular hips, and firm thighs. She chose to wear her skimpiest black lace panties and no bra. The dress she had decided to wear was a long-sleeved, steel blue, silk one that would cling to every part of her shapely body, thus the reason for the skimpy undergarments. The dress contained sewn-in cups, so the bra was not necessary. She slipped the dress on, yes, it fit perfectly. After pulling the close-fitting sleeves down to her wrists, she removed the clip that had been holding her hair up and out of the way. Her hair fell gracefully passed her shoulders and midway down her back. Its natural texture was that of a wavy bushiness and was a texture particularly attractive on her. Just as she finished combing her hair, the doorbell rang. She knew it was Imani. Besides being eternally bubbly, she was also annoyingly prompt. Nia slid on her 4-inch heel blue sandals, grabbed her purse, and ran to open the door. "Let's go, honey. Our fans await us!" Imani said with a giggle as the door opened.

"I'm ready, I'm ready," Nia replied as she stepped into the hallway and locked the apartment door.

The night was warm and the air was sweet with the scent of spring flowers. Seth sat on the ornately carved copper bench on the back terrace of the mansion known as Westville Manor. He was awaiting the arrival of his companions from their respective bedrooms. They all had plans to hit the nightclubs that night, in particular the new one having ladies night that evening. One might say they were all on a serious hunt. Seth was a tall, magnificently built man with light blond hair that hung loosely down his back about 5 inches. Had he been of Greek heritage, he would surely have been referred to as having the handsomeness of a Greek god. However, he was of Scandinavian ancestry and handsome indeed…Oh, yes…he was also a vampire.

The companions wandered out onto the terrace one by one, four males and one female. All were quite attractive people, none could hold a candle to Seth's looks though, and, despite being vampires, the males were all rather envious of Seth's physical beauty.

"I swear, all of you are taking longer and longer to prepare," Seth complained. "One might think you were reticent about going."

"Reticent? What the hell does that word mean? Why don't you just chill, Seth. Everyone is anxious to go. We're all hungry. It's you who is over anxious tonight. What's up with that?" bellowed Terry the more recent, young, and disrespectful convert.

Seth looked at Terry with pissation then turned and started down the path to the car. "Let's go," Seth said with annoyance.

Matilda, the only female of the group, had much feeling for the handsome Seth and always jumped to his defense. "Cut it out, Terry! You always have so much mouth. There's lots of vicious, vengeful vampires out here. You just be glad that Seth isn't one of them," she warned as they all reached the white Rolls Royce.

Seth was not the leader or anything; he was not even the one in the group who had been a vampire the longest. But, aside from being the most handsome of the group, he was also the most sensitive. He felt for others, but was also easily hurt himself, traits left over from his human personality. Some of his sympathies towards others was possibly an outgrowth of his Christian upbringing, 333 years ago. Perhaps he was a bit anxious that night, Seth thought, but not for the reasons they might think. The sooner they could get started, the sooner it could be over for the night. He had accepted his nonhuman status centuries ago and had no humanitarian problems with having to feed on humans anymore. (Afterall, he did not make himself into a vampire; it was forced upon him.) And, he usually did feel sympathy at the demise of his many, mostly innocent, victims. But, still, had not in the past nor even now been ready to destroy himself to save any victims from his forthcoming horror. However, he had begun to feel himself a victim of his own reign of horror. He had grown weary of his present existence and wished for a permanent end to it. He had hoped there was some greater rhyme or reason to living forever, but, in all of his years as a vampire, he had found none.

The white Rolls Royce drove slowly passed the new nightclub. The sign over the door read, 'The Risk', quite an appropriate name, Seth thought, at least so far as that night's work was concerned. There was a large crowd outside the club, that was excellent because it would afford a numerous, but choice menu. The Rolls continued on down the street for two blocks and then turned into a darkened alley. They all poured out of the car, pulling and tugging to straighten their clothes. "Is everybody ready?" asked Jason, the most ancient of the vampires.

"Yeah, sure. Let's move it," answered the irritating Terry.

In an instant, the air was flooded with huge gusts of wind as the vampires took flight. They swooped across the same two blocks in barely a second, landing in an alley at the back door of the club. Jason ripped-off a set of the iron bars attached to the back windows. The window was already unlocked. Jason opened it and the vampires slipped quietly through, it entered into the men's room. Remarkably, no one was using the facilities, so the group entered the building and then the main room unnoticed. They took positions at various sites around the room, each looking for that 'certain someone'. Terry was usually the first to capture his prey. He was never very particular. He was pretty much a vampire slut. No class, no breeding. True to his form he had disappeared already. Matilda was often second, basically because she always had human men 'hitting' on her, so it was just a matter of whether or not she was ready and of how picky she wanted to be in her choice. Sometimes she was picky to a fault, but not that night, she must have been hungry for she, too, had disappeared. Jason followed shortly, as did the other two males, Chi and Arturo.

Only Seth remained, and he was the one who wanted things to end quickly. No one in the club had appealed to him, yet. He was usually as particular about his choice as was Matilda, often even more so. It would be nothing for him to search two or three clubs or roam the streets a couple of hours looking for his satisfaction. Seth looked over at the entrance door, his eyes scanned each new entrant in hopes of spotting that night's delight. Within a few moments, his eyes caught a vision that affected him in a most unusual manner. It was not the usual euphoric feeling he would get once he encountered his desired prey, the anticipation of an excellent meal. But rather, a feeling he had not felt in over 300 years. It was sexual in nature, there was a soft throbbing in his groin that became more intense the closer the vision came to him. He had always thought he was as humanly dead there as everywhere else on his body. Perhaps, the arousal had just never been stimulated. Perhaps, his changing attitude about his situation and the need for a change awakened it. Whatever the cause, he relished the feeling and hastened to interact with the vision of his desire, who was dressed in a long-sleeved, steel blue, silk dress.

Nia and Imani slowly walked through the crowd of people crammed into the club. There was surely a mountain of women, but also a fair number of men. They both walked over to the bar and ordered drinks, white wine for Nia and a whiskey sour for Imani. "Well, let's see what gifts tonight holds for us. We're both due for something good to happen," Imani said happily.

"I agree that we're both due, Imani, but our luck has not been too beneficial lately," Nia replied with a smile.

"It will change soon. You wait and see, Nia," Imani added. At that moment, a good-looking young man in a gorgeous dark gray suit and with dark-brown hair combed into a neatly coiffed ponytail approached Imani. They began a conversation, so Nia turned to face the other way. She wondered what she would do now that Imani was occupied. But, before she could give the matter much thought, she felt a tap on her right shoulder. She turned to see one of the most beautiful men she had ever seen. Her heart began to beat quickly as he started to speak to her.

"Good evening, Madame. My name is Seth Bjorn. I saw you come in and I haven't been able to take my eyes off of you ever since," he said as he smiled at her sensuously.

Nia felt overwhelmed. Not only was he bodily beautiful, but a gentleman. Never had anyone referred to her as Madame, it made her feel special and elegant. She liked it very much. "Good evening, sir. My name's Nia. I'm pleased to meet you," she replied. Somehow she felt she needed to continue the formal tone of the introduction. She shocked herself when she added 'sir' to her greeting. He was impeccably dressed in a perfect-fitting black suit, white shirt, black and gold necktie, and matching handkerchief. His stylish black shoes were shined to the point of mirror-like reflection.

As Nia spoke, Seth's mind was propelled into another reality. Everything but Nia seemed to be moving in slow motion. Nothing seemed real to him but her. His sexual arousal continued to increase despite his attempts to control it. It had been so long since he had been aroused that he had forgotten how much control was actually needed in order to maintain one's dignity. Unfortunately, because of his 'rising' situation, he would have to make the conversation short this time. He thought that next time he would be more prepared and have the ability to keep things more under control…Next time! What was he thinking! His thoughts began to race for he did not know quite what to do. He certainly had no intention of ever feeding on her (nor to let anyone else do so). He could make her one of them. But, he would not do that without her consent and she definitely would not give that now. One thing he did know was that he wanted her. He would not go on without her. At the moment, he would just take her telephone number. Then, he would go feed, meet the others at the car, go home. Then, he would decide upon the best course to follow in his quest for Nia.

"Nia…that's such a lovely name," Seth said gently and adoringly. "I wish I could stay longer, but I really must go. If you would do me the honor of giving me your phone number, I promise to call you tomorrow evening at 7:00 o'clock. Perhaps, we can spend tomorrow evening together," he said hopefully.

Nia was thrilled and saddened at the same time. She was saddened because he had to leave, but thrilled because he wanted to see her again. "Yes, Seth, I would like that very much. I'll write my number down for you right now," Nia replied as she wrote her phone number on a napkin. "Here it is," she added, quickly handing him the paper napkin.

"Thank you, Nia. I will speak with you tomorrow then. Good night," Seth said softly with a smile as he turned and disappeared into the crowd.

"Good night, Seth," Nia called after him. Nia turned back around with the hope of asking Imani what she thought about Seth and to inform Imani of what was said between her and Seth. But, Imani was gone. Nia looked for her around the club for an hour and never found her, so Nia took a cab home. She figured Imani must have been very attracted to that man who had approached her, and, uncharacteristically, went off with him. Nia decided she would give Imani a call the next day and they could fill each other in on the night's events. However, Nia was unaware that the good-looking young man, in the gorgeous dark gray suit, with the neatly coiffed ponytail, who had approached Imani earlier in the evening, was one of Seth's murderous vampire companions, Chi.

Seth stood in the dark doorway of an abandoned building not far from the group's parked car. He caught the sound of singular footsteps coming in his direction. As the steps became louder, he moved as close to the sidewalk as he could without being detected. As the figure moved leisurely passed the doorway opening, in one swell swoop, Seth pulled the figure through the doorway, into the dark hallway, and onto the dust-filled floor. A struggle commenced, but the victim's frantic attempts to escape were futile. No human had the physical strength to defend against a vampire. Seth's teeth ripped into the neck of his prey with a force not known to himself before that night. The blood was warm and sweet. He drank with a passion that enveloped his whole being. His thoughts of Nia helped to produce a euphoria that was more intense than any he had ever known. That night, at least, this must be the release of his desire to have Nia. Yet, Seth was determined that soon he would have her, every inch of her. Then, what euphoria he would experience when finally he was allowed to thrust his penis deep inside of her. Immediately, his mind became enraptured and could hardly contain his thoughts. Even the imagining of a sexual encounter with Nia excited him thoroughly. He finished his feed and returned to the car. The others were all sitting around lazy and sleepy; the way humans get after a big Thanksgiving dinner. They all piled back into the Rolls. Seth volunteered to drive; he was too stimulated to sleep. Upon arriving home, they all immediately went their separate ways. Seth was happy about everyone's decision to scatter; he wanted to be alone.

The morning was bright and Nia had not slept much all night. Her thoughts of Seth did not allow her to sleep much. She was enthralled by him, 'had her nose wide-open', thought he was 'da bomb', or however anyone wanted to describe it. To think he asked for the 'honor' of having her phone number. As the old cliché went, where had he been all of her life. She felt like a kid who had just begun to open her Christmas presents, joyous! She must call Imani right away! Imani's phone rang and rang, but she did not pick-up. Strange, Nia thought, had she not come home? Perhaps she went out early. She would try again later.

The day passed slowly for Nia as she waited for Seth to call. She knew she would be devastated should he not call. In the attempt to occupy her time, she tried on outfit after outfit, hoping to pick the perfect one for her date with Seth. It was 7:00 p.m., and right on the dot, the telephone rang. Nia flew to answer it, almost tripping over the coffee table. "Hello," she said calmly, though her heart was beating wildly.

"Good evening, Nia, it's Seth," he said softly as his handsome face appeared on the telephone screen. Her heart sang with joy! Seth, you called, you called, she thought. They made arrangements for Seth to come to her apartment at 9:00 p.m. and then hung-up. She decided to give Imani another call and was surprised that her friend had not called all day. Once again, Imani's phone rang and rang, but still no answer. Nia decided she would try for a few more days. Then, if she were still unable to contact Imani, would go to the police.

Nia nervously waited for Seth to arrive. She had been ready for fifteen minutes and it was still not 9:00. She sat down, she stood up. She started to go look out of the window, but thought she'd better not. If he saw her, he might think her too anxious. Seth, Seth, hurry, she thought. Hurry.

The group watched as Seth took the keys for the Lexus off of the key rack. "So what's the problem, Seth, you tired of us already? It's only been a few centuries," Arturo said jokingly.

Seth looked at Arturo with a slight smile. They had always gotten along well. "It couldn't possibly be that, now could it?" Seth responded in a friendly way.

"I find it all very mysterious. Why won't you tell us where you're going?" demanded Terry rudely.

"Because it's not your concern," answered Seth with a scowled look upon his face as he walked out of the side door. Matilda, Seth's major supporter, watched out of the window as Seth drove off down the driveway. She was in love with him and did not like what seemed to be happening. She felt some kind of major change was about to occur and was terribly frightened by the possibilities.

Nia looked at the clock. It was 9:00 p.m. Simultaneously, her doorbell rang. She opened the door and for a few seconds her heart fluttered at the sight of Seth. Her eyes met his, then, instantly, they each felt a surge of sexual electricity. They stared at each other for a moment without speaking. The heart of each began to beat at an unnaturally rapid rate. Though in Seth's case, it was no longer a heart kept beating by human energy, but rather by numinous energy. Seth's unexpected erotic passion caused his bodily energy to circulate his blood throughout his body at an exorbitant speed. He felt somewhat light-headed and his heart pounded against his chest with an unprecedented force.

Nia broke the silence. "Good evening, Seth. Please come in and make yourself comfortable. I'll just get my purse and we can leave," Nia expressed with an adoring smile.

Seth walked into the apartment and Nia closed the door behind him. "Fine, Nia. Take your time, though. I'm content just being near you," Seth replied without hesitation.

Could he actually care for her as much as she already cared for him? Nia thought. She prayed it was so. She picked-up her purse and walked back into the living room with Seth. He stood as she entered the room. She walked towards the front door and he followed her. They spoke casually as they walked out to the car, each inquiring about the other's day. Nia mentioned how she had not been able to reach her friend Imani since they were at 'The Risk' the previous night. Seth advised her not to worry, he was sure Imani would turn-up soon. But, in actuality, he suspected that one of his companions had crossed Imani's path last night and that it was not likely she would ever be seen again.

Seth took Nia to the most expensive restaurant in the city. She was very impressed. She would not have cared even if he had taken her to Blue Castle hamburgers, as long as she was with him; well, maybe she would have cared a little. The waiter showed them to an excellent table, gave them menus, and advised that he would return shortly for their orders. Seth thought it best that he provide a reason now as to why he would not be ordering any food. "Nia," he said, "Please order whatever you would like and as much as you would like. I myself will not be ordering a meal, so do not be surprised."

Nia was most definitely taken by surprise. "Why not? I don't understand," she said in amazement.

"I'm not much of an eater. I usually eat once in the morning and then not again until the next morning," he lied.

"Oh, I see. Quite unusual," Nia said. She wanted to say something like, 'so I'll always be eating by myself when I'm with you, unless it's breakfast, huh?'. But...how could she say such a thing to him? He was who he was, she would not try to change him or make him feel guilty. Afterall, he may decide to leave her instead of changing and she knew she could not handle that already.

Seth added cordially, "So, please, enjoy yourself. I will just sip some red wine."

Nia did as he asked. She enjoyed herself. She ordered everything on the menu she ever wanted to taste and Seth enjoyed watching her do so. He received great pleasure from observing and providing her happiness. He maintained a constant smile throughout the evening. But, soon it was time to leave. Seth still had to go feed and return home before daybreak. As they stood in the hallway in front of Nia's apartment door, she hoped with all her heart that he would kiss her goodnight, but it did not happen. He gave her a tremendously hard hug, said he had a wonderful time, and that he would come for her again the next evening at 8:00 o'clock, with her consent. Of course, Nia agreed to the meeting. Perhaps tomorrow, Nia thought, she would get the chance to feel his lips pressed against hers and feel his tongue arousingly filling her mouth. Inducing the rapture she so longed to experience with only him.

Seth opened the door to his bedroom and turned on the light. He was surprised to see Jason sitting on the large, fringed, antique chair in the corner of his room. "What's happening, Seth? Talk with me," Jason said pleadingly.

"Nothing's happening, Jason. What are you talking about?" Seth replied defensively.

"Seth, I've been around you for over 300 years. I think I know you just a little bit," Jason lamented.

Seth knew Jason was right. He and Jason were good friends. He decided he would tell him the truth. "All right, Jason. I'll tell you. Please don't say anything to the others yet. I will tell them in time," Seth responded.

"Fine, man, fine. Now what is it?" Jason asked anxiously.

"I'm in love…with a human," Seth said gingerly.

"What! Are you out of your vampire mind!" Jason exclaimed in a loud whisper.

"Maybe I am. I don't know, Jason. I saw her and I haven't been the same since," Seth explained.

"Well, tell me this, what do you expect to happen now? Do you expect to marry her and then look forward to the patter of little half-vampire feet around the house? Think, Seth! You're dead! You can't get married. You can't have children. You can't have a human life again!" Jason exclaimed again.

Seth looked at Jason in total frustration and pain. He had asked himself the same questions and still had no answers. "I don't know what to do. I don't want to go on without her. In fact, I can't go on without her. There must be a way to handle this so that we can be together. I just need some time. I just need some time," Seth answered in misery.

Jason shook his head in the negative as he got up and started out of the room. He hoped for his friend's sake that a way could be found for Seth to have what he needed. He feared, however, that the other companions would never accept this interracial love between the human race and the non-human race.

Nia had been preparing for her date with Seth when he called and inquired if she would like to drive to the shore that evening and have a picnic on the beach. It was a very warm spring night, so Nia said she would love it. Seth was very pleased. He suspected her tastes were similar to his own. He informed her that he would supply everything and all she need do was to supply her beautiful self. Many of the little things he would say to her made her feel warm inside. Made her smile to herself as well as at him. In just days, she had become some kind of smiling Imani…Imani…she thought, I must call her right now. However, to Nia's dismay, she received the same result, no answer. Tomorrow she would talk with the police.

Seth was as prompt as usual, 8:00 p.m. on the button he was ringing Nia's doorbell. Seth was, afterall, still somewhat a product of his human culture. During his era, a gentleman never kept a lady waiting for him. If anything, he would be early, but even that would be considered a bit rude. Nia rushed to the door with a racing heart. A condition that now occurred at each thought or sight of Seth. She opened the door and they amorously smiled at each other. "Dearest Nia, it's wonderful to see you again," Seth said as he took her hand and kissed it. Nia felt an arousing chill go through her entire body. Yet, she was frightened. She knew that she felt too much, too soon for Seth. She feared there would be a painful ending. But, she could not help herself. She cared for him so deeply. She was sure that nothing in this world could change what they had together.

"My handsome, Seth. I can hardly stand it when you're out of my sight. I long for you when you're not with me," Nia confessed.

Nia's words thrilled Seth. How he had wanted to hear such feelings from her. He knew he would absolutely find a way for them to continue together. He beamed, and then wrapped his arms around her, and she around him. In a few moments, he softly kissed the side of her face as he began to release her. "We'd better leave," Seth whispered reluctantly.

"Yes, I hate to let go of you, but, I guess we should," Nia replied somewhat frustrated again. She had always wanted to date a gentleman. But, with Seth, she would not mind a little non gentlemanly behavior. The most apropos saying at the moment would certainly contain the words, 'be careful what you wish for…' Nia thought.

The drive to the shore was awesome. The night was warm, the moon was full, the sky was clear, the stars were bright, and Seth and Nia knew they loved each other. The beach Seth had chosen was secluded and deserted. Nia helped him spread the blanket, but he would not let her help carry the picnic items.

His 'Old World' sense of chivalry would not allow it. Nia did not mind. She liked being treated like a princess and that is exactly how Seth had been treating her since they met, like a princess. They had both just laid down on the blanket, when Seth reached over and pulled Nia close to him. They laid together, cuddled face to face, their arms around each other, their lips almost touching. Seth slowly moved his hand down Nia's shoulder, then farther down until his hand slid beneath the top of her v-neck blouse. Apparently, Seth's gentlemanly behavior had come to an abrupt halt, much to Nia's approval. His hand stopped as it began to caress her large bare breast and large nipple. Nia thought she would explode as she felt his fingers massaging her nipple, and attempted to restrain herself. Within a couple of minutes, her panties were wet and both of her nipples were hard. All he need do was to make the move and she would be ready to give him everything. But, Seth did not make the move. He would not make love with her until she knew the truth about him. Then, if she still wanted him, he would love her as she had never been loved…with the power of the supernatural.

They remained at the beach until way after 2:00 a.m. They looked at the stars and spoke of wondrous things, cutting it a bit close for Seth. Returning to the city, they said their goodnights to each other, Seth giving his usual frustrating hug to Nia. She thought that since he had fondled her breast for awhile, he might be considerably more aggressive once they were back. But, he only added a quick, sensuous kiss on the lips this time. He informed her that he and his companions were to have a Ball in three weeks, on Saturday, and asked her to accompany him. Nia agreed to do so, and, also agreed to come the Friday before the Ball and leave the Sunday after the Ball. Seth had decided that at some time during that weekend he would tell Nia the truth. He knew he would also have to tell her about her friend Imani, but he would do that at another time. On a Wednesday, two weeks before the ball, Seth told Nia not to concern herself about a gown for the Ball. He had purchased one for her to wear, if she did not mind. Nia told him it was perfectly all right.

Nia was 'floating' over her relationship with Seth, but very distressed about Imani's disappearance. She had reported her as a missing person to the police, but they did not seem very interested. She did not feel they were going to put much effort into finding her friend. Perhaps, Seth would help her, she thought. She must remember to ask him. She always got so flustered around him, though. She could hardly think straight in his presence. As the weeks moved along, Nia contacted the police several times, but they had no additional information on Imani. They were going to keep the case open, but to Nia's disappointment, they needed to move-on to other missing persons. Seth and Nia saw each other every night during that same period of time. But, Nia began to wonder why they never saw each other in the daytime.

It was now the week of the ball, Friday night. Seth opened the large wrought iron gates with the remote and began to maneuver the long winding driveway to the manor. He reached the front door, then stopped and turned off the car. Nia could not believe her eyes. "Seth, I know you said you shared a house with some other people, but I had no idea you lived in anything like this mansion," Nia remarked breathlessly.

Seth smiled. "Come, let's go inside," he whispered softly. He gathered her things and they walked through the front door.

Nia thought the house as beautiful inside as it was outside. Antique furniture was everywhere, and what colors, what designs, such elegance. "Who owns this?" Nia asked.

"Oh, we all do. We inherited it from its owner after his rather unexpected death," Seth explained.

"It must have been a close friend or relative," Nia added.

"Well, you could say we all had the same blood," Seth replied expressing a private vampire joke.

"So, you're all in the same family?" Nia inquired.

The conversation was making Seth squeamish. "Enough of this, come meet everyone," he said nervously as he opened the library door and led her into the room. He had asked his companions to wait for him in the library before he left to get Nia, however, he did not tell them why. Per his request, there they all sat, wondering about the great mystery. As soon as Seth and Nia entered the room, all eyes were on Nia. They all knew at once that she was not one of them. Had Seth brought them some kind of special prey? They awaited Seth's words.

"Everyone, this is Nia, my lovely friend, who will be accompanying me to the Ball tomorrow night. Please be kind to her and consider her blood as that of my own," Seth said.

The companions all looked at each other, all but Jason…Of course, it was no surprise to him. But, he could see, now, how such a beauty could bring a dead man back to life again.

Nia thought Seth gave a strange introduction, but she figured he must know his own relatives.

"I'm pleased to meet all of you," Nia said pleasantly.

There was no answer from the group. Only Jason made an effort to be cordial. "We're pleased to meet you also, Nia. Enjoy your stay with us," he said in a solemn tone.

Nia wondered if she was in a freezer, it was so cold. Had she done something wrong already? She had barely opened her mouth. Seth felt it, too. He had expected at least polite civility from his companions, but, he saw he was not going to get either from them. "I'll take you to your room, Dearest," Seth said gently as he took Nia's hand and led her upstairs.

"I can't believe it!" Terry exclaimed as he flopped back on the velvet sofa. His eyes rolled up to the ceiling and down again as he frowned annoyedly.

"He said he's in love with her," Jason explained sympathetically.

"In love! With a human! How disgusting!" Terry continued to rant.

Jason thought Terry was over-reacting a bit and had never been able to understand the obvious venom that Terry had towards Seth. Especially, since Terry was always the instigator. Matilda sat quietly; a tear flowed from one of her eyes and down her cheek. She wiped it away quickly before anyone could see. It was awful enough that Seth loved another, but to choose a human over her, what an insult. Disgraceful, she thought.

"So, you've known about this, Jason?" Chi asked calmly.

"Almost from the beginning. But, I promised not to tell, so I couldn't say anything," Jason explained apologetically.

"It's a rather difficult situation to accept. I'm not sure I can stand having her around for very long. Aside from her human inferiority, she's a constant feeding temptation," added Arturo.

"The first chance I get, I'm gonna make a meal out of her and throw her body in Seth's face," Terry bellowed recklessly.

"Is that right," Seth said as he walked through the library door.

"Ah, there he is, the man of the hour, the great 'attention getter'. How ironic that Mr. High-class, Mr. Particular, should fall in love with a human. Exactly what you deserve. How low can you get, Seth? Surely not lower than that." Terry continued to hammer nastily.

The mild-mannered Seth had heard quite enough. "You're all just a bunch of hypocrites. Going on and on about the inferiority of humans so you can justify your murdering of them and clear your dead consciences. None of us wanted to be what we are, murdering monsters. Had we each been offered the chance, we each would have chosen to remain human and you know it. So, from what exalted pedestal do you think I've fallen, Terry? From what high and mighty existence? You profess to hate that which you want to be the most, human…I would be well rid of you all," Seth answered back in exasperation. Then, he angrily glared only at Terry. "And take heed, you *sick* bastard…you go *anywhere* near my Nia…I'll destroy you," he added sternly, then turned around and left the room. The library remained silent after Seth departed the room. Then, in a few minutes, except for Seth and Nia, the house was entirely empty. The nightly feeding had begun. And, after spending a few hours with Nia, Seth also had to depart. He wished her goodnight and said he would see her the next day. Nia, while amiable, was rather disappointed with the whole evening. Still, she thought tomorrow should be better. On the other hand, without her knowledge, she would now be left completely alone in the large mansion for several unholy hours.

Chapter 2

Nia awakened a little late in the morning. Since, technically, she felt she was already with Seth, she was not sleepless half the night for want of him. She got up, showered, dressed, and ventured downstairs to see about breakfast. She hoped she would run into Seth, but definitely did not want to see any of the others. As she quietly walked downstairs, she noticed how dark the house was, all the draperies were so thick and closed so tightly that not a ray of light could penetrate them. That's rather strange, maybe they don't like sunlight, she thought. Anyway, Seth had told her to just make what she wanted for breakfast in case no one was up and about when she was hungry. She really wasn't hungry, she was too excited about the Ball. She made herself a few pieces of toast and poured a glass of grapefruit juice. There did not seem to be enough food around to feed everyone in the house. Basically, there only seemed to be enough for one person. They must all be light eaters just like Seth, she thought. Thankfully, she finished eating before any of the others came down, so she hurried to return to her room. She would wait there until Seth came for her. She was almost at the top of the stairs, when two of the men from last night appeared there. They looked at her, and then descended the stairs, passing her without acknowledgment, whispering to each other. Nia just ignored it and hurried into her room, closing the door behind her. Perhaps this was a mistake, she thought, as she walked over to the lattice window. The view was extraordinary. The mansion sat on the edge of a mountain overlooking the metropolis. The clouds seemed close enough to touch and the sun shone bright and warm through her window. She wondered how long it would be before Seth came to see her.

Out of the corner of her eye, she caught sight of something on her bed. She turned quickly to see what it was, to her surprise it was a gown, her gown for the Ball. But who? It was simply gorgeous. Made of yards and yards of white chiffon, it was a sleeveless, off-the-shoulder gown, low cut with a form-fitting bodice. The skirt ballooned into yards of swirling chiffon extending all the way to the floor. She loved it! Next to the gown was a flat, 12 square inch box. Nia picked it up and opened it. Her surprise became even more intense, inside the box were a pair of dangling pearl and diamond earrings, a pearl and diamond bracelet, a pearl and diamond comb to hold her hair, and a 15 inch, three-strand pearl and diamond necklace. There was also a pair of long, white lace gloves and a pair of white velvet pumps on the bed. Seth. What a wonderful man you are, she thought.

In about an hour, Nia heard a knock at her door. "Nia, it's I, Seth. May I enter?" he asked sweetly.

"Oh, yes! Please come in Seth!" she exclaimed excitedly as she leaped off the bed.

As Seth cracked open the door, he could see the light from her window illuminating the room. He could not walk into that, so he called out to Nia. "Dearest, would you please close your draperies before I come in? For some reason, light hurts my eyes today," he explained.

"Of course I will, Seth," she replied as she ran to close them. "O.K., they're closed," she said.

The instant he walked into the room, she threw her arms around his neck, kissing him on the lips. Seth was a little taken-a-back for a moment, he was not used to such an outpouring of affection, but he liked it. "Thank you for the gown and the jewelry. They're truly amazing. You always seem to know exactly what I like," she expressed elatedly.

"I guess that's because we're alike in many ways," Seth replied softly. "I'm pleased that you liked what I selected for you. Now, let me tell you about tonight. I will come for you at 8:30. The Ball actually begins at 8:00, but we needn't be there that early. They're having some kind of meeting first, but it doesn't concern us. Please, do not be nervous. I know you haven't been treated in a kind manner here. I'm sorry. Don't think that it was anything you said or did. It was strictly their problem and they have to deal with it themselves," he said reassuringly.

Nia thought, how could she ever love anyone as much as she did Seth. She had dreamed of such a man, but thought that the only place she would find him was in her dreams. Now...he stood before her, in her arms. They stayed together in her room until about 6:00p.m., laughing and talking and enjoying each other. Then, Seth departed so they could both dress for the Ball.

It was now 8:25 p.m., Nia could hear the orchestra warming up downstairs. The meeting must be over, she thought. She took one last look in the mirror. She had never seen herself look so regal. She thought, she could get real used to this, real soon. Momentarily, Seth was knocking at the door. She opened it and he walked in looking at her with pride. "You look exquisite!" he said as he lifted her hand, twirled her around once, and pulled her close to him.

"I look like a princess," Nia said as he wrapped both of his arms around her waist.

"You are a princess," he whispered sliding the tip of his tongue across her full lips. She quickly tried to meet his tongue with hers, and for an instant, their tongues did touch, but Seth pulled away. The stimulation that each received from just that little encounter betrayed to each what power would be unleashed once they did make love.

Seth also looked gorgeous in his coat and tails. The sides and top of his light blond hair were pulled to the back of his head into a thick braid that overlaid the back of his hair, which still hung free and loose down his back. "Are you ready to face the Romans, Christian?" Seth asked as he let go of Nia's waist and held her hand.

"Yes, I'm ready. Do you really think it's going to be that bad, Seth?" Nia questioned.

"I honestly don't know, Dearest. The guests may be more kind than my companions. But, it really doesn't matter. We have each other," he said as they left her room and descended the stairs.

As they approached the ballroom, Nia could hear the people talking and footsteps moving to the music. Just before they reached the door, Seth let go of her hand and extended his elbow to her. She took hold of his arm and they proceeded through the ballroom door. Immediately, once again, everyone knew she was not one of them. The talking stopped and all the dancers walked to the side of the room whispering. However, the musicians continued to play a waltz. The musicians were human, and, as a matter of fact, were the unknowing entrée' for the night.

"I don't think I can stay here, Seth," Nia said softly.

In view of what had just happened, Seth thought perhaps he should get Nia out of there. With the number of vampires present and their obvious rejection of Nia, it might prove dangerous for her when the feeding was about to begin.

"All right, we'll leave, but have one waltz with me first, will you?" Seth asked warmly.

"Well, I'm not really in practice with waltzing, but I'll try," Nia said apologetically.

"You'll do fine," Seth said lovingly with a smile.

And waltz they did, around and around they swirled to the old Rodgers and Hammerstein 'CINDERELLA WALTZ'. They looked only into each other's eyes. And, for a few moments, were unaware of anyone else in the room as each smiled dotingly at the other. However, no one else was dancing. They were the only ones on the floor. But, soon the music ended. Seth gave Nia a short kiss on the lips that brought whispers and hisses from the crowd. She took hold of his arm once more and they defiantly left the ballroom, returning to her room.

They entered Nia's room and Seth closed the door behind them. Nia walked over and sat somberly on the bed taking off her bracelet and gloves. Her total disappointment with the evening was undisguisable. "Nia," Seth said solemnly, "There's something very important that I have to tell you."

Nia's heart began to beat quickly. She had always hated conversations that began that way. "Yes, Seth, what is it?" she asked reluctantly.

Seth paced back and forth nervously for a moment and then began the truth. "I imagine you have been wondering about some things regarding my lifestyle which seemed somewhat unusual," he started. "Things such as my eating habits, my sleeping habits, my companions, to name a few."

"Well, yes I have," Nia remarked. "The darkness of this house in the daytime and the lack of food or servants for such a mansion."

"Yes, I understand." Seth's heart also began to beat quickly. His fear of possibly losing her to the next few moments became almost unbearable. But, he knew that he must continue no matter what the consequences to himself. Nia deserved to know the truth of him. "This is extremely difficult for me," Seth began again. His breathing became quick and heavy, his face turned pale. He continued to pace back and forth.

Oh, God, look at him, Nia thought, her heart pounding even more now. What could it be?

Seth resumed his torturous confession. "All I can say in explanation to your questions and in explanation of my questionable lifestyle is that I am a being of the night. In truth…I am not human at all. In truth…I am a vampire," Seth said painfully.

Nia thought, the man is crazy! My Lord! I knew it was too good to be true! When will I ever learn?...Still, she implored hopefully, "Seth, please. You're just playing around aren't you?"

"Alas, Nia...no, I am not. I was made a vampire in the year of Our Lord 1699. I was 34 years old. Everyone at the ball, except the musicians, was a vampire too," he added completing his explanation.

No wonder he is the perfect man, Nia thought, he is insane. Perfectly insane. How the hell could she get out of there, she could not spend another night.

Against his prior decision, Seth continued with an equally painful confession. "And...I must tell you that your friend, Imani, became a victim of a companion on the night that we met. Did you not recognize him yesterday in the library?"

Nia thought for a moment then answered, "There did seem to be a somewhat familiar face, but I didn't connect it to that night or Imani."

"Well, at any rate, the one who killed her lives here with me," Seth explained nervously.

Nia was stunned at what lengths he would go to make his story, or should she say psychotic delusion, seem real.

"I can see you don't believe me. I will have to prove it to you somehow. I could let you watch me feed, but I don't think you would like that very much," Seth said.

"You aren't going to bite me are you?" Nia asked in a tone as if she were adding, 'I know you're nuts, but I really hope you don't do that'.

It made Seth smile. He knew she thought him 'mad' and thought any bite he gave her would only be a very painful human bite. "No, I'm not going to bite you," Seth replied affectionately. He slowly took off his coat and placed it neatly across a chair in the room. Then, he walked over to the window, opened it, and leaped out into the night.

Nia screamed in disbelief, "Seth! Seth!" She ran to the window without hope, she knew that the mountain ledge outside her window dropped hundreds of feet before it hit bottom. When she reached the window and looked down, all she could see was darkness and the lights from the metropolis in the distance.

"Nia, I'm over here," Seth called softly.

Nia lifted her head and looked straight in front of her. There about 30 feet away was Seth, hovering over the mountain ledge, his long hair gently blowing in the warm night wind. Her mouth dropped open. She must be having a nightmare. That could not be real. There *were* no vampires!, she thought. In a moment, Seth began to fly back towards the window. Nia began to back away from the window, eventually bumping into the bed. Seth came back through the window and stood before Nia waiting for her reaction. He looked at her with tears in his eyes as their eyes immediately locked together. This was the moment he had feared. Did she love him enough to accept what he had become? Was her rejection of him now forthcoming? Would his heart be torn apart in the next few minutes?

After several seconds, Seth began to walk towards Nia. He watched carefully for any sign from her that this was not what she wanted. He saw none and continued walking until he was a few inches away, facing her, their eyes still locked together. A single tear rolled slowly down his handsome cheek. He had a distressed, almost ashamed, look upon his face that revealed more tears might soon follow. Nia's heart ached for him. It was obvious that his form of existence thoroughly pained him. His deep and continuous suffering was evident. She loved Seth so very much. She could no longer even imagine her life without him, whatever his existence.

She reached up, put her arms around Seth's neck, and pulled his head towards her. Seth plunged full force to meet her lips. Both mouths opened and both tongues found their desire. As his tongue filled her mouth, she thought, there was no difference between his tongue and that of a non-vampire. His was just as warm, just as soft, and just as juicy as any other. But, his was much more electric with its atypical force and atypical speed of movement, far superior to any other she had known. She was wet between her thighs already and Seth had only just started his lovemaking with her. His hands moved to the back of her gown and unzipped it. He pulled the gown off of her shoulders and down her arms until the entire gown fell to the floor. She was left in only her white bikini panties, a white garter belt, and white stockings.

He quickly picked her up from amongst the gown and carried her over to the bed. He watched her large round chocolate breasts shake gently in the air as he carried her across the floor. Her large fudge nipples were hard and pointing at him. Seth sat her gently down on the bed. He must have always wanted her as much as she wanted him, Nia thought. Seth watched her firm thighs and shapely legs as she slipped off her shoes and laid down. He subsequently removed his own shoes, as well as all the rest of his clothing. He was not shy about it, nor did he need to be, his body was absolutely beautiful. Flawless. Muscular. Tan. Tan? How'd he do that?

Seth straddled Nia as he kneeled on the bed then reached around and unfastened her garter belt. He pulled it down, bringing her stockings down with it until they were all pulled-off, then laid the items on the bed. He did the same with her panties. Nia pulled her legs up and opened them so that Seth could lie between them. He became more aroused as he absorbed the enticement between her thighs. Her large engorged clitoris was surrounded by her black curly pubic hair. He gave her a single lick across her entire clitoris and on each large hard nipple. His mind felt as if it would burst from the anticipation of tasting them all in depth. Then, he placed the full weight of his body on top of her. They smiled at each other as he brushed her face with the fingers of one hand. Their lips slowly met, and once again, their tongues passionately intertwined. But, his soon overpowered hers as his deep quick thrusts down her throat provided her with untold ecstasy. She moaned constantly. Nia reached-upward and embraced Seth around the neck; and then erratically stroked the back of his long blond hair as his tongue moved electrically in her mouth, providing continued pleasure. Deeply engrossed in rapture, Seth had 'entered' her before she realized it. Not until she simultaneously began to feel deep quick pleasurable thrusts into her vagina did she realize that he was inside of her. His moans began to match hers in loudness and in frequency. But, this was only the beginning of a night filled with unleashed passions and the gratification of unfulfilled desires.

A lone figure stood in the dark hallway outside of Nia's bedroom door, the envy and hatred building with each moan of pleasure heard through the door. "I'll get you, Seth...and that human, too," was whispered in the air.

Nia awakened in the early morning hours and found Seth gone. She knew what he was doing; she knew what he *had* to do. She reached over and pulled his pillow to her breasts. She hugged it tightly as a tear ran gently down her face. Her tears flowed more heavily when she began to realize that since Seth had been telling her the truth, her friend Imani must be dead. But, after awhile, she fell back to sleep. Seth had not returned, yet.

The next evening Jason knocked on Nia's bedroom door. No one had seen Seth or Nia since the Ball. After several knocks and still no answer, Jason entered the room. He looked around and found no one was there. "Where the hell..." he said, then noticed a folded piece of paper on the dresser by the door. He walked over and picked-up the paper, his name was written on top, so he opened it. It was a letter that read:

Jason,

I have gone away with Nia to live elsewhere. You know it would be impossible for us to stay at the mansion. I know I have broken the covenant, but please do not come after us. Please let us be. Nia will grow old and die, but, unless she sends me away, I must stay with her until that time. Perhaps, some day she will agree to become one of us. For my sake, I hope so. For her sake, I hope not. I wish things had not ended this way. I have known you for over 300 years. I cared for you. Yet and still, you did not support me amongst the others. Why would you not help me? Alas, be that as it may, Nia and I must be on our way now. Maybe I will see you again in a century or two.

Seth

Jason folded the letter back up and put it in his pocket. Maybe sooner than you think, Seth, he thought.

Chapter 3

It had been seven months since Seth and Nia had left the mansion and these months had been the happiest either had ever known. Their new home was a more modest, contemporary one that was built on a beach with one wall of glass windows looking out onto the ocean. Nia stood at the window and watched the waves of the ocean roll in and out, it looked so inviting to her. She thought since Seth was engaged in his nightly ritual, she would go for a quick swim. After changing into her bathing suit, she rushed out of the door, down the steps to the sand, and then on to the foot of the water. A small, gentle wave rolled across her feet. The water was warm; it felt good. She ventured in and began to swim towards the sea. The water was dark and the waves were a little more rough than she had thought, so she decided it would be better if she swam closer to shore. She turned around and began swimming back to land. When she was close to what she thought would be a more safe distance, she felt something grab hold of her ankle. Suddenly, she felt herself being pulled under the water. She struggled in vain as her head sank beneath the water. She began gasping for air as her lungs began to displace air with water, tighten, and signal for relief. Somehow, though, she struggled back to the top. Her head crashed through the ceiling of water, where she was able to inhale the desperately needed air. But, almost instantly, once again, she was dragged under the water, her brief taste of life now lost. Her arms, which had been threshing, now began to feel weak as deeper and deeper she was pulled.

Then, suddenly, she felt herself released again; she found a renewed strength and bolted back to the surface. Once again her head crashed through the ceiling of water, where she gulped in air as if it were going out of existence. That time she swam with all her strength back to shore where she ran as far up on the beach as possible and collapsed on the sand. What was that? she thought with fear, was it an undertoe? She could swear it felt like a hand. She had never been caught in an undertoe. Perhaps, that was how they felt. Whatever it was, she never wanted to feel it again. She slowly walked back to the house puzzled about what had just occurred, and frightened by her brush with death. However, she decided not to mention it to Seth.

Nia entered the house and walked back to the bedroom. She removed her bathing suit and dried off with a flowered towel. She put on a sexy pale-yellow nightgown and crawled into bed. She was still shaken and her chest was beginning to hurt a little, so she tried to rest while waiting for Seth. He came in around 3:00 a.m. and as usual went straight to his bathroom to clean up. They had separate bathrooms to avoid possible blood contamination to Nia by blood inadvertently being left in the room. In about half an hour, Seth came through the bedroom door smiling lovingly at Nia, who had turned on the light and was sitting up now. He wore only a pair of white, short, boxers and his hair was still a little wet from having just been washed. Sometimes, he did not dry it very well. "Nia, dear, you're up late or early, whatever the case may be, are you all right?" Seth asked with a serious look on his face.

"Yes, I'm fine. I just missed you and am glad for your return," Nia replied though she really wanted to tell him about her experience. Yet, she did not know exactly what to say about it and she did not want to worry him. Seth climbed into bed with her and she reached over to the night table and turned out the light. They wrapped their arms around each other and gave each other a very long, passionate kiss before saying goodnight and drifting off to sleep.

The next evening, following an afternoon of jazz and oral sex, (they both seemed to have an equally intense sexual appetite and made love every day) Seth gave Nia a kiss and a hug and left to feed. Nia decided to make herself a light meal, she had not eaten anything but Seth since breakfast. She was still stimulated between her legs from his forceful licks and hoped fixing a meal would calm her down. As she was in the kitchen, she happened to look up and glance out of the windows that faced the ocean. Her heart stopped for a moment when she thought she saw a shadow dash across the deck directly outside the window. She continued to look out the window for a few minutes, but never saw it again. Perhaps, the wind just blew something across the deck, she thought; however, she walked around the house and made sure all the windows and doors were tightly locked. She also closed all the draperies. She finished making her meal and sat down to eat. All at once, she heard a crash outside, stop it! she thought with alarm. She stood up listening for other sounds. Everything was silent but her heart, it was pounding so hard it was almost deafening. There was silence the rest of the night, but Nia could not sleep. This time she would tell Seth about what happened. She was too frightened to hold it in anymore.

She was still in the living room when Seth came back; as usual he went to clean-up immediately. When he emerged into the living room to join her, she rushed over to him and grabbed him around the waist. "Nia, Love, what's the matter?" he asked in a troubled tone.

"Seth, I think someone was sneaking around the outside of the house tonight. I think I saw someone at the window and I know I heard something smash," she said nervously.

"All right," he said as he gave her a kiss on the cheek, "I'll check outside." He walked out of the front door, and after proceeding a short way down the walk, saw a flowerpot in pieces on the pavement. Then, he took a walk around the deck that surrounded the house, but did not see any more indications of a possible intruder. He wondered, though, what his former companions were doing right now. He informed Nia of his findings and asked her to relax and come to bed. She felt better, but still nervous; however she did agree to go to bed.

The following evening Nia was watching a bit of television, but was getting rather bored. Despite the instructions Seth had given her before he left to feed, which were to stay inside, she just had to get some air. She walked to the front door, opened it, and stood in the doorway breathing in the warm salt air. It was so peaceful and calming watching the waves roll gently onto the beach. But, suddenly, she heard another crash; she quickly stepped back inside and locked the door. She did not drink much, but she felt she needed one now. She walked to the kitchen and opened the refrigerator. She saw a bottle of white wine almost full, reached down, and picked it up. When she stood up and turned around, she let out a loud scream. There standing in front of her was one of Seth's companions from the mansion.

"Hello, Nia, remember me? I'm Terry, long time no see," he said with an evil grin.

"How did you find us?" Nia asked in a quivering voice.

"Oh, that was easy. We vampires have sort of a 'homing device' in us. If we can lock-on to the right signal, we can always find each other eventually," Terry explained.

"So, it's been you I was hearing outside?" she inquired.

"That's right and in the water pulling you down. Did you enjoy that romp in the sea?" he said with a chuckle.

"What do you want here?" Nia continued apprehensively.

"What do I want? Why, I want you, Nia. I want what Seth gets from you, sex, that's what I want. Then, the next time I see *wonderful* Seth I can tell him how aroused you were with me. How good you felt to me," Terry taunted.

"I'm not going to have sex with you!" Nia shouted angrily.

"Oh, yes you are," Terry said coldly as he grabbed Nia's arm and dragged her into the bedroom. He threw her on the bed and ordered her to remove her clothing. She made no motion to do so. "You take those clothes off or I'll suck the blood out of you right now!" Terry yelled.

With tears streaming down her cheeks, Nia slowly began to remove her top. Then, from a shadow in the doorway, came a voice. "Leave her alone, Terry!" the voice screamed.

Terry turned around to see Matilda standing at the door. "Mind your business, Matilda. Get out of here," Terry replied as he continued to undress.

"I'm not going to let you do this!" she yelled.

"Why not? I thought you hated her for taking *your* Seth," Terry said tauntingly.

"I don't hate her. It wasn't her fault that Seth chose her over me. He did what he wanted to do," Matilda said sadly.

"Yeah, well, I'm doing what I want to do," Terry replied sarcastically.

"Don't make me hurt you, Terry," Matilda pleaded.

Terry turned towards Matilda with a smirk on his face. "What can you do to me?" he asked smugly.

At that instant, with the speed of the supernatural being that she was, Matilda released a long wooden spear that she had hidden behind her back. It tore into Terry's chest with enormous force and straight into his heart. He immediately collapsed on the floor. Matilda walked over to him and watched as his body slowly decomposed into little piles of dust. His face had a look of disbelief before it crumbled into powder. Matilda looked at Nia and was about to speak, when another voice was heard from a figure in the doorway.

"Thank you for taking care of Terry for me, he was getting in my way," the voice said gratefully.

Matilda turned around, "Jason! What are you doing here? What do you mean Terry was in your way?" Matilda asked with surprise.

"He was playing games with Nia. He wanted to violate her only to anger Seth. I, on the other hand, wish to kill her. To be rid of her once and forever," Jason admitted astonishingly.

Nia's eyes widened and fear gripped her as Jason's words resonated in her ears.

"I won't let *you* harm her either," Matilda said as Jason walked swiftly towards Nia. Once Jason came into range, Matilda attacked him and they began to fight, however Jason was able to fling Matilda across the room. When she got back up and started after Jason again, he swiftly picked up the spear laying on the floor amongst Terry's remains and threw it at Matilda. Again, the spear hit its mark and Matilda collapsed on the floor, in a few moments nothing remained of her body but dust as well.

Now Jason's attention turned to Nia. He again began walking towards her when still another voice called-out. "What are you doing here, Jason?" Seth said angrily as he entered the room.

Jason turned to see Seth walking in his direction. Though, Seth walked passed Jason and straight to Nia, avoiding the piles of dust that used to be Matilda and Terry. "Are you unharmed, Dearest?" Seth asked lovingly as he stood next to the bed.

"Yes, I'm o.k.," Nia replied wiping away her tears.

"Seth, it's good to see you again," Jason said guardedly.

"Cut the crap, Jason. Why are you here and what were you trying to do to Nia?" Seth asked, the anger boiling in him.

Jason paused for a moment and then nervously looked Seth in the eyes. "I'm here because I miss you. I want you back at the mansion. She was the reason you left. She made you break the covenant, so, she should die," Jason responded in his own defense.

"She didn't make me leave the mansion, the 'group' did with their intolerance. She was not responsible for any of what happened. There's no reason for her to die...Besides...why should you miss me so much? So much that you would come after me like this and use some ridiculous excuse to murder Nia?" Seth expressed intensely.

"Why?" Jason paused, then answered with a quiver in his voice, "Because I've been in love with you for more than 300 years."

"What!" Seth exclaimed totally shocked by Jason's answer.

"I'm in love with you," Jason repeated softly. "I know I'm not your prefer-ence, I don't mind that. As long as you were around and I could see you and talk with you and even touch you sometimes, I was satisfied. But, with you gone, I have nothing. I have no reason to exist at all…You said in your letter that you cared for me," Jason reminded despondently.

"Yes, I did care for you once, but only as a brother, nothing more. My heart is with Nia and I will remain with her. I won't be returning to the mansion," Seth said definitively.

Jason stared at Seth for a moment. Then, his eyes filled with tears as he slowly turned and walked out of the room, then out of the house. He strolled along the sand in despair and watched the soothing motion of the waves as the sun began to peek over the ocean horizon.

That morning, Detective Farris and Detective Paulson were both puzzled by what they saw. Apparently, someone had burned something large on the beach. Remarkably, though, some parts of the thing were hardly burned at all. Detective Farris searched through some sort of pockets hoping to find an iden-tifying clue. He found a folded piece of paper…When opened, he saw that it was a letter, which read:

ᘒ

Jason,

I have gone away with Nia to live elsewhere…

Chapter 4

Seth decided that he and Nia should move to another area. He did not expect Chi or Arturo to come after them, neither seemed to care one way or another about what he did. But, he could not be sure, so, it would be best to keep Nia out of harm's way. He decided they would move to the south of France, a vil-lage named Nimes to be exact. He had visited there a little over a century ago and had found it to be a charming place. Based on his descriptions and his obvious fondness towards the village, Nia agreed to move there and helped him make the arrangements. Through much effort, Nia was able to arrange a series of airplane schedules so that it was possible for them to leave the United States during night hours and eventually arrive in Nimes, France during night hours. The arrangements involved a few airplane changes and over-daytime stays at hotels, but it would indeed work out well. Their first flight left the United States on July 4th, Independence Day, perhaps a good omen they thought. Perhaps they, too, would finally be free.

They arrived in Nimes on the night of July 7th, where Seth rented a car and drove them to their new residence. Remarkably, he remembered the way. He had lived at the particular chateau when he was there during the last century. While making financial arrangements, he had found that it was vacant and so quickly purchased it. They drove along a dark winding road that led through a forest and eventually to a large clearing. It was then that Nia first viewed the chateau. It truly was as lovely as Seth had described. It sat upon a slight hill and was a three story rectangular building made of reddish-brown brick and supported in the front by four huge columns made of tan-colored stone. The roof and the base of the chateau had ornate borders surrounding them made of the same tan-colored stone as the columns. There were three rows of windows, a row for each floor, each row consisting of six huge windows bordered in white. The entire chateau was flooded by outdoor lighting, giving the impression as one traveled closer that it was actually daytime. And, gave any traveler a view of the building for miles around, almost as though it was a beacon in the night. The abundant lighting allowed Nia to see that the chateau sat amongst magnificent gardens where multitudes of flowers, seemingly of every description, could be readily admired. Their fragrance filled her senses entirely, giving her the pleasure of a natural 'high'. Seth stopped the car at the front entrance, which was located halfway around the circular driveway.

They both exited the car and then, immediately, a middle-aged man, dressed in a black suit, white shirt, and black tie, came running to greet them, smiling pleasantly. "Welcome! Welcome, Monsieur and Madame. My name is Gabriel. I am the caretaker," he said joyfully.

"Good evening. I'm Seth Bjorn the new owner and this is my wife," Seth replied politely. Nia was taken by surprise when Seth introduced her as his wife, but she loved the sound of it, despite the fact that, legally, it could never be true.

"It is wonderful to meet both of you. Your wife, Monsieur, is very beautiful," Gabriel answered.

Nia smiled at Gabriel as Seth replied proudly, "Thank you."

"I will get your bags immediately, Monsieur," Gabriel said as he hurried down the walkway to the car.

"Here are the keys to the trunk," Seth called out to him as he tossed the keys in Gabriel's direction, then added, "Oh, and please, turn-off most of these lights."

Gabriel caught the keys then called back to Seth, "Yes, Monsieur, I will turn them off momentarily." The lights, though artificial, were in such abundance that they hurt Seth's eyes and irritated his skin.

Entering the chateau, Nia gasped at the elegance and beauty of the interior, which was every bit as magnificent as the exterior, with its Renaissance decor and two grand winding staircases. An enormous crystal chandelier hung regally between the two staircases from the completely muraled cathedral ceiling. The ceiling spanned the entire height of the chateau. The foyer and staircase walls were papered with a very thin-striped, gold and white design giving the illusion from a distance of gold-colored walls. The entire foyer floor and the steps of both staircases were carpeted with rare, valuable, red and gold oriental rugs. And just as outside, there was a multitude of flowers about the place and their fragrance continued to fill the air. The chateau was just as Seth had remembered it, and it was every bit as enchanting now as it had been over 100 years ago.

"This is spectacular, Seth," Nia remarked fascinated with the decor.

Seth smiled and put his arm around her shoulders, then pulled her close. "Yes, it is quite 'something' isn't it?" he responded affectionately.

"Even though it's half the size of Westville Manor, this looks more like a palace inside than the manor, and that's saying a whole lot," Nia said still enthralled with her surroundings.

"Some of this lighting is going to have to go, though," Seth added as he continued to be irritated by the brightness. "And, maybe the caretaker."

"The caretaker? Why?" Nia questioned.

"Because he might see too much, might become too suspicious of some unusual situations. You know, the way you noticed things before you knew the truth," Seth explained.

"Yes, I see what you mean. But, perhaps if we keep our distance from him, don't get too friendly, he won't notice anything very unusual," Nia tried to reason.

"Perhaps. We'll give it a try. I hope we won't be sorry. I would hate to see him lose his job," Seth remarked.

"You're a kind and thoughtful man, Seth. It's hard to remember you're supposed to be evil," Nia said softly.

Seth smiled at her provocatively and replied, "I'm feeling a little evil right now, though. What do you say about going to bed right away?"

"Yes, please," Nia whispered as she reached up and kissed the side of his face.

At that moment, Gabriel hurried through the front entrance laboriously carrying several bags. Breathlessly, he spoke to Seth and Nia in his French accent. "If you will follow me, I will show you to the Master Suite, Monsieur et Madame." They all ascended the staircase on the right-side, made a right turn at the first landing and continued down a long, highly decorative hallway lined with antique mirrors and expensive paintings. Finally, they reached a double-door room, the doors were already open and revealed a room filled with white and gold French antique furniture. Hand painted multi-colored flowers adorned each piece of furniture, including the large headboard of the bed. The emerald green and gold bed coverings and the emerald green and gold draperies that covered the two huge windows, complimented the hand painted leaves on the furniture, as well as the white and miniature-flowered wallpaper. The entire ceiling was a mural depicting a lake and a wooded country scene. The huge fireplace was composed of white tiles about 5 inches by 5 inches in size, each trimmed in gold and each with a tiny hand painted floral design on it. The room was only mildly fragrant from the three vases of flowers placed around it, but that would make it easier to breathe while sleeping.

Gabriel left the bags next to the large armoire, then started out of the room. "Have a good night. If you need me, I live in the cottage just in back of the chateau," he informed them with a smile.

"Thank you, Gabriel. You have a good night as well," Seth said, smiling back at him. Gabriel left, closing the doors behind him.

Nia walked over to the closest chair and undressed until she was totally naked. Then, she began to walk towards Seth, who was standing by the bed and had been watching her with pleasure the whole time. Her soft, long, slightly bushy, black hair blew gently backwards as she moved. He watched her large, soft, chocolate breasts bounce lightly as she sauntered across the floor. He watched her firm thighs move forwards then backwards as her naked hips came closer and closer to him, her black, curly, pubic hair growing thickly between them. Her slightly engorged clitoris peeked invitingly through her pubic hair, looking much like a soft, delicious piece of chocolate candy. By the time she reached him, he only had time to remove his shoes, socks, and shirt, revealing his broad, muscular, chest. She embraced him around his neck; and then kissed his lips, slipping her tongue into his mouth. Seth grunted as he felt her soft, warm breasts press against his bare chest. The hardness of her nipples revealed their location on his body as they stung into his skin.

He reached around and grabbed each firm naked buttock with a hand and began to aggressively squeeze each side while gyrating his groin against her pubic area. Nia felt Seth's penis begin to harden, and in the same instant, he lowered his head and took one of her engorged nipples between his lips. Her nipple filled his mouth and his tongue glided wildly around it for a few minutes. The glides quickly turned to sucks of such force that Nia experienced several orgasms from the feel of it, and let out multiple cries of excitement. A few beads of perspiration began to form on Seth's forehead as he released that nipple and engulfed the other one. Again, Nia's orgasms came, accompanied by her cries of pleasure. She began to feel heavy amounts of moisture flowing from her vagina, then in a moment more, she felt a few of Seth's fingers push their way into the opening. His thumb started to slide backwards and forwards along her wet clitoris as she parted her thighs wider.

Then, he began to continuously slide the inserted fingers in and partially out of her vagina; her wetness began to cover his fingers and hand. He would occasionally pull his fingers entirely out of her vagina and entirely out from between her legs. Then, proceed to lick her wetness off his hand as though licking an ice cream cone. But, he always returned between her legs for more of her sensuous ice cream. Nia began to pull at Seth's pants in an effort to pull them off of him. When he realized her efforts, he joined her in the removal process, holding on to her as he pulled his pants over his feet, and then leaving his pants on the floor. His naturally large penis was now hardened to twice its normal size, and Nia took hold of it with one hand, moving her fingers up and down the shaft and rotating her thumb around its large, wet head, her fingers now covered with *his* wetness.

They stopped for a moment to retreat to the bed, where the lovemaking continued. He positioned his body, on his knees, between her thighs and watched as his fingers massaged her enlarged, slippery clitoris. When her juices began to flow even more heavily, he watched as he again slid two fingers into her vaginal opening and deep inside her, still massaging her clitoris with the fingers of his other hand. Again, he used his fingers as though they were his penis, thrusting them back and forth inside her. Nia responded as if they actually were his penis. She held on to his shoulders, then thrusted her hips and genitals at him in concert with his movements. Her thighs were spread as far apart as she could possibly get them, her large swollen breasts rolled like jello from her movements. She repeatedly cried-out his name loudly, in ecstasy.

Seth loved the sight of her naked genitals, especially when she was thrusting them at him. He loved watching his fingers move back and forth in her vagina and seeing his other fingers play with her clitoris. He also loved the sounds of her pleasure.

When he knew he was near his climax, he guided Nia to turnover. Then, helped her to position herself on all-fours, her buttocks facing him, her legs spread far apart. The position was one he had first experienced with Lucinda, and the one that both he and Nia enjoyed the most. Before he entered her, he prolonged this view of her body for a few moments. As she lowered the front half of her body causing the back half to lift-up and her thighs to spread apart more fully, Seth began to lick her genitals, but shortly, holding one buttock with his hand, he slid his hard wet penis into her. Initially, he pumped her deeply and slowly, however, in a short time, his thrusts became deep and fast, his penis now covered with her juices. He saw her wetness overflowing from the sides of her widely stretched vaginal opening as he watched his penis move back and forth in her. Nia continued to have multiple orgasms and was in the middle of one when Seth stopped moaning and cried-out loudly. He grabbed her buttocks tightly with both hands and held on to them with a vise-like grip, inserting one more extremely powerful thrust into her, reaching his climax. He remained inside her until his climax passed. After a few moments more, he withdrew himself from her. They both laid back down on the bed where they embraced and kissed each other passionately, both still aglow from their experience. But…Seth was more than conscious of the fact that he must leave soon. He still needed to feed.

Chapter 5

The night was dark as Seth walked through the lattice doors of the library, outside into the adjoining garden area. The sky was cloudy so the quarter-moon was not able to provide much light. Seth was very familiar with the chateau and had always left for his feedings from the library when he had lived there in the last century. It was the most secluded of the doorways to the outside and would best hide his comings and goings from Gabriel. Almost instantly, he leaped into the air with a gust of wind so strong, that it caused the petals of flowers to sway violently back and forth and small animals to search for cover.

Gabriel laid in his bed in the dark thinking about his lady-friend, whom he would be seeing in three nights. Suddenly, he heard the loud howl of the wind. What in hell was that, he thought, must be a storm blowing up around here.

He rose from his bed and looked out of the window. The night was still. Not a single breeze blowing that he could tell. He thought he saw a large shadow glide over the tops of the trees towards the north. Heck of a big bird, he thought, and then went back to bed.

Seth flew over the treetops on his way north, 50 miles, to a small village of which he had knowledge. The village was far enough away that its inhabitants would never suspect that the misfortunes that were about to befall them originated 50 miles to the south. He landed behind what he remembered to be a house of prostitution 100 years ago and upon closer observation, saw that it still was. He found these to be convenient places to locate prey, because the people in and around them usually stayed up late. And, because they were working, the prostitutes seldom contaminated their blood with alcohol, thus they were excellent prey. Seth did not like the taste of blood that contained a high amount of alcohol. He chose not to go inside for it was a small village and a stranger would be readily noticed and remembered. No, he would wait for his prey outside, hidden by the darkness, alert and ready to capture his prize.

The weary prostitute did not know what happened when she walked down the dark alley behind the brothel. She had no time to fight or even cry-out for help before Seth sank his teeth into her neck. His teeth sliced through her neck muscles as easily as a knife through half-melted butter. He drank her blood quickly, but with great zeal, he was filled with happiness that night, it being a new beginning for him and Nia. The European blood of the prostitute had a slightly different taste to it than the blood in the United States. Possibly, the European diet had something to do with it. At any rate, Seth drank. The woman went limp, but he continued to drink until he knew she would not live much longer. After finishing his meal, he lifted the woman in his arms, as though a groom carrying his bride over the threshold. He then took flight, traveling 20 more miles to the north, where he landed in a thickly wooded forest and buried the woman, who had thankfully died during the flight. He then flew swiftly south, it would soon be sunrise and not only did he need to be inside, he also needed to avoid detection by Gabriel.

Nia awakened to find Seth lying in bed cuddled next to her, his arm around her waist, his head next to hers buried in her hair. She gently removed his arm from around her waist, then quietly climbed out of bed. She took a short shower rather than a bath in order to limit the noise of running water, trying not to wake Seth. She would take a bath tonight instead. She slipped on a lime-green cotton sundress with spaghetti straps and lime-green sandals, then ventured downstairs to make her own breakfast. Since there were not and could not be any servants in the house on a regular basis, except for Gabriel, she had no other choice. But, she never had servants anyway, so it was no big deal. Descending the staircase, she realized the brightness of the chateau. The sun seemed to streaked through every window. She must ask Gabriel to close all the draperies, and then give him a logical reason to always keep them that way. As she sat in the kitchen eating, Gabriel came through the back door. "Good morning, Madame, Good morning," he said with a smile.

"Good morning, Gabriel," Nia replied smiling as well.

"Madame is looking lovely today. You slept well?" he continued.

"Thank you, yes, I slept very well," Nia answered, a bit flattered by his comment on her appearance.

"Bon, bon. I will continue with my duties now. Do have a pleasant day," Gabriel said as he started towards the interior of the chateau.

Nia remembered about the draperies and called after him. "Gabriel, please close all the draperies in the chateau and turn on a few lights instead."

"Close all the draperies, Madame? But, the sun, she is shining so brightly, it is a wonderful, warm day," Gabriel replied with joy in his heart.

"Yes, I can see that, but my husband is allergic to sunlight. It makes him very ill, so, I must shield him from it as much as possible," Nia explained.

"Oh. Such a shame. A strong, handsome man like that, who would ever have thought it," Gabriel lamented. "Of course, Madame, I will close them all immediately, before Monsieur chances out of the suite."

"Thank you, Gabriel," Nia gratefully replied.

Nia finished her meal and returned to the bedroom, where she found Seth sitting-up in bed. His long blond hair was slightly messed and hung over both of his broad, bare shoulders. Seth had begun sleeping naked recently. She did not know why, but she liked it very much. He looked-up as she walked through the door. "Good morning, My Darling," Nia said lovingly. Seth gave her that perfect smile. Each time she saw it, she was thrilled all over again, just like in the beginning. She loved him so very much; the thought of life without him always gave her a chill.

"Good morning, Dearest. I missed you when I awakened," Seth expressed softly.

Nia walked over to the bed and climbed on it. She stood on her knees and straddled Seth's groin, then lowered her spread thighs until her genitals sat on top of his. She was not wearing panties, so she quickly felt his soft penis between her legs even though the sheets covered it. She put her arms around his neck and they gave each other a very passionate kiss, as he wrapped his arms around her torso and hugged her tightly.

"I'm sorry I wasn't here when you awakened. I was restless and couldn't wait for you as I always do. Maybe I was excited about our new life here," Nia whispered in explanation, looking into his light brown eyes.

"It's all right, Dear, but I worry about you when I don't know where you are," Seth answered affectionately.

"I know you do, Seth. I worry about you as well, especially not knowing where you are half of every night," Nia said in frustration.

Seth smiled at her, "I guess we're just two old 'worriers', huh?" he answered back jokingly.

"I guess," Nia replied smiling as well, but then she continued. "Seth."

"Yes? What is it?" Seth asked lovingly.

"It's an absolutely beautiful, warm, and sunny day. Would you get upset if I drove into the village and did a little shopping?" Nia asked reticently.

Though Seth did not want her to go, he wanted her to be happy. "I won't get upset. Of course, you should go. I want you to go. I'm the one condemned to darkness, not you. How could I care for you and force you to deny what you are," Seth explained less than enthusiastically. He hoped she would feel guilty and change her mind once she saw how sacrificially agreeable he was to the idea.

Nia leaned over and kissed him on his cheek, then whispered in his ear, "I won't be long." She climbed off the bed and snatched her purse from the dresser. As she started out the bedroom door, she looked back at him, "See you shortly," she said with a smile.

Seth gave her a grin and a wave good-bye. That was the first time she had wanted to go somewhere without him and he did not quite understand why. Was she growing weary of him and the life she must live with him? he thought, or was it simply that it was a beautiful day and being human, she wanted to go out in it. Truthfully, he was envious of her ability to venture out into the sunlight. He, too, desired such ability again, so how could he possibly think ill of her request and resulting swift exit.

Nia stepped outside into the sunlight. There was a slight breeze and the fragrance of the flowers still excited her senses, The sight of the flowers was even more glorious in daylight than in the bright lights of last night. She could now see there was a large lake situated to the side of the chateau. It was extraordinarily lovely and had several swans skimming lazily across it. She got into the car and thought she must remind Seth that they needed to buy a car and return this rented one. The car was a convertible and she put the top down to further enjoy the weather. She drove down the cobblestone driveway passed the large, open, iron gates and onto the main road, then made a left turn heading towards the village. Gabriel, who was tending one of the front gardens, watched as she drove out of the driveway. He thought, her life must often be very lonely because anything that needed to be done outside, during the day, must be done by her alone. She drove down the long winding roadway, her hair blowing in the wind. She was glad that the road was wide, because the steepness and winding of it made her nervous and she might otherwise fear driving off the edge. Arriving in the village, she was enchanted with the quaintness of it. It still looked like it belonged in the 19th century. There were a fair number of people around and about, but they seemed to be mostly tourists. Nia found a parking spot and started strolling down the sidewalk, she seemed to be the only person of color in the village, at least from what she could readily observe. She stopped in a dress shop first, where she purchased multiple dresses and other items for her new life. Next, she headed to the jewelry store where she purchased a number of rather expensive earrings and necklaces. Her arms were totally loaded with packages when she stopped at an outdoor table of a restaurant for lunch. As she attempted to place her packages on the table, many of them toppled to the ground. A man rose from the opposite table and began to help her pick them up and put them on the table. He had been sitting there watching her for quite some time as she walked down the main street of the village, in and out of shops. He was a tall, slender young man with medium brown, shoulder length hair. He was clean-shaven and his eyes were a kind of blue-gray color that tended to change into one or the other color depending upon the light.

Nia, who was herself stooping to pick-up her packages, turned her head to see who the person was helping her. "Thank you so much," she said gratefully as they both stood, all of the packages now on the table.

"You're welcome, Mademoiselle. My name is Jeremiah Girroit," he replied, extending his hand.

"My name is Nia Bjorn. Nice to meet you," she answered as she took his hand. However, instead of shaking her hand, he kissed it. Nia was always easily swayed by gentlemanly behavior, so when he asked to join her at her table, she did not immediately say no. Jeremiah quickly took advantage of her delayed answer and proceeded to help her with her chair then sat down in the other chair at her table.

"So, Mademoiselle Bjorn, what has brought you to fair Nimes?" Jeremiah asked.

"I'm here with my husband. We've just purchased a chateau and plan to make this our home. At least for a few years," Nia explained.

"Oh, I see. So, it's Madame and not Mademoiselle," lamented Jeremiah.

"Yes, I'm married," Nia informed amiably.

"My heart is now broken. Here I had finally found my one true love and you are married," Jeremiah teased. Nia smiled. Momentarily, the waiter came over to take their orders. Nia ordered only a vegetable salad and a glass of white wine. Jeremiah ordered a shrimp omelet, a fruit salad, and a lemon drink with lime slices and orange slices. Jeremiah could not help from staring at Nia. She was the most attractive woman he had seen in years. She smelled good, too.

"Jeremiah, please stop staring at me. It makes me feel very self-conscious," Nia requested, though happy about his obvious opinion of her sex appeal.

"I'm sorry, Nia. I just haven't seen a woman of such beauty in a very long time. I feel as though I need to absorb it into my body or burn it into my brain, lest I forget the beauty that sits before me…I may not see the like of it again in many a year," Jeremiah expressed openly.

Nia liked his words very much. Hearing them even gave her a slight tingle. But, she had heard many such romantic comments from her Seth. She checked her watch and saw it was getting late and that she must be getting back home. The waiter returned with their food, placed it on the table, and quickly left them alone, assuming romance was in the air. "Thank you, Jeremiah, those were very kind and gracious things to say. But, now, I must hurry to finish my lunch, my husband waits for me at home," Nia conveyed to him.

"Fortunate, fortunate, man. He must indeed be quite a man to have 'wooed' *you* into marriage," Jeremiah responded enviously.

"Yes, he is quite a man," she answered lovingly.

They quickly finished their meals and Jeremiah paid both bills. He walked Nia to her car where he opened the door for her, helped her into the car, and then closed the door. She started the engine and looked-up at him. "Good-bye, Jeremiah. Thank you for your help and your company," Nia said genially.

Jeremiah looked at her with discontentment in his eyes. This could not be all they would have, he would not allow it. "Have a good night, Nia. I'm sure we will see each other again soon," Jeremiah answered, convinced that he would make such a meeting happen.

Nia drove back to the chateau thinking about Jeremiah. He was a hand-some, nice, man and it was so pleasant eating outside in the daytime with someone. Being normal. She had no friends any more, so had no one to associate with during the day that could go places with her like the village or the beach. Those activities were actually luxuries now.

She arrived back at the chateau around 1:30 p.m., she had only been gone 3 hours, so Seth should have been able to occupy himself sufficiently for that length of time, she thought. She walked inside the chateau and started up the staircase when she noticed Seth sitting in the library reading. She walked back down the few steps she had ascended and entered the library. He laid the book down and rose as she entered the room. She walked towards him and he towards her. When they met, they hugged each other tightly, both sighing in pleasure at their re-uniting. "I've desired you all day," Seth whispered as he slipped his hands under her dress and caressed her pantiless buttocks. "Come with me," he said as he took her hand and led her upstairs to the bedroom suite. Their lovemaking was remarkable, as usual, and Nia wondered how she could ever have had thoughts of Jeremiah. For truly, who in life could be more exciting than Seth.

Chapter 6

Once again, Seth made his exit from the library door. He soared into the night sky, creating a turbulent wind as he flew high above the landscape. Gabriel was about to get into bed when he heard that strange howl of the wind again. What from hell is that? he thought, as he again went to look out of the window. Still no breeze to be seen, but, 'what the devil', there was that enormous bird again. Could that be causing the howl? he thought. He climbed into bed puzzled about the happenings, but, he fell asleep quickly just the same.

The next morning, Nia awakened later than usual. She found Seth already sitting-up in bed, awaiting her arrival to the new day. When he saw her open her eyes, he leaned down and gently kissed her lips. "Hello," he said softly with a smile as he looked into her eyes, his long blond hair brushing against her chocolate-brown face.

Nia returned his smile and whispered, "Hello, my sweet Darling." She sat-up and their arms entwined while they gave each other an 'in depth' good morning kiss. When they finished, Seth held her in his arms and asked softly, "Nia, would you like it if we went into the village tonight? There are at least two nightclubs that I know of and they're supposed to be quite lively." Seth had been thinking about Nia...in particular about her excursion to the village. They had not been out together for a while, so he thought perhaps it was time.

"Yes!" Nia exclaimed, "I would love it."

"Excellent. Then we shall go," Seth replied, happy that he had pleased her.

Gabriel sat in a wooden chair at the inexpensive nightclub in Nimes. He was unable to afford the high-class club on the other side of the village, the one to which Seth and Nia would be going that night. He was watching the crowd dancing to an 'oldie but goodie' song named 'Michelle Ma Belle', when he saw his woman friend, Adrianna, coming towards him. She was also middle-aged, in fact she was a few years closer to 55 years old than he had yet reached. She had short red hair, wore heavy eye make-up, and bright red lipstick. Her face powder was so white that it made her look more dead than alive. She was heavy-set and wore a low-cut, hot-pink dress that was slightly too tight for her. Gabriel rose from his chair and walked towards her as she approached the table. "Bon Soir, My Dear," he said affectionately with a smile.

Adrianna was of English decent and knew very little French. "Good evening, Love," she answered as she leaned forward and kissed him on the cheek. Gabriel held her chair out for her, and then helped her sit down, slowly pushing the chair under her somewhat broad backside. He sat down at the table opposite her since he cared a great deal for her and always liked to look into her eyes. She only visited him a few weekends out of a month because she still lived in England. Sometimes, he suspected she was married, but in the 8 months that he had been seeing her, she had always said she was not and she never wore a ring.

"Blimey," she said nervously, "Have you heard about the bodies they found north of here, Gabriel?"

"Bodies, what bodies?" Gabriel inquired puzzled about the information she was telling him.

"Two of them so far. Both mutilated," she added in a whisper.

"No, I've heard nothing about them. Do the authorities know who they are?" Gabriel questioned.

"Well, one was a prostitute who worked at a brothel almost 20 miles away from where she was found. The other was a young farmer who was on his way home from selling goods at a market. The market and his home were both at least 10 miles from where he was found," Adrianna explained.

"How did they find them, do you know?" Gabriel asked shocked at the news.

"I heard that some hunters were in the woods with dogs and that it was actually the dogs that found them. I guess they smelled something and they began to dig at the ground. One body was buried on top of the other, but, the police think they were murdered on two different days," Adrianna said a little frightened.

"Holy cow. I hope who ever it is does not decide to come down here. What kind of mutilation was involved?" Gabriel asked curious as to how gruesome the acts committed on the victims might have been.

"Basically, it was their necks. There were puncture wounds, like someone or something bit into them. And, whatever it was drained most of the blood out of them," Adrianna continued.

"Sounds like a vampire," Gabriel said with a grin.

"Yeah…right, Gabriel," she said with a cynical smile. "But, the problem is that they do not exist. Well, except maybe in the movies."

"Yes, I guess you're right. I'm sure they will find the murderer soon. So…what would you like for dinner?" Gabriel asked, though he was not dismissing his vampire remark as easily as was Adrianna.

Seth and Nia sat at a secluded burgundy-colored, leather booth in the crowded, romantically candle-lighted nightclub. Nia had on a skin-tight, low-cut, lavender leather dress, a color that went very well with her chocolate-colored skin. The dress had no sleeves and was of a mid-calf length. The outlines of her braless large breasts and nipples were readily visible and caught the attention of every man that happened to see her from the front. Her firm, shapely, pantiless buttocks were also readily observable and caught the eye of every man that happened to see her from the back. But, in particular, her attire caught Seth's eyes. And, he could hardly take them off of her for even a moment. Seth was also a handsome sight in his navy blue, one button, Italian suit and navy blue, silk, open-collar shirt. Again, his long light-blond hair hung free and loose down his back, a style which was most often his preference.

"This is a nice place, Seth," Nia remarked, thrilled at her night out on the town.

"Yes, it is quite nice. It used to be a barn, about 100 years ago," Seth remembered.

"Maybe that's why it's so spacious, it has such a high ceiling," Nia said as she looked upward.

Then, suddenly, a man was standing beside her. She lowered her head to see who had come so close to her since she was not acquainted with anyone in the village. "Good evening, Madame Bjorn. So nice to see you again," Jeremiah said with a smile.

"Mr. Girroit," Nia said with surprise. "Good evening…May I introduce you to my husband. Seth. Darling, this is Jeremiah Girroit. I had some trouble with my packages yesterday when I was in town and Mr. Girroit was kind enough to help me," Nia explained, a bit nervous about the encounter.

"Pleased to meet you, Mr. Girroit. And, if you had occasion to help my wife, I am grateful and indebted to you," Seth said politely, though, he did not like the man intruding upon his evening with Nia.

"I am equally pleased to make your acquaintance. Please believe it was a pleasure to help your wife, and as such, you owe me nothing," Jeremiah replied. He was every bit as polite as Seth and every bit as much wishing Seth would disappear. The orchestra began to play a slow song and Jeremiah thought he would try to take that one opportunity to be close to Nia. "Ah, my favorite song. Madame Bjorn, may I have this one dance before I leave you this evening?" Jeremiah asked brazenly.

Seth and Nia looked at each other, neither one knew exactly what to say. Nia did not want to dance with Jeremiah, not only because she was not interested in him, but also because she felt Seth would not care for it. Yet, she did not want to hurt Jeremiah's feelings, afterall, he had been kind to her. Seth, on the other hand, did tend to be jealous and he wished Nia would decline Jeremiah's offer. However, he did not want to tell her that she could not dance with him. He was not her owner and he knew she would not like it if he tried to control her. Since she saw no great reaction from Seth, and she preferred not to hurt Jeremiah's feelings, Nia agreed to the dance. As she rose, she looked at Seth and smiled. He smiled back and watched them as they walked to the dance floor. Seth watched as Jeremiah put his arms around Nia's waist and she put her arms around Jeremiah's neck. Seth was grateful that Nia kept their bodies apart, so they were not pressed against each other. Nia and Jeremiah started to dance and then started a conversation. Seth had not had a reason to tell Nia that his hearing was abnormally acute, almost akin to canine hearing. And, that he could hear sounds no human could hear. Now, as he sat in the booth alone, he listened to the words that passed between Nia and Jeremiah as they danced with each other to the music.

"Nia, I watched for you around town. I hoped you would take a trip in today. I wanted to see you very much," Jeremiah said softly.

"I like to spend all of my time with my husband most days. I would seldom be coming to town," Nia explained. "But, you and I hardly know each other, why would you look for me all day?"

"You can't say you didn't feel what I felt when we met, when we had lunch together," Jeremiah expressed in disbelief.

"I don't know what you mean. I felt you to be kind for helping me, that's all. I think you have read more into our meeting than was actually there, Jeremiah," Nia replied.

"Why not give me the chance to show how much I care for you. I have the feeling that your husband does not accompany you too many places, and that unhappily, you often travel alone," Jeremiah answered incitefully. "I would change that circumstance for you."

"Why would you think such a thing!" Nia exclaimed shocked at his invasion into her privacy. "Please, don't intrude upon my relationship with my husband. Should we see each other again, let's just say 'hello' and go our separate ways. I am not looking for and do not want anyone other than Seth," Nia told him sternly.

The song ended and Jeremiah, not yet defeated, walked Nia back to her seat. "Thank you for the dance, Madame. It was most enjoyable," then turning to Seth, "Thank you, Monsieur, for the pleasure of your wife's company. I will take my leave now. A pleasant evening and a safe return home to you both," Jeremiah expressed to them as he bowed and walked away.

"Goodnight," Nia replied, happy that he had decided to leave.

"Same to you, sir," Seth answered coldly, his anger towards Jeremiah bubbling inside of him. Even believing Nia was married, the man dared an attempt to take her away from him, and right in front of his face. But Seth's greatest fear had always been that one day a man would come along who would offer Nia love and a normal human life. And, that ultimately, she would leave him.

Shortly afterwards, they left the club and returned home where they went immediately to their bedroom. Seth had been strangely silent, Nia thought. She decided that she would perform oral sex on him. He always greatly enjoyed that and she feared he was quite upset about Jeremiah. Perhaps, that would take his mind off of the club and re-assure him of her feelings for him. Seth undressed and sat on the bed in a pair of navy blue under-shorts. Nia pulled her dress off over her head, under which she was wearing nothing. She crawled onto the bed from the side opposite of Seth and moved on her hands and knees to his side. She twisted her torso such that her bare breasts rested on his thighs while the bottom half of her body laid on its side, her legs lying on the bed, curved around the back of him. He looked down at her, smiled, and placed his hand on the top of her head, then gently began to play with her hair.

She slowly slid her right hand beneath the elastic border of his under-shorts, running her fingers through his thick pubic hair and on to his soft, warm penis. She took hold of it and began to massage it lovingly. In a few moments, she began to feel it start to harden, at which point she pulled it out through the top of his shorts, exposing its long, thick, round, tan appearance. Its large head glistened from the flow of clear liquid that pumped from it. Seth reached down and maneuvered his under-shorts until he had removed them completely, placing them on the bed. He then leaned back on the bed with his eyes closed, propping himself up with both of his arms behind him. He spread his legs as far apart as he could so that she had entry to everything between them. She firmly licked his soft, hair-covered sacks for a few minutes, causing muffled moans from Seth. Then, she licked her way up the shaft as though enjoying a wet slippery popsicle, and upon reaching the top, engulfed the entire large, hard, head with her mouth. She sucked at it as if a baby at its bot-tle. Her mouth began to fill with his warm, clear liquid and she swallowed it down as quickly as possible. Seth's cries became loud and prolonged as he suc-cumbed to the pleasures she was giving him. Being a vampire, Seth had no sperm to ejaculate, so when he reached his orgasm, crying-out in almost deaf-ening moans, his body stiff with rapture, he released a waterfall of clear wet-ness into her mouth.

Nia held his penis in her mouth until she could no longer feel liquid flowing from it and felt it begin to soften. She gently removed it from her mouth, and then softly kissed the head, after which, she sat-up, put her arms around Seth's neck and held him tightly. Seth wrapped his arms around her naked torso, pressing her large breasts against his bare chest.

"I love you, Nia," he said in an emotional whisper. But, he suddenly realized that after all this time, he had never said those words to her. He did not under-stand why, he had surely loved her from the very beginning.

"I love you, too, Seth," Nia replied overjoyed by his words. She was well aware that of all the beautiful things he had said to her over these months, he had never told her he loved her. Nor had she said those words to him. Each had just assumed they were in love with each other and that no words needed to be said. And, indeed, that was true. Yet, it was more than wonderful for both to hear the words finally spoken between them.

Gabriel stood in the dark of his unlighted bedroom looking out of the win-dow. He thought he had heard something or someone moving about in the garden. It was nearly 1:00 am, but he had only come in a short while ago, hav-ing had a sexual encounter with Adrianna at her hotel. As he watched the garden area, he saw what seemed to be the form of a man stirring about amongst the shrubs. It was a dark night and he could only see shadows, however, yes, it was a man. Who the hell is that?, he thought. Is my rifle loaded? But, before he could leave the window to check his gun, the shadow seemed to take flight, quickly spiriting over the tops of the trees. He heard the familiar howling sound of the wind and realized that this, whatever it was, must be the source of the sound. He had seen that shadow before and had thought it to be only an extraordinarily large bird. But, now…he was sure that there was the figure of a man in the garden. Still, from where did the large creature come that had flown into the air? To where did the man disappear? He did not see the man leave. Was he killed by the creature? Gabriel's mind became troubled and confused. But, his heart began to race as he pondered an unspeakable question…Could the man and the creature somehow be one and the same?

Later that morning the day began as usual. Seth and Nia awakened around 10:00 a.m. and immediately proceeded into a very passionate lovemaking experience, both of them practically being sex addicts. Should they happen to end their relationship, each would be hard pressed to find another with the same insatiable sexual appetite. When they finished their lovemaking, they took a shower together, where each washed the other's body, then each dried the other's body with a soft, fluffy towel. The drying exercise was so arousing that Seth was now ready to take Nia to bed again. Nia was also turned-on and obliged him. Seth sensuously asked if he could shave Nia's pubic hair. It sounded exciting to her, so she said it was all right. She laid on the bed naked, her thighs spread far apart. Seth took a battery-operated razor and shaved every pubic hair even remotely visible, occasionally massaging her clitoris with his fingers, causing Nia's large nipples to harden and her juices to flow.

When he finished shaving her, he took a miniature, feathered, duster-like brush and delicately brushed away the shaven hairs from between her thighs. Nia began to squirm and cry-out in pleasure as the soft, gentle feathers stimulated her clitoris. The brush was a sexual tool that they had used previously and was a favorite of Nia's. After removing all of the hairs from her genital area and from the bed, Seth took the tiniest amount of petroleum jelly and massaged it into all of the freshly shaven skin, leaving her pubic area as smooth and as soft as a newborn baby girl. Then, he buried his face between her legs, slipping her now protruding, large, chocolate clitoris into his mouth. Their second sexual session of the morning had begun.

It was after 1:00 p.m. when Seth and Nia finally descended the staircase to the downstairs. When they reached the bottom, each went in a different direction. Seth headed for the library and Nia headed for the kitchen, her newly shaved genitals still tingling from Seth's tongue. Once she joined him in the library, she would entice him into licking her some more, she thought. Upon entering the kitchen, she found Gabriel hard at work cleaning the kitchen windows.

"Good afternoon, Gabriel," Nia said with a kind smile.

"Good day, Madame," he answered somewhat nervously. He was a bit rattled from the events of the earlier part of the morning. He did not pursue any additional conversation. Nia thought his silence odd for him, but figured that everyone had a bad day now and then. She had a glass of orange juice and grabbed a pastry to take with her to the library. She was anxious to have more sex with Seth.

As Seth sat down in the library, in his usual chair, he noticed a long box setting on the large French antique desk by the window. He rose from his chair to examine it. The box looked like one of those in which florists send flowers. There was an envelope attached, Seth opened it and read the contents:

Nia,

It was magic being close to you last night. I care for you in the deepest way. I cannot convey the depth of my feelings in mere words. You have not left my thoughts since our first meeting. I need to see you alone again. I dream of us being together someday and....

Seth could read no more of the letter. It was, of course, signed Jeremiah. The man's disrespect of Seth's 'marriage' to Nia infuriated him. He replaced the letter and left the whole package on the desk for Nia, then returned to his seat. As soon as Nia entered the room, she noticed the box on the desk, women are observant that way. She walked towards it looking at Seth. "What's this?" she asked with a smile assuming it was a gift from Seth.

"Seems you had an early morning delivery," Seth replied coolly.

Nia opened the attached envelope and her smile disappeared as she read the contents of the letter. "Why won't this man leave me alone? Have you read this, Seth?" she asked looking over at him.

"Yes, I've read it. I guess the man feels he's in love with you," Seth answered.

"I can assure you that I've given him no reason to believe I want him. In fact, I've made it quite clear that I only want you," Nia explained, frustrated at Jeremiah's persistence and arrogance.

"I'm sure he will get the message soon. Just try to avoid him," Seth advised, but, he knew that Jeremiah had just sealed his own fate. He would be Seth's first feed tonight, and so the problem would be ended.

Nia gathered the box, envelope, and letter together. She did not even bother to open the box. "I'll go throw all of this into the outside trash bin right now and be rid of it," she said as she started out of the library door.

"All right, Dear," Seth answered softly.

Soon after Nia left the room, in the quiet of the library, Seth's supernatural hearing detected a telephone conversation. It was Gabriel talking to another man about the sights he had seen that morning. He was asking the man for help to investigate what he had seen. The man agreed to help Gabriel and to bring others in on the investigation as well. This could not be allowed, Seth thought. According to what he had described, Gabriel had seen way too much and must be eliminated. Seth would take care of Gabriel before he left for his rendezvous with Jeremiah. How he hated problems. He did not like this kind of killing, but eliminating Gabriel was as much a part of his survival as the requirement of blood.

As for Jeremiah, Seth needed Nia in order to survive, he could not live without her, so Jeremiah's obsession to have her was indeed a threat to his survival. Had Nia wanted to go with Jeremiah, he would not have stopped her, but, since she did not, Jeremiah's open affections were most provoking. Afterall, he had heard Nia tell Jeremiah at the club to leave her alone. But, Seth still had that fear that Nia might leave one day with a human, so why take the chance that one day Jeremiah might win. Yes, Jeremiah had deliberately made an enemy of himself by trying to take away what he thought was Seth's wife. It was Seth's duty to protect Nia from his unwanted advances and to protect himself from destruction as the result of losing her. In the case of Jeremiah, he knew his logic was somewhat twisted and pretty much self-serving, but, his conscience could manage to live with it.

That night Gabriel sat in the dark kitchen of the chateau. He was awaiting a phone call from the man he had spoken with earlier. Since there was no phone hook-up in Gabriel's cottage, he had to make and receive all of his phone calls at the chateau. He wished the man would hurry and call, because he knew the howl would be heard in a few hours and he wanted the man to be there to hear it, and, possibly see the creature. He decided to light a cigarette to soothe his nerves. As he lighted the match, he was startled by the figure of a man standing in the doorway to the hall. Within a second or two he was able to determine that the figure was Monsieur Bjorn. "Oh, good evening Monsieur. You put a start into me for a moment. Is there something I may get for you?" he asked with a smile as he rose from his chair.

"No...thank you. I can get it myself," Seth responded as he walked passed Gabriel. Once he was behind Gabriel, Seth quickly turned and grabbed him by the back of his head and shoulder. Gabriel, though stunned by Seth's actions, attempted to struggle, but in an instant, Seth's knife-sharp vampire teeth sank deep into Gabriel's neck. In another instant, Gabriel's body went limp. His blood was drained until, finally, the life which once existed, existed no more; its spirit now in the hands of its creator. Seth lifted Gabriel's lifeless body and carried it to the farthest end of the most distant garden that surrounded the chateau, then neatly buried it. He then took flight, enroute to his next and final prey of the night, Jeremiah.

Seth entered the club where he and Nia had run into Jeremiah. He searched the club but saw no sign of Jeremiah. Though he did not want to arouse suspicion about himself, he decided to ask the bartender for information about Jeremiah. Immediately upon approaching the bar, the bartender came to serve him. "What would you like, Monsieur?" he asked in a jovial manner.

"Ah, some information, if you would be so kind," Seth replied in a whisper. The bartender looked at him cautiously, as he waited to see what information Seth wanted. "Do you know a man by the name of Jeremiah Girroit?" Seth asked softly.

"Jeremiah, sure I know him," the bartender replied reluctantly.

"Do you know where he lives?" Seth continued.

The bartender looked at Seth for a moment then replied, "Well, if he were living at a private residence, I wouldn't tell you this, but since he isn't, I will. He is staying at the hotel down the street from here called Le Fleur," the bartender said.

Seth smiled at him and then took-out a handful of money from which he pulled a $100 bill and handed it to the bartender. "You won't tell anyone about this conversation will you?" Seth warned.

"What conversation?" the bartender remarked as he grabbed the money and stuffed it in his pocket, then walked towards the other side of the bar counter.

Seth entered the lobby of the hotel Le Fleur and walked straight to the front desk. A kindly looking older gentleman approached to greet Seth. "Good evening, Monsieur. Do you wish a room?" the older gentleman asked politely.

"Good evening, Sir. No, I don't want a room. I would like to know if one of your guests by the name of Jeremiah Girroit is in his room," Seth advised him.

"I will call and see, who shall I say is here?" the man questioned.

"This is a surprise. I don't want him to know that I'm here. Please just say you made a mistake if he answers. I will wait outside to surprise him. I'm sure he will be going out soon," Seth replied innocently.

The older man nodded and rang Jeremiah's room. "The line is busy, Monsieur, so I would say he was in the room," the man said as he placed the phone back on its base.

"That's fine. Thank you very much. Remember, please do not mention I was here if you see him," Seth reminded him. The man grinned and shook his head in the affirmative.

Seth left the hotel and walked across the street and stood in the dark doorway of a closed shop. He would wait for Jeremiah to exit the hotel. Since Jeremiah was a young, energetic man, Seth knew he would not stay in all night. Once Jeremiah exited the building, Seth, would follow him and await an opportunity to attack.

Jeremiah was on the telephone with one of his comrades. Jeremiah belonged to a secret organization known to those with need to know as the Archangel Clan. His comrades had just arrived in town and had called to advise Jeremiah of a 'situation' in Nimes that needed to be investigated. They wanted his help and Jeremiah agreed to help them. They decided to meet in the alley behind his hotel in 5 minutes. Jeremiah grabbed a jacket and quickly walked to the elevator where he rode to the lobby and exited the front door of the hotel. Seth jumped into action as he saw Jeremiah leave the hotel. Seth had planned to see in what direction Jeremiah headed and then keep a safe distance away until his opportunity presented itself. But, to his surprise, Jeremiah immediately darted down the alleyway beside the hotel. Seth quickly crossed the moderately busy street and silently made his way down the alley in search of Jeremiah. As he came to the end of the building, he began to hear the voices of several men.

He stopped just short of the back of the building and peeked around the edge of the wall to the alley behind the building. There was a dim light shining from the light fixture at the back kitchen door of the hotel. Within that lighting, Seth could see the figures of 3 men, including Jeremiah. Seth stood silently out of sight and listened to the conversation of the mystery group. "So, here's the situation. We received a call from a man by the name of Gabriel who said he was the caretaker at one of the expensive chateaus around here. Apparently, he had been witness to some rather strange sights and noises around the chateau and with the mysterious murders to the north, was becoming quite alarmed and wanted us to look into things for him," one man explained.

"I see," Jeremiah answered surprised that he had not gotten wind of anything before now.

"We attempted to call him as soon as we arrived because we told him we would. But, a woman answered the phone and said she did not know where he was and to try later. Perhaps something has happened to him or perhaps he simply wasn't around, but we need to go check-out the place as soon as possible," the second man advised.

"Which chateau is it?" Jeremiah asked.

"Maybe you know it. Chateau de Lumine, at the edge of the Nimes border," the first man said.

Jeremiah could not conceive of it. The chateau where Nia lived? "Are you sure about the location?" Jeremiah inquired uneasily.

"Yes, we're sure. Why? Is there a problem?" the first man inquired puzzled about Jeremiah's reaction.

"I know the people who live there. I find it difficult to believe anything of substance is wrong at that chateau," Jeremiah replied worried about Nia's safety.

"Well, from what we've been told, there's the great possibility that the owner of the chateau is a vampire and the one responsible for the murders to the north. The caretaker seemed to feel that the unusual activity centered around the library area of the chateau. The owner's name is Seth Bjorn, isn't that right?" the second man said.

"Yes, that's the name," Jeremiah answered solemnly.

"What about the woman?" the first man asked.

"She's not a vampire. I've seen her in town during the day," Jeremiah answered, but now he could see that his intuition regarding her traveling alone most of the time was correct. In daylight, Seth could not possibly accompany her anywhere, he would be destroyed.

"She has to know what he is, though, and accepts it. Which makes her no better than the vampire himself," the second man said without emotion.

"Perhaps she's just in love," Jeremiah said in Nia's defense.

"Nice woman to love such a fiend," the first man replied.

Jeremiah did not understand why Nia would remain with Seth either, unless it was against her will. But, he did not really believe that to be the case. Her presence with him was indeed mind-boggling. Yet, the situation gave him hope that he might still have her in the end. Seth left them there to finish their discussion. He had heard all he needed; he knew who they were and the danger in which he now found himself. He would go feed once more then return to the chateau to inform Nia that they must flee the area tomorrow and thoroughly explain to her why.

Seth hurried up the staircase to the bedroom where Nia awaited him. As he entered, Nia could see something was wrong. "What's the matter, Seth?" she asked fearfully.

"Nia, we must leave the country tomorrow night, please make the arrangements first thing in the morning," he said frantically.

"Leave the country, why?" she questioned even more frightened than at first.

"I had to kill Gabriel. He was notifying some people to come here and investigate what he thought were strange happenings at the chateau," Seth explained as he avoided her eyes.

"A man called here for him. Was he already dead then?" Nia asked highly disturbed.

"Yes, Dear, he was, but now, the men he contacted have all but figured-out that I am a vampire and they will be coming to destroy me," Seth informed her unhappily.

"How do you know they will still come, Seth? They can no longer contact Gabriel, maybe they will just go away," Nia answered.

"No, I know them. They're professionals. They belong to a group known as the Archangel Clan. They have been the ancestral enemies of all vampires since the beginning of vampire existence. Generation after generation, individuals are inducted into their army and trained. Then, they travel the world seeking out and destroying vampires. Now that they think they have my scent, there will be no letting go. They will come after me and destroy me unless I can prove to them that I am not a vampire, and, of course, there is no hope of that happening. Also, as fate would have it, Jeremiah is one of them," Seth explained.

Nia was in shock. She had never dreamed that an organization such as the Archangel Clan existed. The fact that Jeremiah was a member of it became a double shock. She had put Seth in danger of discovery without any idea of what she might have done. He had always warned her about associations with strangers, now she understood why. Yes, it was clear, they must leave immediately. Within moments, they began packing things in the effort to avoid undesired hold-ups the next day. The morning brought a period of hustle and bustle around the chateau. They finished packing and Nia dragged everything out to the car. She arranged for them to take an 8:30 p.m. flight to London that night, soon their ordeal would be over for the present.

As the sun set, Seth thought he had better have at least one feeding before the flight. He would not want to be pressured by his hunger to feed on a passenger or possibly become ill on the plane. He left assuring Nia he would return by 7:15 p.m., giving them plenty of time to catch their flight. There had been no sign of the strangers yet, so he thought it would be safe for the both of them if he took this last outing. Since he was leaving Nimes anyway, he saw no need to travel north for his prey. Instead, he went to the outskirts of town and waited in the shadows of a building for his feed. He found a victim almost immediately and he quickly drank his fill, leaving the body where it was rather than wasting time burying it. In a few minutes, he was again in the air on his way back to the chateau.

He arrived at the outside double doors of the library around 7:00 p.m. and immediately walked through them, into the dark silent library room. His supernatural hearing soon detected breathing coming from a corner of the room on his right side. He knew someone was there and within a few seconds he found out who had invaded his home. The man stepped out of the darkness and into the moonlight that shone brightly through the latticed library doors. It was Jeremiah.

"So, you've come afterall," Seth spoke first.

"I'm sure you knew someone would come, Seth," Jeremiah replied in a cold, business-like manner.

"Yes, I've always assumed I would be 'found-out' now and then by others, but I've also always assumed that I would ultimately escape," Seth said undisturbed by Jeremiah's presence. Seth's only concern at the time was Nia's safety.

They watched each other for a moment, each pondering his next move, each realizing that an error in judgment could be fatal. Yet, despite the fact that Jeremiah belonged to a group that was his mortal enemy, Seth had no wish to kill him. He knew he could escape without doing so. Killing that was not required for feeding purposes was always most distasteful to him. He had already reached his fill of it for the night after having killed Gabriel. So…in an instant, with lightening speed, Seth grabbed Jeremiah around the neck, almost snapping it in two, and threw Jeremiah with tremendous force across the room, knocking over a lamp and several vases.

Jeremiah, dazed and in pain from several broken bones, tried to get up from the floor, but could not do so.

In a few moments, Nia came rushing into the library, having heard the breaking sounds. She immediately turned on the library light and saw Seth standing in the middle of the room and Jeremiah lying injured and bleeding in a corner of the room. "Seth, are you all right!" she exclaimed, not concerned about Jeremiah at all.

"I'm fine, Nia. Just get your things and go to the car, Love," Seth replied affectionately. But, just as he completed those words, Jeremiah pulled-out a gun and pointed it at Seth.

Nia screamed out at Jeremiah, "Please, don't kill him! He isn't what you think! He's a kind and gentle man!"

"He's a monster! God willing this silver bullet will rid the world of him once and for all...and send him back to hell where he belongs!" Jeremiah yelled back angrily, then quickly pulled the trigger.

As the silver bullet streaked towards Seth, Nia screamed and jumped in front of him, shielding his body, but receiving the bullet in her own chest. She did not know that Seth's centuries of having been a vampire had afforded him the powers of a Master vampire. Silver bullets could no longer harm him. Seth cried out, "No!" then caught her as she began to sink to the floor. He laid her down gently on the carpet, his heart in anguish at her sacrifice. Jeremiah watched in horror for he never intended to hurt Nia, he loved her. And, by Clan laws, humans were never to be killed by the Clan in the pursuit of vampires. Seth let loose a tremendous roar, then his supernatural speed allowed him to rush to Jeremiah's side and rip Jeremiah's throat to threads before another bullet could be fired. He left the pale Archangel on the floor dead, the blood still gushing from his mutilated throat.

Seth returned to Nia and kneeled by her side. Then, finding her still alive, took both of her hands in his hands. "Nia, Nia. Please, open your eyes for me," he said softly, trying to hold back his tears, anxiously awaiting a response. He watched the spot of blood on her blouse become larger and larger as her life drained from her body.

Nia slowly opened her eyes and upon seeing her handsome Seth, smiled, then whispered weakly, "I'm dying, Seth."

"No, Dear. Don't say that, I will take you to help. You must fight," Seth pleaded desperately, his tears now overflowing and dripping down his face.

"I can't fight...I haven't the strength," she answered weakly. She grimaced several times in great pain. But, as tears began to flow from her eyes and her breathing became exceedingly difficult, signaling the inevitable arrival of death, she struggled to utter. "I cannot bear to leave you, Seth."

"Then don't," Seth begged softly as tears continued to trickle down his face and he continued to fondle her hands.

Gripping his hands as tightly as she could she implored, "God, please forgive this...Seth, make me what you are."

"Nia!" Seth exclaimed in disbelief, "Think about what you're asking. You know the full depth of the existence I must endure. Are you sure it is what you want? It shall be for now and all time," Seth warned with great love in his immortal soul.

"Yes, it is what I want," Nia whispered, her breathing very shallow, her voice hardly audible. "Do it now. Hurry."

Seth's heart filled with happiness. Deep inside, he had always wanted her to become one of his kind. The night he first saw her he had desired such. Yet, he still wished there was another way they might always be together, however, there was not. Seth helped Nia sit-up and held her around her back with one arm. Then, he quickly slit his wrist with his teeth causing a free flow of rich, red blood from the large artery just above his palm. He placed his bloodied wrist against her soft warm lips. "Drink, My Beloved," he said with immeasurable affection and in extreme anticipation of what was to come. She anxiously opened her mouth and gently drank of him. He held her more tightly as her sucking soon caused the fires of orgasm to flash through the both of them. They both began to moan loudly as her mouth engulfed more and more of his wrist and her tongue began to dig into his wound, opening the skin wider and increasing the flow of blood. With renewed strength, Nia grabbed Seth's arm with both hands and proceeded to erotically suck at his wrist, feverishly swallowing his stream of warm and sensuous blood. As they sat huddled together on the floor, the continuing orgasmic exchange of blood caused in each an ecstasy so intense, no human could even imagine it. And, during those few minutes of supernatural passion, they both rejoiced in the knowledge, that because of the love they shared, such rapture was theirs for the taking...until the end of time.

The exchange of blood ended
The transformation began
She died

Then was reborn
Into darkness

Chapter 7

On the run from the Archangel Clan, and despite their encounter with Jeremiah, Seth and Nia made their scheduled flight that night to London. As Nia sat on the plane by the window in their first class seats, she was experiencing a world of wonder. She attempted to begin to function within her newly acquired status as a vampire. Her vision seemed exceedingly strange. Colors all seemed a little 'off' and the lights inside the plane seemed to burn her eyes a bit. As she looked out of the window, she noticed that things at a distance were closer and clearer than they would have been before her transformation. It was almost like looking through binoculars now. She could see farther and with greater sharpness than ever in her lifetime. She began to notice that she was hearing excerpts of multiple conversations, all of the words as audible as if the people were sitting right next to her; though many of the conversations were obviously being spoken in the coach area of the airplane. Amazing, she thought. All she needed to do was to concentrate on one conversation and she would be able to hear every word. She wondered if Seth had the same ability. He had never mentioned it. Suddenly, without any warning, she felt extremely tired. She gently leaned her head against Seth's shoulder, then quickly fell into a deep sleep.

Seth sat with his arm around Nia's shoulders, holding her close to him. It had been a long time since he had experienced his 'awakening'; but he still remembered the psychological battle that was fought between the human that he used to be and the non-human that he ultimately became. Matilda, the one who 'made' him, was not particularly nurturing towards him during his period of adjustment. Though she loved him dearly, the nurturing instinct was just not a part of her personality, human or vampire. Seth was determined not to let Nia adjust in the manner that he had to do it. He would help her in all ways possible for as long as she needed him. It was going to be a very difficult and painful transition period. The physical transformation, though akin to a painful death, was always the easiest part, it occurred automatically and practically all at once. But, learning to live the life of a vampire was literally an attempt to journey from a life being lived in heaven to a life being lived in hell. Not every 'transformed' human had successfully won that battle, Seth himself was almost a casualty. In any event, despite the fact that he was now thoroughly absorbed with Nia and her pending destiny, Seth was still able to sense an un-nerving, dangerous 'presence' in the air. It was like nothing he had ever sensed before and was in very close proximity to him at the moment. It unexpectedly frightened him.

They arrived at the London airport only hours before dawn due to several 'round-about' stops. Nia was somewhat alert now, but still considerably tired. Seth assured her that the transformation was progressing as expected. Her body was recuperating from its own demise. And, coming back from the dead could take a lot out of anyone. Then, he unhappily realized that sometime that evening she would have to make her first 'kill'. Her need for blood would be so strong by that time, he hoped she would willingly do what she must, but, he would not count on it. He considered weaning her along by supplying blood to her either from himself or another source, but he felt it was probably not wise to prolong the inevitable. He remembered how relieved he was once his first 'kill' was done. And, though he still encountered moral dilemmas for a period of time, once he had made that first 'kill', his fear of the 'killing process' quickly dissipated.

Seth engaged a skycap to retrieve their baggage, then he and Nia walked over to the car rental booth where they secured the car that Nia had previously reserved. The valet brought the car to the front doorway of the terminal and the skycap loaded the luggage into the back seat and into the trunk. Then, Nia and Seth were on their way, racing the dawn, enroute to the estate of Seth's boyhood. The place where Matilda first saw him, set her sites upon him, and forced him into the life of darkness.

A pair of unfamiliar eyes watched with great interest, observing every move that Seth and Nia made. They were the same eyes that had watched them throughout their entire flight. The same eyes that were the source of the un-nerving 'presence' that Seth had detected. And, indeed, he was unmistakably correct, these eyes were both highly dangerous and very close.

At about 45 minutes before dawn, Seth drove through the gray stone arch and large black iron gates that marked the entrance to the Bjorn Estate. He traveled as quickly as possible down the winding road. The sun would soon be rising and the mansion itself was still almost 2 miles away. As he drove along the road, Seth began to feel a veil of despair fall over him as he started to remember his boyhood on the estate. His despair turned into a full blown depression as he remembered the life he used to have there and all that he had ultimately lost. Of course, such emotions might develop in anyone who was returning to the scene of so horrific a personal tragedy. And now, in a painful depression, he wished he had chosen another place as their retreat from the Archangel Clan, but, there was nothing to be done about it at the moment.

Nia sat curled in a ball, the side of her head pressed against the car door window. She was in a sound and deep sleep as Seth finally arrived at the front door of the mansion. He was forced to give Nia several firm shakes before she eventually awakened. "Nia, hurry and get out of the car. We must get inside quickly, the sun will be rising in only a few minutes," Seth implored nervously. Being acutely aware of the ramifications of the situation, Nia hurried to exit the car. As she stepped-out onto the gray cobblestone driveway, Seth rushed from around the other side of the car and grabbed her hand, not even giving her time to close the car door. He pulled her quickly to the front double doors of the mansion.

"We'll deal with the luggage later. We don't have time now," Seth stated hastily. He quickly unlocked the front door and at last they were finally inside and safe. Luckily, the caretaker had not yet opened the draperies from the night. Their rushed departure from France had not allowed time to alert the caretaker of their arrival, so Seth would have to leave him a note with instructions as to the draperies and several other things. Though, Seth had not returned to the estate since shortly after his transformation, he would not allow the mansion to fall into disarray. He was always careful to maintain the taxes and always careful to employ the finest of caretakers.

Even though the mansion was dark inside, Nia could still see that it was every bit as beautiful as the other homes they had inhabited. There was a long winding staircase and a huge chandelier that shimmered even in the shadows of the cathedral-ceiling foyer. Seth put his arm around Nia's shoulder and she put her arm around his waist, they then slowly ascended the staircase together. Upon reaching the top, Seth guided Nia to make a left turn. As they proceeded down the hallway, Nia could see the outlines of gold colored picture frames that lined both sides of the long hallway. At the very end of the hallway, they faced a pair of gold-colored double doors, this was the Master Suite. Seth opened the doors and stepped inside by himself. "Wait a moment, while I get some light," he whispered. Seth had instructed one of the caretakers about a century ago to have the mansion wired for electricity. So, he ran his hand along the wall in search of a light switch. He found one and immediately flicked the switch. The lamp on each of the nightstands located beside each side of the bed came on, providing a soft yellow glow to the room.

After settling Nia into the room and literally tucking her into bed (another attack of extreme fatigue had overcome her) Seth proceeded downstairs to write the note of instructions for the caretaker. When he was almost at the bottom of the staircase, he saw the figure of a woman standing in a corner of the hallway. He knew the caretaker was not married nor had any children. Perhaps he had a woman friend who lived with him or had at least spent the night. He decided he would merely greet her pleasantly and inquire as to her status at his home. Once he reached the bottom of the staircase, he found she had disappeared. What the devil?, he thought, where could she have gone? There was no exit anywhere near the area in which she had been standing. The closest one was right in front of him and he knew she did not pass through it. The occurrence troubled him, there was no logical explanation for the happening and he did not like that at all. He turned on the light in the library and walked over to the huge King Henry-antique styled desk. He bent down, leaned on the desk with one elbow, and began to write his instructions. When he finished, he turned-off the library light and set the note upright on the main table of the foyer, then began his return to the Master Suite.

As he walked down the dark hallway, he began to feel puffs of warm air entering his right ear. It almost felt like someone was blowing in his ear. It sent chills through his body and began to sexually arouse him in the same manner as when Nia would blow in his ear. The difference was, though, that the genesis of this stimulation was unknown, thus disturbing. Then, just as he reached the gold doors to the suite, Seth felt a wetness on that same ear. If he had not known any better, he would have sworn that someone had just licked the inside of his ear. Though it definitely felt good, once again, it was a disturbing development. He quickly turned around as he felt something gently stroke the back of his head, but found there was nothing to be seen. However, for one brief moment, he again sensed that extraordinary, dangerous 'presence' which had so frightened him at the airport that day.

Seth entered the room and found Nia still deep in sleep. He hastily undressed and climbed into bed with her. As usual, he pulled her close and wrapped his arms around her lovingly. He was leery about falling asleep himself. He now suspected that whatever the entity at the airport was, it had followed them. It was, at the present, a co-inhabitor of the mansion, its origin and purpose unknown. Later that day, Seth awakened and turned to check on Nia. She was already awake and looking at him. They smiled at each other as their eyes met. Seth leaned over and pressed his lips against Nia's lips and then slid his tongue into her mouth. She began to maneuver her tongue so that it would intermingle with his, as she lifted her left arm and hugged him around the neck, then moved her right arm down and took hold of his large, partially hard penis with her hand. She began to massage his penis forcefully as she slid her hand up and down the shaft, causing Seth's tongue to move more erratically and more forcefully in her mouth and his breathing to become more impassioned.

This was her first lovemaking experience as a vampire and she could definitely tell the difference. Her whole body was more sensitive to stimulation than ever before and she had already had several orgasms. Seth threw back the blanket and sheet that covered the top half of Nia's body. She was already naked, so her large breasts and now engorged chocolate nipples were totally exposed. Seth ran his tongue down her neck and down her left breast until he reached her enlarged nipple. He engulfed it and had begun to fervently suck at it, when he heard the soft moan of what sounded like a woman. It was not Nia; he knew her sounds well. No, this was someone else or something else. He immediately stopped what he was doing and covered Nia's breasts with the sheet. He rolled over to her side of the bed and sat-up on the edge of the bed. He made sure the bed sheet covered his genital area as well.

"What's the matter, Seth?" Nia asked with great concern. "Have I done something wrong? Now that I'm a vampire is there something more I must do to please you?"

Seth turned to answer her, but when he saw she was sitting-up in bed with her breasts exposed, made a comment about it (of course such exposure was never a problem in the past). "Cover yourself, Nia. Why are you sitting around with your body unclothed?" he expressed gruffly.

"What are you talking about? I've been 'unclothed' around you millions of times. Why all of a sudden must I cover myself?" she queried with puzzlement.

"Because I said so!" Seth snapped back. He wished he could tell her the reason for his attitude, but he did not know what he could say. He actually knew nothing concrete and he did not care to frighten her for no reason. It might all be in his head.

Nia knew something unusual was occurring, that was not her Seth. "What's happening, Seth? Please…what's wrong?" Nia asked calmly.

Seth was sorry he had spoken to her in such a manner the moment the words had left his mouth. He leaned back on the bed and supported himself with his right elbow, the bottom part of his long blond hair laid gracefully on the bed. He looked over at her, he could see the unnecessary anguish he had put on her face. "Forgive me, Dearest, I didn't mean to alarm you. I think perhaps the strain of returning to this place has begun to take a toll on my mind. Don't worry. I'll be all right," he said softly. He reached over with his left hand

and grabbed her right hand. Then, pulled it to his lips and gently kissed her palm twice. She caressed his face with the same hand and slid her thumb back and forth across his lips several times. "I forgive you," she whispered with a anxious smile.

They only ventured downstairs once that day at which time they did run across and introduce themselves to the caretaker. He was Mortimer Neville, a middle-aged man from a lower-class area of London. Mortimer had a stroke of luck as a boy when he met a rich gentleman in a London park who took a liking to him. The gentleman offered Mortimer a job working on his estate in the country. As Mortimer would not attend school, his parents were more than happy to give their permission for him to go. It would be an excellent training opportunity for the boy, and also, one less mouth for them to feed. He learned quickly and he learned well and eventually earned the reputation as the best estate caretaker in the area.

Back in their suite, the hunger that Nia had been experiencing since she first awakened that afternoon was felt ten-fold, now that it was sundown. She knew she needed blood. Nia had seen Seth go through such pain a number of times when his need for blood was not yet satisfied. "Seth, the pain is becoming unbearable. Please help me," she pleaded.

"Yes, Nia, we'll be leaving in a few moments. The sun must be completely down before we go out," Seth replied empathetically; he knew all too well what pain she felt. "Do you think you'll be able to do that which you need to do in order to relieve your pain?"

"I don't know. Will you be able to help me?" she questioned meekly.

"Not really. You must be able to attack and secure your own prey. You have more physical strength than any human now. You will be able to easily overpower any human you encounter, so don't concern yourself about that part. Perhaps, you can start with a child and..."

"No! No! Not a child! Never a child!" Nia interrupted horrified at the suggestion.

"All right. All right. Calm down," Seth consoled. "Maybe a woman or a small man then?" he asked in a compromising tone.

"A small man," she replied quietly, now a little less apprehensive.

"Fine. So that's settled. I believe it safe for us to leave now. Shall we go?" Seth said as he extended his arm for her to hold. Nia reluctantly took his arm, she needed blood, but she dreaded what she must do to get it.

They walked downstairs and out to the car. Seth decided they would drive the car to town and park just at the edge of the area, in an unobservable place.

Then, they would fly east to find their meal for the night. Though Mortimer lived in a room beneath the kitchen, Seth had uncovered enough of his background to be certain that Mortimer was a professional. Seth felt Mortimer knew, that except for an urgent task, to remain in his room during evening hours, when the owner occupied the dwelling. Seth did not anticipate experiencing the problem he had with Gabriel again with Mortimer.

As they drove towards town, Nia felt herself becoming more and more nervous. She hoped she would not mangle her victim, she hoped she would be able to perform a fast and clean 'kill'. She was surprised at how easily she was able to distance herself from the emotions of taking a life, at least the life of a grown man. But, Seth had once told her that the lack of emotion towards ending a life was a natural part of the transformation process and not really a reflection on the person's sense of humanity. So, maybe some day even the life of a child would not matter to her, but, not right now. He had also told her that some of the 'transformed' succumbed to the 'awakening' more easily than others. Seth, for instance, had a difficult adjustment to accepting the 'distancing' element. Perhaps, the degree to which one fought the entire process was the reason for the difference in the ability to 'distance'. Afterall, Seth never wanted to be a vampire, Nia requested it.

They reached the edge of town and Seth parked the car in a small clearing amongst the woods that surrounded the town. He took Nia's hand once they had exited the car. "All right, Love, concentrate on lifting yourself and flying above the tree tops," he said instructively. Nia concentrated as hard as she thought she could, but nothing happened. Seth floated upward and hovered just in front of her still holding her hand. "Concentrate harder, Nia. Demand that your body do what you want it to do," Seth prompted sternly. Nia did as he asked, repeatedly whispering to herself to 'rise'. After intense concentration and several commands to herself, she suddenly felt her feet leave the ground. Seth gave her arm a tug and before she knew it, she was looking at Seth's smiling face, both of them at least 7 feet off of the ground. "It will get easier," Seth said reassuringly. He gave her a gentle kiss on the lips in mid-air. Then, they flew-off over the tree tops headed east.

The act of flight was truly glorious, Nia thought. The lights from the towns below as they flew over several, before invading the target town, were enchanting. Together with the canopy of stars and the moon, her virgin flight made for an incomparable view of the countryside even in the moonlight. And, the sense of freedom was amazing. They glided through the night, hand in hand, warm streams of wind blowing against their handsome faces. In what seemed like only a few minutes, Seth and Nia had reached their destination that was slightly more than five miles east from where they had parked the car. They landed at the edge of the small town and found themselves in much luck. There was a carnival being held and there were people straying everywhere, some alone, some in groups or couples. But, of course, Seth was seeking a lone stray, a small man located away from the crowd upon whom Nia could perform her 'kill'. First, though, they strolled through the carnival and looked at some of the sights. They played a few games and Seth even won an enormous teddy bear for Nia. But, her hunger was becoming excruciating, so they had to proceed with the main objective of the evening.

Seth caught sight of an older man who was walking along a path that seemed to lead directly into the woods. "Nia," he said softly, "Do you think you could handle the man walking by himself over there on that pathway?"

Nia quickly turned to look at the man. "Yes, I think so," she answered quietly.

"O.K., let's follow him," Seth said relieved that she had consented to his first choice of victim. He was afraid that she might reject numerous persons in an attempt to avoid that which she needed to do. He was proud that she had accepted her task willingly and without resistance. But then, he knew from the very beginning that she was an exceptional woman. It was the recognition of that superiority which was partially responsible for him being drawn to her in the first place, the other part, of course, was her extraordinary beauty.

Seth and Nia followed parallel to the man as they walked hidden from him amongst the dark shadows of the trees. It appeared that the pathway either went very deeply into the woods or straight through to the other side where there was a clearing and houses. Perhaps the man lived in one of those houses and this was his shortcut home. At any rate, he was the only person in view on the path at the moment, the perfect time for Nia to attack. "Just come-up from behind him," Seth advised. "That way you will not have to see his face and it will be easier for you. Your ability to move quickly has now increased enormously and you will be able to grab him and sink your teeth into him before he even hears you. He will not even know what happened before he dies."

Nia heeded Seth's words. She gathered her nerves. She swiftly exited the trees and positioned herself behind the lone man, grabbing him around the shoulders with both hands at the same time. Seth was right, it was better from the back, and, the man had not heard her approach. She felt a rush of excitement ebb out of her body as she plunged her two newly elongated canine teeth deep into the side of the man's neck. The blood immediately began to squirt out of the two neat puncture holes surrounding her teeth. She pressed her lips firmly against his skin, ensuring that she would receive each drop of delicious, invigorating blood. As she sucked her victim's neck, she felt his warm, wet blood gush into her mouth and pour down her throat. A rush of passion overcame her body providing a pleasurable feeling akin to that of a sexual orgasm. The feeling prompted her to drink with more and more fury, practically sucking the skin off of the neck of her prey.

After a few minutes, the man let-out one loud moan. Seth, who had been monitoring Nia's actions, immediately came to her side upon hearing the moan and abruptly pulled her head away from the man's neck. Nia looked at Seth with annoyance and disappointment in her face. "Nia," Seth said as he gently wiped a few drops of blood away from her mouth with his fingers, "You must cease drinking quickly once you hear that moan. It is the signal that your prey is about to die. You must not drink the blood of the dead, it will destroy you." Nia nodded in understanding. Seth took the body of the man from Nia's arms and carried it back amongst the trees. Nia followed him. He buried the body beneath a large pile of leaves. "How do you feel? Are you free of pain now?" Seth asked.

"I'm good, Seth. My hunger is satisfied, the pain is gone," Nia replied softly.

"All right, wait here until I feed, then we'll return home. I won't be long," Seth said then walked back up the pathway towards the crowds of people. He was anxious to feed and return home. His monitoring of Nia had caused him to become extremely sexually stimulated as he observed her feverish feed. He could hardly wait to 'take' her. He found his prey quickly and fed even more quickly, then returned to the place where he had left Nia. He immediately pulled her to him, he found that he could not wait to return home before 'entering' her. He must have her here and now. He gave her a very passionate kiss and then led her deeper into the woods in the effort to avoid detection by passers-by. He leaned her backwards against the trunk of an enormous old tree.

"This is not very comfortable," Nia remarked hoping he would choose another position. But, uncharacteristically, he ignored her comment and proceeded to lift the bottom of her dress upward to her waist. As usual, she was not wearing panties, so he quickly slid one of his hands between her legs and began to forcefully rub her clitoris. He was doing it in such a rough manner that it was not enjoyable to Nia at all. Then, before she knew it, he had taken out his penis, lifted her left leg, and inserted himself into her vagina. He began to thrust into her fast and furiously, one might almost say violently. Nia cried-out in pain as tears began to flow down her face. "Stop it, Seth! Stop it!" she screamed. He was apparently oblivious to her screams and suffering. He continued to pound into her with his penis, the force increasing with each thrust. Nia started to punch and scratch at his back, her tears now flowing more heavily, her screams more shrill and frequent.

But then, suddenly, Seth stopped. His climax had been reached. And, as if emerging from some kind of 'trance', he regained consciousness of his surroundings and realized that Nia was crying. "Nia," he said in despair, "What's wrong? What's happened to make you cry?"

"Get off of me!" she yelled as she pushed him away, his penis sliding out of her vagina. Seth returned his penis back into his pants, then reached out his arms to pull her back to him, but Nia would have none of it. "Don't you touch me!" she screamed. "Take me back home, *now!*"

Seth was unable to understand. What had he done? he thought. "Calm down. Calm down," Seth replied in anguish.

"Shut-up! Just take me back!" Nia yelled angrily.

Seth floated upward and waited for Nia to do the same, but in the few seconds before she joined him, Seth heard the sound of joyful laughter. It was a woman, laughing as though she had just heard the funniest joke of her life. And, again, for a brief moment, he sensed that disturbing 'presence' from the airport and the mansion. Once Nia reached his side, the laughter stopped and the 'presence' disappeared. Seth distraughtly concluded that something terrible must have just happened between him and Nia, but he had no recollection of it. He would talk with her about it, but not that night.

The car ride back to the estate was one of silence. Neither Seth nor Nia said a word. When they arrived back at the mansion, Nia quickly ran to the Master Suite. Seth followed right behind her. She tried to close the door to the room before he got there, but was not quite fast enough. Since he had made it into the room, she had to request that he sleep elsewhere, but Seth would not bow to her wishes. And, for the first time in their year long relationship, Seth and Nia slept together back to back. A tear rolled down Nia's cheek as she laid there and thought about the night's events and her future with Seth. She feared he was growing tired of her and that his violent sex act was his way of releasing the frustration of still being with her, not having the courage to tell her or just leave her. The violent sex coupled with what had happened when they awakened that day, convinced her that the Seth she fell in love with was changing, and not for the better.

Seth was indeed frustrated with Nia, but only because he was unable to ease her pain. He loved her dearly and would never leave her, but he was afraid he might soon drive her away unless he was able to quickly solve the mystery of the 'presence'. He felt sure that it was the source of his troubles with Nia. The disappearing woman in the downstairs hallway was no coincidence, he thought. She and the 'presence' had a definite connection. She was most probably its genesis. But, what was she? And, what did she want? It was almost dawn; he needed to rest. He would give the matter more thought later.

That afternoon Seth awakened to find Nia was not lying there next to him. He panicked for a moment, but then began to feel sexually stimulated. He felt his penis being sucked. A quick look downward allowed him to observed the outline of a head moving up and down under the covers. He was happy that Nia was trying to make-up with him. He knew he could not possibly go through another night like the last. He relaxed and let himself relish in the rapture she was providing. Nia was exceedingly talented today, he thought. It was becoming the best job she had ever done on him. His moans became extremely frequent and extremely loud as his penis hardened and his pleasure became almost unbearable. She had somehow learned to prolong the foreplay, restricting his ability to climax, and extending his sexual pleasure. Ultimately though, he climaxed, screaming in sounds of ecstasy. After a moment or two, Seth reached down to pull the covers off of Nia's head and to give her an extensive make-up kiss. But, just before he could do so, the bedroom door opened.

"What were you screaming about, Seth?" Nia said with concern as she entered the room. Seth looked at her and experienced a sinking feeling as he immediately pulled back the covers. There was no one and nothing to be seen. Only his own naked body, his penis wet and slowly softening. Had he been dreaming? Did he imagine the whole thing? Was it the entity?

"Seth," Nia repeated, "What were you screaming about? Are you all right?"

Seth looked into her eyes and shook his head in frustration, "No, I'm not," he said softly as he again covered himself with the blanket.

Nia responded as she calmly walked over and sat down on the bed, "We have to talk, Seth. Something's happening between us that we must stop or it will destroy what we have together."

Seth sat-up, reached over, and grabbed Nia by the waist with both hands, pulling her across the bed to his side. "I don't think we're safe anymore, Nia," he said gently as he wrapped his arms around her torso and rested his head on her shoulder.

Nia leaned over and lovingly rested her head against his head. "What do you mean?" she asked in a comforting manner. "Is it the Archangel Clan again?"

"No, I've been seeing things and hearing things and even physically feeling things that don't make any sense to me. It started on the airplane and has seemingly followed us home," he explained.

"Followed us home? What?" Nia questioned with skepticism.

"That's the most fearful part of it. I don't yet know. I have sensed it several times and have unwittingly and uncontrollably interacted with it several times," Seth reluctantly confessed.

"You aren't talking rationally, Seth. I don't understand what you're trying to tell me," Nia answered in confusion.

"I'm trying to say that I think some kind of bizarre force has somehow attached itself to us, or more specifically, to me. I don't know the force. The signal I receive from it is totally new to me. In my whole more than 300 years as a vampire, I have never encountered such a force. I don't know what happened in the woods last night that caused you such pain, but I'm sure that this force, this entity, was responsible," Seth replied apologetically.

"You're scaring me, Seth. Are you truly saying that we're in some sort of peril?" Nia asked apprehensively.

"Yes, My Love. I'm saying I think we're in extremely great peril," he answered softly.

Nia did not know what to believe. Seth had told her only yesterday that he thought the stress of returning to this boyhood home, the place where he had been attacked and forced into the life of darkness, was beginning to work on his mind. Could this all just be the continuation of that stress and not reality at all? How she loved him…more than anything offered in heaven or hell. And, despite the fact that he was obviously distraught and in pain, at that exact moment, she did not know how to help him. As the day progressed, Seth seemed to calm himself. He suggested that they go out that evening to a supper club in town that he had noticed during the drive to the estate. Nia agreed, they both needed relief from the stress of the past several days. They left around 9:00 p.m., driving back down the winding road of the estate and onto the main road. It was a cool night, characteristic of many English nights, but there was a full moon and at least a billion stars in the sky. All and all, it was a lovely night.

The supper club was crowded and there was even a line. Luckily, Seth had made reservations so they hoped their entrance would be speedy. They had to park in an underground parking lot almost four blocks away from the club.

There was absolutely no parking anywhere near the club. Once they reached the front of the club they could see that there were two lines, one for those with reservations and one for those without reservations. The reservation line had only one couple in it and they were about to enter the club. Seth and Nia stood directly behind them. The host asked for Seth's name.

"Seth Bjorn," Seth replied politely.

"Ah, yes. I see it. Please step inside, sir," the man answered as he beckoned for another host. When the new host approached, the man at the door informed him which table was reserved for Seth and Nia. "Please follow me," the new host requested softly.

Seth and Nia did so and were led through a large, crowded, romantically lighted dining room to a quaint, elegantly-set 'table for two' close to the dance floor and the band. The host helped Nia with her chair and handed a menu to each of them. "I shall return shortly," he said as he quickly stepped away.

The dinner went smoothly. Since neither of them actually ate food anymore, they each merely ordered a salad and changed it around so that it would appear to have been eaten at least a little bit. As the night continued, both Nia and Seth felt their relationship re-vitalizing itself. They sat listening to the music and laughing at some of the dance moves they were observing. But then, out of nowhere, stood a woman right in front of Seth. She was pale-skinned with large green eyes and bright yellow hair styled similar to a man's crew-cut hairstyle. She was also quite voluptuous; the way Seth liked his women, though she did not have anything over Nia's body. Nia still reined supreme.

"May I have this dance?" the woman asked Seth in a very seductive tone of voice.

Both Nia and Seth were stunned for a moment; then, Nia became rather insulted. How dare this strange woman walk over and ask Seth to dance right in front of her face. But, Seth, though thrown a little off guard, was somewhat flattered by the attention. He had never seen nor met the woman before as far as he remembered. Still, she did seem somewhat familiar and he felt himself strangely drawn to her. He and the unknown woman gazed into each other's eyes for a moment. After that Seth heard himself answer, "I'd be delighted."

Nia's eyes widened as she watched Seth rise from his chair. What did he think he was doing? she thought. He gave her no consideration at all, just like she wasn't there. Her anger increased as she watched them walk to the dance floor, Seth did not even excuse himself or even look in her direction before he left. She continued to fume as she watched the woman hug Seth around the neck and press her body tightly against his. Nia waited for Seth to push the woman away a bit, but he did not. Instead, he wrapped his arms around her waist and pulled her even closer to him, impossible as it seemed, and each still looked into the eyes of the other. When they actually started to dance, Nia could stand no more. The dance they commenced was of such a lewd nature, it embarrassed her and most others who were forced to observe the disgusting exhibition. It was a bumping and grinding show the likes of which Nia had never seen in public and a dance that Seth had never even done with her in private. She quickly rose from her chair and rushed out of the club. She wanted to fly back to the estate, but, she was too upset to concentrate in the manner necessary to accomplish the task. So, she decided to flag down a taxicab, she needed to get away from there as fast a possible.

Seth and the woman ended their 'dance', then the woman hurriedly said thank you and disappeared amongst the crowd before Seth could ask her name or anything about her. And, truly, once she intermingled within the crowd, she literally disappeared. There was no sign of her anywhere in the club. Even with Seth's enhanced eyesight, he could not detect her. As he walked back to the table, again, he seemed to return to some kind of full consciousness. A state that he apparently had not been in for the past several minutes. Approaching the table, he noticed that Nia was no longer there. He surveyed the immediate area, but did not see her. He did see their waiter, though, and decided to ask him if he knew where Nia had gone. When the waiter saw Seth coming towards him, he straightened-up and produced a smile. Once Seth was close enough the waiter spoke. "May I help you, sir?" he asked in a formal tone.

"Yes," Seth answered, "Did you happen to see where my dinner companion went?"

"Yes, sir. She left the club a few minutes ago. In fact, she left just about the time you began to dance," the waiter replied with a smirk.

Seth rushed out of the front door of the club and found Nia still trying to hail a cab. He called out to her, "Nia!"

She heard him, but did not turn around and did not answer him. Seth quickly walked over to her when he realized she was not going to answer him. He grabbed her left arm and twirled her around to face him.

"Where on earth are you going?" Seth asked breathless from frustration.

"Anywhere away from you! I've had it with you, Seth! I won't hang around and let you hurt and humiliate me any longer! I'm leaving you!" she exclaimed defiantly.

Seth was stunned. "What brought this on? I swear, Nia, you're becoming more and more difficult to understand. What have I done now?"

"That '*I am innocent*' act won't work anymore, Seth. I no longer believe you don't know what you're doing. I believe you're all too aware of your behavior and I won't take it anymore!" Nia continued to exclaim in a voice that could not conceal her pain.

Seth grabbed Nia by her right arm, too, and abruptly pulled her towards his chest. "Nia," he said in a tone of desperation as he looked straight at her, "Please…don't leave me. I know you don't trust me anymore. I'm sorry for that and I'm sorry for all the things that have happened to hurt you. But, you must believe that I haven't consciously or willingly done any of it. I adore you…you are my Love; my only reason for continuing to exist at all. You are the heart that beats within me, and as such, are the very essence of my being, the very owner of my soul. Without you, I cease to be of any value, even to myself."

Nia's eyes filled with tears and the drops began to flow down her cheeks. She heard the Seth with whom she had fallen in love returning to her. She looked-up at him and when their eyes met, the emotions could not be controlled. "My Nia," Seth said softly. Then, they suddenly pressed lips with a passion hot enough to melt the universe, both mouths opened wide. Their tongues rapidly tangled into soft, wet streaks of fire accompanied by rapid and heavy breathing. Nia wrapped her arms tightly around Seth's waist. Seth released her arms and embraced her around her back with such tightness that a little more force would have surely broken ribs. After a few moments, they temporarily interrupted their kiss to return to the car and drive back to the estate, where their act of 're-uniting' could be fully completed.

The entire drive home Seth steered the car with one hand. That was not an easy feat because the closer to the estate they came, the more steep, winding, and dark was the road. However, his other hand was fully occupied under Nia's dress and between her thighs, where he aggressively 'let his fingers do the walking'. Nia held tightly onto his arm, increasing her pressure upon it occasionally and releasing loud moans at the feel of each orgasm that Seth's fingers provided. Once during the drive home, Seth became so heated himself that he had to pull to the side of the road. He engaged in another passionate kiss with Nia. Then, he unbuttoned the top of her dress and indulged himself in several vigorous sucks and multiple juicy licks upon her large brown nipples. That caused her nipples to swell in his mouth from arousal and increased Nia's deep sighs. Her breasts remained exposed the rest of the drive home. Seth enjoyed watching them bounce and shake in movement with the car ride as the moonlight shone a revealing emphasize across them. He loved that they were so big and round and soft. His fingers still remained in exploration between her thighs, though. His amorous interlude with her breasts satisfied him only slightly, but at least enough to make it back to the estate. Still, on that night, Seth's main objective was to provide Nia with as much pleasure of every kind that was supernaturally possible for him. The best was yet to come.

Upon their arrival at the estate, they hurriedly walked inside, quickly ascended the staircase, and rushed down the hallway. Seth burst through the double-doors and smiled as he looked at Nia and held the doors open for her. Once she had entered the room, he excitedly slammed the doors closed and began to peel-off his clothing. Nia had already started that process, and, since she never wore panties or a bra anymore, was now only left with a black lace half-slip to remove. By the time she was naked, so was Seth; he had undressed at an incredibly rapid speed. Seth looked at Nia's beautiful, shapely, cocoa-colored, naked body with the thrill of his first time. His joy over their renewed union inspired the thrill. The love that he thought he had lost was now returned to him and his appreciation of that return overwhelmed him. He walked over to the bed and sat on the front edge of it. His smooth muscular legs were spread far apart exposing his entire genital area to Nia. His usually neat, long blond hair was somewhat array as it draped down his back, the result of the energetic sexual activity in the car.

He waited for her to join him, but instead, she walked in his direction until she was about 4 feet in front of him, stopped, and began to perform an extremely erotic dance for him. Perhaps, she felt she had something to prove, at least to herself. It was filled with pelvic gyrations and pelvic thrusts. Her large breasts with their now enlarged nipples bounced and flowed in the air as her torso and arms rotated in every direction. Seth's semi-hard penis grew a little in size with almost every move that Nia made, and its shaft began to sway involuntarily back and forth from stimulation. After a minute or so, his wetness increased and began to drip onto the floor causing small droplets of moisture to accumulate on the carpet. When Nia came within about 2 feet of Seth, turned her buttocks towards him, parted her legs, and then bent over. Seth could not restrain himself any longer. The sight of her fully spread buttocks and fully spread genitals, which he himself had shaved only a few days ago, being gyrated and thrusted towards him, was too much. He could no longer only watch. He firmly grabbed hold of each thigh and vigorously began to lick her buttocks, her anus, and her clitoris for several minutes. Nia cried out loudly in pleasure multiple times. Then, Seth, again, aggressively slid two fingers into her vagina and used his thumb to massage her clitoris.

Nia continued to cry-out in enjoyment as she felt Seth's fingers 'enter' her and felt the new manipulations to her clitoris, the combination of which provided her with powerful orgasms. Her wetness now covered both her entire genital area and Seth's hand. Ultimately, after several minutes of simulation, Seth was unable to withhold from performing the real act. He removed his fingers, stood-up, and inserted his rock hard, dripping penis into her vagina and held Nia by the waist with each hand. They both released a loud sensuous moan as his large pulsating penis fully 'entered' her. Nia remained bent over, supporting her body by way of each hand resting just above each knee. Then, she and Seth, in almost a state of wildness, pumped themselves into the most explosive climax each had ever had, accomplished by their favorite intercourse position, 'doggie-style'.

When Nia awakened, it was almost dawn. She looked to her right and found Seth peacefully snuggled beside her in a deep sleep, his long blond hair partially covered his handsome face. She felt strange, though. She felt as if she had been awakened by a noise or something rather than just awakened naturally. Suddenly, she realized she was in great pain. In all of the emotional turmoil, she and Seth had forgotten to 'feed'. Now, they would both be suffering until sunset. Then, in a corner of the room, she saw the shadow of a figure. It was the figure of a woman. In the next instance, the woman spoke to her.

"That was a very inspiring act of lovemaking," the woman said in a light and melodic voice.

"Who are you?" Nia asked nervously.

"I am called Sonjaa," the woman replied.

"How did you get in here? What do you want?" Nia inquired still unnerved.

"I go where I want by simply willing it…What do I want? I want your Seth," Sonjaa answered as she stepped out of the shadows and into the moonlight that streamed through the window of the, otherwise, mostly dark room.

Nia gasped as she saw the woman in clear view. She was the same woman from the supper club, the one who had done that disgusting dance with Seth. "You watched Seth and me making love? How? Why?" Nia asked somewhat embarrassed by the thought of having been observed.

"I like to watch. It makes me hot and ready to participate just like I feel now," Sonjaa replied in a sultry tone of voice.

"You weren't standing there or any place else in this room. How could you have seen us, through the keyhole?" Nia asked now with great skepticism.

"My powers allow me to view what I want, when I want, without detection. I can be visible or invisible at will," Sonjaa explained arrogantly.

"Visible to invisible and back again? I don't believe you. What is it that you claim to be?" Nia questioned apprehensively.

"I am a citizen of Hell. My survival depends upon the life force of men, which I obtain by providing them with extraordinary sexual pleasures. I literally love them to death…In ancient times, I was called demon, in modern times, I am called succubus," Sonjaa proclaimed proudly.

Nia had heard of such creatures. But, just as with vampires, she had always thought they were only fantasy or myth and not even remotely real. She had surely been wrong about vampires, so now she must resign herself to the existence of the succubus world as well. She looked over at Seth and wondered why he had not been awakened by their conversation as of yet.

"Do not concern yourself about him. He will not awaken unless I will it so. My powers are that great," Sonjaa bragged.

Nia returned her look to the succubus. "So, what you have just told me is that you want Seth in order to kill him," Nia stated fearful of the answer from the creature.

"My," Sonjaa said in a shrieking laugh, "Aren't you a bright one."

"Why, then, have you shown yourself to me? Why have this conversation?" Nia asked with anxiety.

"Actually, I had hoped to drive you away, but you were stubborn. So now, I want you to know what's coming. It's more fun that way. I like to see the loved ones of the 'soon to be departed' suffer before the fateful act occurs. Adds to the excitement you know," the succubus gleefully expressed.

Nia did not know what to do next. "Is there no way I can convince you to spare him? Nothing I can do to otherwise satisfy your needs?"

"No!" Sonjaa screeched.

"You do know he's a vampire, don't you?" Nia probed.

"Of course! Do you think I'm stupid!" Sonjaa screamed.

The creature's level of irritation was becoming uncomfortably high for Nia. She did not know what Sonjaa's destructive capabilities were and she did not want to find out. "No, I don't think you're stupid. I was only trying to make sure you were informed about his non-human status. Since he is already dead, how could he have a life-force for you draw upon?" Nia questioned as she tried to instill some doubt as to Seth's ability to fulfill Sonjaa's demand.

"That's the best part. I was lucky to find him. Yes, he is no longer human and no longer has a human life-force, but, he is immortal with the life-force of an immortal. It is quite possible that with his force, I may never have to prey upon any man again or at the very least for a long period of time. I would be free to engage in sexual pleasures without carrying the act to the realm of death. You should be pleased that your Seth would save the lives of so many other men by his sacrifice. Not to mention those who would be saved from his 'bite' since I would have destroyed him," Sonjaa reasoned calmly.

Nia thought, Sonjaa indeed talked a good game, but the woman would get Seth only over her 'dead' body, so to speak.

Sonjaa quickly warned, "So, be sure to enjoy this day with him, my dear. It will be your last." Then, in an instant, she disappeared. Nia hoped that she was gone, but if she truly had the ability to become invisible, there was no way of really knowing whether or not she was still there. Seth began to stir, he opened his eyes and saw Nia sitting-up.

"Is something wrong?" he said softly and still half asleep.

"No, Sweetheart," Nia said lovingly as she looked into his eyes and pushed the hair out of his face, "Go back to sleep." After a few moments, Seth was again deep in slumber.

Nia got out of bed, left the room, and walked down the hall to a room in which she knew there was a computer. She sat down and logged-on, into the internet. She was determined to learn all she could about the creature and most of all, some means of destroying it. It was not long before she began to accumulate considerable information on the succubus legend, though it ultimately took all day. The creatures were indeed ancient and extremely deadly. They captured their prey by first projecting a hypnotic trance upon them. This would render the man helpless to its will and also erase any memory of all the events that took place during the trance. So...Seth was telling her the truth all along, she thought, he was not in control of the things he did to her nor was he aware of them. The information continued on to say that in the final stage of entrapment, while the man was in a trance, the succubus would force intercourse with him. Then, while her victim's will was even further weakened by sexual stimulation, the succubus would draw his life's energy into herself, quickly killing the man. But...Nia was still dismayed, she had found nothing on how to destroy the creature.

At that moment, Seth entered the room. He was surprised to see Nia at the computer. Vampires did not have much use for computers except for those who were entrepreneurial. Those with independent wealth, like Seth, did not concern themselves with too much technology. And, because of their longevity, most vampires were independently wealthy.

"What are you doing, Nia?" he inquired.

Nia was surprised by his entrance and quickly changed the screen as Seth walked over and sat in a chair about 5 feet away from her. "Nothing much, just passing time," she replied innocently as she stood-up and walked over to him. She sat on his lap and tightly hugged him around the neck, her head leaning against his. Seth wrapped his arms around her waist and they remained that way for a few seconds before Seth broke the silence.

"Is everything all right, my Love? Is there some way I may help you?"

"Everything is fine," she answered as she kissed his cheek and returned her head to its position against his head. Her heart was in torture because she knew that this might be their last day together and that she would destroy herself should Seth become lost to her. Somehow, she must find an answer to destroying the demon.

Seth spoke again. "You know that with all the excitement last night, we forgot to 'feed'. Are you in as much pain as I am?"

"Yes, Dear, I am. It's truly excruciating isn't it?" Nia replied. She had been so worried about the coming night's events that she had totally forgotten about the pain until Seth's reminder.

"We must leave to 'feed' as soon as the sun goes down. If we wait too long, we will both be too weak to even leave the mansion and we will both perish from hunger," Seth advised, "In fact, I will go prepare myself now. The sun will set within the hour. You will come shortly?"

"I will come soon," Nia said as she rose from his lap and sat back down at the computer.

"O.k.," he said and left the room.

After about 15 minutes, Nia came across an ancient document which was written in some obscure ancient text, but which had been translated into English. At first glance, it seemed to essentially provide the same information as all the other references she had viewed. Her heart fluttered and began to steadily beat at a quickened pace when she reached the last paragraph of translation. There at the very end was the secret to destroying the demon. Salt water. The demon would melt into destruction if somehow a person could throw upon it or push it into salt water. Nia immediately jumped-up and rushed downstairs to the kitchen pantry where she had previously seen a number of buckets. She saw four empty buckets, grabbed them off the floor, and grabbed two large boxes of salt off the shelf. She rushed back upstairs with the items and went straight to the bathroom. She filled the buckets almost full of water and added enough salt so that the water in each was cloudy. She did not want Seth to know what was happening, so she left the buckets of salt water in the bathroom. She hoped she would have the opportunity to reach them when the time came. She breathed a little easier now; at least there was a fighting chance. Nia quickly walked back to the Master Suite to join Seth and leave to 'feed'.

She opened the Master Suite door and was horror-struck at what she saw. Seth was lying on the bed naked, flat on his back, his arms stretched-out to his sides. He was motionless and appeared to be pinned down somehow and unable to move. Sonjaa was also atop the bed naked, on her knees, straddling his groin, Seth's penis already inside of her. A blue mist entirely encapsulated both of them and laser-like streams of light were being emitted from both pairs of eyes. The lights coming from Seth's eyes were yellow; the lights from Sonjaa's eyes were red. The light streams merged to form two straight laser beams that connected their eyes together. Nia could see tears dripping down Seth's face. Was he crying or was it eye strain from the laser lights? Her heart raced as she rushed back to the bathroom to retrieve two buckets of salt water. Luckily, Sonjaa was so involved with her prey that she was oblivious to the fact that Nia had ever entered the room. Nia re-entered the room and set one bucket down, she raised the other one and ran towards the bed. When she thought she was close enough, she threw the entire contents of the bucket on Sonjaa.

Nothing happened! Sonjaa did not even flinch from what she was doing! It was not working! Had the information she found been incorrect? She hurriedly picked-up the second bucket, ran back towards the bed, and threw its contents on Sonjaa as well. Almost immediately, sparks could be seen within the blue mist. Their number quickly multiplied tenfold until they finally absorbed both laser lights and culminated in a small explosion. The explosion broke the connection between Sonjaa's eyes and Seth's eyes, then Seth's eyes immediately closed. In another instant, Sonjaa turned and looked at Nia. The hate in Sonjaa face was so intense, it was unlike anything Nia had ever seen. Within another second, Sonjaa began to shriek in pain, her face and body grew distorted as they began the melting process. The blue mist disappeared and suddenly a turbulent whirlwind whipped around the whole room. It knocked down lamps, small furniture, and everything else that was light in weight. In a few seconds, it centered itself around Sonjaa where it swirled only around her, faster and faster until the melting figure of Sonjaa could no longer be seen within it. Her screams became deafening. Soon after that point, the whirlwind whisked itself over to the window and smashed through, leaving shattered glass sprinkled about the floor. It swirled outside the window for a moment and then disappeared in a puff of smoke; gone forever.

Nia ran to Seth's side and threw the bedcovers over his naked, wet body. She grabbed each of his shoulders and shook him vigorously in the effort to wake him. Seth slowly opened his eyes. "Are you ready to go 'feed'?" he asked softly as he sleepily looked-up at her.

He did not remember anything at all, Nia thought. "Yes…I'm ready, Sweetheart," she whispered affectionately.

Seth sat-up, wearily slid over to the side of the bed, and sat next to her. "I feel awful," he said. "What's all this water? What happened to my clothes?" Then, he noticed the condition of the room. "What in hell happened here?" he questioned wearily.

Nia gently took hold of his hand. He turned and looked at her with an expression of absolute confusion. She slowly began a detailed account of the entire story.

Chapter 8

It had been two weeks since the ordeal with the succubus. Nia and Seth were closer than ever. Nia had noticed that for the last week or so, her ankles and wrists were often swollen. Today, that swelling had gone away and instead had moved to her abdomen. She was reluctant to mention it to Seth. But, she was a bit frightened now and thought perhaps it was some kind of 'vampire thing' of which he might have knowledge. She entered the library, the place where Seth spent most of his days, for he was an avid reader. She found him sitting on the sofa totally engrossed in a book. "Excuse me, Seth. May I interrupt and speak with you for a few moments?" she asked softly.

Seth looked-up at her with a smile. "You're never an interruption to me." He then beckoned to her. "Come. Sit by me." Nia quickly walked over and sat very closely next to him. Seth set the book on the end table and put his arm around Nia's shoulders. "What is it, Love?" he said affectionately.

"Well," she began, "For the last week or so, I've had some swelling around my wrists and ankles. That's gone away, but, now I have swelling in my abdomen."

Seth looked down to where she was pointing. He could see considerable swelling in the area. "Yes, I see that, too," he said with much concern.

"Have you any idea of what it might be? Is it something that happens to vampires on occasion?" Nia asked nervously.

"No, I've never seen or heard of anything like it," he responded worriedly.

Nia was becoming increasingly upset. What should she do? Was she being destroyed from within?

Then, Seth spoke, "I know of someone who might be able to help, if he's still in this area."

"Who would help a vampire?" Nia asked puzzled by his reply.

"Another vampire," Seth said. "He was a physician in his human life and after he was 'made' a vampire, his scientific curiosities carried over into his vampire life. He began to study and experiment with vampire 'patients' and has become quite the expert on vampire ailments. He doesn't live far from here. We can stop by there after we 'feed'. Hopefully, he's still there or at least someone else who knows where he's gone."

"There are other vampires here?" Nia asked in amazement.

"Oh, yes. Quite a few. There's a whole Clan here to which I belong. The Isis Clan. I have been meaning to take you around and get you introduced to everyone, as well as get myself re-acquainted with whom ever is around at this time. As you know, we vampires move around pretty regularly, so there's never a time when everyone is here at once. But, with the succubus and all, I thought we could use a little relaxation before starting with the social obligations," Seth explained.

Vampire social-life. How extraordinary, Nia thought. Then, she remembered the formal Ball back in the United States. Seth had told her that all the guests were vampires and she had thought him insane when he spoke those words. But, it seems that most vampires are an elegant, jet-setting group of "the beautiful people", if you discounted the facts that they were dead and were blood-sucking monsters. Heck…why be so picky?

Seth knocked on the door of what was another huge mansion. It was dark outside and kind of hard to see, but Nia could see well enough to tell that it was a beautiful dwelling. Within a few seconds, the door opened and a short woman with gray hair stepped into view.

"May I help you, sir?" she asked in a quivery voice.

"Is Dr. Firth at home, Madame?" Seth inquired.

"Yes, sir. He's just come back home. Whom may I say is calling?" she answered.

"Tell him his old friend, Seth Bjorn," he replied.

"Wait here, sir. I'll return in a moment," she responded.

Seth turned to Nia and smiled. "We're in luck," he said supportively.

Nia was glad that the doctor was there. She hoped he could provide a happy ending to her problem.

A moment later, a tall, robust man, appearing to be about fifty when he was 'made', came bolting around a corner into the main foyer and straight to the front door. "Seth! Seth, my man! How wonderful to see you!" he bellowed as he threw his arms around Seth and hugged him wildly. The hug was so tight that Seth could hardly answer, "It's great to see you too, Neddelton."

The doctor finally let go of Seth and turned to look at Nia. "And, who is this beautiful creature?" he asked staring at Nia's gorgeous face.

"This is Nia, my companion and lover, and were it legally possible, my wife," Seth answered proudly.

Neddelton leaned over and kissed Nia on the cheek. "So nice to meet you, my dear, very pleasant indeed," he said gently. Nia smiled. She liked him.

"Well, come in, have a seat. What brings you to me?" Neddelton inquired as he guided Nia and Seth into the sitting room. Neddelton sat down in one of the large, cushy chairs while Seth and Nia took seats together on the couch.

"I would like to say this was just a social call, Ned, I truly wish it were. But, we are in need of your medical skills," Seth explained.

Ned's face lost its jovial expression and became totally serious. "What's the problem?" he asked.

"It's Nia. She told me earlier that she had been experiencing swelling around her wrists and ankles for about a week. But, now, that particular swelling is gone and the swelling is in her abdominal area. Do you have any idea of what it might be? I've never known it to happen to any other vampire," Seth said worriedly.

Ned thought for a moment, then answered, "It's not likely you would have heard about anything similar to this prior to now. If it's what I think it is, I've only heard of three other cases myself. The first was reported to have occurred over 400 years ago in a very obscure place. The other two cases were slightly more recent in slightly less obscure locations. I only know about them because of my extensive research into vampire history. Her symptoms seem the same. But, I'm getting ahead of myself. First, let me examine her, then we'll know for sure," Ned advised. He stood-up and indicated for Nia to follow him.

Seth and Nia got up and Seth gave Nia a soft kiss on the lips. "I'll be right here if you need me," he whispered.

"Don't worry, Seth, she'll be fine," Ned called out reassuringly.

In about ten minutes, Nia and Ned returned. Seth stood-up and tried to get a reading of the situation from one of the two faces, but was unable to do so.

"I think both of you need to sit down," Ned requested.

Nia walked over to where Seth was standing and they both sat back down on the couch. Seth took hold of Nia's hand and they waited for Ned's conclusion.

"I'm not sure how this happened. Nia, you must be a recently 'made' vampire, are you not?" Ned asked.

"Yes, that is true. Only about three weeks," Nia replied.

"It's as I suspected. Some time before you were 'made' you became pregnant. You are currently expecting a baby," Ned explained.

"What! How could that be? I haven't been with anyone except Seth for almost a year," Nia answered back in shock.

"Then, it must be Seth's baby. The cases starting from 400 years ago were the same. Recently 'made' female vampires were found to be pregnant by their long-standing male vampire companions. The couples had engaged in sexual intercourse many times prior to each female's transformation and by some act of heaven or hell the male vampires, at some point, produced large quantities of live sperm," Ned continued to explain.

Seth, also in a state of shock, asked, "What happened? What kind of babies were they?"

Ned answered cheerfully, "Just what you might expect. Half-human, half-vampire. They had the ability to function in sunlight, thus could function as a normal human. They could eat regular food, but, also required blood in order to survive. However, they needed blood only every 4–5 months as opposed to every night. They could also fly and had full supernatural strength. And, they retained the ability to reproduce just as any normal human. One could say that for the most part, they had the best of both worlds."

Nia and Seth could not believe their ears. A baby! Their baby! They were both relieved that Nia was not ill, but unsure about the future event. Would they be able to handle it? Afterall, the baby's world would be different from their own. They were creatures of the night, the baby would not be such. Nia wondered if it would be more kind to just abort the baby rather than bring it into a life of half-vampirism. She would discuss it with Seth when they returned home. Seth suddenly remembered the words Jason had spoken to him at Westville Manor, advising him that he would never hear 'the patter of little half-vampire feet around the house'. Seems Jason was undeniably wrong.

When they arrived home, Seth and Nia went straight to the library where they again sat down on the couch. After a brief discussion, they decided not to abort the child. With the initial shock over, they were both quite excited about the news. Though, they could not marry in the human world and the vampire world had no such custom, they could still be a real family now. Their love was complete. It had produced a tangible expression of their great affection for and dedication to each other.

"Perhaps as a half-vampire, the child will find a human with which to mate and produce an even more human child. If the human strain can be continuously increased by the child's offspring through subsequent human matings, maybe we'll be able to give back to the world some of the humans we are forced to take," Seth rationalized.

"We could just destroy ourselves and accomplish a comparable result," Nia reminded. But, she knew neither of them would willingly part from the other in such a permanent manner.

"Won't happen," Seth replied lovingly, "In that, I must be selfish."

Ned had informed them that the 'carrying term' for such a child would be highly accelerated. Those in the past took only 3 months and Nia should expect the same thing, he advised. Since Nia was already one and a half months pregnant, she should expect the baby in less than two months. He also said that once the child was born, the rate of growth would also be highly accelerated. The child should grow at the rate of about 5 years for each month of existence, until reaching the growth of 20 years old. At that point, the growth and development would stop and the child would then become an immortal.

The next night, after their 'feed', Seth and Nia went shopping for infant and toddler clothes, as well as nursery furniture. They bought about $5000 worth of items, even though they knew full well that within the first few weeks after birth, they would have to shop all over again. But, they were excited and had money to burn, so what the heck.

Ned was absolutely correct. In less than two months, Nia gave birth. The baby was a girl. And…because of her exquisite light-bronze color, Seth suggested that they name her Cinnamon. Nia agreed to his choice. Thus, Cinnamon Bjorn was welcomed into the world.

May God Have Mercy Upon Her Soul.

Chapter 9

The months passed quickly, and, once again, Ned had been correct. Cinnamon developed at the rate of approximately 5 years every month. It had now been slightly more than 4 months since her birth. She was, at least in appearance, a full-fledged adult. And, unbeknownst to herself, an immortal now. Following in the images of her parents, she, too, was gorgeous. Her velvety, soft, brown skin complimented her large, light brown eyes and full, perfect lips. Her hair was black like her mother's, but wavy with only a slight bushiness. Its length was almost to her waist. Cinnamon's body was a duplicate of Nia's. Large breasts, a small waist, wide hips, round muscular buttocks, and long, shapely legs. A veritable feast for any man's eyes, as well as a fair number of women. But, she also had a delightful personality. She was happy, bubbly, bright, and caring. Having had no experience with a 'normal' human lifestyle, the lifestyle she did have was perfectly amiable to her. And why not? She lived in a mansion, had plenty of food, plenty of clothes, and two doting parents (though a little strange). Plus, her father had just bought her a brand new Mercedes Benz convertible. What a great life! But, she was soon to have the equivalent of the talk about 'the birds and the bees' with her parents. It was now necessary to explain the whole vampire life to her. She would soon need to be taught how to obtain her life's blood and to learn all of the secrets of vampirial survival.

Cinnamon entered the library where her parents were relaxing. She was on her way to shop in the nearby city. Of course, she would be driving her brand new car. She walked straight to her Mother and kissed her on the cheek. "I'm leaving, now, Mom," she said cheerfully.

Nia smiled and answered, "All right, Honey. Please be careful."

Then, Cinnamon walked over to the chair in which her Father sat. She was definitely a 'Daddy's Girl', which is why she threw her arms around his neck and hugged him tightly as she gave him a huge rather sloppy kiss on the side of his face. "See you later, Dad," she said affectionately.

"Good-bye, Sweetheart. Do as your Mother said and be very careful, beware of strangers," Seth warned.

"I will, Dad," Cinnamon replied, but she wondered why her Father was always so insistent about avoiding strangers. She would have to ask him someday.

Seth and Nia looked at each other and smiled as Cinnamon left the room. They were still in awe at their creation and at times could hardly believe she was actually their daughter. Especially Nia, afterall, she was only 26 years old herself. A particular event had occurred which did cause Seth and Nia some concern. Mortimer, the caretaker, had suddenly quit a month after Cinnamon's birth. The cause would appear to be a high discomfort with their family. He had begun to constantly watch Cinnamon and had apparently taken note of her phenomenal growth and development. Both Seth and Nia had caught him watching her for long periods of time. The whole situation must have become more than he could understand or was willing to remain around, so he up and quit. The hope was that there would be no repeat of what happened in France. So far, there had been no indication of any betrayal by Mortimer, but, the fear was always there now. Seth knew that the family would have to leave the estate in the very near future in order to ensure their safety.

Cinnamon had been shopping for about an hour when she decided to get a glass of orange juice from one of the street vendors located along the busy city sidewalk. As she stood drinking, a young man came beside her, also ordered an orange juice, and stood there staring at her as he drank. Cinnamon was used to men staring at her. But, even though she only saw him out of the corner of her eye, for some reason this young man was making her feel very uneasy. She looked straightforwardly at him and felt her heart start to beat faster as he looked into her eyes and smiled. He was so handsome Cinnamon had trouble controlling her emotions. That was something new for her; she had not yet been affected by a man in this manner. He was tall and muscular with flashing green eyes. His skin was tanned, his hair was almost as light blond as her Father's, but hung only about 2 inches passed his shoulders. She liked what she was feeling, but was embarrassed by and baffled by how difficult it was to control herself.

"Pleasant day isn't?" the young man said cheerfully.

"Yes, it's quite lovely," Cinnamon replied with a shy smile.

The young man liked her apparent shyness, beautiful women aren't usually shy; they're usually confident and often conceited, he thought. "My name is Erin Medford," he said as he extended his hand.

"Nice to meet you. My name is Cinnamon Bjorn," she replied as they shook hands and continued to smile at each other. They slowly released their hands despite the fact that neither particularly wanted to do so.

"Bjorn. That's Scandinavian in origin isn't?" Erin asked.

"Yes. My Father is of Scandinavian descent…my Mother is African-American, though," Cinnamon answered proudly.

"Seems the combination has produced a masterpiece of a daughter," Erin complimented boldly.

Cinnamon smiled even more and felt a rush of warmth surge through her body. "Thank you for such a nice remark," Cinnamon said with unexpected affection.

"You're more than welcome. I only said the truth," Erin responded, now with a tone of affection in his own voice.

Cinnamon quickly finished her drink; her nervousness was becoming too overwhelming. "Well, I must be going. Perhaps, we'll meet again sometime," she said politely.

"Before you leave, might I have your phone number or some way to contact you?" Erin asked anxiously.

Cinnamon thought for a moment; and then decided to give him her phone number. She wondered what her Father might say about consorting with a stranger. But, she was optimistic that Erin was a decent trustworthy person, and so would take the chance. She really did not want him to just walk out of her life. She gave him the number and they went their separate ways.

Cinnamon drove home in a fog of happiness. She was thrilled by her new acquaintance. She decided not to tell her parents about Erin. Afterall, he might not even call her, so she preferred to wait until, if or when, he did call. By the time she returned home, Nia and Seth were preparing to leave on their nightly excursion. Cinnamon was glad because she would not have to submit to '20 questions' now. But, just as her parents were about to leave, the telephone rang. Seth answered it in the Master Suite and within a few seconds opened the double-doors.

"Cinnamon," he called out in an annoyed tone.

"Yes, Dad?" she answered back.

"Come here, you have a phone call," Seth responded irritably.

Cinnamon was ecstatic because she knew it had to be Erin. "I'll take it down here, Dad," she called back to Seth.

"No, you won't. Come here or I'll hang-up," Seth warned sternly.

Cinnamon knew her Father was angry about Erin's call. She would have to be careful about her conversation with Erin since her parents would be listening. She could not understand why they were always so nosey and in her business. As she walked into her parents' room, she found her Father still holding the telephone receiver and her Mother sitting on the opposite side of the bed. They both stared at her as she walked over and took the phone from her Father's hand. She pushed the button that would allow Erin's face to be seen on the telephone screen. He was just as handsome as she remembered and his friendly smile lighted-up the screen.

"Hello, Erin. I'm so glad you called," Cinnamon said sweetly.

"Hi, Beautiful. Happy to see you made it home safely," Erin said with continued affection.

Seth and Nia watched his image closely, but out of Erin's range of sight. "I thought perhaps I might visit you tonight or that you would meet me some place so that we could spend some time together," Erin expressed sincerely.

"I would like that very much," she said as she looked at her parents. Seth indicated to her to have Erin come there that night.

"You may come here if it's convenient," Cinnamon said worriedly.

"No matter where you are, it's convenient. Just give me the address and the time and I'll be there," Erin replied enthusiastically. Cinnamon and Erin made their arrangements and then hung-up the telephone.

"Who is this guy and where did you meet him?" Seth asked immediately.

"His name is Erin Medford and I met him in town today," Cinnamon answered meekly.

"Where is he from and what do you know about him?" Nia asked with concern.

"I'm sorry, Mom, I don't know the answers to those questions," Cinnamon responded nervously. "Please...don't give him the third degree when he comes."

"We have to find out all we can about him and soon. It's essential to our survival. He could be a friend. Or, he could be an enemy of colossal proportions," Seth advised solemnly.

"Why are you and Mom so paranoid, Dad? Is it because we're so wealthy?" Cinnamon inquired with confusion.

"No, we'll explain it to you soon. There is much you need to know. It is vital that you restrict outside acquaintances right now," Seth explained.

Cinnamon was as puzzled as ever. She hoped her parents would hurry with the explanation of the family situation, so that she would know what was going on. Seth and Nia left for their 'feed', with plans to be back around the time of Erin's arrival at the estate. Cinnamon prepared herself for the date with Erin. She chose a very slinky low-cut dress with a hemline so short, it could hardly be called a dress. But, that was the style of young people in the year 2034, so, it was not unusual date attire.

Erin arrived before Seth and Nia returned home. He was stunned when he saw the estate. He had no idea that Cinnamon came from such a wealthy family. His own family was well-to-do, but did not have the wealth of the Bjorn's. His Mother was a member of Parliament and his Father was 'knighted' by the Queen several years ago for all of his charitable contributions and actions. So, they were indeed an upper-class English family. However, when compared to the Bjorn wealth, Erin's family was a relatively minor player. When Cinnamon opened the door, he was again stunned at the vision of loveliness he saw in her. He wondered how he would manage to be a gentleman and keep his hands off of her that night.

"Good evening," Cinnamon said with a bright smile.

"Hello, My Flower," Erin replied in earnest.

"Come-in," Cinnamon said as she stood back from the door so that he might enter. "My parents have gone-out, but will return shortly. You'll be able to meet them then."

"That's fine," Erin said. "It's even a relief. I was rather nervous about the meeting. Your Father was none too pleasant on the phone."

Cinnamon laughed, "He was none too pleasant off the phone," she added and they both laughed.

They had just made themselves comfortable in the sitting room when Nia and Seth returned. Despite Cinnamon's wishes, her parents walked in and did give Erin a necessary 'third degree'. It angered her greatly to see her visitor made so uncomfortable. But, after it was all over, Erin told her it was all right and that she was very valuable to him. His words increased her fond feelings for him and even prompted her to initiate a 'goodnight kiss' upon his departure. Erin was enthralled by the kiss and told her that she had just made-up for any discomfort her parents may have caused him.

Seth had a private investigator research the information provided by Erin. There turned-out to be no indication that he was either a member of the Archangel Clan or supernatural. His references and background information were true to his words. So, Seth and Nia allowed the relationship to advance. They particularly liked the fact that Erin was 100% human and could increase the human element of the family should he and Cinnamon have offspring.

Several weeks had passed and Erin had been with Cinnamon every night since their meeting. On weekends, they were together both day and night, and, though Erin was a computer systems engineer, he always made sure he had time for Cinnamon. Their relationship was deep and loving and very reminiscent of the one which existed between Seth and Nia. They had yet to make love, but, it would soon happen and they both knew it.

One afternoon, while Nia was browsing through a magazine in the bedroom, Cinnamon came to her Mother doubled-over in pain. "Mom," she said weakly, "Something's wrong. I'm having sharp pains all over my body, but, especially in my stomach. Help me...please," she cried.

Nia knew what it was; akin to having her period start, Cinnamon's need for blood had started. Nia and Seth would now have to explain Cinnamon's vampire heritage to her. "Don't fear, Darling. I know what ails you. Let me call your Father in here and we'll explain to you the new circumstances of your life. All of your prior questions regarding our family will be answered and you'll understand the precariousness of our existence," Nia explained empathetically.

Seth and Nia sat down with Cinnamon and explained the whole vampirial history of their family, they began with Seth's transformation in 1699. They answered every question that Cinnamon asked and provided explicit detail of all aspects of the vampire world. After the conversation, Cinnamon retreated to her room and unexpectantly remained there in a depression. She refused to eat and refused to see or talk with Erin despite his many attempts to contact her. Seth and Nia decided to leave her alone for awhile, but, should her depression continue for an extended length of time, they would have to intervene. And, though her pains had disappeared for the time being, Seth and Nia knew the pain would be returning full force shortly. Cinnamon would have to be taught how to 'feed'.

It was a brisk, rainy night as Mortimer sat around a table with friends in the Lighthouse Pub drinking beer and bragging about his new position at the Singletonford Estate.

"I hope I don't see the weird goings-on at the new estate that I saw at the Bjorn Estate," he rattled-off in a liquor induced outburst.

"What do ya mean?" asked one of his many drinking buddies.

"Well, I don't like to talk about my employers, past or present, but, there was certainly strange goings-on at that place," Mortimer continued.

"Like what? You still haven't told us anything," another buddy commented.

"Oh, things like nightly trips out until the wee hours of the night. Never opening the draperies so that the house was kept dark. They strangely always burned lamplight instead of letting in sunlight," Mortimer explained with a tone of suspicion in his voice.

"Oh, so what. Lots of rich people stay out all night. They don't have to get up and go to work like us poor folks," a friend answered.

"What about the drawn draperies? And not a drop of food in the mansion is ever eaten by the owner or his wife…" Mortimer persisted.

"They probably always had hang-overs, couldn't take the bright sunlight or the food," Mortimer's friend explained.

"Oh, yeah…well what do you think about a child that grows from newborn to the size of a 5 year old in the space of one month?" Mortimer answered coldly.

"Either you're crazy or the child has some rare disease we don't know about, that's all," a buddy said.

And with that, Mortimer's circle of drinking friends dismissed the whole subject and started talking about sports. But, someone in the pub had not dismissed the subject. The information Mortimer had revealed in his drunkenness was all too familiar in that gentleman's world. He knew what he must do. He left the pub and hurried to accomplish his task.

Several days into her depression, Cinnamon awakened one night to find Erin standing over her bed. "What are you doing here? Go away!" she begged desperately.

Erin sat down on the bed. "I'm not going anywhere until I find out what's happening. Why have you refused to see me or talk with me? What have I done?" he asked in distress.

Cinnamon sat-up in bed and replied in a whisper, "You haven't done anything. It's not you."

Erin was relieved to at least hear that information. "What is it then? I need to know."

Cinnamon felt that Erin did at least deserve an explanation of her behavior. She gathered her courage and relayed the extraordinary story of her heritage and her burgeoning lifestyle. But, like Nia, Erin was not deterred by Cinnamon's newly discovered circumstance. He loved her dearly and would never leave...or live without her. That was the night that saw them partake in their first sexual experience with each other, again, a mirror of Seth and Nia. Erin and Cinnamon made love until near dawn. After which, Erin kissed her good-bye and promised to return in a few hours. They were going to spend the whole new day together. He then sneaked back out of the mansion through the same route from which he had come, anxious for his rapid return.

Cinnamon remained in bed still naked from her sexual initiation with Erin. The nipples on her large breasts were still engorged from his active mouth, her clitoris was still hard and stimulated from his forceful tongue, and her vagina still dripped with wetness as her thoughts of Erin's penis plunging deeply inside it enveloped her mind. She loved the look of his slightly tanned muscular body. His large delicious penis and other large genital apparati, which were surrounded by a thick fluffy mix of medium blond and dark blond hair. The memory of his bare muscular thighs pressed tightly against her bare graceful thighs as he laid on top of her was arousing and awesome. She loved running her fingers through his head of soft blond hair, caressing his head as she did so, and loved stroking her fingers down his beautiful muscular back. She knew she did indeed love him with all of her heart and would do anything within her mystical powers to please him.

As Erin drove home, he, too, was still sexually stimulated by their encounter. His semi-hard penis grew harder and harder the more he thought about Cinnamon's body. He knew he would have to go home and masturbate in order to relieve the pressure he was now feeling. Being the extremely handsome man that he was, he had always had plenty of sex with plenty of women, almost at the snap of his fingers. But, that was his first sexual experience with a non-Caucasian female and he loved it. The sight, feel, and taste of her soft, brown skin, fudge-colored nipples, and chocolate clitoris were hypnotic to him. And, the fact that he was in love with her made his climaxes the most potent experiences of ecstasy he had ever known.

Seth and Nia were aware of Erin's visit and were happy for it. They were pleased when Cinnamon announced that she would be going out shortly with Erin, they knew her depression must be at an end. Erin came early, as promised, he and Cinnamon left immediately on their excursion. It was a gorgeous day and Erin knew of a secluded area not far away where he and Cinnamon could make love all day without being seen. And, that is exactly what they did, made love all day. It was nearly dusk when they began their trip back to the estate; and was dark by the time they arrived back at the mansion. Erin walked Cinnamon to the door and said that he would go home, wash-up, change clothes, and be back within the hour. Cinnamon asked him to give her at least an hour and a half. Erin reluctantly agreed, gave her an exceptionally passionate kiss, and left for home. Cinnamon went inside and found that her parents had already left for what she now knew was their 'feed', rather than to attend family financial meetings as they had always told her. She walked to her room and began to prepare herself for Erin's return.

Erin, in his anxiousness, was ready way too early to return to the estate. He decided to make a quick stop at the Lighthouse Pub. He took a seat at one of the booths and ordered a ginger ale with lemon. As he sat, his ears perked-up when he heard the name Bjorn mentioned. He did not turn around, but continued to listen to the conversation being spoken two booths away from him. Whoever they were, they knew that the family Bjorn was composed of vampires. His heart almost stopped from terror when he overheard their intention to invade the estate and kill the entire family. He must warn the Bjorns immediately, but, before he could leave, the group got-up and piled out of the pub. There were seven of them, but, they planned to meet several more men just outside of town. Apparently, none of them knew exactly how to get to the estate. Perhaps, that would give him the time he needed to reach the estate first. As soon as they left, Erin darted out of the pub, ran to his car, jumped in, and sped up the road to the mansion.

When he reached the front door of the mansion, he rang the bell and banged on the door furiously, calling out Cinnamon's name. She finally came to the door, but, before she could say anything, Erin pushed his way inside the house. "Where are your parents?" he asked frantically.

Cinnamon became flustered as she answered him. "Upstairs. Why? What's the matter?"

"Call them downstairs, right now!" Erin cried-out breathlessly, his heart beating wildly.

Cinnamon became frightened. "Mother! Father! Come downstairs, quickly!"

Seth and Nia came racing to the top of the staircase. "What's wrong, Cinnamon?" Seth called downstairs with anxiety.

"Sir, there are men approaching the estate this very minute who wish to do you and your family great harm!" Erin called up to Seth.

"Men approaching us? What men? What do you mean?" Seth inquired as he and Nia began to hastily descend the elegant staircase.

"I heard them talking in the pub. They know that you're vampires and they mean to destroy all of you. They should be here at any moment!" Erin explained fearfully.

"The Archangel Clan," Nia said solemnly.

"Yes, My Dear. I'm afraid they've found us again. We must leave immediately, there's no time to gather anything. You and Cinnamon head for the car, I'll get the keys and some money and be right there," Seth instructed.

Nia, Cinnamon, and Erin all started out the front door, but, immediately upon doing so, saw car headlights traveling around the circular driveway of the mansion. The three of them ducked back inside the mansion and bolted the door behind them. Nia ran to the library where she knew Seth kept the money.

"They're here, Seth! They've just driven up the driveway!" Nia cried in terror.

"All right. Down to the basement, all of us. We can leave by the hidden back door," Seth instructed as he tried not to panic. The four of them barreled down the narrow stone staircase, which led to the basement. They could not chance putting on a light that would illuminate the basement windows. So, though they moved quickly, they also had to move cautiously, lest they stumble over each other.

Once they reached the basement, Seth led them in the darkness to the back-door exit. But, much to their dismay, they could see the flashlights of the invaders pass back and forth across the botanical overgrowth covering the basement windows as the men searched the estate grounds. Thankfully, the men had not found the hidden basement door, yet.

"They're everywhere," Cinnamon remarked with a quiver in her voice.

Erin put his arm around her shoulders and pulled her close to him. "I'll take care of you," he whispered.

"But, what can you do against so many?" Cinnamon answered softy. "You'll only get yourself killed if you try to save me. They'll most probably assume that you're a vampire, too."

"She's correct," Seth interrupted. "They most probably will murder you and ask questions later."

"Then, so be it. They will not get Cinnamon without a fight," Erin proclaimed with defiance.

Seth and Nia were pleased to hear Erin's words. It proved he loved their daughter and that should anything happen to them, Cinnamon would have someone left in her world who loved her. The thought afforded Nia and Seth a certain amount of peace, despite the severity of their present circumstance.

"Well, we can't stay here like sitting ducks waiting for them to find us," Seth said reluctantly. "We'll just have to make a run for it and hope that at least some of us make it."

"I agree," Nia answered distraughtly.

"I'll go first," Seth began, "I'll draw their attention towards me. Once they have started chasing me on foot, you three can rush out and head in the opposite direction. Then, when I've led them far enough in the wrong direction, I'll fly-off and meet the three of you at the boat house located near Yardley Lake."

"I won't leave you," Nia protested. "I go with you or not at all."

"Nia, please. There's no time for this. You stay with the children. They will need you," Seth replied.

"They don't need me. They're old enough to take care of themselves…In this world, wherever you go, I go," Nia expressed sternly.

Seth cupped Nia's face with his hand and gently kissed her lips. "All right, My Love. I won't argue anymore. Have it your way," he answered affectionately.

When the flashlights seemed to be moving away from the backside of the house, Seth and Nia decided it was time to make their move. They each hugged and kissed Cinnamon as if it was the last time, just in case it turned-out to be so. Nia also gave Erin a kiss and Seth gave him an affectionate hug. "Good luck to you, boy. And, should things not go our way, take care of my daughter for me," Seth requested earnestly.

"I'll protect her with my life, Sir," Erin replied deferentially.

"Take her to the estate of Dr. Neddelton Firth. It's not far from here. He will know what to do," Seth added.

"I shall, Sir," Erin responded assuringly.

"Good boy. Thank you," Seth answered sadly.

Seth and Nia regretted, now, their delay in training Cinnamon for her vampire life. She had no practice in obtaining her prey or instruction in her flying abilities. Neddelton Firth might have to be her teacher when all was said and done that night. Cinnamon began to cry as she watched her Mother and Father begin their exit from the basement, risking their existence to save her.

"Good-bye Mom, good-bye Dad...I love you," she whispered in tears. Seth and Nia turned, looked at her, and returned a loving, but, heartrending smile. Then, they quickly turned back around and continued their reluctant exit.

Nia and Seth quietly ascended the stairs that led to the yards of the estate. Seth slowly opened the wooden door; it was covered on the outside by shrubbery and overgrowth. He peeked-out into the yard and saw no one in the immediate area, but, he could still hear the voices of the invaders very close in proximity. "Come," he whispered to Nia. She took his hand and they both exited the basement. Once outside, they replaced some of the overgrowth around the door in the effort to keep it concealed a little longer. Then, they hurriedly began to walk in the direction of the voices. Within a few moments time, they saw a group of Archangels still checking under every bush and under every shrub for vampires. As if vampires would be hiding in such places, Seth thought. Seth then said in a tone of dismay and in reminiscence of their first ordeal together, "Well, I guess this is it. Are you ready to meet the Romans, Christian?"

Nia smiled in remembrance and replied softly "Yes...I'm ready."

At that moment, they both presented themselves in full view of several Archangel members. Seth and Nia then began calling-out to the members as they both took-off running towards the woods. The Archangels followed in quick and noisy pursuit. But, the supernatural strength of Seth and Nia allowed them to remain considerably ahead of their human hunters. Once Seth and Nia reached the woods, they dashed through the trees, but, made sure that the Archangels did not lose sight of them. Seth headed towards the old cemetery, which was located a short distance into the woods. There was a group of mausoleums there that Seth was sure would afford them the opportunity to escape and still keep the hunters following in the wrong direction. Some of the mausoleums had underground tunnels connected to the inside of the building. The tunnels had been constructed during the 1300's as a means for the inhabitants of the mansion to reach safety during the frequent feudal wars of the time. The tunnels led to an area completely off of the estate. The only problem was that Seth did not know which buildings connected to tunnels. They would have to quickly go from one to the other in search of an escapable mausoleum.

Erin and Cinnamon heard the sounds of Seth and Nia as they encountered the Archangels. They heard as the Archangels began their chase, and when the sounds of the mob became more distant, Erin and Cinnamon thought they should take their opportunity to run. They emerged from the basement door and found their path to freedom clear. "Let's go," Erin whispered as he grabbed her hand and started running towards the direction in which he thought the river might lay. Neither of them was quite sure where it was from the mansion and in the frantic whirlwind of the situation, neither thought to obtain some direction. They darted through the trees with untold speed, not even looking back to see if they had been spotted. They soon started to see the number of trees thinning and there seemed to be a clearing just ahead. As they approached the clearing, Erin and Cinnamon saw that the clearing was actually a cemetery, and from the look of it, a very old cemetery, filled with multiple old mausoleums and headstones. They both climbed over the rather low wooden fence and began to look at some of the headstones in the moonlight. They thought it might help them determine where they were at the moment.

"This one reads Rosemary Attlewater, born December 12, 1640, died May 24, 1696. Never heard of her," Cinnamon said softly.

"Here's one, Elizabeth Bjorn," Erin whispered.

"That's my grandmother," Cinnamon replied eagerly.

"It reads born April 3, 1650, died October 8, 1699. It also reads 'this mother died of a tormented heart'. Wonder what caused it," Erin remarked.

"1699 was the year that my Father was 'made' a vampire. Grandmother must have thought him dead and mourned him too severely," Cinnamon explained.

"So, we're still on the estate," Erin said.

"Yes, apparently we're still in danger," Cinnamon answered.

Suddenly, they heard the sound of the mob getting closer. They looked-up and saw the flickering of flashlights advancing through the dark woods on the other side of the cemetery.

Cinnamon saw two figures burst through the entrance gates of the cemetery and head straight for one of the mausoleum buildings. "That's Mom and Dad!" Cinnamon exclaimed.

"Are you sure?" Erin asked.

"Yes. yes, I'm sure! We must go to them and let them know we're here! We can all leave together now!" Cinnamon said with excitement as she started towards her parents. Within that split second of conversation, Seth and Nia had already discovered that their first building had no tunnel and had continued on to another building.

Erin pulled Cinnamon back by her waist. "Look!" he exclaimed fearfully.

Cinnamon and Erin immediately crouched down behind a headstone. The mob was already entering the graveyard.

"Search every building and look behind every headstone!" one man shouted.

"We have to help my parents!" Cinnamon cried-out softly as tears filled her eyes.

"There's nothing we can do, Baby. They'll only kill us, too. Your Father told us what to do should this happen. Your parents wanted us to survive them. We must do what I promised your Father I would do," Erin answered back sympathetically. Cinnamon looked at him in despair with tears streaming down her face. "I know it hurts," Erin whispered affectionately as he gently kissed her forehead. "But, we must leave now," he insisted as he pulled her by the arm towards the woods behind them. She took his hand in anguish; and then both ran back from whence they came. They quickly and quietly re-climbed the graveyard fence. And, in another instant, both were gone.

Nia and Seth became panicky as they realized that their second choice of mausoleum did not connect to a tunnel either. There was no time left to continue to search. The children should have made their escape by now, so the new plan was to just exit the chamber and fly away. They quickly turned to depart the building; but, to their distress, saw several Archangel members approaching the entrance. As the band of Archangels crowded through the mausoleum door, Seth and Nia found themselves trapped. Surrounded by the thick, gray, stone walls of the crypt and confronted with an Archangel blocked entrance, they both knew that the end had finally come. A single flashlight found the couple, then the group of hunters shone all of their flashlights upon Seth and Nia, lighting them both in the darkness as if shining a spotlight.

Seth looked over at Nia and took her hand. He was distraught by the fact that he had brought her to this end. Perhaps, he had been too selfish. Perhaps, his great love for her should have demanded that he give her up and leave her to live a normal life. She gazed-up at him with terror in her face, an image that already destroyed him. He smiled at her and gave her a single wink of an eye as a heart-felt attempt to ease some of the horror. She returned a brief, though frightened, smile. Then, they despairingly stared into each other's eyes. Each tortured by what each knew would be the final glance at the other, each absorbed in expressing a silent and final 'good-bye'. But, Seth's mind began to explode with grief over Nia's impending demise. As he held her hand more tightly, his face began to reveal his tormented heart. He could not let them part in silence. His eyes filled with tears the split second before he agonizingly whispered to her, "I love you…Forgive me."

Nia smiled at him with love. Yet, before she could reply, Nia cried-out in pain as two sharp wooden spikes, which had been released from a crossbow type devise, ripped into her chest and rested deep within her heart. The force of the projection slammed her against the back wall of the crypt. Almost simultaneously, Seth met the same excruciating fate. They both quickly slid down the wall and sank to the floor. The Archangels, elated with their conquest, joyfully watched as the bodies of Seth and Nia slowly decomposed into large piles of light gray dust, now harmless, but also, now at peace. Once the destruction was complete, the Archangels strolled leisurely out of the shadowy mausoleum, all gleefully enroute to celebrate at the nearest beer-filled pub. But, in their happiness, they had forgotten about the existence of Cinnamon. She would at least have time to learn ways to defend herself now. The next morning, the crypt was sealed permanently with large blocks of stone marked,

'Danger: Do Not Enter'

The dust, which once composed the handsome bodies of Seth and Nia, remained in the crypt and lay as it fell, undisturbed. Yet, even within that altered state, could still be seen the impression of Seth's hand lovingly and inseparably holding the hand of Nia. Alas, so Seth and Nia would remain throughout eternity.

But, surely a love of such magnificence shall have its song sung by the Muses of the gods forever…and a day.

0-595-31397-3

MB 0JH
Hathersage Rd

Printed in the United States
53692LVS00003B/61

9 780595 313976